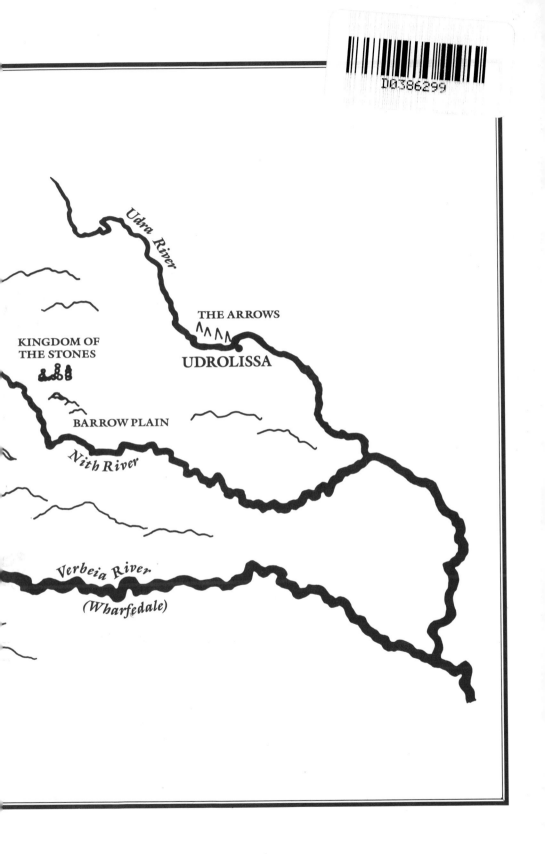

Udra River

THE ARROWS
∧ ∧ ∧ ∧
UDROLISSA

KINGDOM OF
THE STONES

BARROW PLAIN

Nith River

Verbeia River

(Wharfedale)

THE SERPENT'S TOOTH

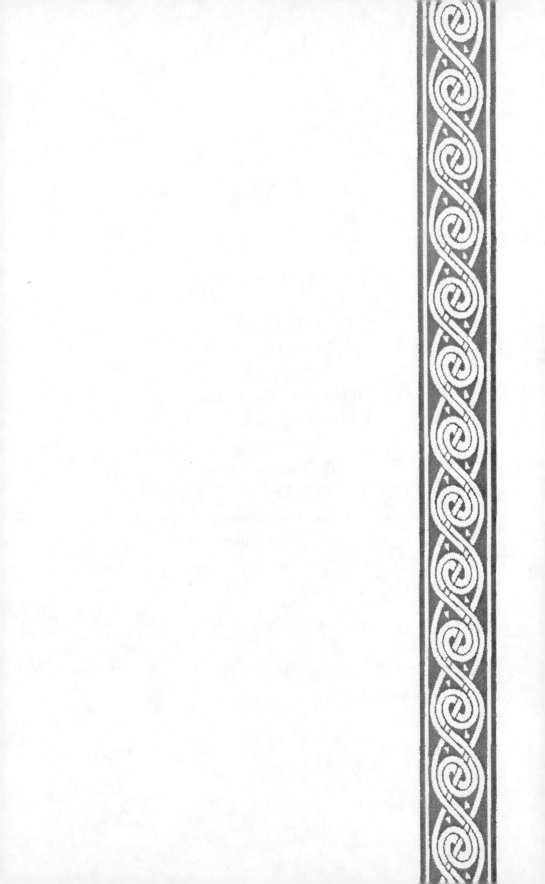

THE
SERPENT'S
TOOTH

Diana L. Paxson

William Morrow and Company, Inc. / New York

It is the policy of William Morrow and Company, Inc., and its imprints and affiliates, recognizing the importance of preserving what has been written, to print the books we publish on acid-free paper, and we exert our best efforts to that end.

Library of Congress Cataloging-in-Publication Data

Paxson, Diana L.
    The serpent's tooth / by Diana L. Paxson.
      p. cm.
    ISBN 0-688-08339-0
    I. Title
PS3566.A897S47 1991
813′.54—dc20
                                                    90-21143
                                                        CIP

Printed in the United States of America

First Edition

1 2 3 4 5 6 7 8 9 10

BOOK DESIGN BY LINEY LI

To Siobhan,

Bear Daughter
Singer to the People

Companion on the Way

ACKNOWLEDGMENTS

Once more I would like to thank Alexei Kondratiev for delving yet further into history to reconstruct the proto-Celtic forms of my characters' names, although in some cases (such as Leir, which would have been something closer to Liger, with the "g" as a barely voiced guttural in the back of the throat), I have retained more modern forms for the sake of euphony. I am also grateful to Caítlin Matthews for sending me an early copy of her book *The Celtic Tradition*, which saved me a great deal of time and trouble in double-checking elements of Celtic culture and religion. The encouragement I received from her and her husband John (also a noted Celticist) during this project has been most welcome. I am indebted to Guy Ragland Phillips's book *Brigantia* for bringing to my attention some of the more colorful examples of north country topography and folklore.

My thanks also to those who provided unexpected information and assistance while I was doing the research, especially Bill Godfrey of the Ilkley Archaeological Group, who took time off from backfilling the summer's dig to give me a lecture on the archaeological history of the moor. Thanks also to Bob Rutland of the Jewry Wall

[9]

Museum in Leicester for his background on the area, and for telling me where to find the village of Leire.

Finally, my gratitude goes to those who gave me moral support during the writing, especially to Leigh Ann Hussey and David Oster for letting me print out the manuscript on their laserprinter, and holding my hand when my computer tried to eat Part III.

PEOPLE IN THE STORY

QUIRITANI of the ISLAND OF THE MIGHTY (the Celts):
LEIR, son of Blatonos also called Leir Blatoniknos,
    high king of the Island of the Mighty

Leir's half-blood daughters:
GUNARDUILLA, daughter of Leir by Aglidet, Lady of Alba
    of the Ai-Siwanet
RIGANA, daughter of Leir by Dara, Lady of Belerion
    of the Ai-Utu
CRIDILLA, daughter of Leir by Fieret, Lady of Briga
    of the Ai-Akhsi, called "Adder" as a war-name

Leir's household and Companions:
ARTOCOXOS (Bear-leg) son of Escutios, leader of Leir's Companions
  BITUITOS the Black
  CADROS the Fair
  CARANTIS
  CATUUEROS son of Ilicos
  DOGBELLY
  DROSTAGNOS (DROST)
  ILIX
  KASWAT
  NODONTIOS
  RAWAL

RED LEG
SIGO
TROST
UXELOS
VORCUNS (Big Dog)
TALORGENOS the oak priest

Chieftains of the Quiritani:
MAGLAROS son of Magloscutios, prince of the Banalisioi (Men of the
    White Cliffs), Gunarduilla's husband and King of Alba
    MORIGENOS son of Maglaros and Gunarduilla
SENOUINDOS son of Brochagnos, Rigana's husband and King of
    Belerion
    CUNODAGOS son of Senouindos and Rigana
BITUITOS of Rigodunon (Fort of the King)
CALCAGOS, lord of the eastern shore
CATUUEROS of the Stone Fort
LOUTRINOS son of Carantis, a chieftain near the Soretia, Cridilla's
    suitor
NEXTONOS of High Fort, also a suitor

QUIRITANI of the GREAT LAND:
AGANTEQUOS (Horse) son of Vorequos, King of the Moriritones,
    (Men of the Sea-Passages) in Morilandis

Agantequos's household and Companions:
NABELCOS, house bard at Moridunon
    CUNO
    GRUNCANOS   } warriors
    KEIR
    BRENNA, wife of Cuno
    SOBUIACA
    GHEMIT
MOTHER NESTA, priestess of the Moriritones

THE PAINTED PEOPLE (Ti n'Izriran):
HULI, priest of the village near Udrolissa
ZAUERET, keeper of the Great House in Udrolissa
GIAHAD, ex-priest, builder of roads

TRIYET, Leir's mistress from Belerion
MLALET, lady of Brannodunon
ZAYYAR-A-KHATTAR, King of the Ai-Zir
ILF, a half-blood warrior in the service of Rigana

The Seven Priestesses of the Ti-Sahharin (Dark Sisterhood):
ASARET of the Ai-Utu (People of the Hare), Belerion
TAMAR of the Ai-Akhsi (People of the Ram), the Dales
ICO of the Ai-Siwanet (People of the Hawk), Alba
ILIFET of the Ai-Ilf (People of the Boar), Midlands
AMAUNET of the Ai-Giru (People of the Frog), Southeast
EKKI of the Ai-Ushen (People of the Wolf), Western Mountains
URTAYA of the Ai-Zir (People of the Bull), Plain of Carn Ava

PEOPLE OF THE OLD RACE (Senamoi) and THE MISTY ISLE
    (Caiactis)
CROW, a failed shaman from the dales, attached to the household
    of Leir
SPEAKER-TO-SPIRITS, singer of the Bear Clan in the dales
ARTONA (Bear Mother) the She-Bear of Caiactis
    SHADOW BEAR
    SPIRIT BEAR   } her daughters

Children of Cridilla's hearth on the Island:
    WILLOW
    WINGFOOT
    GANNET
    WATERDOG
    LINNET

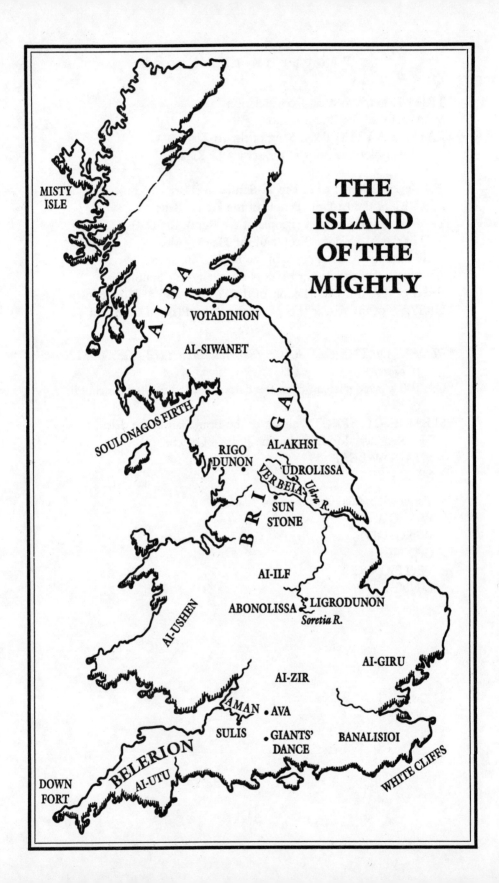

THE
ISLAND
OF THE
MIGHTY

MISTY
ISLE

ALBA

VOTADINION

AL-SIWANET

SOULONAGOS FIRTH

BRIGA

RIGO
DUNON

AL-AKHSI

UDROLISSA

VERBELA

Udra R.

SUN
STONE

AI-ILF

ABONOLISSA

LIGRODUNON

Soretia R.

AI-USHEN

AI-GIRU

AI-ZIR

AMAN

AVA

SULIS

GIANTS'
DANCE

BANALISIOI

BELERION

WHITE CLIFFS

DOWN
FORT

AI-UTU

PLACES IN THE STORY

ISLAND OF THE MIGHTY—*Great Britain*

Alba—Scotland
   Soulonagos firth—the Solway
   Stone of the Young God—Lochmaben Stone
   High Banks—High Banks fort, Kirkcudbright
CAIACTIS, The Misty Isle—Skye
   Artodunon—Dun Ringell on Skye
UOTADINION—Edinburgh

Briga—the High Dales, from the Cheviot Hills to
   the Southern Border of Leicestershire

North:
UDROLISSA—on the Ure near Aldborough, York
   The Arrows—the Devil's Arrows, Boroughbridge
STONE FORT—Stanwick near Darlington, Durham
RIGODUNON (Fort of the King)—Ingleborough, Ribblesdale, York
HILL OF THE WINDS—Penyghent, Ribblesdale, York
R. NITH—River Nidd, York
R. VERBEIA—River Wharfe, York
R. RIPPLE—River Ribble, York
R. UDRA—River Ure, York
   Womb Cave—Victoria Cave, Wharfedale
   Sacred Spring—"Saint" Aldkelda's Well, near Giggleswick,
      Ribblesdale
   Senamoi encampment—Malham Cove, Ribblesdale
   Kingdom of the Stones—Brimham Rocks, Niddersdale
   Barrowplain—Graffa Plain, Niddersdale
   Settlement—near Hangingstone Quarry, Rombald's Moor,
      Wharfedale
   sacrificial stone—Badger Stone, above Ilkley on Rombald's Moor
   Sun Stone—"Swastika" Stone, above Ilkley on Rombald's Moor

South:
ABONOLISSA, Leir's palace on the Soretia—near the hamlet of Leire,
    Leicester
HIGH FORT—Bredon Hill, Leicester
LIGRODUNON (Leir's dun)—Burrough Hill in Leicestershire
R. SORETIA—R. Sore

Belerion—Cornish Peninsula
The DOWN FORT—Chun Castle, Penwith
  Barrow of the Queens—Zennor Quoit
  Womb Stone—the Men-an-Tol
  Mother's Well—Modron Well

Country of the Bull Tribe—Wiltshire
THE SHRINE OF AVA—Avebury Circle
GIANTS' DANCE—Stonehenge
SPRINGS OF SULIS—Bath
R. AMAN—R. Avon

THE GREAT LAND—The Continent
MORILANDIS (Sea-Pastures) Moriritones country—coasts around the
    gulf of St. Malo, border of Normandy and Brittany
MORIDUNON (Sea-Fort), Agantequos's dun—near Domfront,
    Normandy
HILL OF THE HORNED ONE—Mont St. Michel
SANCTUARY OF THE CARNUTES—Chartres
TARTESSOS—Tarshish
GADES—Carthage

PROLOGUE

The shining coils of the river glitter red as old blood in the last light of the longest day, and upon the water, the reflection of the swan floats like a silver shield. But beneath the surface the stream is flowing clear, and the sledgemarks on the shore where the builders brought down the stones for the tomb are merging into the mud again. Only an intermittent ripple of water in midstream shows where the current embraces the sunken stonework, and the carven head with its double faces gazing upstream and down.

Unless you were looking for that riff in the smooth flow, you would never know that the river had changed. But I can feel the drowned gaze of the guardian, one face to the future, and one to the past. And it is to the past that I am facing now, and my thoughts spiral down the stream of the years to the grey plains of the sea that separate the Island of the Mighty from the Great Land.

Near two-score cycles of the sun have passed since Leir son of Blatonos brought the Quiritani over that water in ten swift ships whose sails were white as the wings of swans. He fell upon the land of Briga, killed the king, and made himself consort to the Lady. But his sword was still thirsty, and soon he was fighting in Alba, and that queen also he married, and likewise the queen of Belerion. And where he conquered, he settled his warriors, and put them to building roads and fortresses to hold the land. And they and the others who came after them hailed Leir high king.

And the Lady of Alba bore him a daughter, Gunarduilla, who followed the way of the sword. The Lady of Belerion also gave him a girl-child, Rigana, who was fair as a night of stars. And at last the Lady of Briga gave birth also and died in the bearing. And that child was myself, Cridilla, the last of the daughters of King Leir. Now Gunarduilla's ashes lie beneath a mound in Uotadinion and Rigana's body rests in the Barrow of the Queens in Belerion. But the river Soretia flows above the tomb of King Leir.

Beneath the hushed music of the water I can hear the deeper murmur of the people who wait for me beyond the willows. When I return to them they will hail me as queen of the Island of the Mighty. But for one moment longer I will gaze into the flowing river, and be no more than Cridilla who was Adder of the Bear hearth, Cridilla wife of Agantequos; Cridilla the daughter of Leir.

And strange it is that now, at Midsummer when the triumphant sun turns the shining surface of the river to red gold, it is I to whom the daughter of the queens and the sons of the new tribes from oversea will turn. It was always winter when the course of my life changed before. . . . It was at the Midwinter Festival when I was seven years old that the first spiral began.

FIRST SPIRAL: SERPENT IN THE STONE

Twenty-second to Thirty-first Years
of the Rule of High King Leir

Chapter

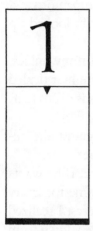

And the blood of the calf lay upon the snow, and she saw a black raven that came down to drink it.

—*The Exile of the Sons of Uisnech*

The Midwinter sky was brightening slowly through the river mist that shadowed the land. The day seemed as reluctant to awaken as I had been to leave the close warmth of my sleeping furs, but at seven, I was already old enough to know that no one in my father's household slept when the high king of the Island of the Mighty was astir. I clung to Leir's shoulders, swaying to his long stride as we plunged down the hill from his feasting hall at Udrolissa toward the sacred stones. I had begged my father to take me to the Midwinter rites in the village before, but this was the first time he had been home for the festival since I had been old enough to go.

The bare branches of oak trees lifted an insubstantial net against the shadows; only the stiff hedging of holly around the enclosure showed blank and dark, and beyond it the four great stones rearing one behind another against the brightening sky. I sensed, rather than saw, the mass of people waiting silently before the entrance. Then the tethered bull lowed anxiously, a ghostly blur in the gloom, and my father's muscled shoulders shifted beneath me. I grabbed for support, suddenly afraid.

"Cridilla," came the growl from below, "you will find yourself riding a gorse bush if you yank my hair!"

Artocoxos Bear-leg, who captained my father's Companions and had lumbered at Leir's heels since before I could walk, looked up at me and laughed.

The callused grip of Leir's big hands tightened on my ankles, and earth and sky resumed their right relationship. Laughter tickled my own throat and I let go of the coarse golden strands of his hair. My father was the high king. How could I fall?

"Will Catuueros of Stonefort agree to join us against the Ai-Zir?" Artocoxos's voice was a low rumble at my father's ear.

My father grunted. "He has no smith in that place. If he wants to be getting any more axeheads it is me he must come to. Every year more of the Painted People"—with a start of interest I realized that he was talking about my mother's folk—"are forced down from the moors. Without axes and ploughshares to buy their service, he will have no one to till his fields."

My attention wandered. I had been listening to such conversations since my birth, as little regarded by my father and the warriors who served him as one of his great hounds.

"It would be easier to fight him," said Artocoxos reluctantly.

"Is your blade getting so rusty?" The king laughed. "If I killed him I would have to find someone else to hold the dun. Think, man—you yourself tallied every warrior who came oversea with us from the Great Land a score of years ago. The gods and our own courage delivered the tribes of the Painted People into our hands! But do you believe these patient farmers would stay so quiet if they thought we were weakening? Catuueros has a strong arm. I do not want his blood, only his loyalty!"

"He does not think beyond his own borders. . . ." Artocoxos was still grumbling, but without rancor now. "Now he is safe between Briga and Alba, but the Ai-Zir have never ceased to challenge us, and Zayyar is a canny leader, and a prince of the old blood as well. If he overruns our southern marches and sets the Ai-Akhsi in Briga aflame, Catuueros may find that iron axeheads can cut more than trees!"

Torches were winding in a glittering stream up the path from the village, and I pounded my father's shoulder. Ahead of them a shadow flickered along the ground.

"See, they will be coming now!"

I felt the warmth of my father's attention returning to me. Leir stood half a head above the men around him. Perched on his shoulders, I could see over the crowd. The torches paled as the mists grew brighter; what had seemed a shadow speeding ahead of the procession was a man.

"Why is he running?"

"He's their singer. He leads the ceremonies."

"Like your oak priests?" I asked.

The king laughed. The priests who had come with my father from oversea were big solid men with striped cloaks and flowing beards. But this man was all angles, running with a curious disjointed grace as if one of the images the villagers put up to frighten crows from the grain had come alive. He darted up the slope toward us, the red rags of a woman's gown flaring out behind him, all a-clatter with bits of metal and bone, and black-ringed eyes stared from a white-painted face as he flashed by. Then the torches swirled after him, and grinning red-clad men whose faces had been painted with red ochre fanned out as the runner began to dodge among the crowd.

"He does not look as if he wants to lead this one," I whispered. "He looks afraid."

"It is the custom," my father answered. "All pretend, to make the people laugh."

I shivered. My older sister Rigana said that once the world had been warmer, before our father's people came across the sea. Were the villagers performing this ritual to bring those times back again? There had been sickness in the village already and the winter was only half done. Those who could read the signs in the land foretold worse weather to come.

There was a swirl of movement and the people backed away. The Companions shifted position around my father. The runner was slumped in the grip of two of the red-clothed men. Then he straightened, and a peal of high-pitched laughter cut through the babble of the crowd. The village men were brown and stocky next to my father's long-limbed warriors, but their prisoner was slim as a reed, with a shock of black hair.

"What breed of man is he?" I whispered as they hustled him to a raised platform of lashed logs next to the last of the tall stones they called the Arrows. The torchbearers spread out to either side, flanking the stones with fire.

"One of the Senamoi, the magic people," came the answer, "the folk who were here before even the Ai-Akhsi came. I wonder where they found him? His tribe usually hold to the moors."

I stared. Before my mother's kindred? But the People of the Ram *belonged* to this land. My sister Rigana said that they had had to teach the festivals of sun and earth to the invading Quiritani, who only celebrated the cycles of the flocks and herds. Trying to imagine a time before that made me feel as if I were losing my balance again.

"When flies grey skies the wren—"

sang the tattered figure, balancing on his perch with a flutter of draperies,

"Glower storm clouds—gather hither
holders, the fire hailing, blazes the flame
to brighten the days,
and strengthen sun—
Come everyone!"

A hollow beating pulsed through his words as he tapped a small drum. His singing had a weird high purity, and I felt the fine hairs rise on my neck and arms. Surely those great shafts of stone were quivering to the beat of the drum!

"When awakens earth
from winter sleep, slow and deep
in hidden heart beats the drum,

bright from frozen flesh is born
the light of life—
all greet the morn!"

I blinked. The stones stood still, but radiance pulsed around
them. The song had mastered them; this was not one of those times
when they danced of themselves and thirsted for the blood of men.
The drumming grew louder; radiance shimmered in the mists and
revealed a tracery of treetops along the river against a pale sky. The
drum missed a beat, I felt, rather than heard, breath drawn in all
around me. Then light blazed suddenly behind the southernmost
stone.

Crows flew up from the trees, clamoring, as a great shout split
the air. A way opened in the crowd before us and they dragged the
bull toward the stones. The long horns tossed, straining the lines
that held it, and the beast bellowed angrily. The red-clad men
marched before it, but as they passed below us, they paused. Artocoxos stepped between them and us, and one of the men spoke
in a low tone.

"They want you to perform the sacrifice, lord," the warrior said.

"Do they now?" muttered my father. "Is it not enough that I
gave them a beast from my own herds, but I must kill it for them?
Have these sheep no priests of their own?" But already he was
lifting me from his shoulders and holding me out to Artocoxos.
For a moment I hung in the warrior's strong hands, then the in-
dignity of the position reached me and I squirmed until he laughed
and set me on the ground.

I did not understand—of course the people had priests. The
man in red was Huli, who came to the dun sometimes to speak for
the villagers. He walked with a limp, and had spiral patterns pricked
out in blue upon his brow.

"Sacrifice by you is greater honor." He bowed to my father.
"Husband of the queen that was, father of the queen that will be!
The sacred blood must be shed to revive the land. Who has a better
right to make the offering?"

The younger men in my father's guard, who understood the old
language well, began to murmur as the old man turned to me and

bowed. I wondered why. My mother had been queen of the lands from the river Udra to the Soretia, but she died when I was born, and I was only the third daughter of the king.

My father laughed and strode toward the bull. Crows called from the bare branches of the ash tree, and the warriors were abruptly silent. The long, twisting horns of the bull had been painted crimson. He was a big beast; his shaggy winter coat rippled white as a swan's wing. I took a sudden step forward and Arto-coxos's strong hand closed on my shoulder.

"Do not be distracting him," he said in the tongue of the Quiritani. "You will see. This is not the first bull the king has killed!"

I looked up at him. Of course my father sacrificed beasts at the Quiritani festivals, but his own gods understood his prayers. This was different. He was drawing the special blade of bronze that always hung sheathed beside his sword, but he had not prayed beforehand, or washed his head and hands. Huli had called it a sacrifice, but did the king believe him? Whether he did nor not, he would be bound by the offering to the land.

There was a scuffle as the beast lunged, and the sweep of a crimsoned horn, then Leir stepped forward and the long knife flashed. For a moment the white body hung above him like a swan before it feels the death in the hunter's dart. Then the blade jerked through the gullet, and the bull fell and twitched to stillness in the mud as its life poured away.

The priest held a bowl to catch the blood. The metallic tang hung heavy in the damp air.

"*When falls the horned lord—*" sang the captive.

> "*Life linked to life, love to the land—*
> *the gift once given now returned, feeds earth*
> *in red flood,*
> *the offering of blood*
> *body and spirit warms,*
> *and holds from harms!*"

He threw back his head, howling as the priest ran past him, splashing blood upon the stones. I staggered and went down on my hands and knees in the mud as a tremor undulated through the soil.

The singer wailed suddenly in no language that I knew, and I tried to curl into a ball.

"Child of my heart, were you afraid?" Hard hands plucked me from the earth and I struck out frantically. "Cridilla, be still. I was in no danger, and you are safe with me!"

I smelled horse and sweat and sour ale. Slowly I realized that my father was holding me. I could hear the steady beat of his heart beneath my ear. I sighed, but I had no words to explain that I had struggled because I did not want to be taken from the earth, not because I was afraid.

Logs had been piled beneath the leafless ash tree, and some of the villagers were disjointing the stripped body of the bull and spitting the quarters to roast over the fire. But most of the men had separated into two groups facing the singer, who brandished something like a flexible baton. With a jarring squeal, he flung it toward the crowd. Red-streaked whiteness whipped through the air. It was only as the first hands grabbed for it that I realized that what he had thrown was the bull's pizzle. Then it disappeared into the press.

"What are they doing?" The huddle of men had become a single creature, heaving and grunting as they fought for possession of the prize.

"It is to make the crops grow." Artocoxos grinned. "Each side will try to bear the talisman away, but it can take hours."

The knot of men swayed, shifting a few feet as someone gave way, then digging in once more. The only movement was at the foot of the high seat, where Huli was binding the tattered man who had sung up the sun.

My father set me down, but I did not get to see what they were going to do with their captive, for he and Artocoxos were already turning back toward the dun and I had to scramble to keep up with their long strides. The scent of roasting beef followed us all the way home.

The sun always seems shrunken at Midwinter, emerging newborn from the womb of the Mother to glimmer for a few hours in the chill skies. But clearly the bull sacrifice had strengthened it. When I looked out the door of the Women's House at dawn the next day it shone from a sky the clear pale blue of a kingfisher's wing, and every pebble glowed.

On the other side of the leather curtains I could hear my older sister Rigana's steady breathing. I had heard Gunarduilla going out even earlier, most likely a-hunting. I wished that she had waited to take me with her, but already another idea was coming to me.

In the home pasture my cows had to compete for the sparse grass with the beasts in my father's herd, but beside the cart-track between the dun and the village there was green grass . . . I bound the thongs of my shoes securely around my ankles, pulled my heavy cloak and my pony's bridle from their hooks on the bedpost, and slipped out the door.

A little smoke drifted above the thatch of the long feasting hall, but no one stirred as I stepped across the frozen mud of the inner compound, pulling the ends of my sleeves over my fists against the bite of the air. In the outer court there were servants about already, bringing water from the spring, building up fires to boil the morning porridge. I begged a heel of barley bread and a chunk of cheese from Zaueret, who had been my mother's servant long ago. She put her arm around me and gave me a swift hug.

"The day's blessing on thee, child—"

For a moment I snuggled into her embrace. "I wish thou wert my mother."

"Art child to the Goddess Herself, little one," she whispered into my hair. "Never forget it!"

Perhaps, I thought as I kissed her. But it was Zaueret who gave me kisses and bread.

"And where farest thou?" she went on as she wrapped the food in a scrap of sacking. "Is it down to the village for the festival?"

"My father says I must not go there alone." I stuffed it into my pouch. "I thought to take my cattle out to graze—the day's too fair to stay inside!" Now that my blood was up I could feel life singing through my veins.

"In the village they will honor thee," Zaueret said. "But stay away from the sacred stones."

I was still wondering what she had meant by that as I kicked Cygnet down the path. I had named her after my father's totem, and with her shaggy coat thickened by winter, the pony looked more than ever like a fledgling swan, but even in the summer she was grey and graceless. Only in her uncertain temper did she resemble the bird, but usually she obeyed me, and on her back I was free.

The cattle gave me standing. There were only six of them now, but the red cow was bearing to my father's bull. Driving my little herd along the cart-track I had freedom and power as my father's people understood them. My sisters owned herds too, but they did not tend them.

The red heifer seemed to feel the air as I did. She bucked and snorted when I headed her back after each attempt to leave the path. Preoccupied by the game we were playing, I did not realize how close we had come to the Arrows. I pushed through a hazel thicket and reined in suddenly, and the heifer, realizing that I had ceased to pursue her, flicked her tail mockingly and began to graze.

The men clustered around the fire at the base of the ash tree were making too much noise to hear me. Their attention was fixed on a bundle wrapped in the hide of the sacrificed bull that was suspended from the lowest branch. They were swinging it back and forth through the smoke from the remains of the fire.

I stopped short, the hair rising on neck and arms as the bundle jerked convulsively.

"Of the year to come, tell us, shadow-walker—"

I hardly recognized Huli. He was wearing a robe of white wool, and from his neck gleamed a golden collar shaped like a crescent moon.

"What dream has come to thee, tell us, tell us—"

"Nothing . . ." came the hoarse whisper. "Smoke and darkness . . . wind and fog. Sighs in her sleep the earth serpent; hatches the sun from a cuckoo's egg. There is nothing. Please, let this one go!"

"Laugh at us, wilt thou?" Huli gestured, and one of the others threw more branches on the fire. Smoke billowed upward. I caught a hint of something aromatic and realized there had been herbs among the branches.

[29]

"Speak, shapeshifter! Thy folk live in spirit land. Hang there thou wilt, till thou dost speak or die!"

The hide bundle quivered and the captive coughed painfully.

"No visions! Would not tell, if visions came. Took land ... Painted People ... killed Old Ones. Now killers slain by iron swords!" A skirl of wild laughter came muffled from beneath the hides, then degenerated into coughing again.

"Prick him—" One of the younger men brandished a bronze boar spear. "Will speak then!"

Huli swung his head back and forth. "Take care—we learned long ago how the curses of the Old Ones bite when they die!" Grumbling, the boy stepped back. Huli looked up at the man in the hide.

"Now death comes to the Painted People too, and not from swords. Too much rain—in fields stands the water, in houses die the men. What must we do? Breathe deep, let the smoke take thee, man of the moors. Ask the spirits why!"

Smoke billowed up from the smoldering logs. The hide jerked, and I heard a long high trail of syllables, repeated again and again until it became a song.

"Too much—" said one of the men. "He dreams again."

"No matter. Wait until the herbs wear away. He will answer in time."

Carefully I eased back through the hazel copse and onto the path. If they turned they would see me standing there, and my father forbade fighting among the subject peoples. They might be angry if they knew I had seen them breaking his law. But although the sun was still shining, even after I retrieved my cattle and got them to the grass, for me the day was clouded. How could I help that poor man trussed up in the hide without bringing down my father's wrath upon the villagers?

The land sloped gently toward the river, strips of stubbled cropland divided by thin traceries of beech and the thicker blur of hazel thickets whose lower branches still bore a few withered leaves. The air above the ash tree was a-flicker with wings, and in the distance I could hear ravens telling each other the news. I sat beneath an oak tree, plaiting dead grass into braids and listening to the chewing of my cows, and my thoughts went round and back again. What could I do? At worst, the king would be angry with the village. At best, he might laugh at me. My sisters could not help—they were of Alba and Belerion, not of this land. For the first time, I wept because I was only a child.

It was only when I began to shiver that I realized that the sun had been covered by real clouds. Snow-heavy as a wet fleece, they were piling up to the westward, and only a shimmer of dimming light showed where the sun had gone. I told myself not to be foolish, for at Midwinter surely it was clear weather that would have been unnatural. But I could feel the sense of wrongness in the air.

There was something wrong on the earth too—only two of my cows could be seen. By the time I found the others, the clouds had sunk nearly to the treetops, and the light was going fast. A touch of cold air damp with the promise of snow fingered my brow as I drove the cattle along the path, and the bare branches rattled like bones.

When I neared the ash tree I let Cygnet slow, but I heard no sound. I herded the cows into the lee of the hazels and reined the pony around them. The trunk of the ash was a straight shadow above the scattered ashes of the dead fire, but it still bore its strange fruit, swinging in slow circles in the strengthening wind.

Dead, I thought. I kicked the pony's sides to urge her closer, and felt the first flicker of hope when she went willingly. She would have smelled death; the black birds who waited in the treetop would have been busy already if a corpse had hung there.

"Singer," I called, using my mother's tongue. "Dost live?"

The bundle quivered. "Down . . ." The voice was only a whisper. "Lost between earth and sky he is, and never the wiser. Like thee, at home in neither world. Flies in the wren's kingdom soon . . . oh, cut him down. . . ."

I frowned. On foot I could not have reached him. But I was tall for my age, and I had practised standing on Cygnet's back before. Would she allow it now, with the storm coming on? Carefully I nudged her until we were next to the hanging man. Through the folds of the hide I could see one dark eye.

"Why hangest thou from the tree?"

"Hung my master on the worldtree until he understood all wisdom . . ." came the whisper. "Death only dost this one see. . . ."

That was no explanation. I tried again.

"How came these folk to capture thee? What dost thou so far from thy hills?"

"Wandering . . . no place of rest upon earthmother . . . only fear. . . ."

"The oak priests say another body is sought when the spirit goes," I told him, measuring the distance. "Why be afraid?"

"Dreams . . ." he answered me. "Fangs and claws to tear the soul. Hast seen them in the dark?"

I stared up at him, remembering times when the shadowed thatch above my bedplace gave birth to shapes that writhed up the carven houseposts and I kept silent only because I was the daughter of a king. This was the first grown person who seemed to know that those nightserpents were there.

He jerked and the twisted rope that suspended him from the tree quivered like a bowstring. On my cheek I felt the cold kiss of the coming snow.

"Be quick, lady of the high place—"

Again I stared, for how could he know I was not from the village? And why had he addressed me as if I were a queen?

"Quickly, ere lost be the spirit between the worlds."

I warmed with an odd surge of protectiveness, like the feeling I had when I watched my first cow give birth to her calf. I unsheathed the bronze dagger my father had given me at Samonia and gripped the blade between my teeth. Then, humming reassuringly and praying that Cygnet would not stir, I got my feet under me and very carefully stood up on her broad back. I struggled for balance as the wind gusted, but now I could get a grip on the hide and, just barely, reach the rope with the blade.

Choosing a spot where the hemp was frayed already, I began to saw. The first strands parted swiftly, for my father had taught me to keep a good edge on the bronze, but I knew that the blade would soon dull. The blood roared in my ears, or perhaps it was the rising wind. I could hear voices telling me to run away. I heard drumbeats, and told myself it was the pounding of my heart.

But the hempen strands were parting. The rope groaned and the captive jerked. Cygnet stirred restlessly.

"Be still!" I hissed. "The knife—" Then the last strand began to give way. Someone shouted behind me and the pony took a step forward. I clutched at the hide for support and suddenly we were both swinging. The world disappeared as a flurry of snow whirled past, then we fell through the void.

I lay in darkness, fighting to breathe. Then the weight that was crushing me quivered. The captive had fallen on top of me and was squirming free.

"Cridilla . . . the Lady. . . ." A confused murmur of voices mixed with the whistling of the wind. "Only a child!"

Six of the village men were staring down at me, Huli closest. I struggled upright.

"Didst think we would leave him to the snow, lady?" he asked. "Our thanks to thee. We will take him now—"

"For death delayed is still afraid!" came a whisper from the bundle beside me.

"What will ye do with him?" I asked then.

"What is that to thee?" said the priest. "These be not thy mysteries."

"But I rescued him—" My knee hurt from the fall, and I could feel a change in the mood of the men around me, but the need to protect was still strong, and I was the daughter of a king.

"No strayed hound pup is this for thee to nurse, honored one," Huli said gently. "Masters of magic are the moor folk, and we need that power."

"Not for sacrifice—" I knew well that except at the times and places when their auguries required it, the oak priests had forbidden the people to offer men.

"Dost thou so betray thy mother's blood?" asked one of the men.

"She would not speak so if our women had her fostering—" added another.

"Then take the man, and take her, and raise her as a queen!"

"Art mad? The sea-king is a wolf with one cub—he would set our thatch aflame about our ears!"

I shook my head, trying to understand. What had I done to them?

"Child, take him we shall, with or without thy will!" Huli said to me.

The captive's struggles had freed him from the hide, and he emerged from its folds like a hatchling, snow-powdered hair standing in stiff spikes and eyes white-rimmed with fear. One of the men lifted his staff and I tugged my cape off and threw it over man and hide.

"The shelter of my cloak for him!" I cried. The earth quivered beneath my feet. "He is my man now!"

"Lady, listen—" Huli began, and then the whirl of snow solidified into tall riders. A long spear snaked between me and the priest.

"The king!" they cried, backing away. "Comes the king!" Only Huli held his ground.

"Lord, tell the child. The man is ours, for our rites. It is not for thee to interfere. . . ."

Leir nudged his horse closer. The cloak that swathed his shoulders made him look even bigger, but his head was bare. Even the snow feared to fall upon him; radiance flared, haloing his body with a shimmer like pale fire. *The god Lugus looks like that,* I thought, gazing up at him, *when he grasps his spear!* He had only Artocoxos and Vorcuns with him, but the villagers did not move. The man I was trying to save gripped my leg and I could feel his body quivering.

"My prize, my captive now!" I jiggled from one foot to the other and began to grin. "Da, I want him. They mean to kill him. Let me take him back to the dun!"

The spearpoint lifted another fold of the bullhide free. The gaze of the captive met that of the king, black eyes locked with blue. The fine tremors that had shaken the singer began to ease. Beneath the smudged face paint I could see the ridges of ritual scars covering cheeks and brow. What was he, I wondered, when he was not half-mad with fear?

"Are you a free man?"

The captive frowned, striving to follow the Quiritani words.

Then he shrugged. I remembered what he had said. What did freedom mean to a soul as demon-haunted as he?

"If you enter my household, you belong to me, like my hounds, like my horses, like my spear."

"Yours." His gaze never left the king. "While sun and moon rule the sky!" Something in his gaze suddenly altered, a dead coal leaping into flame.

"What do they call you, man of the moors?"

He hugged himself, looking up at the black birds that still waited in the trees.

"Crow . . . you call this one Crow. . . ."

At that, one of the younger village men took Huli's arm, whispering. The priest shook his head, then he looked at me.

"Perhaps this is thy right. Thy duty also, lady. Save us when thou shalt come to thy power. . . ." He made the sign of submission and turned away.

"Artocoxos," said Leir. "Put the lad on Cridilla's pony. The princess will ride with me."

Wrapped close to the warmth of my father's body, I realized for the first time how cold I had been. Snow was falling thickly now, but the horses knew their way back to the dun.

"My cows—" I said suddenly, remembering.

"Already on their way home. We found them before we found you," came his deep voice, close to my ear. "I came searching for you when the snow began to fall. I did not expect to be rescuing a raiding party." One of the other men laughed.

"She is his daughter, to be sure," said Artocoxos. "Did ye see how she stood over the poor lump, like a swan at the nest when the fowler comes nigh?"

"They would have killed him, and he had helped them already," I said finally. Surely it was because my father had come that the village men had given in. It was only Huli's last words that still seemed odd, as if he had given up his captive not because of the king, but because of me.

Everyone in the dun seemed to be at the gate, waiting. I saw Gunarduilla, tall and fair as my father, and Rigana's dark, vivid face at her shoulder. Her coloring was like that of the man I had rescued. It had never occurred to me before that she had so much of the blood of the old people. It was she who pushed through the crowd with a warmed blanket to wrap me in.

I let Rigana fuss over me, though Gunarduilla's wry grin told me that she understood that I had not been out that long, and it had not been that much of a storm. But it pleased Rigana to mother me. Indeed, she and Gunarduilla, being so much older, were all the kin I had to play the mother's role. It was only when the story the men were telling had passed through the Women's House that they began to look at me differently.

The people drew away and I saw the man I had rescued sitting by the hearth with my cloak still around his shoulders. The snow had washed the last of the paint from his face, and someone had given him a cloth to dry his hair. He was younger than I had thought him, wide-eyed at the confusion of sound and color that must have been strange to him, and still wary, like a half-fledged bird that has been swept from the nest before it is quite ready to fly.

"His name is Crow. I rescued him," I said proudly.

"One of the witch people!" Gunarduilla made a warding sign.

"You took him from the villagers?" asked Rigana. "You interrupted the rite?"

"He was just hanging there. He would have died." I looked from one to the other. Crow watched as if he knew we were discussing him.

"If they had been finished he would not have still been there." Rigana gripped my shoulders. "You broke the ritual—Goddess knows what harm you may have done."

"She is too young," Gunarduilla said soothingly. "Do not be frightening the child, sister. She does not understand."

"Then she had better learn," came the swift answer. Shadows gathered in Rigana's dark hair. "They have taken everything else from us—" She glared toward the other end of the hall where the warriors were laughing. "Will they take our gods away as well?"

"But Crow does not belong to the village!" I exclaimed. There was something wrong with her reasoning, but her eyes were flashing green with anger, and I could not find the words. "And father said no killing—"

"*Him!*" All her venom precipitated in the word. "If it were not for him, defiling the royal hill, there would have been no need for the ritual!"

I stared, feeling oddly guilty without understanding why. The king was her father too. I suppose it was then that I first realized that my sisters did not love him as I did. I hugged my arms, feeling a cold that had nothing to do with the snow.

"In one nest, sister cygnets rest," said Crow, his dark gaze turning inward. "Peace is best." Then he laughed.

I closed my eyes, dizzied by a sudden tumult of wings.

Chapter

The man said to her, "Is this the time that my lying with thee will be easy?"

"I have not made a tryst with thee, verily," said the woman. But they stretched themselves down together.

—*The Second Battle of Mag Tured*

From all the years of my growing there are some days that are still sharp in my memory, though I do not always know why. Although I was fostered mostly at Udrolissa, at times I journeyed with my father to my sisters' lands, and my memories of those visits are vivid in a way that is different from the unrolling fabric of my childhood in Briga. From my ninth year, for instance, I remember the visit to Belerion when my sister Rigana was given in marriage to Senouindos son of Brochagnos.

Belerion thrust like the horn of a cow from the southwestern tip of the Island of the Mighty into the sea. It had been rich once, when traders came each summer from Tartessos and Gades to the islands they called the Casseritides to trade for tin. Sometimes they came still, even though now men made their swords from iron. But the traders who did get through said that there was war in the lands around the Middle Sea, and whoever held the Pillars of Hercules could bar the gateway to the Ocean. The old days, when the people of Belerion grew wealthy on southern gold, were long past.

Rigana used to sing of those times, though they were as much
a legend to her as to me. Now, when I looked out across the golden
shimmer of gorse-bloom to the dancing blue of the sea, I imagined
I could see the trading ships standing in toward shore, their painted
sails big-bellied with wind.

"Cridilla!" The vision vanished at Gunarduilla's call. I turned
and saw her beckoning, her hair as brilliant as the flowers.

Beyond her, the dark blue robes of the priestesses were like
moving shadows against the moorland, in shocking contrast to the
bright robes of the other women waiting there. I had heard many
tales about the Wisewomen of the Sacred Ground, but this was the
first time I had seen more of them than a single dark figure whispering to Rigana's mother, who had died of a wasting fever at the
Midsummer just past. I wondered if the death of the queen had
something to do with my father's sudden willingness to marry his
second daughter to one of his men.

Slowly I made my way to Gunarduilla's side. We had come over
from the Down Fort with the other women earlier that morning.
But Rigana had been with the priestesses for a week now, preparing
for her marriage. Gunarduilla rested her hand on my shoulder. She
had inherited our father's height as well as his coloring. After a
summer outdoors chasing cattle, my own earth-colored hair had
been bleached almost as fair and my skin was the same golden
brown.

The priestesses formed a semicircle, robes billowing as the wind
swept over the rise. The number of the priestesses of the Ai-Utu,
the People of the Hare, was always seven, and they lived in a row
of round stone houses set upon the ridge above the ancestors'
mound. The folk who served them lived in the hollow below, where
the road to the estuary went by.

Belerion was a land of wind and sky, whether lashed by storms
or luxuriating beneath the golden embrace of the sun. That same
wind lifted my hair and I took a deep breath, savoring the mingled
perfumes of late summer flowers and the sweet smell of stacked
sheaves drying in the fields.

"Why do they wait?" I asked.

"They are waiting for Rigana." She grinned, and I thought of other times we had waited while our sister made up her mind which necklet to put on, or how to pin her shining black hair. But when she emerged from the largest of the houses, she was dressed simply in a sleeveless shift of the same dark blue as those of the priestesses, and her unbound hair flowed down her back. All her attention was on the earthenware bowl between her hands.

I felt rather than heard the beat of a drum as Rigana took her place at the end of the line. For a moment she turned, and I saw her eyes, wide and unfocused as if she were still blinded by the darkness from which she had come. I waved, but she was following the priestesses over the top of the ridge. Then Gunarduilla hurried me after them.

The other women were already grouped around the barrow. Some of the rocks that covered it had fallen away to reveal the huge uprights, man-high, that supported the interior cavity. The entrance was an oblong of pure blackness that drew the eye into depths beyond the mind's comprehension. Then the darkness rippled, as if the empty space were filled by shifting, sinuous coils. I shivered, remembering tales of the great serpent that lies at the heart of the world. She was the First Mother, but Her children had rebelled against Her, and even now She sometimes raged.

Rigana knelt before that door into darkness, touching the earth with her brow, and held out the bowl of milk in her hands. Gunarduilla pushed me forward, and I felt a breath of cold air from the mound.

"Listen, sister!" she said in my ear. "And learn what you must do when the king has sold you to some man as old as he is, so that the children you bear will belong to your land!"

My land . . . Rigana's land . . . And Gunarduilla's land was Alba, where *her* mother still ruled.

"But they're all our father's lands, aren't they?" I asked.

"Because he conquered them," Gunarduilla said fiercely.

I looked up at her. "But he is the king!"

Her grip on my shoulder tightened painfully. "Little fool! The people accept him because he married our mothers. The Ai-Utu will accept Senouindos as Leir's deputy here because he is marrying Rigana."

"My mother is dead already . . ." I still did not want to understand.

"Cridilla, if your people obey King Leir, it is because of you!"

I stared at her, remembering suddenly the day when I had rescued Crow from the villagers. They had saluted the king, but first
they had bowed to *me*. I shook my head.

"I do not want to be a queen."

Rigana sat back upon her heels, lifting her hands in salutation.
Gunarduilla sighed.

"Never mind, little one," she told me. "Watch now. There will
be time enough for you to understand these mysteries when you
are grown."

"Listen, ye Old Ones who in darkness are dwelling—"

Rigana pushed the bowl of milk farther into the barrow, and
it seemed to me that a mist went up from the smooth surface as it
entered the shadow of the stones.

"Kneels now to serve you, your most distant of daughters,
stripped of her sovereignty, pleading for power and begging your
blessing! Accept now the offering, ancient ones, ancestors!"

Once more she bowed her head, and shadow flowed out from
the entrance to mingle with the dark waves of her hair. The current
of air from inside the barrow seemed cool now; it was the air outside
that had become unpleasantly warm. I swayed forward, and only
Gunarduilla's firm grip on my shoulder kept me from falling beside
Rigana.

"What is it?" I shielded my eyes against the brightness of the
day. "What is inside?"

"What do you feel?"

Through laced fingers I saw one of the priestesses watching me,
and I hid my face against my sister's shoulder. Unbidden, my lips
shaped words.

"It is cool inside . . . and peaceful. They are saying to wait . . .
be patient . . . to each cycle its season . . . they abide."

Another hand, cool as the air from the mound, stroked the damp
curls back from my brow. My eyes fluttered open and I saw the
priestess.

"The power is in this one. She must be trained," said the woman softly. She was not as old as I had thought her, though threads of silver streaked her brown hair. "And soon. . . ."

"Her father will not let her go now," Gunarduilla replied. "But perhaps in time he will let her be trained by the She-Bear on the Misty Isle as I was, for he has no sons."

"When comes her bleeding time, let word be sent to me. Her right to the Mysteries cannot then be denied, if he wishes to retain sovereignty."

Rigana was getting to her feet, and the priestess moved to help her.

"Who is she?" I whispered when she had turned away. There was no reason why I should think her beautiful, but she drew the eye. Had my own mother looked that way? For a moment I wanted to run after her, to climb into her lap and let her strength keep all the strangeness at bay. Then Gunarduilla put her arm around my shoulders, and I leaned against her gratefully.

"She is Asaret," said my sister. "She is the Mother here, and great in the councils of the Ti-Sahharin, the Seven Wisewomen who watch over the land. When the Quiritani came into the land they cut out the tongues of the old priesthood, except for a few whom they kept to teach them numbers and the meaning of the sacred stones, and buried them in the holy hill, but the priestesses they dared not touch for fear of the Lady of the Land. Her interest honors you."

I frowned. As I became accustomed to the sunlight again, already I was forgetting that moment of mystery.

"Look, they are leaving us behind!" I tugged at Gunarduilla's arm.

The Womb Stone was an hour's brisk walk along the ridge trail. By the time we got there I could hear the others laughing. They brought out skins of ale and bread and bilberries, joking as the women do when there are no men to hear. I understood most of it, for I had watched cattle bred and children born, though I could not always see why they laughed.

"Wilt slip through the stone now, Rigana?" asked Mlalet, who was Lady of Brannodunon. "If 'tis easy, so will thy man's rod slide into thy cauldron, and the babes come smoothly after!"

Now they were all urging her on. Blushing, Rigana pulled the shift over her head. Her breasts were small and high, but her haunches were heavy, the triangle of pubic hair startlingly black against her white skin. Naked, she kissed the first of the upright stones that flanked the Womb Stone. Then she wriggled through the hole in the center stone, which was waist-high and round as a wheel, and crawled across the grass to salute the upright stone on the far side.

"Slick as an eel!" Another woman laughed. "She will pop out the babes like piglets."

"Daughters—" said my sister, tossing back her black hair. "From my womb only daughters will spring."

I wondered how she intended to manage that. If we could make our cows bear mostly heifers, every man would be rich as a king.

"With two sisters," said someone, "perhaps it will be so."

"What a disappointment for Senouindos! Fine bull of a man that he is." This was the Lady of Brannodunon once more. She lowered her voice. "The old queen's bed he shared when the king was not by, but never did she bear to him."

"Bitch," said Gunarduilla to me in Quiritani. "Was she lusting after him herself?"

"So then, well matched are they," said another, "for since she came into her power, our princess has tried the paces of every likely lad in the land!" The comment had been pitched too low for Rigana to hear it, but it did not sound like a criticism.

"He is well enough, if an outlander lord we must have," Lady Zana of Dubodunon answered briskly. Considering that all of these women of the old Ai-Utu blood had Quiritani husbands, and were living in the new forts that my father had ordered his chieftains to build, I was surprised that she should question it. But I already knew better than to say so to Gunarduilla. My sister could be as stubborn as a heifer, slow to trust and even slower to revoke a given loyalty, and her first allegiance was to her mother's ways.

"He is but man, when all's done," said Zlalet, "that can be led around by his rod. An' he has the welcome of thy thighs at night, Rigana, thou wilt have the rule of him by day."

After that, the conversation became uninteresting. The fuss that men and women made about coupling mystified me. I wandered out onto the moor.

Poor soil and grazing sheep kept the gorse low here, and the little pink-purple bells of the heather trembled in the breeze. I settled onto my haunches, watching the blue flicker of a butterfly with delicately spotted wings. For a moment it hovered, and I stretched out a finger to give it a resting place.

I started to rise, then froze, for the sun-dappled shadow beneath the interlaced heather stems was moving; a zigzag of white and dark brown uncoiling beneath my hand. I stared into glittering black eyes as the wedge-shaped head lifted, and a slender forked tongue flicked out to taste my skin.

"Stay still—" came a calm voice from behind me. "Become part of the land."

I could not even nod. My thigh muscles were beginning to scream already, but I forced myself to think of nothing, to become as much a part of the moor as the purple grasses or the stones. Stones . . . abruptly I remembered how the darkness had lain coiled inside the barrow, and I felt consciousness shrinking to a small point in which all the world was only one point in the pattern of the adder's shifting scales, beneath the sweep of the butterfly's blue wing. The mote that was myself floated between them, and for that moment, I desired nothing more.

Then the world flowed into motion. Awareness returned, and I saw the adder sliding into the patterned heather once more. Behind me, the priestess let out her breath in a long sigh.

"The blessing of earthmother is thine . . ." She knelt beside me, gazing at the place where the serpent had disappeared. "Upon thee be laid this prohibition: never to slay a serpent, since hast been spared."

I nodded. I knew already that I must not kill a swan, for that free, fierce bird was my father's totem. This was another, like the rule against eating the meat of the horse, which was the Quiritani totem, except when it was a sacrifice.

"Could it have killed me?" I still had no sense of danger, but I could see the fine sheen of sweat on Lady Asaret's brow.

[45]

"Well grown as thou art, perhaps not, but would have made thee ill."

"Oh . . ." I considered that, wondering why I had felt no fear.

"Art royal, child of the twin tongues, and to the queens is given the serpent power," she said as if I had spoken aloud. "It is the Goddess who thus blesses thee. Understanding will come with thy womanhood, never fear."

Which goddess? I used to wonder sometimes if my own mother were really an immortal who had returned to the Otherworld. The shining ones sometimes mated with mortal kings in order that heroes might be born. But why should a goddess take on human flesh simply to give birth to me?

I looked at Asaret curiously. Always I had thought of womanhood as an ending of freedom, but now I felt a prickle of anticipation. It would be no heathland adder, but the Serpent of the Deeps Herself that would obey me when I was a queen.

The warriors charged toward us, white skin reddened and sweat-sheened by the sun. One man stumbled, and I heard the crack of bone as he fell. His sword went cartwheeling through the air, narrowly missing the man who came after. I shrieked from a throat already hoarse with shouting, and clutched at my father's arm.

"Artocoxos! Artocoxos! Go!"

The chief of my father's Companions was in the lead, but Senouindos was close behind him, a broad, heavily muscled man surprisingly fast for his size. They raced naked as they sometimes went into battle, carrying their swords and oblong shields. Vorcuns was next, running like a hound. His long legs took one stride to Senouindos's two, and he was coming quickly, thigh muscles bunching and sliding beneath his fair skin. Rigana lifted her head like a mare scenting the stallion, and perhaps Senouindos saw it, for suddenly he put on a burst of speed and passed Artocoxos, leaving Vorcuns, spent and laughing, behind.

Only the oak priests paid any attention to the man who had gone down. Everyone else crowded around the runners, who were panting and grinning with the sweat pouring off their skin. A shift in the wind brought us the scent of roasting meat from the dun whose new drystone outer walls were already man-high. Senouindos had worked hard to make it a stronghold that would please his chieftain.

Leir pulled off one of the gold bands that clasped his upper arm and handed it to Rigana. He had proved his own strength already in the wrestling, and was dressed once more in richly chequered tunic and breeches, with the crimson cloak that had come all the way from the Middle Sea.

"Here is the prize, daughter. Do you be bestowing it, in earnest of the greater reward you will be giving him soon."

My sister's face was expressionless as she took the arm ring, but her eyes moved up and down the body of the man before her. Though he was only my father's age, he had had the white hair that gave him his name since youth, but the sweat-slick muscles crisscrossed by the pink and white lines of old scars were round and hard.

Rigana was dressed for the feast in linen shift and a long-sleeved gown of fine blue wool, with a deep border of patterned weaving at the hem. The embroidery at its neck and wrists was scarcely visible beneath the treasure of gold and amber she was wearing, her hair had been plaited and arranged in convoluted coils held with golden combs and pins, and more ornaments secured the floating white veil.

I am a queen and the child of queens whose line has ruled this land since the sacred circles were set up to watch the sun, said her splendor, *and you are a beast from beyond the sea. . . .* But as Rigana looked at him, her lips parted a little, and something stirred behind her eyes like the coiling darkness in the mound. I fidgeted, and touched my father's arm.

"Da—on the moor today I almost touched an adder!" In all the excitement of the games I had forgotten it. For a moment he went very still, then he smiled down at me, his eyes the deep and shining blue they went when he spoke of battle, or played some hard-fought game.

"Did you now? And did it bite you?" His voice was controlled.

I giggled in spite of myself. "It ate me up, and now it's hungry for more. Da, when will the feasting start?"

"Soon, little sister," said Senouindos, forcing his gaze away from

Rigana to look at me. The sweat was drying on his skin, but in his throat a pulse fluttered still. I pressed closer to my father's side. "Do you smell the roasting?"

I took a deep breath, my nostrils flaring as they identified pork and venison, and my stomach growled. The anger faded from my sister's face, and she laughed.

"The men will be wanting to bathe before the feasting, but the meat should be almost done. Perhaps Zana will let you carve off a piece to see." Her glance challenged Senouindos. "I know, waiting is hard for the young."

"And sometimes for those who are older," he answered her, "but I can control my appetite until it is time. . . ."

I looked around for Crow, and glimpsing the tuft of feathers that crowned his leather cap bobbing through the crowd, I ran off in search of him. I had not told him about the adder either. If I could beg some meat to give him, perhaps he would tell me why the snake had not bitten me.

The rim of my father's great drinking horn was banded in bronze around which serpents pursued each other, head touching tail. Their cold smoothness touched my lip as he tipped the horn. Then I tasted the mead and swallowed eagerly, knowing that I would get no more. Mead was for the warriors. I tilted my head back even farther to catch the last of the sweetness, sticking out my tongue to trap a final drop as he lifted the horn away.

One of the women brought a pitcher to refill the drinking horns. She was young, with full breasts that bobbed against the loose weave of her shift, and curly dark hair tied back with a thong. She was just a serving girl, but as she knelt to pour the mead the king pulled her against him. Her eyes widened, but she knew better than to try to draw away.

"What are you called?" After a moment he repeated the question in the old tongue. The girl's grey eyes met the king's burning blue gaze. Very slowly, he smiled.

"Triyet . . ." came the whisper, and he nodded.

"Wilt serve me, lass. Dost understand? More venison now, for my trencher is bare!"

"And thy dog be hungry also, lord," came a voice from under the low table as she darted away.

I jumped, scattering the straw, and peered beneath the rough boards. A pair of brown eyes, alight with mischief, looked back at me. If I had not heard the voice I would have thought some animal was lying there. Leir tugged, and Crow came blinking into the light, his dark curls all on end and his garment of pieced furs stuck about with straw.

"Here's a bone for thee, then." The king tossed a half-gnawed rib into the air. With a fluid somersault Crow was beneath it before it fell. He caught it between his teeth, and fell to worrying at it like a hound. Senouindos laughed. But Rigana, who sat between him and the king, did not smile. Gunarduilla, on my other side, snorted scornfully and looked away.

The boards had been laid over boulders in a rough circle inside the fortress. A series of circular stone huts had been built inside the inner wall, which was nearly twice the height of a man and as broad at the base as it was high. This was a land rich in rock, but they had not the timber for roofbeams to make the houses very wide. Still, there was room to pen the more valuable animals inside the walls, and a dependable well. As Senouindos had promised, it was a secure stronghold from which warriors could ride out to meet ships that came either to the sheltered bay of the Rock of Belerion or the more open waters of the estuary that faced the western sea.

I took another bannock from the basket and began to chew. A bowl full of bilberries was passed along, and I grabbed a handful, savoring the tart sweetness of the juices as each one went down.

Crow finished with his bone, leaped into the middle of the circle with his characteristic boneless grace, and began to juggle the hard little apples that grew wild in the sheltered vales. His gaze had gone unfocused, as it did sometimes when he danced. He moved to a drumbeat that no one else could hear, and the bits of metal and bone tied to his garment jingled merrily. Some of the men began to beat time, clapping faster and faster and laughing as the dancer spun ever more furiously.

At last the pace grew too quick for even the nimblest juggler, and the apples went flying. Most of them flew over the heads of the feasters, but one struck Artocoxos, who caught it before it reached the ground. Another hit the Lord of Brannodunon, who was only restrained from climbing over the table to throttle the juggler by the fact that now almost everyone was laughing at *him*. But there were a few, men and women, who watched Crow with a different kind of appreciation in their eyes.

The last of the apples rolled across the dirt to me.

In the meantime Artocoxos had decided to pass on the favor by tossing his apple to Vorcuns, and then for a few moments everyone was scrambling for fruit to throw at friends and enemies while Crow stood blinking. Somehow the apples all missed him, and by the time the men tired of that sport the awareness had come back to his eyes. A gesture from my father brought him back to us. He crouched, panting, behind the king.

"Let children play while they may; soon ends day!" he said breathlessly.

"Bide for a time, till they are calm again," said Leir.

Crow nodded, shivered, and looked at the apple in my hand.

"Here," I said. "You lost the others—" He took it, a swift smile lighting his dark eyes.

As things quieted, they lit the bonfire in the center of the circle, and Talorgenos, the oak priest most skilled at word-craft, stood before it. At his feet sat another priest, with the eight-stringed bow-harp in his hands.

"*Now shall I sing of the son of Blatonos—*" The harp thrummed and the warriors fell silent. As the slow summer dusk failed, the first stars were awakening in the eastern sky.

> *Blood-kin of the swan-king, who swift o'er the sea*
> *Flew free. No power had the Dragon of the deep*
> *To keep him from the fertile shore. . . ."*

"Nor earth serpents to keep us from landing upon it!" breathed Senouindos. "Those were the days of glory, were they not, my lord?" He did not notice how still Rigana sat beside him, or the look that passed between her and Gunarduilla.

Leir was staring past the singer into the flickering flames, and

I wondered what he was seeing there. I thought of the land from which he had come as an endless expanse of saltmarsh and forest where everyone was always at war.

"But those days were long ago, and now your daughter has grown to an age to marry," said Rigana with poisoned sweetness.

Leir looked at her. "Child, Senouindos is a brave man, and steadfast. He will guard you and this land. I have tried to do my best for you. Do you understand?"

I could see her struggle. Couldn't *he* see how she must feel? Then she forced a smile and patted his hand.

"Surely I am grateful, father. Senouindos and I shall do very well." The harp spoke again, commanding attention, and once more the bard began to sing.

> *"By furor of storm and sea-wave wracked,*
> *Cracked upon the rocks the courageous craft.*
> *Laughed then Leir, to his lips set horn—"*

"I remember!" cried Artocoxos. "I was half-drowned. Your first and greatest deed, lord king, was to squeeze me dry!"

"Do ye remember the storm, then?" said Senouindos. "The waves were like moving mountains, monsters with maws open to swallow us whole!"

"And the planking groaning like a pregnant cow," added old Uxelos. "As wet inside as out, but no hazard to heroes. I mind when the mast began to split, an' I was up with the rope before it could fall, binding it round."

"And I was the one," said another man, "who was first, when the rocks snapped our oar blades, to push us free with the stump of my oar."

"He grabbed it from his brother, then was sick over the side . . ." said Crow softly, searching the grass for a fallen bone. I kicked him, and his eyes widened as if he were only just realizing he had spoken aloud. But the warrior who had boasted was glaring, and I knew Crow had made another enemy.

Fortunately no one else seemed to have heard. The younger men, those born in this country or come over in later shiploads in answer to Leir's call, listened enviously. Their turn for bragging would come later, and as long as there was ale to oil their throats they would go on.

> *"First on the shore to follow the chieftain*
> *Was Senouindos, wise and worthy warrior.*
> *More valiant the deeds that followed, the reward,*
> *His lord bestows, the radiant maiden.*
> *Laid in one bed, may they make a son;*
> *One hero-born, to mingle the blood*
> *Of his father and grandsire in glory!"*

This morning, Rigana had prayed for a girl.

As the thrumming of harpstrings faded, a twittering of flutes came from behind us. During the singing, all the older women had withdrawn from the circle. They stood now before the largest of the houses. Silhouetted in the doorway was the priestess.

For a moment no one moved. I gazed from the dark figure in the doorway to the priest whose robes glimmered pale in the light of the fire.

"Now are the torches of the night alight in the heavens!" cried Lady Asaret in the old tongue. "Now are the stars auspicious for the marriages of queens. Let the royal woman be brought to her bridal!"

Two of the women came forward as Rigana rose, and Gunarduilla and I fell in behind them. It was so still that I could hear the whisper of her gown across the grass. Then the flutes began to play once more. As the women closed around us, I heard uneasy laughter from the circle of men by the fire, growing louder as the servants brought them more mead.

But for Rigana they had made an enclosure of wicker screens between the hut and the wall of the dun. The priestesses disrobed her, helped her to stand in the wooden tub, and poured the water over her body. I stood in Gunarduilla's shadow, half afraid they would notice me and make me leave, half wishing I could run away. Some of the women were whispering together; there was a burst of muted laughter. The weight of expectance in the air made me twitch like a nervous mare. Goose flesh pebbled Rigana's white skin.

"Take courage, sister," said Gunarduilla softly, "and remember thine inheritance. When the man lies between thy thighs, he will be thy prisoner."

Then they were toweling her dry and rubbing her with scented oils. As they led her into the house, a sudden shout of laughter erupted from the fire circle. With considerably more speed and less ceremony, the men were disrobing the bridegroom.

They marched Senouindos to his bride with a man on each arm, as if they were putting the bull to the cow. But he was grinning. It was only when they opened the door and he saw Rigana's white body by the glimmer of the rushlights, with the embroidered linen of the bedcloth over the mattress of sweet-smelling herbs behind her, that the smile faltered.

"Be welcome to my dwelling, lord. . . ." She held out the bride-cup with the gesture of a queen, and I remembered that in my father's language that was the meaning of her name.

Then someone pulled me away and they shut the door.

The dun was full of people, but I was alone. At this moment the hut behind me was the center of the world, but I did not belong there. I heard my father laughing, but as I started forward I saw that he had one arm around the girl who had served the mead. With the other he was pulling down her shift so that one round breast was bared.

In a moment he would have her down on the grass. The other serving girls were faring likewise, while the wives had withdrawn to the women's enclosure, or were off to their own beds with their men. It was always thus at weddings, so why did I feel as if everyone I loved had abandoned me?

"Once was a well in a cavern where lived a young maid . . ." said a quiet voice beside me. "Do you ask, where this was and why she stayed? Will you listen? Follow, and shall hear . . ."

A shadow leaped lightly to the wall of the dun and darted up it, hardly seeming to touch the stones. I choked back astonished laughter. Could I do that?

The stones were rough, and I was bruised and breathless by the time I had scrambled to the top after him. From here the fire was a dying coal. Crow sat cross-legged, gazing at the stars that flickered in the sky-sea like reflections in a forest pool.

"She lived *in* the well?" I gasped. "Was she a person at all?"

"A person, but why human? Sometimes she was Maiden-Guards-Well, and sometimes Sugë the serpent, black as waters in caves where light never comes; white as eyeless fishes who swim there."

I thought of the snake I had met that morning and shivered. Everyone knew that there were beings who could appear in the shapes of men or animals. Had it been only an adder I saw? Then another question occurred to me.

"Why did the fish have no eyes? How did they get there?"

"Why have eyes when is nothing to see? This was in the morning of the world, when man and beast talked together. All things different then." He grinned at me. "A story of the hill people. You want to hear?"

I drew up my knees and clasped my arms around them, nodding vigorously.

"One night maybe badger dug through top of cavern, maybe tree root came in, but through hole above, Maiden-Guards-Well saw something sparkling. She wanted it, she called to it, but no answer came."

"It was a star, wasn't it?" I exclaimed.

"The first star," Crow said. "Maiden could go down, deep to heart of earth, but how to get out of cave? She became serpent, curling and coiling, coiling and curling around the well. Water excited, began to rise, filled cavern. Sugë spiraled up through hole and out as fountain, higher and higher, wanting the brightness. But now every drop of water reflecting starlight. Water filled heaven with river of stars.

"She could not find the one she looked for. She fell back to earth, waters spreading everywhere, filling hollows, making streams through every fold in mountains. Now land rich with water, and sky bright with stars. But Maiden, weeping, sank back beneath earth again."

"Because he had left her . . ." I said bitterly. In the silence, I realized that I had brought my father with me, even though we were alone. But above us light flowed in a glittering stream across the sky.

"Just now he does not need this one, does not need you," Crow said in a different voice, and I knew, without understanding, that he was feeling the same way as I. "He is a star."

From the hut below us I heard my sister Rigana's triumphant cry.

Chapter

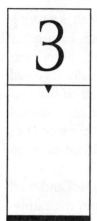

Now when Cuchulain went alone across Alba,
he was sad and gloomy and weary for the loss of his
* comrades,*
neither knew he whither he should go to seek
* Scathach.*

—*The Wooing of Emer*

B y the time the last of the wedding feast had been consumed, Rigana seemed content with the husband to
whom Leir had given her, and Senouindos went about
with a triumphant grin. I was less amused by the smile
on the face of the girl Triyet as she realized that Leir meant to bring
her along when we went north again. I tried not to mind. There
had been many women, but I was the king's favorite child.

But in the end she did make a difference. It was because of a
quarrel between us just after my eleventh winter that my father sent
me away.

Since the last full moon it had been raining, a steady, soaking
downpour that kept folk indoors. Leir's hall at Udrolissa was large
enough for the king and his Companions to sit down together to
their feasting, but I was glad to escape at the first glimmer of
sunshine. From the walkway inside the palisade I could see that the
season had been advancing despite the rain. Woods that had been
a dark fretwork of bare branches were veiled now with pale green,
and the meadows glowed where new growth had pushed through
the sodden mat of last year's grass. After the mixed reek of wood-

smoke and wet wool and the scents of men who had been cooped up together for too long, the sweetness of the rain-washed air was dizzying.

My father's wolfhounds had followed me to the wall, splashing gleefully through the muddy pools and leaping upon each other with ferocious growls and wildly wagging tails. They were long-limbed beasts with coarse, brindle grey fur who usually surveyed the world with lordly disdain. But today they seemed to have reverted to puppyhood, and when I climbed down from the wall they extended their game to me. Laughing, I tried to fend them off, but in moments muddy paws had undone all the care I had taken to keep from being splashed as I crossed the yard.

Shouting, I sank my fingers into the nearest furry ruff and tried to wrestle the dog down. I turned my face aside from the carnivorous stink of hot dog breath and laughed, putting forth my own strength exultantly as we rolled over in the mud and came up again. The next few moments were a blur. Only gradually did I realize that someone was shouting my name.

"Cridilla!"

White-tip whuffed and sat down suddenly. I wiped mud from my eyes and saw stiff folds of saffron wool and, above them, Triyet's accusing eyes. Her mutterings faded as she saw that she had gotten my attention.

"Rolling in the mud with the dogs! Cridilla! Wilt wallow with the pigs next? Get up now and wash thyself. Is this a proper way for a woman of the Royal House to behave?"

It might as well have been Rigana, the accent of Belerion pattering quick and sharp against the slower speech of the north. But Triyet was not my sister. One-eye nosed at my shoulder, panting to resume our game. I tugged at his ears, then shoved him away.

"In the old days, a princess would not have been allowed—"

"In the old days, there would have been a whipping for such words from thee!" I replied, shaking off dogs and getting to my feet again. These days Triyet wore embroidered linen instead of coarse wool, and necklaces of gilded bronze glinted upon the generous bosom that my father so admired, but sharing his bed did not give Triyet a mother's rights over me.

"My folk had their own farm in my grandmother's time!"

"Now thy seed is sown by a Quiritani lord!" I replied. Her cheeks blossomed with red blotches that went vilely with the saffron wool.

"Half-blood bitch!" she muttered.

My eyes narrowed. "Not so little, vixen!" I hardly had to jump to reach Cygnet's back anymore. "My father's dogs are more nobly bred than thee!"

"Unbridled brat—"

"High-tailed mare—" I waggled my rear like a breeding mare presenting herself to the stallion.

"Oho—she has you, lass! She has you now!"

The roar of my father's laughter silenced both of us, and the dogs surged toward him. For a moment Leir looked like a rough-topped pine awash in a swirling, furry grey sea. His eyes danced, then he barked a command and the dogs began to flop down in the mud beside him.

"Wilt *encourage* her?" Triyet was still furious.

Behind the king Artocoxos and several of the Companions were gnawing on their moustaches to keep from grinning. Zaueret and the other women had come out from the kitchen hut to see. The last time that Triyet and I had engaged in a shouting match it had been my backside that suffered, and I could see the lines of laughter in Leir's face tightening into a frown.

"She is my daughter," he said quietly in Quiritani.

Triyet tried to draw herself up in regal indignation. It was not entirely successful. After two years of good feeding, she was plump as a partridge.

"Discipline her thyself then, lest she be mistaken for a slave!"

My father stilled as he did when something he would not put into words disturbed him.

"Are you so much better, woman?" But instead of "woman" he used a word that had the connotation of a heated stone that one puts into the bed to warm it. "You have given me no child."

I frowned. Only Leir's queens had ever borne him children because the women of the duns gave his mistresses herbs to prevent conception. But I had not realized that Leir did not know.

Triyet's eyes widened. Bracelets chimed gently as she reached out to him. I watched curiously, wondering once more how such a simple alteration in the lines of her body could bring him around.

But this time, Leir simply looked at her. "You'll not speak to my daughter so again." His gaze moved back to me, and though his expression remained severe, it seemed to me that laughter leaped in his eyes, like lightning in a summer sky. "And you . . . will wash before you return to the hall."

I thought that would be the end of it, but when I did come in, still damp around the edges and shivering because the promise of spring had faded with the light and it was cold, I felt a tension that kept voices subdued and glances wary. But I only noticed that for a moment. While I had been outside having the top layer of my skin scrubbed off, my sister Gunarduilla had arrived.

"What is wrong here, child?" she asked when I had finished hugging her and telling her about the mud and the dogs and the rain. She had wintered in the north with her mother, and I was surprised to realize how glad I was to see her again.

"Oh—" I cast a quick glance across the hearth and suppressed a giggle. Triyet was sitting next to the king, but they were not touching. He was deep in conversation with some men from the midlands. Rumor ran that the war arrow was going round the villages of the Ai-Zir, and several Quiritani chieftains dissatisfied with their holdings had joined them. Clearly, Zayyar-a-Khattar had finished licking the wounds he had gotten in the war four years ago. While Zaueret was scrubbing me I had heard the warriors speculating hopefully on the prospects of a summer's campaign.

"Triyet scolded me for getting so dirty, and he stopped her. . . ." I watched in admiration as Gunarduilla raised one golden eyebrow.

"I did wonder how long she would last," she said quietly.

"What do you mean?"

"Do you remember a woman called Blaracca?" Gunarduilla said then. "Very fair, the wife of Brendigenos, whom Leir killed for rebellion."

I nodded. My father's rule had been a history of such conflicts, but I did remember the woman a little. She had been sweet-voiced and rather shy.

"But what does she have to do with Triyet?"

Gunarduilla laughed. "There have been many Triyets, many Blaraccas, little one. Our father has had one woman after another ever since he stopped marrying queens!"

"And do they all end up fighting with him?"

"I suppose they do." She grinned. "Leir Blatoniknos has never been an easy man."

I shrugged. He was my father. How could he be different?

"Never mind, little one. It does not matter." Gunarduilla smoothed my hair. "I have an errand outside. Do not let them take my meat away!"

When she had gone, I concentrated on my forehead, trying to imitate her lifted eyebrow, but when I touched my face I realized that all I had managed was a frown. With a sigh, I began to gnaw once more on the meaty beef bone.

When we had finished eating, Triyet retired to her boxbed with ostentatious dignity. In one corner of the hall two of the younger warriors had stripped off their ornaments and were wrestling. Artocoxos and Vorcuns moved pieces across a gameboard while the women they were currently sleeping with looked on. Talorgenos sat in a corner with one of the younger priests, who twisted the pegs of his bow-harp as he tried to get the strings in tune. If there was to be war, the priest's songs of past valor would be much in demand.

The dogs had received the same rough scrubbing as I had been subjected to. Now they sprawled in an untidy patchwork of grey and brindle and brown between Leir and the hearth. Crow lay among them, his tattered fur garment blending with their hides so that it was hard to distinguish between dog and man. All I could see of his body was the oddly defenseless curl of one sinewy hand.

As soon as Triyet had gone, I burrowed in beside him, pillowing my head on Storm's furry flank and stretching out broadside to the fire. After weeks of smoked pork and salt beef, the fresh meat the hunters had brought in had been inebriating. The dog licked my face and then lowered her head with a gusty sigh. Warm, full, and tired, I let my eyes close.

"I do not share Triyet's hysteria," said Gunarduilla sardonically, "but I understand it. Are you really raising your daughter to companion your dogs?"

I heard Leir's deep laughter, half opened one eye, and glimpsed my sister sitting on the bench beside the king. But nobody sounded angry. I slid back into the warmth of the dogs and the fire.

"Did you think that I spoke foolery? Look at her now!"

"What harm?" came my father's deep reply. "The beasts will not hurt her, nor yet will the long lad. Let her lie!"

"Harm! No indeed—for surely in all their fur you can hardly tell them one from another! Let him be Basajaun if it amuses you—" She used the old word for the wildman that lived in the deeps of the forests. "But what warrior will take your daughter Maitagarri, lying there!"

"I am not a wildwoman!" I sat up suddenly, tumbling off Squealer, who had pillowed his gaunt head on my thigh.

"Are you not?" Leir laughed again, ruffling my hair as if I had been one of the dogs. "Then you must be something even more fierce and terrible; a she-bear, perhaps, or even the great worm of the dales!"

"If I am, then I am going to eat *you*!" I flung my arms around his leg, thick as a tree trunk beneath the wool of his breeches, and began to worry at the chequered cloth.

"Fierce, yes," said Gunarduilla, "and what are you going to do with all that valor? This one will not be content to spin by the fire. I will hold you to your promise, father, for her sake and for your own. You must let Cridilla come to Caiactis with me!"

What promise? I let go of my father's leg, staring. She had spoken before of the island where the warrior women taught their skills, but I had thought it was a child's tale. I felt a vibration between them like the tension when a warrior catches his opponent's blade on his own. The bold curves of Leir's nose and brow were repeated in the blunt lines of hers; the firelight struck the same gold from their hair.

"Wild swans soar high, where do they fly?
Who can bind them? Who can find them?

[62]

*Let go the cygnet now and learn,
How the splendid swans return!"*

Crow's singsong faded. He had not opened his eyes. Perhaps
he had not even been aware he was speaking. This time it did not
matter, but the warriors murmured against him when he prophesied
someone's death before a campaign.

I turned to tackle him, but my father's hand closed on my
shoulder.

"Is it truly so?" Leir said softly, looking down at me.

"Da—you won't make me leave you!" I grasped at his fingers.
Even the dogs were not so solid and comforting as my father's
hand. His gaze went from me to my sister with a sudden flicker of
hostility.

"The cow has betrayed me," his voice hoarsened. "Will you steal
my little heifer away?"

"Of course not, father," Gunarduilla said carefully. "Neither
Cridilla nor I would ever hurt you. She will return to you stronger,
a mistress of the sword!"

"Will you turn her into just another such shield-maiden as yourself, then? Where will I find her a husband?"

Gunarduilla's smile challenged him. "Would it be so ill a thing
to have two daughters who can guard your back?"

Leir laughed, and the other men, who had been trying not to
show that they were listening, echoed him. Talorgenos had taken
his place at the king's left hand. He could move amazingly unob-
trusively for such a massive man. I met his slow, reflective gaze,
and felt my stomach clench, for his presence had turned this conversation into a council.

"You will be much in the midlands this year, and the next as
well, fighting the Ai-Zir and strengthening your defenses there,"
Gunarduilla went on. "There is no place for the child. Cridilla grows
too big to be ruled by your servants. Will you leave her to run wild
here? Better to let her go with me! You know that she will be safe
on the Isle."

Leir sat back and reached for his cup. "Wise One, have you
counsel?" he asked Talorgenos.

The priest bit down upon his thumb, a practice by which his kind were trained to unlock their knowledge. After a moment he gave a little shudder, and came back to us again.

"She is the luck of the land, the daughter of the ninth wave; she is the cup in which your life is held. But when the seedling stretches away from earth's shelter it must grow strong enough to weather the storm. High king, your bond was given when the child was born. Oak and earth and fire remember. This morning the omens of change were in the air. I think that you will have to let her go."

Leir's gaze had gone inward in that expression I called his "king look." It usually meant that he was planning something. Crow sat up, thrusting the dogs aside, but my gaze was fixed on my father's face, as if by memorizing the winged eyebrows and the broad, weathered brow, his jutting cheekbones and the long line of the jaw still covered with winter beard, I could keep him forever.

"Safe? Perhaps, but I suppose she must learn to fight some-time. . . ."

"I have your word on it, then—" Gunarduilla held out her hand. As Leir took it, I pulled myself up, no longer caring that everyone could see my tears.

"Child of my heart—" He drew me into his lap and I clung to him, trying to find room for legs and arms that had somehow gotten longer since the last time I sat this way. I felt the strong beat of his heart beneath the rough wool of his tunic, and was comforted.

"Didst fear would be abandoned by thy Da?" His beard tickled my ear. "Never, my little one, never think it—this is but for a time, and then wilt return to me."

It was drizzling when we rode out from Udrolissa, and no one could see whether the moisture on my cheeks was rain or tears. I sat straight on Cygnet's round back and pretended that this journey was like any other. But there were memories for me in every rain-swollen stream and copse of budding thorn, and every oak tree within a day's ride of the dun was an old friend. We skirted fields that had been won from the forest with iron axes and iron-shod ards, and men who labored to scratch new furrows into the sodden

earth looked up from the ploughshare as we rode past. By afternoon we were in the deep forest that clothed the rising land where
the Nith splashed down from the dales. As the sun sank, the shadows lengthened beneath the trees. Several times, I thought I
glimpsed something moving behind us, but I could not tell what
it might be.

That night we guested at a cluster of huts that clung to the slope
below the sacred springs. Gunarduilla went up the hill to speak to
the priestess, but I stayed by the fires. I had rolled myself in my
cloak for the night and was already drowsing when I heard whispers
above me.

"Will she be safe then, in thy northern land?" It was the voice
of an old woman. I let my eyes open just a little and glimpsed faded
blue robes and a profile as cragged as a moorland tor in the glow
of the dying fire.

"What is safety, Mother Tamar?" Gunarduilla asked. "But my
blessing on those warriors whose challenge draws the swan-lord
southward, else never would he have allowed the child to go away.
She will be taught things that there is need for her to know."

I felt a tingle as the priestess touched my hair. But I kept my
eyes shut, pretending to sleep until they went away.

Later still, when the fire was only a glow beneath the ash, I
became aware of another presence near. An angular, furred form
bent over me and I gasped, wondering if Basajaun himself had
come, but a muttered word and a touch upon my eyelids sent me
spiraling down into sleep again.

In my dreaming, I sped across a glimmering silver sea set with
islands that the parting mists alternately veiled and revealed. Ominous humps that seemed carven from the bones of night became
abruptly luminous as the light shifted. I pressed forward eagerly.
And then, suddenly, it was a grass-grown meadow over which I
was running, racing someone I could not quite see. I thought it
was my father, but when I risked a glance I realized that the other
runner was no taller than I. The radiance of his golden hair glimmered on the grass before him, then for a moment, his head flamed
red as fire. And in that moment he blazed ahead of me and was
gone.

When I woke I would have thought it all a dream, but on the fur beside me lay a crow's black wing feather and a morsel of Zaueret's sweet preserve, and though I still did not understand about the boy, I knew who the shadow in the forest behind me had been.

In the morning we resumed our journey. The road ran through thick woods, starred with early violets, and late snowdrops nodded beside the streams; creamy primroses were opening wherever there was a little sun. Soon we were winding westward up the vale of the Verbeia. The lifting mist revealed the high green rim of the moors beyond the trees, shading to purple and brown as the grasses gave way to the hardier vegetation of the moor. Sometimes we saw smoke from hut circles tucked away in the folds of the hills, and a few flocks of sheep drifted across the green, but for hours at a time we rode through a landscape that seemed empty of humankind.

"Empty?" said Gunarduilla, pulling her pony back beside mine. "Is the forest empty when you see no animals there? The dalesmen have learned to keep cover, since the Quiritani came. It is true, though, that now there are places in those hills where only the witch-people go—the Senamoi, from whom Crow came," she explained.

"They pitch their skin tents in the lee of a hill for a little while and then move on, hunting across the hills. In the time of your mother's grandmother, when seasons were warmer, it was different. In those days there were cornfields where only sheep can find food now. But the Goddess turned Her face from us and hid the sun. Now it is the sheltered bottomlands for whose possession men war."

"Is that why the men of the Ai-Zir in the south are going to fight our father now?" Her words had reminded me why I was being sent away.

Gunarduilla answered with a snort of laughter. "They fight because they are men!"

"If that is such an ill thing," I responded, "then why are you dragging me north to learn to use a spear?"

"A man fights for glory, a woman from necessity!" She turned, eyes blazing, and Cygnet tossed her head as I inadvertently jerked the rein.

"On the Island you will learn to track a deer and snare a bird as well as how to kill a man with lance or sword. You will learn how the wolf fights, how the eagle dances in the air, and how the salmon slips upstream. If you are very good, you may learn the way of the Bear. Boys and girls both train there, but it is the female warriors, women of a line older even than our own queens, who rule. If your mother had been a warrior, perhaps the Quiritani would not rule this land today!"

"But you and I are Quiritani too," I objected. Gunarduilla had always talked this way, but it did not make sense anymore. I saw her face set into hard lines that made her look suddenly like her mother, that brown, crabbed queen of Alba whom I had only seen once, when Leir was making one of his annual visits there. For a time we rode without speaking beneath whispering alder trees.

"Once I thought so," Gunarduilla said finally. "Leir's blood and my mother's warred within me, until I thought to take my blade and let it all flow out into the land and so have peace. We have two tongues, sister, but the spirit cannot live divided. I have chosen, and once I take oath I do not change. In my heart, I am my mother's child."

"I never knew my mother," I whispered. "This is nothing to do with me." I wanted to dig my heels into Cygnet's sides and gallop away.

"Little sister, did no one ever tell you how Leir won this land?"

"Talorgenos has chanted the story a hundred times in the hall!"

"Not the whole story!" She laughed bitterly. "He sings how the heroes battled the waves, but does he tell how the warriors of the Ai-Akhsi were scattered, searching the sodden meadows for stock washed away in that storm, when the Quiritani came?" I shook my head, unable to answer her.

"Then listen! This is how Zaueret, who lived through it all, told the tale to me. The people of the Great House knew of the coming of the Quiritani by the smoke of burning steadings, and later by the flames that opened like pale flowers against the darkening sky.

The full war-host would have made short work of the sea-raiders, but there was no time for them to gather, and so, when the line of torches flowed up the road toward the Great House above the Udra, there were only the warriors of the household to oppose them, and the king with his two half-grown sons."

"Sons . . ." I stopped her. "Did my mother have children before me?"

"Did you not know it? Queen Fieret had sons, yes, but they never grew to be men," Gunarduilla went on. "She waited inside with her women; she waited and heard the clangor of iron on bronze, and the cries. And they say that her face did not change when Leir thrust back the hangings that covered the doorway and stood before her with the blood of her children still red on his hands.

" 'Your man is dead,' he told her in the rough gabble the traders use. 'Now this place belongs to me. . . .'

" 'I grieve for him, but it changes nothing. The land is mine, is me—' she answered him.

" 'Then I will take you!' said Leir, and he shut the door.

"Fieret did not resist him. She had known this must happen, for how could a war-leader rule except through the queen? Only before she would accept him she laid upon him the *geas* that he should never curse a woman. She was older than he, almost past bearing, but they say that Leir loved her. Perhaps that came easier because he was so much away, riding first to the north to conquer Alba and marry my mother, Aglidet, as he had married yours. Then he went campaigning south to set his heel upon Belerion and took Dara of the Ai-Utu as his third queen."

"And my mother," I interrupted. "What was she like? What did she feel for him?"

"For Leir I think she came to feel kindness," Gunarduilla said reluctantly. "But I only saw her once, before you were born. She was a very soft-spoken woman, but there was strength in her, like one of these hills." She gestured toward the high sweep of the moor.

"But when she gave birth to me she died . . ." I said flatly. "My father would still have her if it had not been for me."

I had always known that, but I had never really thought about it before. I had no memory of my mother, only of Zaueret's warm breast and her lullabies. I suppose my first knowledge about my birth had come from women's gossip overheard when they thought me too young to understand. It was my fault that people left me, or sent me away.

"Fieret was not forced to have another child, even though Leir desired an heir for the north," Gunarduilla said then. "You will be taught how to prevent conception when your moon blood begins to flow. Never think it any fault of yours, Cridilla. The queen chose to bear a daughter to be lady of this land."

"Father said last year that I was growing to be very like her."

It had been in the autumn. We had been driving the cattle down from the hills to the home pastures, making camp along the way when night fell. I remembered stars, and the sound of men singing, and the nutty flavor of grain parched in the fire. All the other chieftains must have been busy with the same work as we were, for there had not been a whisper of trouble for weeks, and during those few golden days Leir had ridden like a wildman and laughed like a boy. And he had shared all that exuberant joy with me.

"He told me . . ." I swallowed, "that he had loved her very much. It is my fault that she died."

"I'm sure he believes that he did," Gunarduilla said dryly. "It is astonishing how often death improves a relationship. Leir has had eleven years to idealize his first queen—although, in the case of your mother, there was not much he needed to forget. Fieret never openly opposed him."

I felt tears prick behind my eyelids and looked quickly away. The king had never loved Gunarduilla's mother. How could she understand? *I won't argue with you either, Da—I'll make it up to you.* I cried silently. *Only please let me come home again.* But Cygnet plodded steadily onward, and the bare-topped hills did not reply.

For the next two days we moved west through the dales, angling northward as the great hump whose summit was slowly being carved into another of Leir's forts hove into view. The Painted People had built a few hillforts before the Quiritani came, when the climate changed and the crops began to fail. But it was my father's folk who needed the security of the summits to control the countryside. Rigodunon, the fort of the king, was the greatest so far begun.

For the rest of that week the great mountain was our companion, but presently we came out into sight and scent of the sea and turned due north through a country of long lakes set among tumbled vales. Ten days after we had ridden out from Udrolissa, we descended into the green fields where the Soulonagos firth cut deeply into the land. More blue hills blurred the horizon, but on the plain before us, a stark shaft of lichened grey marked the beginnings of the land of Alba. We paused to honor the Young God by laying wreaths of primroses upon His standing stone. Then we turned westward toward the Misty Isle, into Gunarduilla's country.

Timbers creaking with strain, the boat came round into the wind and headed back toward the jagged rocks of the shore. My stomach responded to the changed motion with a renewed queasiness that sent me groping for the side. Ever since we had boarded at High Banks over a week ago, I had been sick, to the crew's amusement and Gunarduilla's thinly veiled exasperation. Who would have thought that a daughter of the hero who had tamed the sea would have no stomach for sailing at all?

I clung to the rail and fixed my eyes on the wildly sculptured shape of the land before me, trying to ignore the heaving grey mountains to either side. There were shadows beneath those glassy slopes, eyes that watched, tendrils beckoning. After the first day I had learned better than to eat solid food in the mornings. But this was the last island.

The boat's motion eased as we rounded the point and slid into the protected waters of the deeply cut bay. The faded dun sail flapped and thrummed as it was pulled around. I sat up, finding relief in even so small a change in the motion. Behind us other sails danced across the waves. The folk of the north clung to the rocky coasts and the islands. Overland travel in these lands was tortuous, but the sea-roads were open, and fishing vessels thronged these waters like ducks on the river at home.

I took a deep breath. Mixed with the salt tang of the sea I smelled green grass and pine. The shrouding mists thinned suddenly, and sunlight woke color from the rugged slopes and slashed a stroke of brilliance across the sea. Silver splashed down the mountainside and wound through the green meadow at the head of the bay. For a moment a rampart of stone sprang into view, then the clouds closed in again and there was only the rocky hillside.

Timbers shuddered beneath me as the boat grated up onto the pebble-strewn strand. One of the warriors blew long and mournfully on his horn, and from somewhere among the pines came an answer. Then Gunarduilla hauled me to my feet, and from the rocks came a wave of moving bodies whose yammering drowned out the calls of the gulls. I clutched her arm, recollections of Crow's tales of rock goblins mingling with memories of the faces I had seen in the sea.

Gunarduilla was laughing. We were surrounded by skinny shapes half-clad in fur and leather, gabbling in a mixture of tongues. Bright eyes gleamed through tossing sun-bleached hair, scratched arms and legs blurred into a swirl of brown limbs. I let go of my sister's sleeve. If these were children, they must not think that I was afraid.

But they were like no children that I had seen. They quivered like my father's dogs, equally eager for fight or for play. And like the hound pack, a single whistle stilled them instantly.

I took a quick breath, eyes widening as two dark-haired warrior women preceded a figure thick-bodied with muscle through the silent crowd. Sturdy legs showed below a leather kilt, stout arms emerged from a bearskin cloak that flowed down to its heels. Gold glittered from ears and neck, and a gold-studded leather band confined many braids of greying hair. As the cape fell away I saw sagging breasts above the muscled belly and knew even before my sister spoke who this must be.

"They call her the She-Bear—Bear Mother—Artona in our tongue. The other two are Spirit Bear and Shadow Bear, her daughters," Gunarduilla said softly. "Speak humbly. On this island, she is greater than any queen."

If I had trusted my voice, I could have reassured her. This

woman reminded me of my father when he was getting ready for battle, and the humor that gleamed in her slitted grey eyes did not reassure me at all.

"Gunarduilla! Eh, but art grown like a pine tree!" Bear Mother opened her arms and Gunarduilla moved into an embrace that could have crushed her. "So this be th' little one!" Bear Mother added, letting her go and looking at me. I stood straight, forcing myself to meet the edged glance of those eyes. "Will be another tall one like thee, Gunarduilla, and fronts me without fear!" She laughed. "Daughter of a royal dun, 'tis certain. Let the child-pack try 'er, then will we see what's bred in th' bone!"

"The crossing was hard for her—" Gunarduilla began, but the warrior woman stopped her.

"All th' better. All must start th' same. Wouldst have me coddle th' maid?" The children behind her quivered, and my stomach knotted. I looked at Gunarduilla in appeal, but she shook her head. The She-Bear frowned once more at me.

"Wilt learn to be a warrior, lass? Wilt accept all challenges, speak truth always, and obey?"

As those eyes fixed me, I felt something stir within me that was not fear. Perhaps the sun had pierced the clouds again, but I saw light flaring from a swordblade, and I knew that if I assented, one day I would wield that blade upon a battlefield. I shuddered with mingled anguish and glory, but the other way lay only shadow. I looked at the mistress of battles and brought up my arm in the salute the young men gave my father when they marched out of the dun.

Trading our escort for the horde of children, Gunarduilla and I followed the She-Bear up the winding path into the fort the flicker of sunlight had revealed, and I drew strength from the solid ground. There were stone huts built against the walls, and one larger round house thatched with straw. They fed us on venison and oatcakes and thin beer, and Gunarduilla joked with Bear Mother and her daughters and the two men who seemed to be the only other adults here.

Murmuring to one another, the children watched me, and through half-lowered eyelids I scanned their ranks, distinguishing with difficulty between beardless boys and girls whose breasts had not yet grown. Most of them were like my mother's people, sturdily built with hair from fair to brown. But there were two long-limbed black-headed girls like Crow, and a boy whose red hair flamed like a torch in the gloom.

And then, suddenly, the meal was over. The She-Bear gestured to one of the dark girls.

"Willow. Here be Cridilla, thy new mate—in the Fieldmouse hut will she lie till a' wins a place in a clan. Show her th' way."

I turned to Gunarduilla, but her face was like stone. "Sister—" I whispered. Could she hear me?

Waiting for her to reply, I pulled off my cloak and unclasped the belt from which my pouch and bronze dagger hung, and gradually I began to realize that no answer was going to come. My father had abandoned me and now my sister was deserting me too. After a moment's consideration I unpinned the brooch from my neck as well. I was sorry about the rest of my clothes, but in any case they would not last long here. Gunarduilla looked at my preparations and lifted one eyebrow, but I refused to meet her eyes.

They were waiting for me in the yard. Willow stepped away as the ring closed around me, and I settled into a crouch, conscious of the other eyes that were watching through the door.

"Will ye tackle me all at once," I asked, "or choose a champion?" A boy who looked about nine edged forward, and I guessed that he had been the latest to arrive before me. Then we grappled, and all awareness narrowed to scuffling feet and straining limbs.

The first lad was sinewy and strong, but I was faster. After a few moments he rolled away and the next one came after me. "Quiritani bitch!" someone hissed in my ear. Teeth and nails and elbows scraped and gouged, and I heard my tunic tear. My father's dog pack had been kinder. I realized then that it was going to be a dog fight indeed unless I could reach the leader and win or submit swiftly.

But keeping my feet seemed to be as much as I could do. I fought mindlessly, determined only to do as much damage as I could before they bore me down. Presently the breath began to rasp in my chest; even rage could not move my arms and legs quickly enough to block the blows. Then I was dimly aware of someone behind me who was not attacking. I shielded face and belly with my arms and felt a little strength flow back into me.

"To the wall," came a Quiritani voice in my ear. I felt my companion move and followed. Something bulked up before us. I touched stone and turned, feeling another shoulder against my own. Sharp edges poked my back and buttocks, but the support let me catch my breath, and I punched viciously at the first face that came near.

For a few moments more they came on, then there was a space before us. The whistle calling them off was only a formality. Gasping, I closed my eyes, feeling the ringing in my ears begin to fade and sensing that there were a number of places that were going to start hurting very badly, very soon. I knew that Gunarduilla was still watching from the doorway, but I would not look at her. I blinked sweat, or perhaps it was blood, out of my eyes, and turned to my companion.

Even in the dimming light I recognized the flame of red hair. It was the long-faced freckled boy I had seen earlier. His lip was puffed now and bleeding, but he gave me a crooked grin.

"Agantequos son of Vorequos of the Moriritones, your ally," he said thickly as I smiled back. "They call me Horse, here."

Chapter

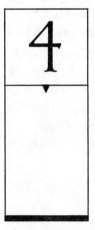

4

Eight hundred years she was thus, until she brought forth a manchild, and on the day he was born he was stronger than his mother. They began to fight . . .

—Rennes, *Dindsenchas*

For two years I lived on the Misty Isle with never a word to remind me of home. Days of sun and storm merged into an endless present as I learned the skills of survival. By the time I could afford to remember once more, I was separated from the child I had been by a gulf as deep as the sea. I was cold or hungry often, exhausted or exhilarated, sharing with my hearth-mates every joy and pain. But I was never bored. I took to my new life as the cygnet takes to the skies, and never imagined it could end.

And then my father came to take me home.

It was summer. Between one step and the next I stilled at the osprey's piercing whistle and squinted upward until I saw the bird's sharp silhouette against the sky. The deep, slow beat of arched wings bore him past the shoulder of the hill, serene as if he saw nothing more interesting below him than the wind ruffling the grass.

"He is telling his mate that here is no good hunting," said Horse. "Look at the tracks—'twas midday when those of the Eagle hearth passed this way!"

"Since 'tis falcons we are now, we ought to be listening," whispered Gannet, freeing a strand of wiry brown hair from an over-hanging spray of pine.

"They are too far ahead to be overtaken," said Linnet, frowning.

Willow and Wingfoot nodded agreement, and Waterdog, who looked so much like Crow, sighed. In the two years since I had come to Caiactis the seven of us had become a unit, passing together from the hearth of the Fieldmouse to that of the Falcon, learning the ways of the Hare and the Otter as we grew. We had taken oath to help each other through our testing, to pass all the higher grades together until we won admission to the kindred of the Bear.

Right now it was the Eagle hearth whose feathered standard we must carry off without ourselves being captured.

"Do we climb the crags, then?" Willow asked fearfully. "I'll slow ye down!"

" 'Tis the only way to get behind them. . . ." Horse replied.

The Old Woman lifted above the curve of the moor before us like a mountain sculptured from shadow at the beginning of the world. It would be a hard climb, and Willow had no head for heights at all. I tightened the belt that held my doeskin kilt, and gave her a smile. My leg was the same color as the leather, crisscrossed with old scratches, burnt brown by the sun.

"I will follow you," I told her. "I won't let you fall."

"Thanks, Adder!" She called me by the name that I had won the first time I used my teeth in a fight.

"Try ropes," said Horse suddenly. "If we are linked by ropes we can get everyone over the rough parts—"

The plover's egg freckling had run together over Horse's back and shoulders into solid brown, and the rest of him was faintly pink, as always, beneath the downing of coppery hair. I saw the gleam in his blue eyes and thought it was a good idea. Horse's notions usually were.

"Old Lod down the glen has a rope he uses to pull stuck sheep out of the bog—" I said slowly. We all began to grin.

Two hours later we were looking down at the inlet. I squinted at the glitter of sun on water, and brought up my hand to shade my eyes. Nothing stirred on the slope below us, but there was something on the sea. . . .

"What is it?" Horse was at my shoulder. He was long-sighted, and I eased back a little to let him see. "A boat," he said presently, "on a heading for the dun. There's a horsetail standard at her bow."

Even for Gunarduilla they wouldn't fly the royal standard, I thought numbly. For the first six months I was on the Island I had cried myself to sleep each night, hoping that my father would send for me, hating Gunarduilla for her treachery. And then I had begun to find my place among these wildfolk that the She-Bear was training into warriors, and after a time, I even ceased to dream.

"Your father. . . ."

I nodded, remembering Leir's golden laughter, and the excitement that made the air crackle around him, and the undercurrent of fear. It was simpler here. The others fell silent, waiting to see what I would do.

"I do not wish to go."

"Be glad that you can," he said softly. He put an arm around my shoulders and I leaned against him. "My Da sent me here three years ago, to keep me safe from his enemies. If he is dead, I must go back to Morilandis and kill them, when I am a man."

"If the king takes me away I will return!" Suddenly it seemed dreadful that Horse should be abandoned by everyone. Since that first fight, we had stood shoulder to shoulder. And the others—they were my real family.

"Adder, you must go down to them," said Gannet. "We will capture the Eagle for you, and give you your feather when you return!" Their grins were back and my heart lifted, and for the moment, everything was all right again.

Leir had brought me back to my own land and people, I thought as I looked at the chieftains assembled beneath the council trees below his new fortress, but they no longer felt like home. Perhaps that was why my father had taken me away from the Island. But it would need more than a month to change me from Adder of the Misty Isle to Cridilla of Briga once more.

The woven cloth they had stretched to shelter us pulled and sagged as branches moved in the breeze. Here, where Briga met the midlands, the summer sun was warm. The light that filtered through the loose weave chequered the faces of those who had come to the Assembly like the patterns in the tunics they wore. Light and shadow, dark and bright, their semblance changed with each shift in the breeze, as deceptive as their words. To discern the reality beneath appearances was the quest of the king. On the Misty Isle, we were not so colorful, but if someone told Bear Mother a thing, you could be certain it was true.

"I appeal to you for justice, high king!" Nextonos was on his feet, presuming on his status as one of my father's old comrades-in-arms. "Give me payment for the cattle your laborers slaughtered, and the blood-price for my herdsman too."

"Lord, those laborers were building *your* road!" answered Gia-had the road-builder. He was one of those spared from the old priesthood of the Ai-Akhsi for the sake of his skill with numbers, a magic the Quiritani did not know.

"From the ridgeway to the marsh crossing south of here the path is cleared now as you ordered, the streams bridged, and the low places filled in. Was it not your will that we should be supplied by the clans through whose territories we passed? Nextonos's man was breaking your law when he refused us food!"

Leir looked down at them, frowning. The rough planks of his high seat were covered by the hide of the white mare they had sacrificed to make him high king, his white rod of kingship was in his hand. I sat upon a cushion of sheepskin, holding my father's feet. It was the custom that the king's feet should lie in the lap of a maiden when he sat in judgment, lest he forget the Goddess from whom his sovereignty came.

It seemed strange, when a month before I had been ranging the uplands of Caiactis like a wild thing, to uphold a king. I wondered why I had been chosen while my sister Gunarduilla waited in the dun. My other sister, Rigana, had a baby son now, called Cuno-dagos. They seemed like strangers to me now. Indeed, I was half a stranger to myself with my hair bound into braids and confined by an embroidered band. The wool of my new tunic scratched my skin, but Bear Mother had taught us how to sit still.

"It was your right to ask, indeed," said Nextonos, "but you

attacked the herd like wild wolves! What did you expect my man to do?"

"We did ask—" the road-builder began. "We could have starved—"

"He never—"

"Hold!" Leir's voice cut through their babble. "Not wolves are ye but dogs, to snarl so over your dinners!" The white wand stabbed toward the chieftain. "You knew that the road-builders must be fed and scanted the giving. For failing in your duty you will pay six cows."

Nextonos's face reddened and something almost palpable thrummed in the air between him and the king. His hand was clenching and unclenching at his side, and if men had been allowed their weapons, I thought he would have gone for his blade. But before he could do anything, Leir had turned, his fierce gaze stilling Giahad's smile.

"And you! Did you think this roadway you are making was for your own pleasure? Had I no obligation to aid my people I could sit at my ease in my own dun!" He gestured across the meadow toward the rampart of the fortress that would be dedicated to-morrow. "But I can give no help if I cannot reach them. If you go to killing the folk for whom the road is building, what use will all your labor be?"

"He still owes me a blood-price!" the chieftain cried, scenting an advantage.

"He does indeed—" said the king. He glanced down at me, and the glint in his eye told me what he would say. I mouthed the words with him. "He owes you six cows!"

Everyone within earshot began to laugh. Old Calgacos from the eastern shore slapped his knee, shaking his head, and even Bituitos of high Rigodunon smiled. The men of Alba were whispering be-hind their hands, and the delegation of Banalisioi men from the white cliffs on the southern coast frowned thoughtfully. If the king had overcome the litigants by force, the chieftains would have ad-mired him, but to see the opponents outmaneuvered with words was better still. Leir's laughter rolled out like the sea roaring and Giahad and Nextonos sat down, glowering.

"Listen, my comrades," said the king when the laughter began to fade. "Are we too proud to learn from the people who were here before us? We have even more need of swift communications than they, for though you are breeding up tribes of your own with a will"—there was laughter at this as well—"we are still few in this country, and we must stand together. It was because our people could not unite in the lands across the sea that we are here today!"

I considered that curiously. My father wanted the roads for control, or, as he said, for unity. But what had the old people used them for?

"We have talked long, brothers, and my throat is growing dry. Let us refresh ourselves, and when the sun touches the top of that oak tree, return to the council."

Speech roared around us like an undammed stream as the men began to rise. Artocoxos drew close to the king, murmuring, and after a moment drifted away in the direction that Nextonos had gone. Leir swung his feet out of my lap and eased to the ground, stretching.

"Is that what you wanted me to learn?" I looked up at him.

My father grinned. "It went just as I told you, did it not? If you know how men think, you know what they will say. It is not so hard then to think a step ahead of them."

"What will they do now?"

"Talk until their anger cools. I've sent Artocoxos to make sure they're supplied with ale and kept away from their weapons. By the time they wake up tomorrow, they will think it was funny too."

I got to my feet, feeling a trickle of perspiration wind down my spine. What I wanted was to strip off these clothes and disappear into the forest that skirted the hill. But it was more than pride that kept me standing, straight and still, by my father's side.

I had tried to hate him when he came for me, but he was like a bonfire against the grey stones, warming all within range. And he had known that he must be gentle as a tamer of beasts until I came willingly to his hand.

By the time we headed homeward I was beginning to remember how I had loved him. Two years on the Island had not made me any better a sailor, but my father held my head each time I was sick over the side, and when we reached shore, the two years of separation might never have been.

Leir had predicted my reactions as precisely as he did those of his men. But I did not care. It was enough to stand with him here.

"The chieftains are afraid, of course, that I will use these new roads to control them," he was saying now.

"And will you?"

"For the greater good, to make this island all one kingdom someday. When I was a boy in the Great Land I heard a trader tell of countries where great lords ruled for as far as a man could march for many days. Even before I set foot on her shores the Island of the Mighty fought me, but through subtlety of wit and strength of will I shall gain the mastery."

I stared at him. These fortresses he was building began to have another significance now. I had thought they were to protect the southern border of Briga from the Ai-Zir, but their meaning was rather different when one remembered that Leir was also king of Alba and Belerion. The stronghold of Ligrodunon that we were dedicating on the morrow would sit at the center of the Island.

"The chieftains only understand their own tribal lands." Leir drew my arm within his own. "My father thought he could fly. Perhaps I am mad to think that I can bring this whole isle beneath me, but my name will live on the lips of the poets even for having tried!"

I frowned. The north was my land, just as Belerion was Rigana's, while Alba belonged to Aglidet and Gunarduilla. Each land had its own goddess, and yet Leir had married all of their queens, covering them each in turn as the stallion mounted his mares. . . . Was it the same?

"Do you understand?"

You do not lie to the war-leader. . . . In two years, Bear Mother had drilled into us an uncompromising truthfulness. You could boast of your own deeds shamelessly, but however highly colored, there must be facts behind them. You could accuse another, but you must be able to prove your words. Lying was the one crime that merited exile.

The king was waiting for my answer. *He needs me to understand him,* I thought, *or why would he be telling me this dream?* Truly, in that moment, I wanted to agree with him, but my tongue remained bound.

After a moment he laughed. "Never mind, my heartling, how could I be expecting you to see what I cannot even say? For now, it is enough that you are listening."

. I put my arms around him, and his body felt as solidly rooted into the earth as the walls of his new dun. *This is the truth,* I thought then, but like my father, I was sensing something for which I knew no words.

The calling of the carynxes shattered the stillness of the morning air; long swan-curves of horns blaring until the air itself blazed with sound. Earth throbbed with the deep heartbeat of drums. I felt that beat pulse through me, wanting my father, who was with the priests, or Gunarduilla, who had stayed inside the walls, or Crow, who was nowhere to be seen. Beside me, the chieftains' wives stirred, pointing. Striped cloaks billowing as the wind took them, the oak priests were coming through the gate of the dun.

They fanned out to either side. Talorgenos appeared between them, the half mask of his goose-feather headdress pulled forward, his shoulders swathed in a roan horse hide. Following him, dressed all in white with a mantle that trailed behind him on the grass, walked the king. A shrill whinny echoed the blare of the horns as men led up a fine three-year-old grey stallion never ridden by a man. The ribbons of woven grass seemed too fragile to constrain such power, but the horse moved as if he came consenting.

The priests said consent was required for a true sacrifice, and this one must be valid, for it was to dedicate the fortress that would be the heart of Leir's power.

The bloodtree was set in the ground before the gateway. It was a rowan with trimmed branches from whose top a carved bird eyed the assembly. The priests and the chieftains circled round it, the women facing them. I looked back as they drew me into the line and at last glimpsed Crow hovering at the edge of the crowd. One of the older warriors who was kind to him sometimes had a hand on his shoulder—protective or possessive, I could not tell.

I felt a trickle of perspiration wind down my back. The day was as fair and bright as those that had preceded it. Talorgenos stepped forward, and the silver bells on the white branch in his hand caught the sun in a burst of light. My father turned to face him.

Their eyes met and held as Leir freed the brooch that held his white mantle and let it fall. Then his hands moved to the broad belt studded with plates of gold. As he unlatched it, his kilt fell away. The women quivered, seeing the sun gleam on his broad chest and the swell of his thighs. He reached for the ropes that held the stallion, and the slide of his muscles beneath his skin was like the ripple beneath the satiny coat of the beast he held.

"Do you hold him—" Talorgenos's voice came muffled through the mask. "Together shall ye journey, and together be sanctified."

The stallion's proud head dipped as Leir drew the horse toward the tree. A swift toss looped the rope around the pole, and the bird carved at its top quivered eagerly. Talorgenos circled them, the silver branch providing a constant shimmer of sound. The branch followed the sweet curve of the stallion's back, saluted the proudly lifted tail, then trembled above the head of the king.

Leir's head tipped back, and suddenly he cried out, "Here is the Tree that grows in the world's sweet center. They shall become immortal who ascend this Tree."

The horse shifted nervously away from the constant shiver of the branch, winding his headrope ever more tightly around the pole until he was held fast. Men set pots fashioned of the gritty local clay in a circle around him, barring his return. They sprinkled herbs on the coals inside them; sweet smoke began to rise in drifting veils.

"The head of this horse is the dawn!" cried Talorgenos, and the drumbeat quickened. *"The sun is his eye, and his breath is the wind."*

The stallion stood shivering. The white was beginning to show around his eyes now, though my father was stroking his head and murmuring. Talorgenos shuffled more quickly; the voice in which he was chanting was not his own.

"His back is as broad as the bowl of the sky,
The sun rises in his forehead,
And sets in the crease between his quarters."

Talorgenos swept the branch along the stallion's back and the plume of a tail lifted in challenge. Lightly the branch brushed the shining flanks, and the stallion's pizzle peeped from its sheath of skin. He stamped, clearly growing uneasy, but still he did not try to break away.

"Through his phallus flow the rivers," cried the priest. *"And he pisses rain."*

The drums thundered suddenly. The horse's head jerked but the tree trunk had been well planted and stood fast. The trumpets shrilled, and a sigh of anticipation whispered through the crowd.

"This horse is the earth and the stars of heaven.
This horse is the steed that journeys between the worlds;
This horse is the offering."

Now the priest was at the king's shoulder. I glimpsed the gleam of the double-bitted axe of bronze in his hands and felt my own heart battering against the cage of my breast.

"Come, my swan, let us fly to the Otherworld!" cried the king. The axe lofted like a butterfly on the wind. An uncontrollable shuddering rolled through my flesh. Then the winged blade swooped down.

Crimson flared from the blade as the pale body rose, its mane like a swan's lifting wing. The head flopped back against the pole and red life-blood pumped from the heart that did not yet know its death and poured into the bronze cauldron, a scarlet shower blessing priests and warriors and dyeing the king with the same crimson. The sweet stink of blood mingled with the sharp scent of the herbs on the warm air.

"Now you are flying, now you are soaring into the air!" Talorgenos cried. Artocoxos caught the king as the bloody axe slipped from his grasp. "Now he bears you into the heavens; now he carries you into the land of the gods! Hear the thunder of his hoofbeats

as you gallop across the cloudfields! I see the throne of the Great
One, the Great King leaning upon his mighty scepter—he stands,
he smiles, he accepts the sacrifice!"

A thunder of sound rolled across the meadow as the people
began to cheer. Crow was crouched on the ground, shuddering.
Already the warriors had pulled the stallion's body onto its back
and were stripping the skin away. In moments it had been torn
from the flesh and suspended from the pole. Another swift stroke
opened the belly; Talorgenos peered into the steaming entrails.

I saw my father's lips move, but could not hear the question.
The oak priest bent and shook his branch above the sacrifice.

"A good harvest and a good season see I," he proclaimed. "There
is fat clinging to the coils and no spotting. But there is a knotting
here, there will be war!" The warriors cheered, but I saw limbs red
with their own blood and blinked, forcing the vision away.

"I see long life to the king, prosperity for the land."

Talorgenos sliced a gobbet of red meat from the stallion's thigh
and pressed it to Leir's lips, carved more and gave them to the other
men. Then the butchered limbs were carried to the cauldron.

Someone doused the king with a leathern bucket of water and
he shook himself, shuddering. They arrayed him in his kilt and
mantle, but he was still leaning on Artocoxos's shoulder as they
began the circuit of the fortress. Talorgenos dipped a rowan branch
into the cauldron and splashed the blood of the stallion against the
packed earth and the wooden bulwarks. I glimpsed a kind of shimmer where it spattered, like the steam in the sweathouse when water
is thrown upon the stones. Then they moved around the outside
of the dun.

As the drumming and the chanting grew fainter, I caught my
breath and stamped my feet to connect to the earth again. I had
never gotten dizzy at a sacrifice before. But I had seen something
like this once— Memory supplied an image of tall stones black
against a Midwinter dawn, and a painted face with frightened eyes.
Slowly I turned. Crow was on his feet again, watching the departing
procession with mingled fear and longing in his gaze.

When they completed the circuit the king was walking steadily
again, but it seemed to me that about the fortress a bright mist was

[85]

rising. Nine times in all they ringed it round. With the last of the stallion's blood Leir sanctified the gateposts, and between the carved posts I saw a shimmering veil.

"You shall stand fast!" The king drew a line between the gateposts. "No enemy shall pass between you. This hill shall be sacred forever!"

It was like the breathless moment between the lightning and the storm. Like an echo from the heavens came the sound of a chariot wheel being rolled over stones. Suddenly there were clouds on the horizon, but the thunder had rumbled from somewhere closer. The god was laughing, and I heard his laughter through the people's cheers.

One of the priests dipped the rowan branch in the blood bowl and began to sanctify the people. The press of the crowd carried me face-to-face with my father, and I saw his eyes still wide and unfocused, and a splash of red upon his brow. Then the blood touched my lips and the drumbeat pulsed through my limbs, and I was dancing with the rest of them, knowing in my flesh that the power in the earth and the air and the blood that had been shed in offering were all one.

"Now the place is sanctified," said the king. "The exchange is sealed by the blood of the stallion, his power for the blessing of the gods."

They had set benches before the shrine inside the walls; one large seat for my father, and to either side, lower ones for Gunarduilla and for me. Leir drank deep from his mead horn, and I edged away, for sitting next to him was like being too close to a fire.

Ligrodunon had been a sacred hill long before my father planned his fortress. The new walls sheltered the feasting hall, a few houses, and the rectangular shrine, over whose images the last of the stallion's blood had been poured. Outside, the people were busy at their feasting. Within the circle sat the chieftains and their women, and the servers were already bringing out casks of mead and ale.

Still dizzy from the rush of energy I had felt at the sacrifice, I tore off a generous hunk of bread and began to gnaw at it. Gunarduilla looked white and wary and for the first time I noticed that six warriors of the Ai-Siwanet, her mother's people, sat beside her on the grass.

"These roads we build are growing longer," the king went on. "The peace that we have made with our cousins in the southeast is holding, and to bind our tribes ever more closely, Magloscutios of the White Cliffs has sent us his younger son Maglaros to rule with my daughter Gunarduilla in Alba."

"And how will you feel when he gives you to an old man to seal his alliances?" Gunarduilla had asked me when Rigana was wed. But she was the one who was being married off now. Her bride-price was the support of the southern Quiritani, but from that, she would reap no benefit. It was this Maglaros who would get a country to rule.

I wondered what sort of bargain she would have in her husband. Maglaros was a young man, and tall, with strong-springing auburn hair. Two gaunt black hounds lolled beside him, and from time to time he would fondle their silky ears. But there was something ungenerous in the set of his mouth. Or perhaps he was just apprehensive, facing a bride who looked more ready for battle than the marriage bed.

"By what right will he rule in Alba, O my father?" Gunarduilla's voice was cold. For the first time since we had sat down, Leir turned to look at her.

"By right of the bride-treaty, daughter," he replied.

"I have made no treaties, nor have I consented to become a bride. . . ." Clear in the stillness came the sounds of distant revelry. Gunarduilla stared around the circle, and as her eyes met mine I glimpsed appeal.

When the child-pack attacked me on the island, you looked on and smiled, I thought then.

"You are my daughter—" he began, but her voice was an echo.

"Your daughter, not your slave! Am I to be bartered like a heifer at a fair? No man enjoys the friendship of my thighs against my will, and no man claims Alba but through me!"

The hawk-feather clusters bound into the hair of the Ai-Siwanet warriors trembled. The Quiritani men were leaning forward, eyes agleam with anticipation of a row, but the faces of the women were like masks.

"Through you and through me!" Leir's voice had gone harsh suddenly. "I gave you life, girl, and I can destroy you!"

"Then kill me!" Gunarduilla rose, ripping at the neck of her tunic. "Let my blood feed the earth!" In the sunlight, her breast was like the breast of a swan. Maglaros looked at her and something kindled in his gaze, but Leir was rising; I felt the air pulse around him and my belly went cold.

"Da—do not!" I began. I had thought I hated my sister for abandoning me, but I could not bear to see her battered by our father's wrath.

He did not even notice me. Face-to-face in the glimmering sunlight, Gunarduilla had never looked more like him.

"Kill you? That would be wasteful!" Leir snarled. "If you will not bear a man's weight upon your belly, I shall tether you to a post like a wayward mare and condemn you to bear my guests on your back up the hill." Even focused in another direction, his anger was like a blow.

"King of the Quiritani, you shame yourself and me!" Gunarduilla's face went first white, then red. "Would *you* so tamely surrender your sovereignty? You won the land by conquest; let this man do the same. He who would rule me must defeat me before I will give him a sheath for his sword!"

"A fight, let them fight!" Nextonos shouted, and the others roared. Leir had not expected this, but furious as he was, he understood her. Maglaros got to his feet, his pale glance shifting between Leir and Gunarduilla.

"Lord king, I will try my strength against the maiden. It is an honorable challenge, and a worthy prize."

She looked at him with a wary calculation as if for the first time she were seeing him as something more than one of the straw figures the villagers put up to frighten crows from the grain.

Leir was still dangerously flushed, but the aura of danger around him had diminished. The king had not survived so long without knowing how far he could try the temper of his men. They had drunk and eaten. They were ready for some entertainment now.

[88]

"Fight then," he said to Gunarduilla. "If Maglaros wins he shall be your master, but maiden you shall live and die if the victory is yours!"

I bit my lip, seeing hidden thoughts still moving behind his eyes like trout in a forest pool. What my sister had asked for was not maidenhood, but the right to choose.

One of the Alban warriors brought out Gunarduilla's weapons. Ai-Siwanet and Quiritani took up position around the ring. Two of the southern tribesmen were helping Maglaros to strip, and Gunarduilla began to do the same, as unself-conscious as if they had been on the practice field of the Island, with Bear Mother waiting to lacerate both victor and loser with an analysis more brutal than any blade. Suddenly I wanted very badly to be back there, with the lean fare and the hard beds and the cold wet wind off the sea.

Gunarduilla had grown big-breasted and put on flesh in hip and thigh, but she was still long and lean in body, and she moved with the casual grace that was the mark of Bear Mother's training, holding sword and shield as if they had grown in her hands. Against her white skin the vivid blue tattooing of the Island's hearth-kindreds showed clearly—wolf and eagle, stag and salmon rippled in abstract curves across her shoulders and back and thighs.

Maglaros's movements were more careful, and his body bore the crimson tattooing of battle scars. But those livid markings were all on his legs and arms. This would not be his first fight, and he had not survived the others by exposing himself recklessly.

"Come on then, Banalisioi craven—" said Gunarduilla, stepping into the circle. "Or are you less eager for my embrace now that you have seen my claws?"

"I have killed a hand of foes in the combat of champions and scores in battle. I do not fear the weapons of a shield-maiden, though there are daggers in her glance and barbs upon her tongue!"

"And iron in her hand!" Gunarduilla exclaimed, leaping toward him.

Maglaros's shield took the first blow. His sword came around, but she was no longer there. Her blade stabbed in, he shifted; iron clanged and slithered as he deflected it and pressed past her guard.

Gunarduilla twisted and thrust her shield against his with her whole weight behind it. I saw him rock, but she was the one who bounced back again, pivoting lightly away as she realized that she did not have the mass to move him.

Men breathed again. Now the combatants had taken each other's measure and were settling to their task. Gunarduilla began to weave from foot to foot, her sword a flicker of light as it caught the sun. A muscle twitched along Maglaros's shoulder blade. Gunarduilla growled low in her throat and flashed in again, and when she spun away a thin line of red was springing up along Maglaros's arm. It was first blood, but no one seemed to care. I realized suddenly that Gunarduilla was out to maim her enemy, while Maglaros must keep her alive in order to win.

She will have to kill him, I thought as I looked at the immovable line of his back. *He will never give in.*

Again Gunarduilla attacked, and this time her recovery was slower. She was well trained, but no longer in training. She came at him a third time, counting on his immobility, and his sword and shield moved together to knock her back. Perspiration laid a fine sheen over her flesh; her face was crimson and her eyes blazing.

She shrieked like a wild beast, and some of the warriors drew back, muttering. But it was not the cry of the Raven of Battle that unmans warriors, and Maglaros's eyes only grew more watchful. He waited as she launched herself once more, but this time he moved as she came for him. She tried to evade, but tiring limbs would not obey her; she was still turning as his arm lifted in an overhand cut that twisted down toward her unprotected head.

I heard the sound, like an axe bouncing from a tree trunk, while my mind was still trying to understand what I had seen. Gunarduilla's sword and shield were already spinning from nerveless hands and she was falling as I realized that Maglaros had hit her with the flat of the blade.

All around me, watchers let out pent breath. Maglaros stared down at the woman who had challenged him, lying now on her back with outflung limbs, then he let sword and shield slip to the grass. Gunarduilla whimpered a little and began to move, and it was then that I realized that Maglaros still had a weapon after all. As Gunarduilla opened her eyes he cast himself upon her, forcing himself between her thighs.

Their mating was like the ferocious coupling of the wildcats that roam the hills. Even as her nails gouged his back, her muscular legs were vising around his body, flesh striving against flesh in search of an impossible victory. When he grunted, was it with strain or passion? Was it fury or triumph that I heard in her reply? Even I could feel the energy that pulsed between them, but whether it was attraction or hatred I did not understand, and in the years that followed I sometimes wondered if they themselves knew.

Presently he rolled off of her, his manhood flaccid now. She lay panting, staring up at the sky.

Maglaros got to his feet. "Come, Lady of Alba," he said coldly. "I have lain with you and it is time to seal the bargain with the wedding feast." He held out a hand. She said nothing as they helped her to dress, nothing as he led her to the place where the southern tribesmen were sitting and they took their places there. A sudden gust of cool wind ruffled the dry grass.

"Let us drink to the wife of Maglaros son of Magloscutios," said my father.

I will not marry, ever. . . . I told myself then.

As the others lifted their drinking horns in acclamation, I made my way to the back of the shrine. The wind was blowing more strongly now. Suddenly I could bear the weight of my festal garments no longer. Gasping, I stripped off the gown of patterned wool and opened my arms to the first cleansing spattering of rain.

Chapter

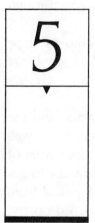

Not a man of them was taken till his hair had been interwoven into braids on him and he started at a run through Ireland's woods; while they, seeking to wound him, followed in his wake. . .

—*Silva Gadelica*, I: 92

G ulping air, I leaped forward, exulting in the swift bunch and release of the hard muscles in my calves and thighs. This race was my final testing on the Misty Isle, the goal I had aimed for every day of the two years since I won my father's permission to return to the Island. I was fifteen winters old that day, and if I survived this, I would be admitted to the hearth of the Bear.

I heard the rustle of leaves and knew that my pursuers were coming through the oak copse behind me. I had come that way too, but I did not think any branches had brushed me. The intricate braiding of my hair was still intact, the tufts of down still clung to the hazel wands I bore.

I plunged down the hill, only peripherally aware of the infinitely varied greens of the grass and foliage through which I ran. Fallen leaves carpeted the slope; it looked like soft footing, but there could be a hidden branch there, and I dared break none. The She-Bear and her daughters could track a moth upon the night breeze. If I left traces of my passing I would fail as surely as if I let my pursuers run me down.

DIANA L. PAXSON

The pace itself was no problem; any one of the youngsters the She-Bear was training could overtake a deer or run the width of the Island and back without growing tired. But I must pass through the land like a spirit, leaving it undisturbed.

My ears told me that the others were coming out onto the slope behind me; my eyes scanned the terrain ahead. *Seek speed, not haste. . . .* The She-Bear's words echoed in my ears. *Run as the deer runs, in beauty.*

I had put the first, essential distance between myself and the youngsters from Wolf hearth who were pursuing me. I was well warmed, but not yet sweating; muscles hardened by four years of training were obedient to my will. There had been many challenges in the time I had been on the Island, increasing as I passed from the Falcon hearth to that of the Salmon, where I learned poetry, flew with the Eagles and ran with the Wolves and came finally to the hearth of the Red Deer. Beyond this there was only the hearth of Bear Mother herself.

It had been almost two years now since I had seen my father. If I won this race I might become one of the teachers, and then I would never have to go home.

There were pines ahead of me, twisted by the wind. I leaped for their soft shadow, passed the first of them, and slowed. Now I understood why this path had been made so inviting. A great pine had fallen in a tangle of branches and blocked the way. If I back-tracked I would run straight into my pursuers, but the branches reached brow high. To get over that I needed wings.

This obstacle must be the first challenge in the testing; I had known it must come, but not when.

"An' dost have no wings, then, daughter of the swan?"

I stumbled, staring around me. Was Shadow Bear hidden some-where, or was she speaking to my soul? *Don't question it!* I willed the tension in my back to ease.

Shadow Bear had given me the answer. But I couldn't fly. . . .

I would have to jump over the tangle with no idea where I would land. The feathers on my hazel wands quivered as I maneu-vered them past the trees and I realized then that perhaps I had something that would help after all.

[94]

I looked hard at the tangle, then forced myself to backtrack a few paces, got a good grip on my sticks and began to run.

The pines flashed by me; then the deadfall was ahead. I leaped, arms lengthened by the wands I was swinging forward, stabbing down at the rough trunk and feeling them bend as I lifted and they took my weight for the moment before my own momentum brought legs and body up, and over the upper branches. Then I was falling, bringing the wands down like wings to steady my landing, knees and ankles bending as I touched earth again.

I shook my head, waiting for my sight to clear. I had been lucky, for this side was carpeted with fallen pine needles. Once more I heard the howling behind me, but I thought that soft laughter sounded from the woods as I ran on.

I stretched into swift motion. Though I still had only two feet to run on, I felt as if I could fly.

In the past year I had grown woman-high. I was taller than Horse now, though he still outweighed me, for my body was all lean muscle, with breasts barely budded, and buttocks tight and hard like a boy's. The rough fare we ate on the Island built strength in the legs for running, and power in the arms and the long muscles of back and belly for throwing the lance and lifting a shield. They said that we girls would not get our moon blood until there was some fat as well as meat on our bones, and I was glad.

The path still led downward. I began to hear the chuckling of the burn, where alder and sallow fought for nourishment on the crumbling ledges of stone. I began to slow. Another test must be coming, and seeing how the foliage stretched over the water, I guessed which it would be.

The ground fell away before me. I slid down a bank and saw a barrier of green. The gap between it and the ground was no higher than my knee. Someone hallooed on the ridge above me, and I jerked as if my back already felt the bite of the sharp-pointed lances in my pursuers' hands.

"Dost flinch from th' wolf's fangs? Must take th' low road to escape this enemy!"

That was the voice of Spirit Bear. I swayed forward, trying to locate her, and the movement recalled the sinuous path of a serpent through the grass. They had called me Adder. Could I move with the snake's lithe motion now?

I launched myself forward, hazel wands lifted so that my upper arms and elbows took my weight as I hit the ground. It was damp; I could feel the water near. As I squirmed beneath the green leaves, springy branches brushed against me. I bent with them, trying to slip beneath the pliant stems with a motion as sinuous as they.

And for a moment, then, it was easy. This must be what they meant when they spoke of swimming, for I found myself flowing through the aqueous space beneath the alders like an eel swimming upstream.

Then a last, lithe twist of my body brought me into the sunlight again. For a moment I lay panting, unwilling to lose the cool support of the earth. But the stream was sparkling ahead, and beyond it stretched the open moor. I shed the serpent-shape with a quick contraction that brought me upright, a swift jump took me over the water, and I began to run again.

The wind was cool on my flushed skin as I leaped through the heather. Pride pulsed through me like strong mead. Beyond the next rise was the last slope down to the shore, and the rocks where I would make my stand. The only thing missing was Horse, running by my side.

Just below the ridge was a thicket of birches. To one side jagged rocks rose sheer and on the other the ground fell steeply away. To go through the birches would delay my pursuers more than it would me. I slowed, striving to retain my rhythm, but the closer I got the more impenetrable those pale tree trunks seemed.

A glance back showed the wolf pack strung out along the moor and coming fast. Now there was no time to go around. Desperation sharpened my concentration.

"Art a spirit, child. An' dost see spirit in all, wilt fly free 'twixt th' worlds."

From the midst of the birches came the voice of the She-Bear.

How did a spirit move? My eyes unfocused, and for a moment I saw the tangle of dappled silver trunks and branches as a pulsing pattern of brightness. I must be a current of energy undulating through a pattern of energies like my own.

"Know that all things are light. . . ."

Myself included? I felt that I was moving in slow motion, but my momentum carried me forward. Shimmers of silver flowed around me, birch trees bent around me as I passed.

I understood that I was through them when the world began to grow solid again. Before me was the edge of the moor, and the sea-smell, and the wide blue sweep of the sky. I felt my own flesh settling back into human form, as if for a moment I had been something other. I could not stop to question, for from the other side of the thicket I heard muttering as my pursuers wondered if I had gone around or through.

The sea was booming against the shingle below. A single leap carried me halfway down to it; fleet-footed I danced over a tumble of boulders, and dropped down into the belly-deep hollow among the largest just as the first of the wolf pack appeared at the cliff-top above.

Finally I had a moment's leisure to wonder how they had followed so swiftly. Did they have to overcome the same obstacles, or had there perhaps been a glamour upon me so that I did not see the easier path?

It did not matter. I had outdistanced them, and my good bull-hide shield was ready to my hand. This would be the first time I had battled in earnest without Horse beside me, but I felt invincible, and as my foes pelted down the slope I shrieked my battle cry.

Silent, they spread out in a half circle around me. There were nine of them, naked, with blackened faces and wolftails tied into their matted hair. Sunlight glinted on the well-honed blades of their spears.

—Nine spears, and even though my shield was made of hard-ened bullhide, if those points struck straight on they would go through. By law there was no honor-price required for those who died during their training on the Island, whether they were killed by accident or in the trials. The brothers and sisters of my own hearth could not help me. A gull swooped low over my head, and

I kept myself from flinching with an effort of will. Then I saw on the cliff-top above us the shadow-shapes of the She-Bear and her daughters in their mantles of dark skins.

I reminded myself that I had asked for this testing, and settled my feet more firmly in the sand.

A long wolf howl split the silence. Seabirds rose screaming; the air was full of frantic wings and serpent-shapes that darkened the air. Before I could think how to meet them I was taking the impact of the first three aslant on my shield while I lashed out with one of my hazel wands and knocked four more aside. A blur in the air was my only warning that two of the lances had been cast a breath later, but my arms struck up and outward, and the last two spears glanced by to either side.

My skin was on fire. I burst upward from my pit, roaring. Shadow Bear told me later that my braids had been intact when I reached the boulders, so it was then, I think, that the thongs that bound the end of each lock burst free.

It took me longer to realize that no one was attacking me. There were people all around, and the clamor I was hearing was the sound of their cheers.

Sparks flew up in puffs of golden stars as Gannet threw another dry pine log on the fire. I tore a mouthful of venison from the piece of haunch Horse had just given me and wiped my mouth with the back of my hand. I could hear the sounds of satisfaction all around me as the rest of the Red Deer hearth-kin did the same. Up and down the beach fires burned brightly, and scents of roasting meat mingled with the smell of the sea.

"You were very sure of me, to be hauling so much food all the way from Artodunon out here," I said between bites. "What if I had failed?"

"It would have served for the funeral feast, wouldn't it now?" The answer Horse gave was eminently practical, and Wingfoot and Willow, who were sitting nearest, laughed, but there was an edge in his voice that troubled me.

"Huh—" I punched him. "Did you doubt that I would win?"

I realized that I had never heard of anyone who had failed this testing and still survived it. I was glad that thought had not occurred to me before. The brand-new Bear tattoo still smarted on my belly, but I did not care. There was meat in abundance and casks full of heather beer, and the lean faces of those who had become closer to me than my own sisters shone in the circle of light cast by this fire.

Horse gave me an odd look, then grinned suddenly. "With you coming out of that pit like the Lady of Ravens in a rage? In another moment we would have had to dump one of the casks over your head to cool you down."

Linnet and Gannet giggled, and even Waterdog began to smile.

"And waste all that beer?" I drained my horn, and Willow took it to be refilled.

Someone at the fire next to ours had brought out a drum and was holding it up to the flame to tighten the skin. In a few moments a resonant beat was pulsing across the sand. Willow came back with my beer and I poured it down. This was not the thin stuff they usually fed us, but a headier brew sweetened with honey, because I was a warrior now. I felt the drum beat in my belly and pushed abruptly to my feet.

Horse stared up at me. "Are you well?"

Well . . . what a pallid word for this joy! The stars danced above me as the children of the hearth-clans danced on the shore. Emotion frothed within me like the head on the beer. Suddenly all that I was feeling burst free in a long howl.

> *"Ai . . . ai . . . ai . . . the Adder am I!*
> *All of ye here, behold me and fear!*
> *Among bears, a bear, face me if ye dare!"*

Two of the littlest girls squealed and tumbled aside as I swayed toward them.

> *"A deer in my leaping, a swan with wings sweeping,*
> *Ai . . . ai . . . ai . . . a warrior am I!"*

[99]

My arms lifted. I was too drunk to dance, but the power of the deer surged within me, and breast and shoulder muscles felt the deep pull of great white wings.

> *"With eagle's sharp sight, a fierce wolf in the fight,*
> *Salmon sleek and wise, a hawk in the skies,*
> *A wildcat for cunning, a fieldmouse swift running,*
> *Both hunter and prey, by night and by day,*
> *Serpent hid in the grass, swiftly I pass . . .*
> *Hunting ghosts through the trees, spirit sight sees. . . ."*

A rush that owed nothing to the beer pulsed up my spine. Who was I? *What* was I? I felt my own shape slipping and knew that in a moment I would understand.

> *"Ai . . . ai . . . ai . . . the Adder am I!*
> *All of ye here, behold me and fear!"*

Then the sand came up to meet me. When I could see again, I was lying by the fire, and Bear Mother was bending over me.

"Adder. Where didst thou learn the song?"

The words were my own, but the pattern and tune? I frowned, trying to remember, and saw in memory firelight dappling beech trunks in a forest far away, and a slender form whose cheeks glistened with tears as he sang.

"A man called Crow—" I stammered. "From the high moors —my father's man . . ."

"'Twas one of the Old Race taught thee?" Teeth that were still strong and white despite her years flashed as Bear Mother grinned. "So! Sing not that song again, child, till dost learn what it means!"

I nodded. My head was throbbing, and my stomach churned. As they moved off, Shadow Bear looked back over her shoulder and winked at me. But I was already on my way to give up the contents of my belly to the waves. Offshore mist hid the horizon, and at my feet the dark waters hissed hungrily. As soon as I could, I hurried back to the fire.

"And until you learn to drink like a warrior, you had better not pour down so much beer," said Horse when I returned.

I kicked him. "Take care, my lad, lest I spew it all over you! Is it that you envy me?" It seemed to me that his face flushed, though it was hard to tell in the light of the fading fire.

"Envy! Can you really believe—"

Then he pushed himself abruptly upright and strode away.

"Has Horse had too much to drink too?" asked Linnet, holding out a basket of bannocks.

I shook my head, but I had no more idea what was wrong with him than she.

People began to drop off to sleep soon after, curling up where they were on the sand. I wanted to go find Horse, but all the stress of the day had suddenly caught up with me, and all I could do was to accept half of Gannet's cloak beside the fire.

Snowy pinions swept strongly downward, catching the wind; my neck extended, and the steady beat of wide wings sped me upward. The world I had transcended spun away. Clouds boiled up before me, I burst through the mists and suddenly I was gliding across white billows that covered the heavens like the waves of the sea. Rejoicing, I stroked upward, seeking the Light. . . .

"Why so surprised, swan-daughter? Did not know you have wings?"

I skipped a beat, head turning, and glimpsed a dark blur beside me, a crow whose clumsy wingbeats kept him level with me no matter how powerfully I flew.

"Why did you never tell me?" I asked. "Who would stay earth-bound when he could seek the skies?"

"Is why. You keep this form too long, maybe lose your own! And wings are not the only wonder," the answer came with a sudden *carkk* of amusement. "You are serpent as well as swan, and, if you want, the deer and other things. All shapes are in your own."

"Show me—" came my cry.

"Is the shape of the battle serpent you take next," he replied. "Go back to hearth-kin, Adder! Fangs needed now!"

Wind roared in my ears. I plummeted downward, inward, sucked back into an awkward shape, flailing, flailing—

—Rough wool scraped my arms as I fought free. Someone was screaming behind me. I twisted upright. The beach was a-swirl with shadows shifting in dim silhouette against the grey, predawn sky. Sparks sprayed as someone stumbled through the remains of a fire.

A long wolf howl lifted above the shouting. I fumbled my arm through the shield strap and reached for the hazel wand. My head pounded in time with my racing pulse.

A dark figure loomed suddenly above me and I glimpsed the brown gleam of a blade. Fear shocked through me. but my body was already reacting. Bronze boomed against my shield and the wand rapped smartly. There was a howl as the enemy sword flew free, and my stick whipped around to connect with a satisfying thunk against bone.

My attacker staggered as I leaped for his fallen sword, but before he could recover I had tossed my stick to my shield hand, grabbed the hilt of the sword, and thrust into him. With a stifled gurgle he fell.

My breath came in harsh gasps as I watched the life fade from his eyes. *Like a dying deer . . .* In the strengthening light I could read the tattooing that covered his skin. He had been a man of the Pig People of the northern isles.

The wind blew mist between me and the others as I looked for Horse. Dim figures struggled around me like warriors in a dream. I plunged toward them and blinked as something too huge to be human reared up from the press, striking right and left like a sow-bear defending her cubs.

Another figure leaped forward. I saw black hair tossing and the flare of a blue blade. That was Spirit Bear, naked as the men who attacked her, and laughing. I shook my head to clear it, and suddenly the figure behind her became Bear Mother, a long knife flickering in each hand. But the sounds she made were no woman's war-cry, and even as I knew her, she was changing, bear- and woman-shapes flickering in and out of focus with dizzying speed. Where the clawed hands descended, foemen fell.

Already tumbled forms lay still around her. But from the sea more blue-spiraled shapes were coming, and children scattered across the sand before them. Above the baying of our enemies, their yells sounded thin as the piping of gulls.

Two of the Falcon hearth girls were helping another limp toward the cliff behind us, pausing at intervals to snatch rocks from the beach and hurl them at their foes. I darted between them toward the oncoming enemy, wondering whether even an adder's agility would help me against three heavy men with swords. As I settled into a defensive crouch, a thrown lance took one of them in the throat. The other two charged me, cursing. Bronze clanged as I knocked the first man's blade aside. I staggered and went down as the second sword split my bullhide shield.

I rolled over and over, trying to free my arm, and came upright with my hazel wand swinging in my left hand and the captured sword stabbing in the right. My enemies were strong, but I was far swifter, a fury uncoiling through me that I had never felt before.

As they came at me I hissed defiance, struck and twisted and hit out again. My war-name rang in my awareness like a battle cry.

"Adder!"

That shout did not come from my throat! I twisted, slashing, and glimpsed fiery hair. Then a lance thrust past, and Horse was at my side. Back-to-back, we settled into the pattern in which we had fought so many times before. Painted totems writhed toward me from an oblong shield as an islander charged.

"Give way!" I screeched in Horse's ear. I ducked, stabbing, as a blade sliced the air where my head had been. Horse grunted, but I was pulling my point from the islander's thigh and dared not look to see. My foe fell back, yelling, and his companions hesitated. I straightened and felt Horse stagger beside me.

"To the cliff," he muttered. "Get our backs against it . . . safe. . . ." Safety? In that moment of respite, I wondered. Bear Mother and her daughters were still the center of a writhing knot of warriors. If Horse had been whole, I would have tried to join her, but most of the children who could run were retreating, and through the thickening mist I could see another boatload of is-landers surging toward shore.

[103]

A little farther down the beach the cliff was broken where a small burn tumbled to the sea. "That way—" I nudged his shoulder with mine and felt something wet and warm. "Can you run?"

"I *won't leave*—" he began, but the islanders were coming in again and I sprang past him. His blood burned my skin. I shrieked as I had when the Wolves attacked me, sword and stick striking in a single blur of motion, over and over again. When my foes turned to flee only Horse's grip on my arm kept me from leaping after them.

"I'll run now," he gasped, "—keep you from more madness. Help me, Cridilla—"

The sound of my own name broke the spell. Seabirds screamed as I got my shoulder under his good arm and half dragged him toward the stream. The same fury that had driven me at the foe lent me the strength to get Horse to safety. It was not until we were well into the ravine that the burn had cut across the slope above the cliff that I dared to stop and let Horse slump against me while I tried to clamp the great gash in his shoulder closed with my hand.

"Was that a shout?"

For a moment every nerve tensed to defend or flee. But beyond Horse's harsh breathing, the only sounds I could hear were the musical chime and gurgle of water in the burn and the osprey's distant call. I sank back on my elbow in the bracken, looking down at him. The madness of the fight seemed a nightmare. Now I felt the fear.

"It is only a bird, seeking her dinner in the sea."

I smoothed his sweat-soaked hair, nearly the color of the blood that stained the pad I had bound over the gash in his shoulder, and lifted the locks back from his brow. Against the dark blood his skin looked appallingly pale, but at least the bleeding had stopped. If I could keep him warm and quiet, he should be safe now.

"Do you think that the islanders are still hunting us?" he whispered.

"I don't know. . . ." The sky beyond the fringe of fern that edged the ravine was flushed with soft color. It was going to be a fair day.

"I saw Willow fall, and Wingfoot. Do you think they killed everyone?"

I bit back a sharp reply, knowing him half-dazed with the shock of his wound, and realized that I was afraid to learn the answer. Here, where the lip of the ravine overhung the burn so steeply, I had found a bit of ground that was almost smooth, if not quite level, cushioned by tufts of moss and last year's bracken and screened by young alders and new fern.

How long, I wondered, could we stay hidden here?

"Stay still—" I told him. "I want to see what wood is here. I think these branches would filter the smoke of a fire. You need food, and there are fish in this stream."

"Do not be trying it. If they come searching, they'll see you." He turned his head fretfully. "You should have left me! You could have gotten well away!"

"You were away already!" I retorted, sitting back on my heels. "Why did you come back to fight for me?"

Horse grinned, and something in my belly clenched suddenly.

"What? Leave you all the glory, and you so proud of the Bear on your belly already that you could scarcely speak to me? There would have been no living with you, lass."

"And I suppose you let yourself be wounded so that I would have to carry you away?" I flared. "Agantequos son of Vorequos, even now can you not speak truth to me? Without you, I would not be living at all!"

Slowly, the laughter faded from his clear eyes. "You did not know what you were doing. You were outnumbered, and you were battle-mad."

"But you were not," I pressed him. "When we were safe by the fire, you ran away. Why? And why did you return?"

He tried to shrug, and I bent forward to keep him still, but I could not make him look at me.

"Cridilla, it was not envy!" he said suddenly. "Do you think that after I had watched you knock away those lances I could have been anything but glad? But whether you had passed the test or failed it, our companionship was ended, and until you came to this island I never had a real friend!"

[105]

I stared at him. "Nor I—" I whispered, "nor I. . . ."

"In the testing I could not try to help you." He reached out to grip my arm. "But when you battled the islanders, there was no one to keep me from your side!"

"Horse, I will not let this be an ending!" I exclaimed. "We'll form our own hearth! I'll train you for your own testing as soon as your shoulder heals!"

"And after?" Once more he grew somber. "You belong to this land and I am an exile. One day your father will take you home and you will not come back again."

"I will not leave you!"

At last his gaze met mine, and I flinched from what I saw in his blue eyes.

"Cridilla! You are not yet a woman, though you are a warrior, and I am not yet grown a man. But I am close enough to manhood to know that I will never find a woman to equal you."

"I swore not to marry," I said, "but if I should change my mind, I promise it will be for you!"

"Will you kiss me to seal that vow?"

I looked at him. Was Horse laughing at me again? His curving lips looked soft, nothing like Maglaros's sneer or Senouindos's tickling beard. And suddenly I wanted to touch them.

"If I do that, will you be good and let me take care of you?"

"This time. . . ."

Swiftly I pressed my mouth to his. His good arm came up in an awkward hug and I stretched my length against his, feeling his heartbeat shake his chest, abruptly aware of the heavy throbbing of my own.

We are comrades . . . I thought. *That is all!* But I knew in that moment that whatever had happened to Bear Mother and the others, Horse was right. Things between us were never going to be the same again.

Chapter

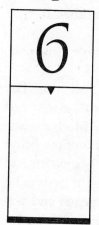

6

One Samain Eve Ailill and Maeve were in the rath of Cruachan with all their following . . . Great was the obscurity of the night and its horror, for it was that night the demons always showed themselves. Each man went in his turn to brave its perils, and it is rapidly that he returned to the house again.

—*The Adventures of Nera*

"Crow, do you hear? Your brothers are calling you—"

Below the banked walls of Ligrodunon, birds were fluttering into the leafless trees like bits of ash blown from the embers of the sky. Crow tipped his head, listening until the harsh echoes of their calling faded into the stillness of the fallow fields. In the past few dawnings frost had silvered the stubble and the last of the leaves. It hardly seemed possible that it could be Samonios already. But half the year had passed since the attack on Caiactis. For a third of it, I had been home.

Behind us the yard of the dun was a-bustle with preparation for the festival. I could smell meat cooking in the great cauldron, aromatic with wild garlic and herbs—joints of pork and beef bound up in cloth bags and all boiling together.

"They find scraps from the slaughtering on the ground by the pens," Crow said softly. "They summon others to the festival."

"So they too celebrate the year's dark turning . . . well, I wish them joy of their feasting," I replied.

This week they had been killing the beasts we could not afford to feed through the winter, and not even the freshening wind of early evening could entirely cleanse the air. With every breath I remembered the scent of the blood that Horse had shed defending me. Men and beast all bled the same. And some gave their lives so that others could live.

Thus Bear Mother had died, covering the retreat of those children whom the first onslaught had not slain.

Was that why I felt so restless this first night of Samonios? The oak priests taught that on this night the spirits of the dead returned from the Otherworld to visit their clans. Had Bear Mother made me her kin when she pricked her totem into the skin of my belly? Could she find me, so many marches south of the Island that had been her home? I had never seen a spirit, but tonight everything was strange. I watched as the sun pulsed and flattened and was netted by the black branches and the shadows crept out from beneath the trees, and felt suddenly cold.

"Not to be bitter, little one—" Crow's face was still in shadow. I could not keep the tremor from my laugh.

"I am as tall as you are, and a warrior, and I am beating my wings like a caged bird against these walls!"

"Everybody captive; few can see bonds. Even you."

"I thought that *you* would understand!" I tugged at the heavy wool of the gown I wore, chequered in subtle golds and browns. In the first weeks after the king's men had brought me home from the Island, the cloaks and tunics of the Quiritani had stifled me, but despite the fat that four months back in the king's house had put on my bones, I was beginning to lose my resistance to cold, and that made me afraid.

"What blind man sees, brings others ease,
What's dark as night gives singer sight—"

He laughed suddenly, and folded his long legs beneath him so that he seemed to be perched on the wall. "But not for self. Not ever, now. . . ."

I moved closer, trying to see his expression, and realized suddenly that though he still looked like a boy, there was a threading of silver in his soot-colored hair. When had that happened? Was everything that I thought secure in danger today?

"Why not, Crow? On the Island I sang your song and Bear Mother told me it was a song of power. If I could sing it now, I would wing northward despite the season."

"Even silly geese know to fly south in fall." He cocked his head to one side.

> *"Caged birds, indeed, the crow and swan!*
> *Is freedom gone?*
> *When darkness falls, who looks for dawn?"*

"Oh, how does my father bear with you?" I cried.

One winged eyebrow quirked as he turned to me. "Leir is his own law. Like the sun, like the sea . . ."

"Then why does he need you? Why do you stay here?"

At that moment one of the tree-carved images of the gods would have seemed less still, for in the air around the sacred statues there was always just the hint of a shimmer, but Crow had drawn all his energies inward. In the fading light, with a length of rough grey wool draped round him, he seemed less substantial than the spirits. I reached out, but did not quite dare to grasp his arm.

"Crow! Do not go away from me!"

"Does flower need the bee or oak the mistletoe? Does rain need the sea?" He gave me a crooked smile, and for a moment his earth-brown eyes were unguarded and vulnerable as those of some wild thing.

"This one left first home . . . will not run again, even now, when he feels the coming of the spirits, and is afraid. Will not leave you . . . or *him* . . ."

I looked where he was looking, and saw my father crossing the yard with his unmistakable arrogant stride. He, at least, would always be there. I was grateful for his strength even as I resented the high-handed way in which he had brought me back to his protection.

As a child, I had assumed that my father's dun was the center of the world. Nor had I wondered what Crow had been before the villagers of Udrolissa captured him. But now I too had been up-rooted. He had lost his destiny. Was the same thing going to happen to me?

"Crow . . ." I swallowed. *Teach me!*

His gaze moved over me with an opaque and unrevealing ap-praisal that reminded me painfully of Bear Mother. *He has the knowledge . . .* I thought, *Why does he play the clown for us here?* But slowly, he shook his head.

"What could this one give? You are growing. You will have other teachers soon . . ."

"What do you mean?" I began, but he was already turning. I heard a step below.

"Cridilla! So, child, there you are!"

Though he scarcely stirred, the authority I had glimpsed in Crow was abruptly gone. As Rigana climbed the ladder to the walkway, he seemed to grow smaller.

"The acorn grows as 'tis bent—but can'st not make an oak of a rowan tree!" He looked from me to my sister and sketched a mocking homage, and then, as she began to frown, was suddenly off in a clatter and tinkle of bones and bells.

I stared after him. In all the time we had been talking, his ornaments had made no sound at all.

Rigana shuddered. "How do you bear that creature? He makes my skin crawl!"

"Our father—"

"The king dotes on him, I know it," she interrupted. "But that does not mean he is fit company for the Lady of Briga!"

"There has been no Lady of Briga since my mother died!" I answered her. "Those days are gone."

"Are they?" She smiled oddly, and I folded my arms across the new swell of my breasts, uncomfortable for different reasons now. Rigana was looking at me as my father looked at a heifer he was going to bring to the bull.

"Indeed, you are a tall lass," she said finally. "But you are shaping well. In time you will understand."

I felt myself going red. Bear Mother and her daughters had had women's bodies, and they were warriors, but I had not had much chance to work out since my body had begun to change. Last summer I had worn my flesh with the ease of a young doe, but next to Rigana's fine-boned perfection, I felt misshapen and clumsy now.

"Poor child, it is hard indeed. But there is power in that body you are growing. When your courses begin you will begin to learn its mysteries. Even Gunarduilla does not know how to use them, but she is a battle-mare. You will be fairer than she. Are not the young lads watching you already?"

I glared at her, sure she was mocking me. Horse had cared for me, but he was my comrade. It was Rigana whom the eyes of the warriors followed when she moved with the mead horn around the hall. We had even laughed together because the woman who shared my father's bed these days was jealous.

"Did you climb up here just to say that to me?"

Rigana lifted one winged black brow. She had come fully into her beauty. Her belt was studded with medallions of worked gold, and cinched tight to prove that her waist was still slender even though she had borne a child. Above it, her round breasts strained against the crimson wool of her gown.

"Are you a child still, Cridilla, or do you even know why you are so cross with me?" She smiled oddly. "Well, it does not matter now. Your father is calling for you. The torches of Samonia are lit, and the folk are gathering."

Already I could hear the sound of singing from below.

"Shadows gather, darkness nears, night is winging nigh
Light the torches, bring the wood and build the balefires high.
Winter winds blow chill—
Fire fends off all ill!"

I looked beyond her and saw the yard a-glitter with points of flame. To the westward, fire bloomed already from the summit of Beacon Hill. From the settlements in the valley of the Soretia the people would be watching. They always used to hold their own Feast of the Dead near first harvest, but these days many were coming to celebrate it at the same time as the Quiritani.

"Torches serpent-circling round, sain the hall with light,
Beacon blaze between the worlds and bring the spirit sight,
Show the souls the way—
Evil keep at bay!"

My breath caught as the flames within the fort flowed together and encircled the hill with a serpent of fire. The singing grew fainter as the procession moved on.

"Torches' flame defies the dark, doorways open wide;
Dead and living here clasp hands and clan and kin abide.
Blessèd ones draw near,
Be welcome without fear."

"Come," said my sister more gently, "let us go down to the festival."

My father's feasting hall was long in the fashion of his homeland, with fire in a trench that ran down the middle. Boards laid across logs kept the food above the fresh rushes upon which the warriors were sprawling. There were raised couches for the chieftains near the end of the hall, across from those of the high-born women. The king's place was between them at the head of the fire, with Crow crouched beside him, as familiar and unacknowledged as one of the dogs.

Rigana's couch of honor was next to mine, but early in the evening she had joined the women who were bearing mead to the warriors. Men's voices grew softer where she passed. I could hear her laughter and the musical clash of her necklaces each time she bent to refill a drinking horn. Only Senouindos did not seem to notice her graceful passage through the hall. He had a skinny slave boy to keep him supplied with drink, and since the torches had been brought into the hall he had paid little attention to anything except the contents of his bowl.

I shifted uncomfortably on the cushioned softness, wanting the rib of a fresh-killed deer to gnaw on and a seat on an old hide flung across a packed-earth floor. Not that a deer rib would have been much use to me this evening. I was not used to such abundance.

A few bites of juicy pork had been enough to set my guts to griping and I had dared do no more than taste the slab of beef my father had awarded me.

I bit off a piece of bannock heavy with honey and let my hand drift downward. A warm muzzle poked into my palm and the rest of the bannock vanished. A moment later Storm's gaunt grey head lifted hopefully above the table and I thrust it firmly down again. The dogs were curled close around me, and no one seemed to have noticed where most of the food I had been given had gone.

Crow moved among the people, juggling daggers and arm rings and oak apples, turning somersaults and walking on his hands to make them laugh. There was a stir at the end of the hall, and he came upright in a rain of miscellaneous objects, gathering them deftly into his patchwork cape as a drum beat out a swift summoning.

"Drink, O warriors of the Quiritani, to the glory of dead heroes!" Talorgenos stood at the far end of the fire, the plumage of his goose-feather headpiece casting winged shadows against the lime-washed plastering of the wall. His trained voice carried, and the hall was abruptly still.

"Let us praise our brothers Uratos son of Ilicos and Bituitos the Black, who were slain by the men of the White Horse vale. Brethren of the sword and shield, we salute you and bid you be welcome—" He tipped the silver-mounted ceremonial horn and sent a thin stream of mead hissing into the fire. In a single endless swallow, the warriors drained their horns.

The cowhides that hung before the doors had been tied back, and the fire leaped in a sudden wind that sent smoke swirling. To my watering eyes the smoke seemed to solidify and for a moment I saw the shapes of men.

I sat up, wiping my eyes on the back of my sleeve. The air was still again, and the smoke had become a dim haze that was filtering up through the thatch above the beams. But Leir had not yet drained his horn. Slowly, silence spread once more through the hall.

"For Uratos and Bituitos," said the king, "and for Trost and Uxelos and Red Leg, and all the other good lads gone. They are blessed, for they died fighting, but we feel their loss!"

[113]

I drew up my knees and pulled my shawl around my shoulders, for the first time really looking at the people who surrounded me. The warriors seemed younger than the men I remembered from four years ago, long-limbed and cocky. Their elaborately limed and braided hair framed smooth faces with tenderly nurtured moustaches above smooth chins.

I had noticed as soon as I returned that the war-band was smaller, half full of men whom I did not know, but I had supposed that our tried warriors were fighting elsewhere. The king had ordered that I be brought south to Ligrodunon, but it had been Artocoxos, big and burly as ever though his beard was grizzled as a bear's pelt now, who welcomed me. Indeed, I had hardly seen my father until he returned for the festival. I had intended to be cold to him whenever he finally found the time to try to charm me. But he looked, not old, but weary as I had never seen him before.

Leir was heaving himself to his feet, his drinking horn held high. This night his hair fell from its binding atop his head like a horse's tail, its gold darkening to chestnut with a threading of white that gleamed copper in the light of the fire. His face showed the strain of the recent warfare, the skin weathered like rubbed oak, flesh just a little loose on the heavy bones.

"The heads of my foes grin above my gateposts, but my sword is still unsatisfied. Everywhere our enemies gather. Their depredations in the south you all know. The Ai-Zir have carried off cattle— That is no new thing," he added as someone laughed. "And a thing understandable; for who among us has not done the same? But to kill the cattle when they have taken them, not at the proper season but wantonly, is an abomination . . ."

A bloated cow with stiffened legs accusing the air . . . the plaintive low of an abandoned calf calling chorus to the cawing of the feeding crows. . . .

I forced myself to focus on my father's words. He was speaking not of the casual raiding that went on constantly among the Quiritani, but of something more serious. In much of the Island, the Painted People were still unconquered. My gaze moved to Rigana, who was sitting on the edge of her husband's couch now, kneading his shoulders. Even she was watching our father, but I could not read her gaze.

"I thought that we could all live together, but no longer. This is one island, it should be one people!"

"War!" came a cry from among the younger warriors. "Let us kill the Ai-Zir and make their lands our own!"

Fire that fills the sky and blood that spreads across the land. . . .

I blinked. I had never seen a village burning. Where had that image come from? I had not been sick since I left for the Island. I wondered if I was going to be ill now.

"We are too few," came an objection. "Let us make treaty with them, and have peace until we can breed up more warriors or bring them over the sea." There was a murmur of agreement.

"Well enough, if they were men of truth who could honor a treaty once made. We had treaties with the tribes from beyond the rift in Alba. But for the past three months my daughter Gunarduilla and her husband have been beleaguered in Uotadinion, because the tribes have laid waste the countryside. She is with child at last, and cannot fight free. And that is not all. You all know the oaths that protect the sanctity of the Misty Isle—the warrior women are of the old race, but they are beyond kinship or boundaries. For the past four years Cridilla, my youngest, has dwelt in safety there—"

Leir turned to look at me, and I saw the blue spark of fury in his eyes. Was he angry with me?

"But this summer raiders killed the She-Bear and most of the children in her care. If my daughter had not already been herself a warrior, she too would have died!"

No, it was not anger, but anguish, that I saw in his gaze . . . My heart beat heavily. Suddenly I was seeing a vision of my own body lying in its blood like a slaughtered cow. But was that me? Surely the figure was shorter, heavier, with blood pooling between its flaccid thighs.

That did not happen! It is not me! I gasped and ground the heels of my hands into my eyes to make the picture go away.

A murmur of outrage swelled in the hall. "Let the maid herself tell the tale!"

"Tell us, daughter, how the She-Bear of the Isles died!" said Leir.

I opened my eyes, drawing on Bear Mother's training to regain control. They were all looking at me now. I remembered that I had my own war-band to grieve for, held out my horn for one of the servers to fill, and got to my feet, facing the king.

"There were five bands of children on the Island, the youngest only six years old," I began. Swiftly, I told the tale.

Less than half that number had survived the raid. A few who had nowhere else to go were still with Spirit Bear and her sister. I would have stayed, even though death had voided my oaths to Bear Mother and there was no school for me to teach in anymore. Horse was with them. He had been still too weak to travel when Leir's warriors came to claim me, even if it had been safe for him to go where he might be found by his own father's enemies. Horse was starving in the north, and I was here, in this well-fed, fur-lined prison, alone.

"Therefore I ask you who are warriors to drink to those who, had they lived, would have been worthy of your company. I invoke the spirits of Bear Mother, of Willow and Wingfoot, Gannet and Waterdog—" The list went on. . . .

I tried to blink away memory that brought the faces of my dead before me as wind gusted again through the open doorways. Leaping firelight harried the shadows around the hall, bright and dark and bright again, bewildering vision. There was an ache deep in my belly and my skin felt cold. I waved smoke away from my eyes, but suddenly I was having trouble seeing.

A slender girl with a tangle of dark hair moved at the edge of my vision. I turned, trying to see as she faded into the shadows once more. *Willow* . . . I thought. *I called her, and she has come . . . the dead are returning, and this year I can see them!*

Shaking, I opened my eyes again. For every warrior who gnawed a pork bone or poured mead down his throat there was a shadow who fed on the haze of energy that glowed around the food. A war-band twice the number of the men Leir could field filled the hall.

"It was warriors of the Ai-Zoma, the wildcats of the islands, that did this thing—" cried the king. "And these are the enemies that threaten my oldest daughter and her unborn child. Our enemies in the south are defeated, but these folk snarl and spit like a wildcat daring to come after the lambs because the dog is dead. Will we allow them to mock us?"

"Let them mock the men of Alba. What use to shed our blood there?" I saw a shadowed corrie, where ravens croaked out the tally of the slain. . . .

"In battle I will be a hero! They will all sing my praises—" I looked around, then realized that Leir was still speaking. I had not been hearing those comments with my physical ears.

"When spring opens the passes, let us teach them who rules this land!" Artocoxos was on his feet, shaking his fist. If his sword had not been hanging on the wall behind him, it would have been in his hand.

Swords flared in sunlight above faces made animal by rage. . . .

"And who rules the Quiritani? This war is for Leir's gain!" A lance was blurring through the air . . .

"Where will it end, when the Wildcat tribe are all slain?" Sudden shadow of a lifting shield. . . .

"I will slay them all, and the bards will make songs about me!"

I clapped my hands over my ears. I felt as if I had suddenly been stripped of my skin. What was happening to me?

The warriors were all shouting. Artocoxos and Senouindos stood beside the king, hammering on the table for emphasis, while Rigana smiled. The shades of the slain were growing more solid, as if they fed on the energy of men's rage as well as on the offerings. And the slaves were bringing more mead for the warriors. Tonight there would be enough to feed them all.

I looked desperately around the hall, saw Crow and began to move toward him. His dark eyes were white-ringed, like those of a frightened horse. His gaze focused where mine did; he saw the same things I saw. But as I watched, the warrior whom he had been entertaining asked a question, and Crow nodded, shivering. The man lifted his cloak and Crow crept beneath it, burrowing close against his side on the narrow couch. Then the cloak dropped to cover them. I could just see Crow's head against his protector's shoulder, and the warrior reaching to caress the dark brush of hair.

I stopped short, understanding that Crow had found his own refuge from the ghosts of men who were neither kin nor kind. I could not seek comfort from him now, and I thought that even if I had gone to him, he could not have helped me. We would have been like two children, huddling together for fear of the demons of the dark.

But what could I do? The hall was in an uproar. Men were calling on Talorgenos to kill a bull and sleep within its skin on this night when past and future clasped hands, to prophesy the outcome of the coming war. The spirits thronged around me in swirls of icy air, holding out eager hands. What did they want from me?

"Did I not say it, girl? Hast already the power—"

I gasped, for though this speech, like the others, sounded on the inner ear, I knew the accent well. A furred form was taking shape from the shadows. I recognized the stiff, pricked ears of the hood, saw gold gleam pale beneath it, less bright than the piercing grey eyes.

"Artona . . . Bear Mother—" A whisper was all I could manage, but I need not have spoken aloud.

"Didst think a' could lose me by comin' so far? Watchin' over all my children now . . ."

I laughed weakly. We used to think the She-Bear must be served by spirits, for whatever one's misdeeds, she always knew. But now *she* was the spirit, helping me. . . . Crow had said I would find other teachers. This must be what he had meant.

"I feel sick, my guts are cramping, and I am afraid!"

"Then seek th' privies, child. Outside is clean air to clear thy head. Why stay here?"

Of course that was what I should do. Why had I been unable to think of it before? The warriors were drinking and beginning their battle boasts already. Surely no one would care if I left the feast now. I wrapped my shawl around me and started for the door.

* * *

I came out into a world where the wind was given shape by darkness. Drifting cloud alternately revealed and veiled the stars. There was a damp chill in the air, a sense of shifting forces as winter neared. Torches streamed wildly from the doorposts of the mead hall, laying wavering pathways of light across the fading grass. Light gleamed on the white bone of old skulls set into niches in the walls of the shrine and made the shrinking lips of the newer trophies curl in illusory self-mockery.

At this hour all the living were within doors, but although the thronging spirits remained in the hall, the windy darkness was all a-whisper with other voices. Perhaps the scent of blood had awakened them. They spoke of festivals and sacrifices here in days before ever Leir Blatoniknos built his earthen walls.

"She-Bear, what have you got me into?" I asked. "If I go out into this, will you ward me?"

"My folk be older even than these . . ." came the answer. *"Not to fear!"*

I had never felt anything quite like the dull ache that was throbbing in the pit of my belly, even the time that I had got into the green apples, or when I was sick at sea. I hurried toward the privy pits, choosing one where an occasional flicker of torchlight let me see my way. Late at night after a festival, drunken warriors had been known to fall in.

Relieving myself did not help much. But it was only when I started to get up again that I noticed the dark smear of blood upon my thighs.

I am wounded . . . Memory showed me once more my father's vision of that woman who was like me, lying dead with the blood flowing from her womb into the straw. *Now I pay the price for being born!* I touched myself, and smelled the scent of slaughter that all day had filled the air.

"Is not Death that flows from thee, girl, 'tis Power . . ."

I looked up and saw the She-Bear, seemingly solid in the wavering light, as if the energy in my blood had at last enabled her to take a form that I could clearly see. Other spirits hovered beyond her, but her presence kept them at bay.

"My moon blood . . ." I said, understanding at last. I had not wanted it. I did not see the use of it, except to draw hungry spirits that I did not want either. "Do a woman's courses always come with such pain?"

"Will flow th' more easily an' thou dost not resist it., Go now to th' Women's House. Tell Zaueret t' give thee yarrow an' red clover an' chamomile."

I found myself smiling. Even a spirit, however powerful, could not brew me a pot of tea.

"If canst smile, child, hast learned a thing that no ill can conquer!"

I straightened and shook down my skirts. They were stained already, and the wind was chill. I was already at the doorway of the Women's House when I realized that Bear Mother was fading in the light.

"Do not leave me!" I whispered.

"Not to fear. Will come always when dost have need of me," came the answer, and then she was one with the wind.

"Is someone behind thee?" asked Zaueret, turning from the hearth as I came in. "What dost thou need, heartling? Dost look so pale!" I shrugged, suddenly aware that though my woman's blood was flowing, a heartwound that had been bleeding since I saw Bear Mother's corpse was now healed. I wondered if perhaps someone would always be behind me now.

"Some rags," I muttered, "and a pot of yarrow and red clover tea."

For a moment Zaueret stared. Then her round cheeks creased in a grin.

"Lady . . ." She bent before me as I had seen the tribesfolk bow to Rigana in Belerion. But never, never before, to me.

In moments, it seemed, all her girls were bustling around me, and I had been bathed and provided with the necessary supplies and put to bed in the enclosure where the women of the dun sometimes withdrew for privacy when their courses arrived. And it seemed scarcely longer before Rigana was there, looking down at me with the same secret smile she had worn that afternoon.

"I *knew*! Ah, sister, all day I have been feeling the change in you—but I hardly dared to hope that your time was coming at last!"

"Hope?" I laughed, but less bitterly than I would have earlier. Zaueret's tea was working already, or perhaps it was simply understanding what had happened to me that had eased the aching within. "Is a woman's first moontime always so strange?"

Rigana laughed. "It is not usual for a girl's first blood to come to her on the hallows, 'tis true. But it is the best of omens. Oh, my dear, what a queen you will be!"

"What do you mean?"

"Your initiation, child, what else? The ceremonies in which you gain the use of your power. In the morning I will send messengers to Lady Asaret and the others—" She sat down on the side of my pallet and took my hand. "If the weather holds, they could be here in another moon, and we will have time before Midwinter to journey to the Womb Cave for the ritual."

"The cavern up in the dales near the Hill of the Winds?" I asked in disbelief. "In the middle of winter? Father will never let me go!"

Rigana looked at me and laughed again. "Leir will have nothing to say to it, my dear. These are Women's Mysteries, and he dare not interfere. Nor will he try to do so. Even a Quiritani sword-swinger fears to meddle with a maiden's moonpower until it is trained. And you are the Royal Daughter of Briga. It is to his advantage for you to come into your full power as Lady and queen."

I must have still looked dubious, for as she rose she patted my hand.

"Sleep now, my sister. Let your body complete its transformation. And do not trouble yourself about our father—until your initiation is over you will not set eyes on him or any other man."

Chapter

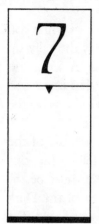

*You are whiter than the swan on the swampy lake,
you are whiter than the white sea-gull of the stream,
you are whiter than the snow on the lofty peaks,
you are whiter than the love of the angels of
    Heaven.*

—Scots Gaelic folk charm, *Carmina Gadelica*

The season's first snow had fallen the night before. Above the limestone cliffs of the scar the fells shone in the morning light, and white sparkled from the fallen oak leaves on the slopes below. A wisp of smoke was rising from the fire where the priestesses were heating stones for the sweathouse, their breathing making white puffs in the still air. I sat enthroned upon piled saddle blankets, trying to pretend that all this bustle had nothing to do with me.

After Samonios, we had journeyed up from Ligrodunon by easy stages, through moors and meadows leached of all color by the cold. But the sacred rowan branch that was borne before us was all a flutter with tassels of bright yarn; we passed through the countryside accompanied by the sweet sibilance of its silver bells. No man of either the old race or the new would have dared to delay us once he had seen the cow skull that was bound to that sacred staff.

When the gentle alternation of forested vales of half-cleared slopes began to give way to open sweeps of stony moorland, I felt an unexpected tremor of excitement. And then, beyond them, I glimpsed the sacred mountains that watched over the land. It was only at that moment that I had begun to realize that it *was* my own land, and that perhaps there was some purpose to all this ritual.

"Amaunet came in from the country of the Banalisioi while you were sleeping," said Rigana, beside me. "That brings the tally up to five"—she counted them off on her fingers,—"Lady Asaret, who is their senior; old Tamar; Ilifet, the one in the pigskin cape; and Urtaya of the Ai-Zir, who guards the stones of the Goddess on the plain."

I opened my eyes at that, for at last report, the People of the Bull had still been our enemies. But as Rigana kept telling me, this ritual was more important than the wars of men. It must be, to bring the Ti-Sahharin out at this time of year. Three of the Dark Sisterhood had come from farther than we had. I wondered if it was true that the great priestesses could take the shapes of birds and journey upon the wind.

"But it may be that there will be only five if the snows hold Ekki in her western mountains, for there's little hope that the Alba folk will be able to get through this year," Rigana went on.

I sighed. I did not like thinking about how Gunarduilla was faring. I could not even begin to imagine her pregnant, and I did not want to wonder whether she would live to bear her child. Better to distract myself by speculating on what was going to happen to *me*.

The lives of my people, whether Ti n'Izriran or Quiritani, were governed by the great cycles of ceremonies that marked the seasons of men's lives and of the land. I had grown up with them, but this was the first time that I had been the focus of a ritual. If I had been an ordinary girl, a week or two in the Women's House would have been enough to prepare me for my passage. But from one moon to the next the women had lectured me on the workings of the female body, and how to deal with men and children, and now it was nearing Midwinter. What in the name of Dana's tits was left to tell me, and why could it only be communicated here?

"Are you impatient, little sister?" Rigana laughed. Her hood had fallen back and her hair seemed almost shockingly black against the bright snow. I looked at her in surprise, for her tone was playful.

"When they initiated me at the Mother's well and the Barrow of the Queens—and it was during one of the stormiest springs I can remember—I thought the ceremonies would never end."

"Why do it then?" I ventured to ask. I had faced my testing on the Island with confidence in my body's ability to meet my demands. But now my body had betrayed me, and after what I had seen at the Feast of Samonia, I was beginning to doubt my spirit as well. Even the water from the sacred spring seemed to whisper mysteries as it trickled from the scar above us through a stone-lined channel to the pool.

"Because we *are* the queens—" Her voice had deepened, and I shivered. "And our fertility is the fertility of the land. Of all of the Mother's children only man has to be taught Her law. In each land the cycle of life is unique, as each woman is all women, and yet herself alone. Each woman must be courted differently. So it is with the land, and how shall the men who come into it understand that without our teaching?

"The knowledge will be lost if we do not do these things. Our desires and discomforts are nothing beside that need. Already we are threatened. In the White Cliff country the line of the queens is dead and only the priestess is left to carry on.

"You see Urtaya—" She pointed to a rather heavy-set woman wrapped in a red bull's hide. "She brings the greetings of her queen, but her Lady is old, and has borne only sons. Some of the priestesses are old as well, and it is hard to train their successors in the lands where the Quiritani rule."

"Is that why Gunarduilla took me to the Misty Isle?" I asked. "Was Bear Mother part of your sisterhood?"

"Artona's wisdom was of an order older even than ours," came a voice from behind us. "You are fortunate to have had her teaching."

Rigana made a sign of salutation, and I nodded awkwardly,

recognizing the woman who had kept me from being bitten by the adder when I was a child. Lady Asaret did not appear to have grown any older. But today she wore ornaments of jet and amber and a cloak pieced together from the skins of hares over her robe of dark blue wool.

Two of the other priestesses had followed her.

"Lady," said Lady Ilifet, "hot to cracking are the stones, and the ground prepared around them. Are ye ready here?"

"Sweep all the coals away and uncover the stones, and let Lady Tamar prepare the enclosure. The Maiden awaits her cleansing." She turned to me. "Dost understand?"

Three priestesses lifted the big beehive hut of interlaced hazel saplings, carried it like an overturned basket to the fire, and lowered it around the pile of glowing stones. As the women draped hides over the structure to hold the heat inside it, I began to strip off my warm clothes.

I was hungry, for since sunset the evening before they had kept me fasting, and after this cleansing there was still the vigil to get through. If I could. . . . Perhaps it was shame, to seem unwilling after all the trouble they were taking for me, that made me nod.

"Now it begins!" said Rigana fiercely. I sighed, and let her pull my gown over my head.

"I will do it," I told her, straightening. "But I still do not understand . . ."

"When you come out of the Womb Cave you will know—" She faced me wide-eyed, and for a moment I thought that I could see into her soul. "Oh, my dear one—when you understand what it means to be a queen, then you and I and Gunarduilla together will renew the world!"

Waves of heated air pulsed through the close darkness around me, even more shocking after the chill of the air outside. I clung to the cool damp of the hut's earth floor, not caring what these women thought of me. The priestesses sat in a circle against the wicker wall, female forms made dimly visible by the glow of the heated stones. Someone was murmuring a prayer to Earth our Mother. After a few moments I became conscious of the musky odor of women's bodies mingling with the spicy scents of the herbs they had scattered on the stones.

A rattle hissed suddenly, startling me upright again.

"Listen, my sisters, now are we in the place of beginning; now are we in the place where all is made new."

Lady Asaret's voice sounded different here.

"Sa . . . sa . . . it is so . . . it is so—" The other women swayed.

"Do not cling to thy mother, for she must die, and a mother thou thyself shalt be."

"Be it so," I answered, for I had never known my mother's love. And yet as I said it I felt a pang of loss, and in that moment understood how much I had longed for her.

The rattle spat stone once more.

"Do not dote upon thy father," came the voice from the darkness, "for he will die, and thou shalt bear children to another man—"

Did I set too much love upon my father? Sometimes I thought I hated him. Well, I had no wish to take any man as husband, so perhaps it would not matter if I assented to this too.

"Do not gaze backward at the games of childhood, for the time comes now for building the world anew . . ."

I frowned. I did not think the men who had died beneath my blade on the Island had been killed by a child! But it was true that the bragging of the warriors in my father's hall at the Samonia sometimes sounded like the boasting of children at play.

I had chased cattle on Cygnet's back with an unthinking joy that now, when age had claimed her, I was unlikely to know again. The king had promised me the pick of his herds, but however much I might come to love a new horse, I would still remember the possibility of loss.

It was not the joys of childhood that I must relinquish, but the ignorance that had kept me from valuing them.

"What was childish in my past I now release—" I answered at last.

There were more questions, too many of them addressing traits that I hoped I had outgrown. I had indeed often been roaming the woods when there were chores to be done. I could not veil the truth, even when tact was necessary. Unless I was pressed it was hard for me to speak out in company. Someone, perhaps Zaueret, must have told them what to require of me.

But they did not ask me to give up my hard-won skill with arms. Perhaps they feared that Bear Mother's ghost would haunt them, or perhaps they also understood that arms borne of necessity were not a childish thing. Finally the rattle silenced the questioning.

"What thou wert is ended. What shalt thou be? Receive now a new name—Black Sow or White Mare, Dark Serpent of the Depths and White Raven that links Earth with Sky—" Other names followed until my head whirled. "The image of the Lady art thou, and all Her faces must thou wear . . ."

By now there was only the faintest glow from the stones. I peered into the darkness around me, sensing, rather than seeing, that the other women were there. It should have been growing cooler, but the air was still stifling. I felt as if I were melting into the muddy ground.

"This is the Goddess who is Mother of All; She it is by whom the world is destroyed at the end of each age, that from Her it may be reborn. Goddess art thou, that in the cycle of thy womb dost each moon manifest this mystery!"

"This is the power of the blood of the moon," came a voice from the other side of the circle, "blood shed for life, not for death; for cleansing, not in impurity. This is the blood-sacrifice of women. This is the blood that makes fertile the field, thy body's proof of immortality. . . ."

Women's voices chorused around me, resonant as if they were being spoken now and forever in every time and place that women performed the ceremony. I fought to breathe against the heat and the pressure. Surely there were more here than the five women who had entered the hut with me. In the air above us invisible presences gathered, queens and priestesses in a line unbroken since the days when the great stone circles were established in the land.

"In thy moontime, thou dost walk in power," another woman said. "To men without knowledge, this is a thing to fear. Not understanding, their own magic goes awry. For this reason we go apart when our flow is greatest, or learn the means by which our energies may be contained. For this reason, choose this time to work thine own most cogent spells. . . ."

I nodded, remembering how the spirits of the dead had thronged to me, and understanding that my own body gave me a power that the men could gain only through sacrifice.

"Like unto the ebb and flow of the tides in the Great Sea are the tides of thy body; salt-sweet blood, salt sea water, both answering the call of the moon." This voice was deep and low.

"Like unto the waters that flow in the secret hollows beneath earth's surface is the blood of thy womb; from those springs flows the life of the world, easing the thirst of the body, feeding the need of the soul." The words were a breath that spoke to more than the body's ears.

The voices faded. I sucked in air, and found myself on my knees, clutching at the muddy soil.

"From earth and water cometh thy power, to annihilate or make new. Swear now, thou who art the vessel of the blood of queens, to serve the land as the land shall require. Not death but life shall be thy offering!"

An expectant silence pulsed around me. I remembered how the blood of the white stallion had fountained beneath the axe, and how, for a moment, I had sensed my father's appalling vulnerability. There had been so many sacrifices, substituting for the final offering. And yet what they were asking of me was in its own way more terrible.

"All that lives must die so that all that has died may be reborn. This is the work of woman. Thou hast the power to destroy or to heal, so that the sacred waters may continue to flow. . . ."

I did not know if those words were spoken aloud, but the pressure around me had become unendurable.

"I will . . ." I whispered, and felt an answering tremor in the earth beneath me. Yet still I did not know what that oath might mean.

"From earth and water didst thou come; from earth and water thou shalt be reborn!" Lady Asaret sang out triumphantly. "Now do we give birth to thee. Shed thy old life, Serpent of Briga, and emerge made new—"

The skins were thrust aside from the doorway and daylight streamed through. Someone's arms closed around me in a quick embrace. The light was blocked as she released me and crawled through the opening. Then the next one hugged me, and the next. The last woman pulled me toward the doorway. I covered my eyes as she dragged me into the light.

Lady Asaret waited at the edge of the water, and the other priestesses had formed into two lines between me and the pool, grasping bunches of birch rods. But more people had arrived while we were in the sweathouse. There was a new priestess, and behind her, next to Rigana, I glimpsed Gunarduilla's golden hair.

Until this moment I had not realized how much I wanted her. But I had no time for rejoicing. Someone pushed me forward. I bit my lip as the first birch branch stung me, and began to run.

"Maiden shed a skin!" chanted the priestesses. "Maiden shed a skin! Cast the old aside, rebirth what is within!"

I pressed forward, but they were all around me; new sweat blinded me; my overheated skin was on fire. Four . . . Five . . . I counted as I passed them. And then, before I could come to Lady Asaret, I saw another in my path, and this woman was blue as any warrior with the totems pricked into her skin. I felt her lash fire my flesh and recognized the warrior's subtle shift in balance and the swing of her arm. *Bear Mother*. . . . I turned, dashing sweat from my eyes, holding out my arms.

There was no one there.

But Lady Asaret was laughing, drawing me into her embrace and into the chill release of the pool.

"Didst see her?" she cried. "O blessed child! Seven priestesses! Seven of us were here, after all!"

They crowded around me, scrubbing my glowing flesh with rough cloths as if they would remove my skin. I staggered, and strong hands upheld me. I had been released from the close darkness of the sweathouse into the bright air, and all my griefs were gone. Consciousness swung dizzily between the confines of my body and the whole wide world.

"Hold me—" I whispered, "or I will float away!"

Lady Asaret's arms enfolded me against the sweet softness of her breasts and the firm swell of her thighs. *Why did they want me to give up my mother?* I wondered hazily. *My mother is here!* I clung to awareness of the delicious coolness of the water they were pouring over my heated skin, and the firm warmth of women's hands.

"Let my arms hold you, daughter—art safe with us here . . ." the priestess crooned. My head dropped to her shoulder. I was weeping, and I did not know why.

"Art cleansed . . . art renewed . . . art made whole . . ." came the whispers. Their hands touched me softly now. Gradually the sobs that were shaking my body eased.

My blood pulsed strongly through my veins, so that I felt only pleasure in the touch of the chill air. I had never been so clean. That sense of lightness remained, as if I were not quite contained within my body, but I could see clearly once more. Every stone and tree seemed to shine with its own light, and the other women—angular or full-fleshed, breasts pendulous or firm—were all suddenly beautiful.

Lady Asaret took a bowl, of jet worn smooth with use, and held it under the lip of stone where the water fell into the pool. In a niche above it stood a figure carved from some dull metal. Above the bell of its skirt two round breasts jutted from the straight torso. The features were blurred with age, but it seemed to me that she smiled.

The priestess lifted the bowl to my lips and I gulped down the sweetness, gasping as it refilled my body with the moisture I had sweated away. But surely it was something more than ordinary water. I felt as if it were replacing the very blood in my veins.

"Beloved, we have rebirthed thee—" said Lady Asaret as she helped me back to the solid ground. "All that we know, we have given thee. It is for the Goddess to speak to thee now."

"Art weary, little one?" asked Rigana, reining her pony closer. "'Twill not be long now—dost see that shadow? 'Tis there the cavern lies. . . ."

We were moving along the base of the scree below a broken wall of limestone. After my cleansing, they had carried me in a horse litter across the river, turning up the dale and taking the path that climbed the long cliff toward the crags, a journey of somewhat over an hour.

A soft-voiced command brought the horses to a halt. Gunar-duilla helped me out of the litter and I found myself glad of the assistance, for I was still not entirely connected to the world.

"Are you well?" I whispered, hugging her. Her belly was just beginning to round. There was a new wariness to her eyes, but she seemed strong as ever, and her fair skin was glowing from the cold.

"I am here, little sister—is not that an answer?" For a moment her glance met Rigana's, then her attention returned to me. "It is yourself you must be thinking of now, child. This chance will not come again. Journey boldly, and bring back a fair vision for us all!"

Westward, the long, tiered shape of Rigodunon watched over the countryside. The dales lay quiet beneath the snow, with no hint that their stillness had ever been disturbed by humankind. What was I supposed to learn here?

Lady Asaret came back down the line, her skin boots crunching on the snow.

"Behold the Womb of Briga—enter it, and be reborn!" The priestess pointed to the cave. "Cold it will seem, yet warmer is the cavern than the air outside. Now the sun is high. When she returns to this spot again we will come also. Dost understand?"

I nodded. The oak priests lay for three days and three nights in darkness, awaiting their visions, and Crow's people initiated their singers in worse ways, half-drowning them in icy water, or hanging them from trees. I had no reason to fear a single night in a cave.

But as we climbed, the shadow in the crag became the maw of some great beast that was waiting to devour me. From the entrance I looked back at the world I was leaving. *Death waits for me here* . . . I thought then, but whether of the body or the spirit I did not know.

Then I bent beneath the overhang, and went in.

Light from the entrance showed me a rough mud floor that sloped toward the back of the cave, growing deeper as I picked my way downward and the passage widened. The stepped planes of the ceiling were broken here and there where the rock had shifted. I stumbled, and saw a shattered pot and the green of corroded bronze. It was a harness fitting, the sort of gift one might leave to propitiate a ghost. They had called this cavern a womb, but once more I wondered if tomb might be a better name.

The end of the cavern curved ahead. As I heard the scrape of the stiff hide they were dragging across the entrance to the cave, I moved toward the illusory shelter of one of the shallow bays in the wall. For a few moments longer a line of light was visible around the edge of the opening, then that too disappeared as they began to pile up the stones.

Blackness flooded in around me. The darkness of the sweathouse had been stifling, but compared to this place, it seemed friendly and secure. I was acutely aware that I was in a space nearly the size of my father's banqueting hall, and although I had seen nothing worse than myself before they took the light away, how could I be sure?

I strove to hear above the rush of blood in my ears and the rasp of breath in my lungs. Slowly I became aware of the breath of cold air on my cheek, a distant drip of water, the rattle of a falling stone.

You are a warrior of the hearth of the Bear! I told myself. *Will you shame your teachers?*

I was suddenly convinced that I would gain nothing here but a sore throat and sneezes, but I owed it to those who loved me to carry through. I felt my way forward to the wall of the cavern, and began to lay out my furs.

Eyes strained in vain to find meaning in the blackness that surrounded me. I shut them, but in another instant they flicked open, frantically seeking light. I remembered Crow's tale of the Maiden who guarded the well, and began to realize why the blindfish had given up their eyes.

I could not close my ears, and the small noises I heard somehow only made more apparent the lack of any sound with meaning. How had the Maiden endured with only her own thoughts for company? I wanted to scream, but I feared what any noise might evoke from the darkness. I huddled into my furs, shuddering.

After an endless time I realized that nothing had happened . . . nothing was going to happen . . . there was nothing and no one here but me.

There was no way to tell time here. I was hungry already, so the state of my stomach was no clue. I cycled through awareness of each fear and discomfort several times before it came to me that I might as well try to do the work that I had come for. Certainly there was nothing else to do here.

"Goddess," I whispered into the darkness, "whether you are called Ava or Dana or Sugë, Jan-et or Verbeia or Tamar, I hail you as the High One, the Briga from whom we name this land. . . ." I paused, wondering what I should ask Her, and remembered the ghosts who had gathered so hungrily in my father's hall.

"If you care for us at all, then hear me. Your children are killing each other. The fields are fertilized with the life-blood of men."

I sat back, a little surprised at what I had decided to say. Whether or not the slaughter mattered to the Goddess, for all my warrior training, it mattered to me. I had sought honor when I raced across the Island, but that was before I had seen the blood of my friends running down to mingle with the waters of the sea. Men might fight for gain or glory, but everyone knew that the most dangerous beasts were females protecting their young.

More time had passed by the time I had finished exploring the implications of that for myself as a warrior. What else should I ask?

"Mother of Everything, I never knew the mother who bore me," a new prayer rose within. "Was it my fault she died? My sisters desire me to take her place; sometimes I feel that my father is wanting me to fill her place too. I want him to love me—" Suddenly I remembered the strong warmth of Leir's hand on my shoulder and my eyes filled with tears. "But I am not my mother! I cannot be what they want me to be!"

A female animal will die to save her children. I thought then, *but why did my mother die? What compelled her to risk her life giving birth to me?*

"Lady of Briga, are You concerned with this land only, or with all? What does my father want with all his warring? Is there no way to Your bed but blood? My sisters say that Leir rules the regions of this island only because he married their queens. But he sowed death in their fields ere ever he sowed life in their wombs. How can he belong to this land?"

I drew breath, and realized that I was shaking. Was I concerned for my father, or for myself?

Lady, I said silently, *help me! The blood of my father and my mother are at war.* . . . I understood now what Gunarduilla had once told me of her own struggles. If at that moment I had held a weapon, I might have let my blood flow into the earth around me to end that conflict.

But I had no means of harming myself, and after a time my pulsebeat slowed, and I calmed.

Perhaps there was some point to this vigil after all. For the first time in my life, I had been given the opportunity to think things through. Strange sparkles danced before my eyes, disappearing when I tried to look at them. But now I was not afraid to close my eyelids. I tucked the furs back around me and settled down in a hollow between two stones.

Images presented themselves to my mind and faded before I could claim them as I sank deeper into the friendly dark. I found myself sitting in my father's feasting hall at Ligrodunon. Crow was tumbling to amuse the warriors. They were laughing, but his eyes were sad. I called out to him, but he did not seem to hear.

My spirit fled to the north, and found Horse carving bone into a knife handle, working it in smooth curves like the limbs of a slender girl. But again and again as he labored the knife would halt, and he would sit, staring. A woman in a cloak of bear fur came into the hut behind him. Then she put her arm around him, and I saw no more.

Wider and wider spread my vision. I saw farmers sorting through their seed-corn, and warriors honing the long iron blades of their spears. I watched as a girl strained on the birthing chair and the women around her chanted spells, while the head of a newly slain warrior still dripped red from a post outside the door. I saw deer pawing snow away from feed in the northern mountains, and wolves loping patiently on their trail.

And then, at the same time, it seemed that I was back in the feasting hall. But now the torches had burnt out, and the warriors snored on their benches against the wall. Only at the end of the fire trench did a flicker of flame leap now and then from the coals, highlighting the bold planes of my father's face, kindling a spark in his open eyes.

"Is she well, think you?" he whispered. "Tell me—will she be the same when she comes back to me?"

Something stirred beside him, and Crow sat up, thrusting aside the dogs.

"Lord," he began, "how can this one know?" The king's hand closed suddenly in the fur of his cape. Sky-blue eyes stared into earth-brown.

"You know . . ." growled Leir. "You do not fool me with your games! You know everything. . . ." Crow whimpered and the dogs stirred uneasily. Abruptly, the king let his captive go.

"But I am here," I called to them, *"cannot you see?"*

Neither man turned. Crow sat back, rubbing his neck, then laughed. "The cygnet flies in ancient skies, but where she goes the serpent knows. . . . Wouldst hear a story, lord?" Leir nodded and took a long swallow from his horn.

"This is the story of Maiden-Guarding-Well," said Crow. But this time he told it differently. Now it was the Star that shone down through the opening to search out the Maiden, and she fled from him, but everywhere her waters were forced upward in springs and fountains, and everywhere that she burst into the open, he was there.

"That is not the right ending!" I cried. *"That is not the way the story is supposed to go—"* But they could not hear me. They would not hear me—

The hall disintegrated around me, and with a snap that jolted my bones I was awake, sitting bolt upright and staring into the dark.

It was *cold*. There must have been a change in the weather, for the air around me was like ice. Shivering, I gathered up my fur robes, but they were icy where they had fallen away from my body. I breathed deeply, trying to make the blood sing in my veins as it had when I emerged from the sweathouse. But the chill seemed to grow deeper. The cold coiled around me, and my extremities began to grow numb.

This is the death I sensed waiting for me . . . I thought then, but my mind was growing numb too, and it was hard to care. I felt my body slump as sensation left me . . . no, I was sinking, being swallowed by an ice serpent that sucked me into oblivion.

These were the icy waters whose embrace I had feared when I crossed the sea. But now they had engulfed me, and there was no way to go but down. . . .

Oddly, the deeper I went, the more I could move. I had no body, but some essence remained that followed the current toward an unimaginable goal. Gradually I became aware that the resistance that channeled it was stone. The rock was porous, and water permeated it everywhere.

I felt the weight of water around me, forced up through smooth passages by pressure from below. I gave myself to that movement with a growing excitement, and a voice that was and was not my own cried, *"Water is the Life of the Land!"*

I was a serpent made of water, twisting and turning, an upwelling energy that could not be denied. And then I burst suddenly into freedom and felt myself expanding, scales becoming feathers, feathers extending into wings. But still my sinuous neck was that of the serpent, and my sharp bill bit the sky.

Below me, the land lay still in the grip of winter. But I could sense the moving water everywhere, swirling sluggishly beneath a shell of white in lake or forest pool, flowing strongly beneath the ice in river and spring and stream.

Light blazed suddenly. Harsh voices were calling a name I once had known. Dim figures hastened toward me.

"Blessed Briga, she's frozen! Look, there are crystals of ice in this fur! Rigana, throw down the blanket—"

I beat frantic wings against the hands that strove to bind me to flesh once more, but they were too strong.

"Cridilla, can you hear me? Oh, I told them how it would be! If she dies, the king will kill us all! Cridilla—"

I blinked. It was Gunarduilla who was carrying me, Gunarduilla who was calling my name. The light grew stronger. Now others were helping her. Women stripped off fur gloves and boots warm from their own bodies and slipped them on my limbs. A babble of words assaulted my ringing ears.

"The vision—" Rigana's face appeared before me. "Cridilla, what did you see?"

I stared at her, wincing as my hands and feet began to throb with pain. "The serpent . . ." I croaked, and suddenly they were silent, listening. "The serpent and the swan are one. . . ."

Rigana looked at me uncomprehending. "She is delirious—" said someone. "Do not be expecting sense from her now."

I let my head fall back against Gunarduilla's shoulder. As I gazed at the blank sky I felt a cool kiss against my burning skin. From the sky came falling the cold white feathers of the swan.

SECOND SPIRAL: THE FLIGHT OF THE SWAN

Thirty-sixth Year of Leir's Rule

Chapter

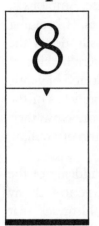

8

*"Thy reign will be subject to a restriction,
but the bird-reign will be noble,
and these shall be thy taboos . . ."*

—*The Destruction of Da Derga's Hostel*

I n winter, the cold locks up the life-giving waters and
numbs the land, as if nothing will ever move again. Looking back, it seems to me that the four years that followed
my initiation were all one wintertide. Whatever changes
had been wrought by my vigil remained as invisible as seeds awaiting
the long-delayed kiss of the sun. The priestesses returned me to my
father's house to be nursed back to health. Rigana went south to
her lovers and Gunarduilla returned to her northern wars. But I
remained with the king in Briga until my nineteenth year, the companion of his journeys and the confidante of his strategies, and
thought myself content.

It was just before the Feast of the Maiden, when water dripped
steady as a drumbeat from the thatch of the great house that my
father had built near the river Soretia, that things began to change.

That day it seemed to me that things long frozen had been set
moving everywhere, and in myself not least of all. For so long my
path had been as set as the white crusts that night still left in yard
and field. But now each morning turned them into pools that were
churned to mud by the feet of messengers. The air itself was clam-

orous with the disputation of warriors and the roar of running water and the cries of returning birds.

A dozen of us had ridden out from the king's house, Ambiolissa, early that morning, packing bows and nets in hopes of bringing down some waterfowl. Our horses splashed clumsily down the muddy path, but in the meadows the new lambs were frisking as if they had wings. The watershed of the Soretia was a land of gentle undulations. Since yesterday, it seemed, the outer branches of the trees that clustered in its hollows had changed color. Now their tips were swelling with new green. I felt my own throat swelling with a shout, or perhaps it was a scream.

Was it the scent of the air that reminded me suddenly of the Misty Isle? My legs trembled as I suppressed the urge to kick my mare into a headlong gallop across the fields. I told myself that it was only reaction to having been too long inside. Even my father must have been chafing from inaction, or why were we plodding through the mud today? Our stocks of food were not really that low.

We were not the only ones to be taking advantage of the sunshine. On the higher, better-drained ground, the folk of the nearby village were readying their fields for the plough. From the slope above came a pure piping, and as we drew closer, the words of the song.

> *"Frost flowers melting, buds on the bough,*
> *Grows the earth greener, wanting the plough;*
> *Hearken and waken,*
> *Heavenly Maiden—lend life to the land!"*

As we neared, one of the farmers stepped out into the road.
"Ho, father of warriors—a boon!"

Leir pulled up, expecting the usual appeal for charity or justice, and the rest of us reined in behind him. The king's cloak of chequered green and grey and white was thrown back over his shoulders. In the past few years his hair and beard had imperceptibly turned from gold to silver. In that clear morning air, he looked as if the light were shining through flesh and bone. In the distance I could still hear the song.

> "Lambs in the meadow, swans on the nest,
> Sows to be breeding, mares still at rest,
> Harken and waken,
> Heavenly Maiden—lend life to the land!"

My mare sidled fretfully, sensing my mood, and I reined her down. Artocoxos was, as always, a half length behind his lord. I rode on my father's left side, with the others strung out behind us. The high king's customary winter retinue had grown a bit during the season just past. In addition to the Companions, two of the chieftains, Loutrinos son of Caranti and Nextonos of the High Fort, seemed to be spending most of their time in our hall. I tried not to notice how often their glances rested on me.

Leir had been benefiting from men's ambitions to become his son-in-law ever since my first moon blood came. I did not mind that, so long as it never came to anything, and often it seemed to me that my father had no more wish to see me wed than I. But Loutrinos and Nextonos had been more persistent than most of my potential suitors. I had dressed today in my oldest brown tunic with a laced doeskin vest and a frayed cloak striped in brown and grey, but I could feel them watching me as we waited for the king.

> "Day out of darkness, sun out of cloud,
> soil through the snowdrift, life from the shroud;
> Hearken and waken,
> Heavenly Maiden—lend life to the land!"

"What does the ploughman ask?" Loutrinos was a big, powerful man who had been only a few years in the Island, and his command of the old speech was not good.

"He asks the king to cut the first furrow—" I said in a low voice. "It is the custom here, for the lord's power to bless the land."

"In my land also." Loutrinos edged his mount closer to mine and Nextonos began to scowl.

The king was shaking his head impatiently. The ploughman saw me watching, and bowed deeply, but in his eyes I saw appeal.

"I believe that they want me as well," I said swiftly, and was urging my horse to the king's side before either man could respond.

"We have not the time to go poking at every field 'twixt here and the river!" muttered Leir. "What did the man do last spring when I was in Belerion? Can these folk not even furrow their wives without my being by?"

"Now then, Da—you know well that he would do the thing himself in your name, were you not here. And this one act will serve for them all. . . ." I laid my hand on his sleeve and smiled.

"Is the ard prepared?" I asked, still holding on to my father's arm.

"It is, lady, with fennel and salt, with soap and manseed," the ploughman answered, "and the offerings to the Mother have been made."

I turned to my father. "It will take only a moment, do you see? And then we'll be off to the riverside!"

"Will we?" asked Leir. "This morning Talorgenos heard a raven croak from the top of an oak tree, and I have had strange dreams. But I suppose nothing's served by arguing here." With a sigh he swung down from his stallion, and I followed him.

The ploughman led us to the end of a long rectangle of stubble covered with a scattering of drying dung. The ground was springy beneath my feet. Closer to the earth, I could smell the heady scents of moist earth and new green. The first spring herbs were already poking through the cold soil, and the starry yellow flowers of colts-foot, good for colds and coughs, glowed at the edge of the field. My father was still frowning. Couldn't he feel the life in the land? I grinned with delight, and Leir smiled indulgently.

Taking his hunting spear, he strode to the corner of the field. Light blazed from the bright blade.

"Thus do I serve thee, Lady—" cried the king. "Open thy womb! Bring forth abundantly for the good of men!" In a single clean motion the spear flashed down and scored a moist gash in the soil.

"My thanks to thee, lord. Now will she be fruitful indeed—"

said the farmer with satisfaction. Folk had materialized all around us. A boy switched at the flanks of the shaggy black oxen to drive them into position, and another man brought up the ard. None of them were watching us now.

Leir shook his head ruefully, as if he too understood that he had been as much a tool in this as the oxen or the plough, and started back toward the horses. It was then that I realized that the throbbing in the earth was the vibration of hoofbeats, approaching at great speed.

The king straightened, and the authority that had seemed to depart from him after the furrowing rite stiffened him once more as three men on shaggy ponies so splattered with mud that one could not tell their color came into view.

"Zayyar—" they cried, and the hands of the warriors went to their swords. "Zayyar-a-Khattar, the great bull of the Ai-Zir, is dead!"

The faces of the warriors slackened with disbelief or incomprehension, but in my father's eyes I thought I saw loss. Then he began issuing orders, and in moments messengers were riding off in all directions. This news changed everything. For nigh on ten seasons, the war-host had marched south each year as soon as the cattle had been driven to their summer pastures. What would they do now without an enemy?

By the time he had finished, only a few of us remained.

"Will you be returning to the hall, lord?" asked Artocoxos.

Leir shrugged wearily. "What for? Zayyar will not come down upon us with his war-band now, and it will be the Spring Turning before the chieftains arrive for the Council. Let us go on with our hunting."

I watched him curiously as we moved out again. I had thought he would be overjoyed at the death of his old enemy, but his gaze had gone inward. As we drew closer to the river the air grew clamorous with the spring hosting of the waterfowl, but he did not seem to hear.

The others were not so abstracted.

"They'll be for making peace," exclaimed Artocoxos, "before the grass sprouts on the old man's mound."

"You sound disappointed," I said curiously.

"Ah, 'tis like that first great fight of mine with the bear who clawed my leg," he said, sighing. "It was a hard battle, but I missed the beast when 'twas over. I knew I was alive, fighting him. He was a worthy foe!"

"What about the old bull's nephews? Won't they be squabbling over the high seat?" Nextonos inquired. I wondered if he feared that the fortress the king had set him to building on one of the more prominent hills to the north of the watershed would not be needed after all.

"Well, that's just their difficulty, now," said Artocoxos. "There's three bull calves butting heads on the plain of Ava, and not one of them with half the balls the old man had. By the time they finish fighting each other there will not be enough of a following left to any one of them to defy a foe."

Loutrinos nodded wisely. His lands lay more southerly, and I suppose it was a relief to him to know that the men of the bull would not be driving off his herds this year.

Who, I wondered, were the young men who had been blooded on this long war going to fight now?

Ducks flew up squawking as we neared the banks of the Soretia, and Leir lifted his hand.

"Be still, and let your silence honor the passing of a noble warrior!" The other men wilted beneath his glare. Then his look softened. "In any case, we'll get nothing for supper with such a company. We must divide up into pairs—"

"I will be happy to escort the princess," Nextonos began. The king looked from him to Loutrinos, whose mouth was already opening to make the same offer, and for the first time since the news from the south had come, his lips twisted in a smile.

"Partner yourselves as ye will. The lady Cridilla hunts with me."

One by one, like chieftains speaking in Council, the waterbirds were taking up their conversations again. I had learned to sit still on the Island, and in his chequered cloak my father blended into the faded brown and new green of the reeds. As we settled into our places, the mallards began to move back into the open water once more.

"Just like Loutrinos—" I whispered, pointing at one glossy fellow, just beginning to come into his summer plumage, who was paddling determinedly after a speckled female.

"And Nextonos?" Leir nodded toward another, moving to head the first drake off while the duck swam unconcernedly away. His gaze lifted to mine and I grinned back at him. "Do they trouble you?"

I shrugged. "Only if they trouble *you*. Let them dream about me if it serves your policy, but remember that when I lay ill for so long after my initiation, you swore I should marry no man not of my own choosing!"

Behind us the furry catkins of the the pussy willow were opening, swaying branches shadowing the brown water near the shore and the king's face as he frowned.

"The matter of your marriage will come up again at the Spring Council. The chieftains are determined to see you husbanded. . . ."

I looked at him, lifting one brow in Gunarduilla's fashion, a trick that after long practice I had finally made my own.

"Why? My sisters' marriages have given me no cause to envy them—" I drew breath, wondering how much of the gossip about his older daughters the king had heard.

It was common knowledge that Gunarduilla and Maglaros quarreled constantly when they were not making war, and Rigana's appetite for men was known to everyone in Belerion except Senouindos. But if my father had not learned how his daughters had dealt with the husbands he gave them, it was because he did not wish to know.

And they were my sisters, though we had not seen much of each other in recent years. I had no reason to expose them to my father's wrath.

"Perhaps I am selfish," he said ruefully, "to keep you here with me. But to whom else can I speak so? To my warriors I must always be the chieftain—"

And to your women, the stallion . . . But now that I thought about it, these days the women who shared his bed were mostly there to keep it warm.

"I am the drifting cloud," I said aloud. "I am the moving stream. So long as I am free your words are safe with me. . . ."

The duck that looked like Loutrinos paddled off, and now the rotund little grebes came bobbing after, the pale fluff of their cropped rear ends flowering momentarily as they dove. Teal moved busily among them, adding their own colors to the gathering. I had glimpsed the white curve of a swan's back a little upstream as we moved into position and knew that his mate must be nearby, thatching their nest among the reeds.

There was a shout and a splash downstream, as if someone had missed a cast and fallen in.

"No harm done," I whispered as the birds began to settle again. "Some mistakes carry their own punishment."

"Some victories do the same," said Leir suddenly. "It is not the young men only who will wonder what their skills are good for now that the Great Bull is no more."

I thought of the tattoos upon my back and belly that no one ever saw. I still worked out with the warriors, but my sword had stayed in its sheath since I returned to my father's hall. I flexed the long muscles of my calves carefully, so as not to disturb the birds. Had it been I who had raced the wind across the Misty Isle?

"Is that a greylag?" I asked quickly as something moved among the reeds.

"Too early," my father replied. "But with the sunset, they will be dropping down to rest. 'Tis only a heron, do you see?"

I glimpsed the bird's grey back and then the graceful pale neck recurving as the head lifted, a fingerling trout clamped in its beak. *Sister, good hunting!* I thought then. For the first time in many months I was wondering whether this was all that life was going to hold for me. In that, my father and I were alike, though I did not tell him so.

"The land still needs a king . . ." I said aloud.

"Shall I beat my spear point into a shoe for an ard? I dreamed last night," he said softly, "and wondered if the omen was meant for me. . . ."

"What did Talorgenos say?"

Leir grimaced. "With all his mouthing about ravens and omens he had no time to listen to me! If he wants to know what the king is dreaming, let him ask the birds!"

"But the birds do not speak to me, father," I said gently. "What was the dream?"

"I stood by a lake and saw a flock of white swans going up two by two, and each pair of them was linked by a golden chain. The only sound was the humming of their beating wings. I had never seen anything so fair as those white shapes rising. I wanted to go with them, but I was earthbound. But when the last of them circled the hall, I saw that his chain was broken. I cried out to him to take me, for I was a son of the swan. . . ."

"And then?" I prodded as he fell silent.

"Then came thunder, and a voice crying, *The chain is broken, the oak is riven; victory goes where the curse shall fall!* And the swan circled thrice about my hall, and then he too was gone. I woke weeping, and now I understand, for who is left to challenge me? Perhaps Zayyar was the lucky one; he died fighting, even if it was only a boar."

I stared at him. "Surely there is more to kingship than winning battles?"

Leir shrugged. "Since I came into this land I have never had the chance to learn. . . ."

He could say such things to me, I thought then, as he could say such things to the birds and the reeds. The king's fingers, that were so certain on the haft of a spear or the hilt of a sword, now picked restlessly at the grey wool that covered his knees. His knuckles seemed swollen, the veins a blue embroidery beneath the weathered skin. How long had they been this way?

Why are you surprised? came a voice from deep within. I shook my head as if a gnat were buzzing in my ear, for it was not possible that my father should grow old.

"Now you can be finishing your road," I said a little desperately.

"Indeed, so I can." His mood seemed to lighten. "And look, there are the greylags coming in!"

I looked up to see the flying geese stitching a precise chevron across the sky. Leir was rising, avoiding any sudden movement that would give warning, his bow ready in his hands. I was still reaching for my own weapons when he loosed his first arrow; I saw the slim shaft pass beneath a gander's lifting wing. He turned in place as the geese planed down toward the river, coming in toward us and upstream. A second arrow sped; I could not see where it fell; and then the third as they reached the water, and we heard a frantic commotion of wings in the reeds.

Now the rest of them were up again, calling frantically, and the ducks were adding their own hysteria to the din. I loosed a few arrows into the fluttering mass, and then the flock was off again to some less treacherous resting place.

"You got one bird, at least—" I said when the clamor had subsided. "Let us go see!"

Stiff from long sitting, we picked our way upstream through the reeds. Presently we heard something struggling in the water and then the air hummed as one of the nesting swans burst toward the sky. Leir parted the reeds. When he did not move, I waded in beside him, peering around his shoulder.

The bird whose blood was laying a spreading stain across the water was the other swan.

"It was my arrow—" I said into the silence. "I take the guilt upon me. Let it lie where it fell. . . ." I was suddenly hot and then icy cold again.

I plucked at his sleeve, trying to draw him away, but Leir shrugged me off and stepped down into the reedbed, reaching for the fallen bird.

"My arrow." He held up the hunting barb he had plucked from the swan's white breast, and I saw the distinctive black and grey fletching. "And my fate . . ."

The swan's great wings trailed like the folds of a white cloak as he lifted it and clambered back onto the bank. The wound was a crimson flower in snow.

"Da, the men must not see this. You will not be bringing that bird back to the hall!"

"Shall I become a skulker in shadows? A doer of deeds that the daylight must not see?" His voice gained in power. "Never have I disclaimed any act of mine since first I took up arms!"

"But this one was none of your willing!" I flared back at him.

"Do you think that matters now?" Beneath the anger, I thought I saw the same sorrow I had glimpsed when Leir heard that the prince of the Ai-Zir had died. "I will never deny what I have done!"

His face was darkened by a shadow as the swan's mate soared above us. Once, twice, a third time it circled widdershins, then it stretched out its long neck and winged toward the setting sun. The king laid the dead bird upon the earth, fumbled for his hunting horn, and blew a long, clear call.

There was a babble of astonishment when the warriors saw what game we had gotten, but a glare from Leir silenced them. We mounted in uneasy silence, the pack horse dancing nervously as the net bag that held the mallard and teal the other men had shot was balanced by the dead weight of the swan.

As we moved through the tangle of alder and willow between the river and the fields, Artocoxos came riding up. I saw him whiten as he glimpsed the swan.

"I suppose it was one of the warriors who killed it—" he began, and I smiled sourly, wondering if Leir would listen to his old friend where he had not heeded me.

The king turned on him. "The arrow was mine. The shot was mine. And it is I that will eat this bird!"

"My lord, listen—" Artocoxos kneed his mount closer, his voice a deep rumble that was meant to be a whisper. "All here know of your *geasa*! If you bring that thing home, the whole countryside will be talking of it in a day. They will say it is an evil omen, that Zayyar's ghost has cursed you, or worse things—" He was babbling. His eyes showed that he knew it, and when Leir held up his hand the old warrior's voice failed.

"This is no man's work but my own—" the king said loudly, and I saw finally that it was just because he *did* believe us that there would be no retreating now. "Earth and sea and heaven rise up and cover me if I deny what I have spoken, for I will not go back from my word!"

I jerked back on my reins, and realized only then that it was the force of Leir's anger that had driven all of us back from him. In his face the battle-mask was showing, his eyes protruding, veins throbbing visibly beneath flushed skin. No one dared to stop him as he lashed his horse down the path.

Through the silence came the trickle of running water across a stony ford where a rain-swollen rivulet snaked down to join the Soretia. There was a flurry of white among the shallows as the king's horse splashed into the water, and a great white swan shape beat heavily into the sky. Water sprayed in a crimson fan against the sunset sky as the horse reared. Then the reins whipped free as Leir fell backward in a curious boneless slide and the horse went down.

I was flinging myself off my mare even as I lashed her forward. I dodged among the flailing hooves to get to the king. My father lay still with his legs splayed up the stream bank and his head in the water. More water sprayed over us as the king's stallion heaved itself upright again, but by then I had Leir's head in my lap and was trying to use the warrior's heal-craft I had learned on the Island to probe for broken bones.

"Not dead?" There was anguish in Artocoxos's whisper as he threw the stallion's rein to another man and slid back down the bank to kneel beside me.

"He lives—" I settled Leir's head more securely against my knees. The king's mouth sagged open, his face was still flushed, his breathing stertorous and slow. More carefully now, my fingers probed the contours of his skull. "But he may have hit his head, falling."

"Lady," the warrior inclined his head to me. "Shall I set the men to cutting poles for a horse litter?"

"Do it"—my lips twisted—"and hope Leir wakes before we get him into it, and curses us out for fussing so!"

Artocoxos got to his feet, roaring orders at the men who hung back in a silent half circle on the bank above us. They moved off more quickly when the old warrior began to use the flat of his sword. Nextonos and Loutrinos started toward me, apparently under the impression that the orders did not apply to them, and found themselves braiding ropes into a harness for their own mounts to carry the litter when it was done.

Had the sun gone down already? The sky was still that pale clear color of flame, but there was no warmth in it. It must be the icy water in which I was sitting that made me so cold. In the distance birds called plaintively, winging their way toward home.

"Da—can you hear me?"

There did not seem to be any indentation in Leir's skull. I fingered the knobbed column of the spine, but if there was a break there, it was small. I looked into his face once more. His breathing seemed a little easier, but his features were slack and still. I laid my hands against the two sides of his head, wishing I had learned more of Lady Asaret's magic.

"Leir Blatoniknos, listen to me!" My voice cracked and I realized that I was not as calm as I had believed. "Wherever your bruised spirit is wandering, come back to your body now! If there is great damage I must know where it is before we can get you out of this stream!"

He took one long breath and then another, and his eyelids fluttered, but it was only the left one that opened. I shivered as it stared through me into the sky. From behind me came the hollow thunk of swordblades biting into the saplings along the stream. *Hurry!* I thought. *I am afraid!*

"Da, where are you hurt? Will you not look at me?"

He grimaced, and gradually the vague gaze narrowed until it was focused on me.

"Fier. . . ? Fi . . ."

I bent closer. "What is it, father? I cannot understand—"

He drew a rasping breath and tried again. "Fiereh—?"

Slowly I realized that he was trying to say my mother's name.

"I am Cridilla, father—now tell me what is wrong!"

The grey eye continued to consider me suspiciously, and then, still mostly with the left side, he frowned. I felt the water's chill rising through my limbs.

"Who . . . hi' me?" he asked.

"No one, father," I answered him. "Your horse slipped, and you fell."

"Can' move . . . arm. . . ."

Swiftly I began to probe the area around the right shoulder blade and down the long bones of the arm. He did not wince—indeed, he did not seem to be feeling what I was doing at all.

"Lady," came a call from above, "we've laid cloaks across the horse litter. Can we be moving him now?"

"*Hit* me . . ." Leir repeated, and when he looked at me, there was suspicion in his eye. "Wan' Fiereh!"

I waved them forward. There was nothing out of place that I could see, and Leir's skin was beginning to grow cold as my own.

"Why in water?" he said a little more clearly. "Drowned. . . ."

"Father, we're going to lift you," I said carefully. "You've had an accident, and we are taking you back to the hall. . . ."

"*Not* hur'! Rest . . . no message—" He forced breath into his lungs. "Don' tell men!" His eyes closed once more.

"He must have hit his head," I told Artocoxos as the men levered Leir into the horse litter they had made. "He's still dazed. . . ."

"I've known it to happen, after a head blow, or a fall," the old warrior answered carefully. "You there—move slowly now! D'ye think you're carrying a sack of grain?" He darted forward, steadying the litter as they hoisted it up between the horses.

I stood where he had left me, half soaked and shivering. *It is only the cold . . .* I told myself, *only the cold that is tying this hard knot in my belly and making my heart pound like a drunkard's drum.*

"My lady—" Loutrinos was leading my mare and smiling. My fist clenched as reactions I thought I had forgotten urged me to strike him down. "They're ready to move out now. We must hurry to reach the hall before the sun goes down!"

Dusk was weighting the world with shadow as we came in. Men came out to the gates with torches, voices growing shrill as they saw the litter and curiosity chilled into a fear that was more explicit, if not so deep, as my own.

"Why are you all flopping about like so many netted cod? Of course the king is alive. He has only had a fall—" Artocoxos's rumbling voice sounded almost amused. Was it only I who perceived the edge of strain? "Come now, lads, and let us bear him in by the fire."

"What is it?" Talorgenos was suddenly at my knee. "What has happened?" I glimpsed Crow emerging behind him in a tumult of dogs.

"Not a word about your omens, priest!" I hissed as I slid off my mare. "It is a healer we are needing now, and if you doomsay I will stake you to the doorpost with your own staff!"

His gaze moved past me to the packhorse where they were unloading the ducks that the other men had brought down, and I realized that I had forgotten to get rid of the swan. His eyes widened. I saw him shiver then, and knew what icy finger had touched his spine.

Crow stood still behind him and his lips moved. I took a swift step to his side, but before I could clap my hand across his mouth he howled. I felt sound strain his breast as I held him.

"You too will be silent, amantanos—" I felt him stiffen as I used the Quiritani word for a witless one. This was no time for him to come out with one of his cryptic prophecies. "Get the dogs out from underfoot here and hold them. We will care for the king." My grip on his arm must have been painful, but he made no sound as I released him. As he darted off I heard him whimper, and the dogs, tails tucked and ears flattening, pattered after him.

"Artocoxos—" I cried, and the old warrior turned toward me. "Get that evil thing out of here before any more of them see!" He looked at the bird and nodded, his face twisting with an emotion that he could not hide.

"I will tell you everything—" I turned to Talorgenos again. "But now, in the name of the Mother, let us get the king inside!"

Chapter

9

*A modest woman is a dragon, which none comes
near.*
*The daughter of a king is a flame of hospitality,
a road that cannot be entered.*
*I have companions that follow me to guard me
from whoever would carry me off against their
will . . .*

—*The Wooing of Emer*

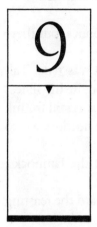"*E ya, ai, eya ai . . . eya . . . ai!*"
The children's skipping song grew clearer as I
came through the gate of Ligrodunon, swerving to
avoid a serving girl with a basket of hot bannocks
wrapped in a linen cloth. It was hard to believe that near two moons
had swelled and faded since my father's accident, but the meadow
outside the dun was filling with warriors and servants as the chieftains came in for the Council, and there was hardly room inside for
the ones who must be lodged within the walls.

"Who are these for?" I pointed at the basket.

"Take one now, mistress, while they be warm." She smiled shyly.
"These are Zaueret's baking, and be sure those greedy sows in the
Women's House will leave thee none."

I lifted a corner of the cloth, breathing in appreciatively. The
heat from the bannocks was welcome, for though the spring sowing
had begun, there was still a bite to the morning air. It had been
raining, but now a light wind was shepherding the clouds away.
Pale sunlight glittered on puddles and sent moisture steaming from
the thatch of the feasting hall.

"Lady, how does the king today?"

I kept smiling. I should have expected the question—it was only what every other living soul in the dun was wondering, and most of them less polite about asking.

"Well enough. The wetting did no good to old bones, but there is naught to keep my lord from the Council!"

I smiled, hoping devoutly that what I had said was true. Talorgenos said that the king had been elfshot. I thought his illness had been no more than a chill. But though the king was still fretful, he was getting his strength again. Sovereignty was not lost for so slight a cause as tumbling into a stream.

"May the Mother bless him!" The girl covered the bannocks, and went on toward the House of Women.

May She bless us all! I thought as I continued toward the feasting hall.

> *"Wildman dance, wildman play,*
> *Wildman jump, wildman pray!*
> *Eya, ai, eya ai . . . eya . . . eya . . . ai!*
> *Eya, ai, eya ai . . . eya . . . eya . . . ai!"*

I stopped short as I saw who was leaping through the rope's spinning coils. A children's game it might be, but they had gotten Crow to play. Flapping his arms, he jumped from one foot to the other as the rope swung round.

"Higher, higher!" cried a boy's treble. "Go fast now!"

The two little girls twirling the rope pumped furiously, their faces red with effort. They seemed to be working as hard as the man who jumped and jingled between them.

"Eater of carrion! Amantanos! Jump, Basajaun!" another boy cried, and something sped by Crow's head and spattered against the wall.

> *"Wildman spin, Wildman leap,*
> *Wildman laugh, Wildman weep!*
> *Eya, ai, eya ai . . . eya . . . eya . . . ai!*
> *Eya, ai, eya ai . . . eya . . . eya . . . ai!"*

My own laughter faded. Why did he stay to be tormented? Then I saw the elaborate clothes the children were wearing, and frowned. The older boy's hair was dark, and there was something to the tilt of his head . . . he turned and I recognized Cunodagos, Rigana's son. The girls must be her twin daughters, then. They resembled her more than they did their father—who might have been almost anybody except Senouindos, if gossip were a guide. The younger boy was dressed as richly, his hair a foxy brown. *Morigenos,* I thought, my sister Gunarduilla's only child.

I started toward them, and Crow did a desperate handspring out of the ropes and fetched up at my feet, breathing hard.

Cunodagos turned, his face reddening with wrath.

"Good day, nephew—" I said through a set smile. "I am sorry to take your playfellow, but the king has need of him."

His face changed as if he had put on a mask. It had taken him a moment to realize who this woman in the worn brown cloak must be. Morigenos, less experienced, looked guilty. There were smears of mud on the far wall too, and I guessed that the clod I saw had not been the first one thrown. The two girls had dropped the rope and stood panting, seeming almost as glad of the rescue as Crow had been.

"The king cannot bear to be without him for long," I went on. "I doubt that he will have much time to play with you."

"It is the high king's dog," said Cunodagos. "I had heard. . . ."

I rubbed my palm against the rough weave of my tunic, stifling the urge to apply the flat of it to the rosy cheek of the boy who was smiling blandly back at me. Only the knowledge that I had no time to embroil myself with children kept me still. Instead, I smiled sweetly, leaving Cunodagos to wonder how much I had seen.

"Get up—" I said to Crow in a low voice, and then, when we had left them already beginning to quarrel among themselves, "Why did you not call for help, you silly man?"

"Though seed of Leir on rocky ground doth fall, 'tis better still than none at all. . . ." The sooty lashes hid his eyes.

"What about the king—what about me?" Long practice led me through the tangled meanings. "He is well!" I said angrily. "And neither he nor I will ever cast you out!"

Crow shrugged and picked dried mud out of his hair. "When king goes from's wits, hath no need for amantanos, and you marry soon. . . ."

"Is that all that worries you?" I laughed. "I have my father's promise that he will not force my choice, and what man, think you, would care to wed such an adder as reputation makes me? You saw how that child looked at me just now!"

"This one has eyes. . . ." He shook himself like a dog, and the sour mood fell away. "But Serpent is not doomed to live unloved —dost know the tale of the Varncliff Worm?"

"I do not, but come back to the king's house with me and I will hear!" I said, relenting. Perhaps, I thought, the story would amuse Leir.

Crow began as we were walking. It was a tale about a king's daughter who was enchanted by a wisewoman of the old race whom the king had mistreated, and transformed by her into a great serpent who lived in the cliffs of Varn. The serpent was always hungry, but the more she ate, the greater she grew, and the bigger she got, the greater her hunger.

By the time Crow got to the part where the serpent had consumed all the sheep and the cattle, and all the stores of grain and even the men they offered her as husbands, we were pushing through the hide curtain that partitioned the king's bedplace from the rest of the hall.

"Where . . . have y' been?"

He was awake, then, and coherent. I turned, willing myself to forget other mornings when he had hardly been able to talk at all, and held out my basket.

"Getting you more herbs for tea, father. The coltsfoot did your cough so much good before—"

Leir grimaced, but he seemed to be in a good humor. I noted with satisfaction that both sides of his face were twisting. He *was* better, then. I had been a fool to be afraid.

"And Crow is telling me one of his tales—"

"Speak then, lad," said the king to Crow, who stood fidgeting in the doorway.

"Listen then—" he said, turning a quick cartwheel. "And maybe old ears hear what young ones do not understand!"

Leir patted the foot of his bed, and Crow perched himself cross-legged upon the furs.

"There was a young warrior—long ago he loved the maiden. He hear of the trouble and brought gifts to the wisewoman, asked her how to get the girl free from the spell. . . ."

I added another stick to the kindling in the small hearth and turned to glare at him, beginning to see where this would lead.

"And what did . . ." Leir coughed, "the wisewoman say?"

" 'You take seven buckets and fill them with the milk of seven white, red-eared cows,' the woman say. 'And you go to Serpent wearing a war tunic made of seven thicknesses of elkhide. She'll want the milk, but before you give her each bucket, you make her shed a skin.' And the warrior did what she say," Crow went on, "and when the Serpent want to drink the milk, he say, 'Serpent, shed a skin!'" Crow's eyes sparkled with a gentle malice that I knew too well.

"And then?" asked the king.

"I hope she ate him!" I said under my breath, but neither man seemed to hear.

"The Serpent hisses, 'Why should I shed a skin with you all armored? Mortal, take off a tunic!' And he did that, and the Serpent coiled and twisted and slithered out from her topmost skin, and she drink the milk that he offer her. And for the second bucket of milk and the third and all the rest of them until the sixth it was the same. And at last there was the pile of elkhide tunics, and there the pile of cast-off skins."

I spat on one of the stones that were heating in the fire, and when it sizzled, grasped it in the split hazel tongs and dropped it into the cauldron to heat the water. In a few moments the scent of the coltsfoot leaves was diffusing through the room. I looked around for the honey.

"And what of the last skin?" asked the king.

Crow gave his high-pitched laugh. " 'Man, take off thy tunic!' she say, and 'Maiden, shed a skin!' he answer her. And he did, and

[161]

she did, and they stood there, man and maid. Then he poured the last bucket of milk over her, and the enchantment was gone."

"And then . . . he took something else from her, eh?" Leir chuckled and I glared at both of them.

"He was her husband." Crow's gaze was unreadable.

"Do ye think . . . th' lass will marry?" asked the king.

"Crow, you begin to make me sorry I rescued you—" I turned, the ladle in my hand. Then I realized that Leir had stopped laughing.

"She will desert me . . ." my father whispered. "Another man will steal her away. . . ."

"She will pour boiling tea over both your heads if you do not stop this foolishness!" I exclaimed. "Da, I am *here!*" Hot liquid splattered my hands as I set the pot down. "Look at me! Please look at me!" I knelt beside the king's bed and grasped his arms. Slowly, far too slowly, his gaze came back from whatever Otherworld he had been staring into and focused on my face.

"Wilt stay by me?" he asked. "*She* left me alone!" His color had come back, but the flesh seemed somehow to have loosened its hold on his bones. I realized in horror that the brightness in his eyes was tears.

"Da, what other boon have I ever been asking?" I said softly. "By what god shall I swear it? Unless you should curse me from your door yourself I will never go!"

Someone was arguing in the other part of the hall. I glared toward the door hanging, but the voices grew louder.

"Nonsense, I am his daughter! Of course I can go in there. . . ."

I got to my feet. "Gunarduilla is coming, father. She must not see you this way. Let me sponge your face a little—so—and quick, run the comb through your hair."

The king blinked tiredly as I readied him, but by the time my sister reached us his eyes were hard once more, and the only evidence of sickness was the tea I was ladling from the bowl.

"But I am not going to marry anyone!" I paused in midstride and turned to face Rigana. "I already told you so!" Her face had a pale glow in the sunlight that was filtering through the infant leaves of the beechwoods below the dun, and her eyes shone green and luminous like the water in the stream.

"You cannot blame me for asking. It is one of the three great questions of the Council. We sound like oak priests, don't we, dividing everything into threes, but it is true."

"I've already heard the one about our father's health," I said sourly. "What is the third?"

"Oh . . . they want to know if we're going to conquer the Ai-Zir."

I nodded, and we began to walk once more, our footfalls silent on the new grass. The dark young warrior who was escorting us was even quieter than we. He had the grace of a hunting cat and eyes like a good dog. Rigana had called him Ilf, so he must be half-blood. I wondered if he shared Rigana's bed.

"So, I can see why they need to know if father is fit for battle, but why the sudden interest in me?" I said finally.

"Well, whose lands border the country of the bulls? Don't tell me that you haven't thought about it, Cridilla!" Rigana was looking at me as if I were a stupid child. "You could double your territory in one campaign!"

"I am not queen of the Ai-Zir."

"She who was their queen is dead too, last summer." She stopped, smiling, as we reached a clearing where the first of the primroses were opening. "So you see . . ."

I was beginning to. It was not stupidity, but worry over my father, that had kept me from understanding the news that had come to us just before his fall.

"Are you thinking that I will challenge you for it?" I said then. "Briga is big enough for me!"

"But will it be big enough for the man you marry?" she said patiently.

I sighed. We had been over this before. I had been glad to get out of the sickroom and let Gunarduilla sit with our father, but I was beginning to wonder.

"The king has sworn he will not make me marry," I said flatly. "Perhaps I will take a lover when I want to bear a child!"

The warrior behind us hastened forward, then fell back abashed as he realized that Rigana was only laughing.

"Oh, little sister, little sister! Just when I think I understand you, you surprise me! So you will rule as they did in the old days, without making any man king at all! And you are a warrior-woman—yes, I remember those pictures tattooed on your flesh where no man can see—so you will lead your own war-band as well!" Seeing a dry spot near a patch of violets, she spread out her cloak and sat down.

I had assumed that our father would still be the king. I stood awkwardly, looking down at her.

"Sit, child—" Rigana said, smiling. "You tower over me like a young tree!"

Next to her, I felt like one, I thought as I settled myself cross-legged nearby—something thick and knobby, like an oak, while Rigana was a hawthorn, prickles hidden beneath the delicate flowers. Our escort jammed the butt of his spear into the soft ground and leaned back against one of the trees.

"I am not really laughing, sister." She patted my hand. "It is none so bad an idea, if they would allow it, but we cannot yet bring back all the old ways. For now, we have to let the men think they own us. In the darkness, no weapon they forge can defend them against the power between our thighs. But the time is coming when men will remember why they must count descent from their mothers. Then the old clans will have their lands again, and the festivals of the Goddess will be celebrated by the queens."

"Do you think so?" I lifted one eyebrow. "I have seen that son of yours, Rigana. Do you truly believe that he will let his little sister rule?"

"Her children will be his heirs, anyway." Her voice grew sharper. "If you and I and Gunarduilla stand together, we can accomplish it. That is why we must get you mated to a man you can rule. It cannot be fear of lying with a male that makes you resist the idea of marriage so. . . ."

I felt myself coloring. "I wouldn't know. I've never tried."

Rigana laughed again. "You silly child! Have you never gone into the wood with some likely lad to gather greenery for Belos, or lain down in the fields on Midsummer's Eve? Your hair has a gloss like polished wood and your skin takes the glow of the sun. You've filled out well too—" She looked me up and down appraisingly. "You would not lack lovers if you did not cover your attractions with those appalling gowns."

I smoothed the dull wool of my tunic self-consciously. I knew that she was teasing me, but I could not drive the heat from my cheeks and brow.

"Has no one unpinned the brooch at your shoulder to cup your breast and tickle the nipple until it grows hard?" She was leaning toward me, but she had pitched her voice to carry. "And has no man held you so that you can feel his desire, or caressed your inner thighs until his fingers found the melting softness at your core?" She continued, and I realized that the stories I had heard about her experience hardly did her justice. "It is very sweet, Cridilla, to cradle a man between your thighs and to hear him cry out with need. . . ."

There was a stifled sound from the direction of the tree, and suddenly I understood why Rigana was speaking so loudly. If she was not sleeping with the young warrior, she must be trying to seduce him, or perhaps she simply enjoyed making him squirm. I felt an unaccustomed heat in my own flesh, and my breasts were tingling. I shifted position uncomfortably.

"Rigana, at the moment it is no matter whether or not I would enjoy being mounted by a man—"

Her lifting hand interrupted me. "Because our father promised you that you need not marry—I know. Do you think that he is going to live forever? Or have you simply been too close to him to see? Leir is old, Cridilla—*old!* When he dies do you really think that they will let you rule the land alone?"

I realized that I was shaking my head in simple, meaningless negation of her words.

"It was only a fall," I said stupidly. "He is getting his strength again, perhaps not to lead a battle, but others can do that. Who else can make all these chieftains come together like sheep into a fold?"

"You, and I, and Gunarduilla—" She leaned forward, striking

the soft earth with each word. "We could do it. If we stand together, the Goddess will rule once more!"

Had She ever ceased to do so? Surely I had found Her during my vigil in the cave. But slowly I realized that what Rigana wanted was for the Goddess to reign supreme and alone. I could see the three of us with gold torques gleaming from our necks and ravens circling above us, riding at the head of an army like the three-fold Quiritani goddess of war. Leir had feared that a husband would steal me away from him, but my sister's temptation was far more dangerous, if only he had known.

She was still watching me, her eyes bright in a face that passion had made even more pale. She had never seemed so beautiful.

"Rigana, I cannot answer you. Leir still lives, and that is all I understand. But I will not stand in your way if you want the Ai-Zir lands. . . ."

"*Leir lives* . . ." my sister mocked me. "But one day he will fall. I am not tormenting you with these thoughts for my own pleasure! You are my sister, and I care about your happiness. You are not his wife, Cridilla, but you might as well be! You must not waste your life tied to an old man—I know!"

As she drew breath, I remembered Senouindos and shut my mouth again. Even our father had ceased to run after the women in the past few years, and his virility had been remarkable. Rigana had some excuse for her love affairs. But the idea that our situations were at all alike was monstrous.

"You are looking murderous . . ." Rigana sighed. "Do you think me greedy for power? I will not deny that I enjoy making men do my will, sister, but that is not what Gunarduilla and I are striving for. We must restore the old ways before Mother Earth herself rejects us. The climate is worsening. Two years ago the harvest failed. It is a sin against the land to vest sovereignty in a king. Do you wish your people to perish for no fault of their own?"

"You are not making sense, Rigana!" I exclaimed. "Leir has reigned for over thirty years. If the Goddess were displeased, we would all have starved by now!"

"In his time, Leir Blatoniknos did the Lady good service," said Rigana slowly. "But how well can he serve Her now?"

"You will see at the Council!" I said desperately. "Leir is still strong. The king still has his power!"

"Perhaps. But remember what happens when the king stallion loses potency. . . ."

I shook my head, smelling once more the iron tang of the blood of the horse that had been killed to dedicate the dun.

"We are not beasts! It is not the same!"

"We are all Her children, nourished at Her breasts, sprung from Her womb," said Rigana implacably, "and we all owe Her the same debt at the end!"

The king stood in the carven doorway to the feasting hall, talking to Senouindos. He looked tired, but it was not obvious just how much of his weight was supported by his staff, and the slackness on the left side of his face was obscured by his flowing moustache and beard. From the yard, I could watch him without being noticed. Gunarduilla's husband had stopped me as I returned from bearing a message to Artocoxos, and I did not wish to arouse his suspicion by hurrying back to the king's side.

"Do you think we will make war on the Ai-Zir?" I asked loudly.

Most of the forenoon's session of the Council had been devoted to our old enemy. The chieftains were still arguing, while my father's Companions leaned on their spears in deceptive laziness, lest any of the discussions should come to blows. They were good men, from the newest mixed-blood lads, Tomen and Drostagnos and Zanis, to veterans like Vorcuns and Nodontios who had been with Leir for years. For the past four years I had trained and hunted with them as if they were the brothers I had never had.

Maglaros moved closer and smiled, sunlight striking sparks from the auburn in his greying hair.

"Two moons ago there would have been no doubt of the answer. It has always been our lord's intention to bring all the south under his hand. We would be in their laps by now, if it were not for the king's . . . illness."

"A chill—" Use had made the answer habit by now.

"Of course," he agreed blandly. "But it has delayed things. And given people time to talk. . . ."

I shrugged. "Was there ever a time when they did not? If it were not this, it would be something—speculation, perhaps on your campaigns in the north." The punishment Leir had begun after the raid on the Misty Isle had been continued by Maglaros and Gunarduilla, and with no light hand.

"Or wagers on who your husband is going to be—" he said in the same tone. "If there is one. Gunarduilla tells me that you have sworn not to take a man."

At least it was a different question. I looked at him curiously, and refrained from saying that his wedding to my sister had sparked that resolve. He had coarsened during the eight years since he had become Gunarduilla's husband. I would be quicker in a single fight, I thought, measuring him, though he might outlast me on a battlefield.

"Marriage can be . . . limiting, although your sister Rigana does not seem to have found it so," Maglaros said then. "Are you perhaps more like her than you are like Gunarduilla?"

He drew one callused finger down the shining length of my braided hair. Stung by Rigana's criticisms, I had dressed for the occasion in all my amber necklaces over a long gown of saffron worked at hem and sleeves in dull green. I was beginning to be sorry I had made the effort. I shut my lips tightly as he went on.

"You don't need to marry to have a man for your bed, and so long as you have your father you need no protector. But one of these days, Leir will no longer be king." He must have taken my silence for agreement, for he moved closer. "Do you think that you can rule alone, little sister? You will need a man behind you then. But you could manage without a husband if you had a powerful . . . friend."

I was growing a little tired of his pregnant pauses, but I kept my gaze carefully on the ground. He edged closer, and I wondered if he were going to try to kiss me here in front of half the Council of Chieftains.

"Maglaros," I said evenly. "I appreciate your brotherly concern. I am glad to know that there is someone in the Council who has my welfare so strongly in mind."

"Shall we swear alliance, then?"

I allowed myself a glance at the king. "I can decide nothing now, when I am so anxious for my father," I said quickly. "But I will remember your words."

"And think about them . . ."

With a quicker tongue I could have told him exactly what I thought of his proposals, but I had not the skill.

Maglaros grasped my hand, and pressed a wet kiss into the palm. I jerked it back, a warrior's discipline keeping it away from the dagger at my side.

The hollow booming of the council horn stilled all conversations. Talorgenos was summoning the chieftains back inside.

"I must go. My father needs me!" I was dithering like a flustered maiden, but in another moment I would have given myself away. I hurried into the hall, and when I thought he could no longer see, I rubbed my palm furiously against the skirts of my gown.

I stopped to regain my composure behind one of the pillars as the chieftains swirled past.

In the past years, Leir had reigned mostly from Ligrodunon, and foreign craftsmen had found him a good patron. The pillars had been carved and painted with the swooping spirals that were replacing the concentric circles and meanders of the older style. Hangings of brightly woven and embroidered wool helped to insulate the walls.

When my cheeks had cooled, I went down the aisle to the high seat. Leir was already settled, eyes closed as if he were gathering his strength for the afternoon's fray.

"I am here, father—" I touched his knee. Leir opened one eye.

"And none too soon. They are bellowing like penned cows. Artocoxos, it is time to begin."

I grinned up at him, then untied the thongs of his shoes so that I could take his feet into my lap. They were cold.

Artocoxos lifted the speaker's staff.

"We had determined that the time was ripe for an attack on the plain of Ava just after Midsummer, when the cattle are settled in the hill pastures, and the crops are in. Now must we decide what forces are to go, how commanded and supplied."

"Not so quickly—" came a voice from the king's right. Bituitos of Rigodunon was getting to his feet and holding out his hand for the staff. "It seems to me that before we commit our strength in new lands, we should secure our defenses at home. Our lord's older daughters are already wed to strong fighters who can defend their lands, but the youngest has no husband. Surely it is only good sense to ask what will become of Briga if the king should fall?"

Suddenly the hall was buzzing like a hive. I cast an anguished glance up at the king. *Remember your promise, Da—remember what you swore to me!*

"I have no wife, and I am wealthy." Loutrinos unfolded his bulky limbs. "And you all know my reputation in war. I will speak for the maiden if it is acceptable to you all!"

"But he has been only a few years in this country!" Nextonos darted forward. "I know the land and the people, and I am building a strong fortress on my hill. Give the girl to me and I will defend her."

I don't need a defender! I screamed silently, glaring around the hall.

The air became clamorous with debate over the rival claims. It was only when my father's feet twitched that I realized how tightly I was gripping them.

"Wait . . ." he growled in a low voice. "Do not be antagonizing them."

Even through this commotion I could have made myself heard. The She-Bear had trained us to project our voices through the din of a battlefield. I was beginning to understand why Rigana wanted power. They were antagonizing *me.* . . .

"If she takes a man of Briga it will give him too much local power—" said someone.

"What about a prince from the western mountains, or a man of the fens? The lady Cridilla's marriage should bring us an alliance!"

"An entanglement, more likely!" came the answer. "Let us not commit ourselves to defend other people's borders until we have secured our own."

"It would make them too strong!"

The din increased. I could feel the tension in Leir's body, but so long as he held his peace I must hold mine.

"Let her take a husband from over the sea then, who has no ambitions here!" From near the door came a voice that cut through the babble like a sword cleaving straw. "I offer the lady Cridilla a husband from Morilandis in the Great Land."

I jerked, staring, and the shouting died as men jostled and turned. Above the heads of the others, fair and brown or grey, I could see a flame of red hair. Suddenly my mouth was dry. Even when the others drew aside to let the newcomer through I was telling myself it was impossible. Horse had never been so tall.

A pale-haired fellow with the bulk of a harp strapped to his shoulders preceded him and another, who was solid as an oak, marched behind. Two big red-blond warriors walked to the left and the right of him, but one did not notice them as their leader came up the aisle.

Horse used to wear a deerskin kilt and a mantle of moth-eaten fur. This man walked in a tunic of saffron wool with gold wire gleaming from the embroidery at its hem, and a cloak of deep crimson from the Middle Sea that should have, but did not, clash with his hair. A necklace made from the teeth of beasts he had killed was the only jewelry Horse had owned, but this man's neck was weighted by a torque of twisted gold almost as massive as the one my father wore.

And Horse had been angular as a foal, with bones poking through his scarred and freckled skin. This warrior's long bones were sheathed in lean muscle, his face all carved planes beneath skin burnished to a ruddy brown. He came to a halt before the high seat and stood as if all the splendor of my father's hall were only the setting for his honed grace, as the spiraled bronze sheath embraces the gleaming purity of the sword.

But the hair on him was still bright enough to light a fire, and when he turned, I could not deny the smile. Everyone else was a shadow, and he the sun.

"Agantequos son of Vorequos, chief of the Moriritones and King of Morilandis, salutes you, lord, and claims the hospitality of your hall!"

"It would seem that you have it already," growled the king.

"Only with your goodwill. But I have traveled far—"

[171]

"At least you do not come in secret to steal our treasure!"

"It is an honorable offer I am making for her, and I have the wealth to back it, in cattle or in gold."

He still had not looked at me, and suddenly I was grateful, for surely the pounding of my heart must be shaking my amber beads. Then came an appalled suspicion that he had forgotten what I looked like. I straightened, frowning. His glance shifted as if by chance, and I saw in his eyes the same look they had held when he persuaded me to kiss him so long ago.

Until this moment, it had been easy. Until now, my greatest fear had been that the chieftains would force my father's hand. But I had known what it was that *I* wanted. Until now. . . .

"He can claim guest-right, but not the lady," said Maglaros. "You cannot marry her out of the Island, lord."

"Only for part of the time," said Horse. "Her first daughter could inherit Briga, and her first son the lands that belong to me."

Now the fat was well and truly in the fire. It sounded sensible enough, but in one sentence, Horse had managed to affirm both the mother-right the Painted People believed in and the father-right that the Quiritani were attempting to impose, upsetting virtually everyone in the hall.

"Hold!" the king's voice roared suddenly. "You have the right to advise me, and so I have let you brangle. I have heard your arguments, at a length that becomes tedious. But I am the maiden's father, and I am the king. It is for me to decide . . . and by the word that I have given, it is for Cridilla to choose!"

My father knew that I did not want to marry. He knew that there was not a man of this land who had ever stirred my pulse. But he did not know what had passed between me and Horse when he lay wounded on the Misty Isle. By the oath that my father had sworn to me, I could choose to go, yet by the oath I had sworn to him, I had to stay.

And for the first time since I had left Caiactis, I did not know what I wanted to do.

"This is foolishness," came the whisper. "She has bewitched him!"

"Leave off your fears for Briga," rumbled Leir. "I can defend it, and my child. And when we have taken the land of the Ai-Zir, she will have an even greater inheritance."

Rigana's face paled, and Senouindos was frowning. Gunarduilla looked troubled, but Maglaros's bland face showed nothing at all. Had he come to me with her connivance, I wondered, or was he betraying us all? The rest of them were shouting again. Horse had moved to one side, a little surprised by the uproar. I could feel his gaze upon me, and looked resolutely away.

"King of the Quiritani, are you then immortal?" Loutrinos cried. "The river denies it, and the swans!"

I bit my lip. We had tried to keep that story from spreading, but of course Loutrinos had been there.

"If the king be unfit, then 'tis our right to choose another," came a voice from the back of the hall, not quite bold enough to let his face be seen. "And we will do so with or without your blessing, old man!"

I scrambled aside as Leir's feet thumped down on the footstool.

"I am the king!" His voice reverberated through the hall. "By conquest and oath and service. Dare any deny it, let him face me, and I will blast him from this hall!"

Men recoiled from his wrath like wheat bending beneath a strong wind. He seemed twice as tall as other men, but the veins in his temple were bulging ominously.

"Go!" he screamed, "everyone—this Council is done. At the Midsummer hosting we'll see who rules here. Get you gone from my presence! Out, all of you, now!"

I thought I heard thunder, but maybe it was only his voice resonating in the timbers, or the vibration of men's feet as they trampled toward the door. Artocoxos shepherded them outward, casting anxious glances over his shoulder. I sprang to my feet as Leir's voice failed him. Then the great door slammed shut, and he began to sway.

Chapter

And he thought that at the second bound or the third he would come up with her. But he was no nearer to her than before. He drove his horse to its utmost speed, but he saw that it was idle for him to follow her.

Then Pwyll spoke. "Maiden," said he, "for his sake whom thou lovest best, stay for me."

"I will, gladly," said she . . .

—*Pwyll Prince of Dyfed*

After the Council the oak priests killed a bull, and Talorgenos lay all one night in trance, wrapped in its hide. By water should Leir be healed and the land made whole, said his vision, and the most powerful healing waters in the Island were the springs of Sulis, where a great king had been cured of leprosy long ago. It was there that the high king must journey, and although Leir's illness had left him more stubborn and contentious than ever, he agreed.

The springs lay hidden in the hills between the country of the Ai-Zir and the Sabrina estuary. They were also on the road to Belerion, where Senouindos was gathering his forces. To our own people, Artocoxos gave out that the visit to the sacred waters was only a rest-stop on Leir's journey to inspect the men of the southwest, and the stories about the king's illness a ruse to deceive the enemy. It was a good enough tale, and I had not realized what a prison Ligrodunon had become until we were on the road.

We moved slowly, for Leir still tired quickly, but it eased my heart to see how his strength increased with each day of exercise. The Companions and part of the war-band rode with us, and Talorgenos and his students, and women to attend me, and the trackers and the dogboys and the dogs. In time of war the king had sometimes traveled with a smaller retinue, but now that he had been challenged, it was important that he be attended like a king.

My suitors came with us like stallions after a mare in season, tossing their heads and flaring their nostrils whenever any of the others got too near. If Horse had not been one of them, I might have laughed. Among so many, even his skill at stalking could not get him close to me. He was depending on me to create the opportunity for us to talk, but I did nothing.

With Zaueret going back and forth between the royal party and the war-band, I could find out all I needed to know without seeing him. His reputation had been spreading among the men. They said that Agantequos son of Vorequos was indeed a chieftain of the lands just across the Narrow Sea. Morilandis lay near a sacred rock that rose from the water by the shore. His Companions boasted of the vengeance he had taken upon his father's enemies. They said that many great warriors followed Agantequos now. And he was young, and strong, and he had a talent for teasing. But those things I already knew.

I told myself that my father needed me and I had no time for dalliance. But in truth, I think I was afraid.

Two weeks of travel brought us to the banks of the Aman and we followed its windings into the wooded hills in which the hot springs lay. This was limestone country like my own dales, scored with narrow, steep-sided valleys sharply cut by the streams. Here in the hills the Aman ran deep and swiftly, navigable to small boats, but with few fords.

The weather held clear and bright as we journeyed, and the fields were full of flowers. There were geese on the river, and ducks of all kinds, but we saw no swans.

And then we glimpsed the stone banks of a dun on a hill across the river and below it, a swirl of mist among the dark masses of the trees. Here the Aman made a deep loop and broadened to a ford. I caught a whiff of something that smelled like rotten eggs on the wind. Two rivulets of steaming water emerged from the forest to empty into the river, and I realized that the trees before us must shelter the sacred springs.

Women clad in dark blue robes were waiting on the other side of the ford. Talorgenos urged his pony across the water ahead of us, bearing a hazel bough.

"Cridilla—" My father's call brought me back down the line. "Who are they?"

I lifted a hand to shade my eyes, wondering if Lady Urtaya would be here. That could have been awkward, though the shrine was supposed to be neutral ground. But it was Lady Asaret to whom Talorgenos was giving the bough.

"One of them is the priestess from Belerion, and I suppose that the others belong to the shrine."

"Will they lodge us in the dun? I will not lie like a beast on the ground. I hope they are not too holy here to cook a hot meal."

He was tired. In the course of this journey I had grown to know that tone well. I said something reassuring and summoned young Zanis to go to the priestesses and request admission to the sacred springs.

"Who is the goddess who is worshipped here?" My voice had dropped to a whisper. There was a silence that stilled the spirit beneath the oak trees. At the far end of the pool reeds rose from black mud, but nearer, where gravel made a firmer border, the boulders were stained the red of the fresh-spilled blood. A bright flame flickered on the stone altar beside the pool.

"She is the fire and the water; She is power upwelling from the depths," said Lady Asaret softly. "Call Her Exalted One, if you will—Briga in your tongue. She is beyond all titles."

"But what is Her true name?" Suddenly it was important to me to know.

The priestess shook her head. "Here we call Her Sulis, the opening, the womb of the world, but Her true name can only be spoken by the heart. Let the fire consume you; flow with the water, and then perhaps you will know how to call Her, and She will hear. . . ."

I looked once more at the reddened rocks and thought that the pool was like an entrance to the Lady's womb.

"What about my father? Will they be bringing him soon?"

"While you are here, the king is not your responsibility. When he has rested, he will come to bathe in the healing waters of the eastern pool. Each day he will come, so long as he stays. But this is the women's sanctuary, and this is the fire that no man may look upon. It is your own purification that should concern you now."

The pool was waist-deep and blood-warm. I tried to hold my breath, breathed in convulsively and coughed as the reek caught in my lungs. One of the younger priestesses giggled. I took another, more shallow breath and found that I could bear it. My skin was tingling where the water touched it. Slowly I allowed myself to sink down into the pool.

"Here there is comfort; here there is rest;
Arms to enfold you, soft pillowed breast;
You have only to be. . . ."

Somewhere, women's voices were singing.

"Let the Mother hold you . . . let the Mother heal you," came the whisper from around me. "There is nothing to fear, you are secure and at ease. Sa . . . sa . . . sink down now and be at ease."

"Here is no turmoil; here is no storm;
Here is no hatred; none here to harm;
Here you are free. . . ."

It was like being swallowed by some great beast. Wind fluttered the scraps of cloth that had been tied to the branches as offerings. I could not remember when I had been so at ease; certainly not at the cleansing I had undergone at my initiation, but then I had not been in need of healing. I closed my eyes dizzily and felt someone's strong hand holding my head above the water. There was some reason I had come here—something I ought to be trying to do, but I no longer cared. Time flowed away and was lost in an eternal present of pure content.

"Here is the center; here is the spring;
Here is the secret, the source of everything;
Eternity. . . ."

"Cridilla, return now . . . come back to your body—"

The voice was so gentle; why should I resist it? Gradually I found myself inhabiting my flesh again. But there was a difference. I felt lighter now. I had been carrying my father since the day he killed the swan. And I only understood this now because for a little while the burden had been taken away.

> *"Here is the home and here is the heart;*
> *Here you remain although you depart;*
> *Returning to Me. . . ."*

Lady Asaret was holding out her hands. I sighed, and then pulled myself to my feet, shaking out my wet hair.

"Now, child, you may make your offering," said the priestess.

No blood was shed at the sacred springs. It was a place where even sworn enemies could seek healing in safety. Here, no violence might be done to any living thing. Even the war-band, which lived on meat, had to camp away from the sanctuary. Talorgenos had warned me, and I had brought grain and oil for the sacrifice.

Newly clad in a dark robe like the ones the priestesses wore, I followed Lady Asaret to the sacred fire. There was a thatched canopy built over the altar, supported by four sturdy pillars carved with meanders and circles and spirals that flowed down into the ground. On one of them I made out a male face surrounded by wildly writhing beard and hair, and on another a carving of the three mothers. Across from them was a seated figure with a beard, and on the fourth pillar a crudely carved figure of a woman crowned with the crescent moon, with bare breasts and a stiffly flared skirt, itself incised with the same patterns as the trees. I stared, trying to remember where I had seen such a thing before.

"Yes—it is very like the goddess at the holy well where you were initiated—" said the priestess softly. "But the image in the dales is the older, for as the years pass, even oak decays and must be carved anew."

"Then I am still in my own country . . ." I said, looking up at the image, and the hollow eyes seemed to look back at me. "For the Lady is here too."

"You may find Her in stranger places than this, before you are done . . ." said Lady Asaret. "But now it is time for you to make your offering."

The lads whose turn it was to guard the king were dicing in the meadow in front of the grove while Nabelcos, the bard that Horse had brought oversea with him, played for them. It was easy duty, while their lord was in the sanctuary and the rest of the warriors were keeping watch on the Ai-Zir. Artocoxos had his work cut out to keep them from fighting each other, just to have something to do.

When I came down from the Women's House on the third morning after our arrival, I found my three suitors stalking each other among the oak trees. I stopped short, for three days at the springs had been enough to restore my energy, and I wanted exercise. But it was too late. They had seen me, and were closing in.

I folded my arms across my breasts and looked from one to the other, wishing I had worn a plainer gown. But it would not have helped me. Nextonos or Loutrinos would have married the high king's daughter if she had stood up in a sack, and Agantequos had been accustomed to seeing me in nothing but a doeskin kilt in the days when he was Horse and I was Adder of the Misty Isle.

Loutrinos held out a bunch of flowers, smirking a little because he had it ready and the other two had nothing. One had to give him credit for persistence. Zaueret had been passing his bouquets on to me every day since our journey began, and I had been feeding them to my mare. He was wearing a fine tunic of creamy wool woven with colored bands, sweating in it, because even for spring, the weather was warm.

There was no help for it but to take the flowers. They were bright as the sunshine—primroses and cowslips and the first yellow asters. I touched them gently; it was not their fault that I did not like the man who had picked them.

Nextonos shouldered past him. "Lady, where no healing was needed, the springs have only increased your beauty! Will you walk with me?" He was not so overdressed as his fellow chieftain, but his leather vest would have been more suitable for riding.

I looked past him. The woods clung thickly to the slopes above us, green and cool. I had leaped like a deer upon the rocky heights of Caiactis. This was not the Island, but suddenly I wanted to know these west country hills.

"I will walk, but who will walk with me?" I smiled sweetly. "The man of you who first finds me at the top of that hill will have my company . . ."

I handed the flowers to Zaueret, who was listening with brows raised, and after a moment's thought, I handed her my shawl as well. It was a pity that my feet were no longer hard enough for me to run barefoot, but my slippers were soled with bullhide. Still smiling, I began to kilt up my gown.

"What word shall I give thy father when he asks for thee?" asked Zaueret. The waters were performing their healing magic, but though he grew stronger with each day, the king's need for me was like that of a child who has lost a favorite toy, and clings to its mother until a new one is given it.

"Tell him that 'tis for a short time only. Before the evening meal I will be back again, and all the better for the exercise!"

Loutrinos was watching in amazement. I looked at his girth and knew that he would be left behind soon. Despite his age, Nextonos was in far better condition, and he was eyeing me with growing determination. Horse looked deceptively sober, but the light in his eyes betrayed him. He would be certain that I was arranging this just for him. I gave him a quick, sidelong glance. In the old days, when we had been the same size, I had been able to outrun him. He was taller now, and heavier—how had he ever gotten so tall? He could probably outfight me, I thought, looking at his shoulders, but could he overtake me in thick woodland and on a hill? And would his woodcraft be good enough to follow if once I left him behind?

I did not know whether I wanted him to catch me. But every breath of the sweet air sent new life singing through my veins. Any man who did match my speed was going to know that he had had a run!

I gave them all a warrior's salute, and then I was in motion, trotting slowly at first to loosen my limbs, though I am sure that

Loutrinos thought it was to encourage him, then beginning to step out so that by the time I reached the woods, I was going as fast as a cantering pony can run.

My first breath of the green smell of the forest was like strong mead. Suddenly I felt as if I could run forever. I heard the men crashing through the bushes behind me, and remembered how I had raced the wolves on the Island, and laughed.

The west country hills were thickly clad with hazel and beech trees. I could hear someone coming behind me—Nextonos, by the panting. But of the three men, it was the one who I could not hear who worried me. Would he be angry at my teasing? A trader from the lands around the Middle Sea had told us a tale once of a princess who had tried to outrun her suitors. A golden apple flung down in her path had conquered her. What trick, I wondered, might Horse be planning to distract me?

And why, indeed, was he pursuing me? He had a land of his own to tend, and the wood was still green in his high seat there. Surely there were girls in his own tribe; girls with golden hair who could bring him useful alliances.

A log gave beneath my foot and I nearly went down. As I recovered my balance I realized the real reason why I had kept Horse at arm's length all this time, and that was because he did not belong to this land. I might not share all my sisters' ambitions, but I would never give Briga away.

Ahead of me I saw young alders; there must be water near. As I slid down the bank something exploded from among the leaves. I nearly fell, then grinned as I saw the white scut of a young doe.

Run, sister, and lead them astray! I slacked my pace, treading carefully. Now I could hear the water, and I knew that if I could get among the rocks, not even Horse could track me.

I had reached the headwaters of the stream that came down the slope below the dun. It was low for this time of year; bare rocks poked through the flood like bones. But its bed was a path a child could have followed. I was breathing in harsh gasps now, but I pushed myself upward, leaping surefooted from stone to stone. As the stream narrowed, the trees clustered more thickly, but beyond them I could see the level sweep of the down. I burst through pliant

foliage and found myself on a steep grassy incline beneath a limestone outcrop, completely surrounded by trees. Shaded by hazels,
the water trickled from a gash in the rockface into a basin carved
by water in the living stone.

I scooped up water, gulping thirstily, and began to strip off my
clothes. Then I knelt beside the stone basin once more and began
to splash the cold water over my limbs. The water was as pure as
the water of my own hills. I was warm enough to welcome the
chill, for the spring sun blazed like a fire behind me, drying the
droplets as soon as they touched my skin.

Presently I began to feel cooler. I rocked forward onto my knees,
peering into the pool. I could see my reflection in shifting fragments
as the waters stilled; here the slope of my nose and there my brow,
a hazel eye gleaming beside them, and a tendril of wildly curling
brown hair. I leaned farther, and glimpsed a swirl of tattooing and
the dark eye of one of my nipples winking back at me from the
stream.

All these are parts of me, each of them is a reality . . . I thought,
drawing a finger through the water to stir those elements into yet
another image, shaping a monstrous beauty like the hag maidens
in Talorgenos's tales. *But where is the center? Which is the truth of
me?* Tremors rippled through me as they pulsed through the water.
I stared, feeling the essence of identity itself beginning to unravel.
I was shifting . . . what would my new nature be?

And then, from that almost forgotten part of the world that
was not myself, I heard a sound. . . . There was a sigh, the sound
of cloth brushing branches. . . . Blinking, I turned.

What I saw was the white skin of a man's belly, upon which
the image of a bear pricked out in blue stretched and contracted as
the muscles moved. I recognized the tattooing of the Islands, but
for a moment my dulled mind could not comprehend what a man
so marked was doing here. His upper body was hidden by the folds
of his tunic, but as he pulled it over his head I saw chest hair like
copper wire glint suddenly in the sun.

An instant before he extricated himself from the garment, I knew
who it must be. But even as I saw the flame of red hair and heard
him swearing, another part of me was still denying it. The Horse

[183]

that I knew had a boy's skinny body. And when had he won admission to the hearth-kin of the Bear?

Carefully I got to my feet. "Does this mean you've won the wager?" I said conversationally.

The turn of his head was like the movement of some wild thing. His blue eyes widened, and then I saw that though he had a man's body, he could still blush like a boy. When he answered, his voice was controlled, but in his throat a pulse beat fast.

"In all truth, it does not. I lost you on the mountainside. But I am very thirsty from the run. Let me drink from your sweet waters, lady, and then I will go."

He had pursued me, but now he sounded afraid.

"The waters belong to the Mother—" I parted the alder shoots and stepped aside. "You need no permission from me!"

"Do I not?" For the first time, Horse smiled. Abruptly I became aware that both of us were naked. That had never mattered on the Island. There, I had been as familiar with his body as with my own.

But then both of us had been children, and he was looking at me as if he had never seen me before. It was true—he was not Horse, he was Agantequos now. Covertly, I appraised him. His long bones were sheathed in layered muscle, his skin milk-white except where face and arms were exposed to the sun; blue veins corded his shoulders and arms. His male parts, nestled in their cloud of fiery hair, had grown as well.

The boy I remembered had sometimes moved awkwardly, but this man bent to the water in a movement of controlled power. He was as thirsty as I had been. He would be hot too. As he started to straighten I splashed water at his curved back, retreating as he whirled. Sunlight slipped through the screen of leaves and touched each droplet with fire.

"You wanted cooling, did you not?" When I saw his expression I began to laugh.

"Did I?" he snapped, then the laughter began to dance in his blue eyes. "Then you must complete the task. Bathe me, Lady of Briga. With your father and his people wallowing in the sacred waters like a herd of pigs at a ford, there's no room for a poor wanderer to dip in his toe. Do you wash me, lady, that I may be healed."

"Are you in pain, then?" I asked him. "You do not look ill." I plucked some soft dry grass and compressed it into a scrubbing ball.

"I am wounded where no one can see," Agantequos said solemnly.

"There's little I can do for that, but I'll scrub your back for you."

He was still grinning, but he turned, and I soaked the grass and began to bathe the smooth muscles that ran into his shoulders. As we grew silent, a warbler in the buckthorn bush began his commanding "tuc-tuc" once more. A frog grumbled once from somewhere among the rocks, and the insects resumed their peaceful hum.

Agantequos's skin was surprisingly smooth. The totems of the Island's hearth-kindreds rippled beneath my hands, unmarred by the sword scars that I had seen on the front of his body, except for one angry dimple in the salmon's tail.

"A spear did this—" I said accusingly.

Agantequos half turned. "Here is where it went in—" I saw another mark, much larger, in his side as he lifted his arm. "But it touched nothing vital. The blow I gave in answer was better; it pierced the heart."

"Who was it?" This was not the kind of slash and gash men usually got in battle, but the deliberate blow of a challenge fight.

"It was the man who killed my father." Agantequos touched the golden torque that rested upon his collarbone. "I returned to the Great Land when I had completed my training, and lived like a wolf in the woods while I scouted the country. And when the time was accomplished, I came into his feasting hall and faced my enemy, and when he lay bleeding, I wrenched this gold from his neck, and the warriors who had followed him hailed me as their king."

"Horse, I am glad!" I knew how his exile had pained him. "And now you are secure in your father's high seat at last?"

"Oh, there are some ill-bred dogs that still sometimes snarl, but I can bring them to heel." He grinned.

"Even when you are away?" I said sharply, remembering how incessantly my father had traveled to keep his warring chieftains in line. "You should not have come!"

"My people were only one of the things I was lacking, Cridilla. The other one is here. . . ."

He touched my shoulder with fingers rough from the abrasion of swordhilt and spear. An involuntary shiver passed through my skin. I stepped into the water, but he moved with me. His hand stroked down my arm, as a man will do with a skittish mare, and my flesh tingled where it passed.

"I cannot leave my father," I whispered, watching that strong hand move back and forth upon my skin. "I cannot leave my land. And you cannot give up Morilandis for me."

"Cridilla, do you know how beautiful you have become?"

What did that have to do with it? I looked at him, and my breath caught. Rigana had said that men would desire me, but I had thought she was flattering. Was it the light in Agantequos's eyes that told me he believed what he was saying now?

"Your hair shines in the sunlight like an oaken spear shaft polished by long use, but it's a living color, like a chariot-pony's hide, and just as smooth—" He was touching my hair now, as if I were the mare, and the curls sprang back around his fingers and clung. I looked at them in wonder, then shivered as his hand slid down my shoulder once more.

"Your skin is softer, like the petal of a flower, or the downy underside of a new leaf in the spring . . ."

"It is brown—" I objected, looking at the whiteness of his chest and belly. Would his skin be as soft?

"It is golden!" He turned me so that the light fell full upon me through the whispering trees. But what I saw was the sunblaze kindling in his hair.

". . . Kissed ripe by the sun. Shall I envy her?" His voice grew lower. "Or shall I imitate her? So. . . ." And suddenly he bent and I felt the softness of his lips against my shoulder with a tingle that seemed to leap instantly through the rest of my body from my arm.

I pulled away. "Stop that!"

"Didn't you like it?" His blue eyes were dancing.

"That makes no difference! Nothing can come of it!" I rubbed my arm where he had kissed it as if I could make the tingling go away.

"It makes a difference to me," he said calmly. "But if you will not let me touch you, I must depend once more upon my eyes. Your body," he continued dispassionately, "is as supple and elegant as ever, but now it is powerful. Your limbs are round and smooth, but I can still see the slide of the muscle beneath the skin. And you still run well. You are balanced, and there's a rhythm in your movement, like the leap of a deer."

I remembered the stag tattooed upon my back, and how I had run on the Island, and realized just how good this chase through the forest had been.

"And you have grown like a half-wild roan stallion I had for a time"—I tipped back my head to appraise him—"all strength and stubbornness!" Some men slowed as they grew older, but I thought that Agantequos would always be quick-moving, with the same alert turn of the head that I remembered from when he was a boy.

"Your breasts are like the round smooth hills where the sheep graze," he went on as if I had not spoken, "and the swell of your hips is like the curve of the downs that shelter the secret valley and the sacred spring. I want to graze upon those hills, Cridilla; I want to drink from that sweet spring. . . ."

His voice had grown harsh suddenly and I took another step away.

"No more—no more! I should not have allowed you to begin."

"But you did," he answered, "and now there is only one ending."

"I cannot marry you," I repeated over the buzzing in my ears, trying to find meaning in the words.

"I want to lie with you—" he shouted. "Can I make it any plainer? I wanted you even when I was too young to know what for! We were two halves of one whole, Cridilla, and I am weary of being alone."

"I am for no man's taking!" I whispered. "Can you possess the salmon that swims in the stream?" Without thinking I was easing into the flowing pattern of defensive movements I had learned on the Island so long ago.

"Then I shall be the otter!" Water splashed up between us in a shining veil as he landed in the stream. His darting attack matched my sinuous evasions. His hand fastened on my arm, but wet skin slid through his fingers and I leaped back up onto the far bank.

"Can the otter take a falcon?" I taunted him, then regretted it as a leap more powerful than my own brought him after me and a sweep of his arm brought me for a moment hard against him. I slipped away, but here I was backed against the cliff face. I faced him, hands ready.

"The eagle can knock her from the skies," he gasped, lifting his arms to embrace the air. We circled, limbs remembering movements learned in patient practice long ago.

The patch of grass on which we were circling was far too small for this. I glimpsed the bright tangle of my clothing on the other side of the stream, but whenever I tried to swoop that way, my opponent was always there. The world narrowed to this stone-encircled sphere, and fluttering in my throat I felt the beginnings of panic.

"The wily hare can escape you!" I cried suddenly, feeling the power in my legs as I sprang for the rocks behind me. Then from behind me I heard the wildcat snarl.

The fringe of waving grasses at the rim of the hill sprang up before me. I pulled myself up and crouched, panting, taking in the sweep of grassland and the encircling trees. Then I heard the hunter, and sprang to my feet.

He had praised my running. I would run now, in the swiftest form I knew.

I flashed into motion like a doe bolting from cover as he came over the edge behind me. The trees blurred as I picked up speed. My pursuer leaped as I leaped, matching me bound for bound. He was the wildcat no longer. If I had been able to turn, would I have seen antlers sprouting from his brow?

"Run—" came the breathless taunt from behind me. "What

shape . . . can evade me, when the signs . . . pricked into your flesh
. . . same . . . as my own?"

I turned to answer him, missed my footing, and he slammed
into me and bore me down.

As I sprawled upon the grass I felt myself changing once more.
And though he bore the Bear tattoo as well, at least he would know
he had been in a fight when we were done.

I flung my arms around him, fingers stiffening into claws that
ripped across his back. My lips had drawn back; my teeth grazed
his shoulder, then I was flung free. Over and over we rolled, clawing
and tearing. Sweat-slick skin slid and stuck and parted as we grappled. From my throat came a sound that was not human. I twisted
and squeezed, not caring how he battered me, and as he tried to
push me away, I sank my teeth into his arm.

It was the taste of his blood that stopped me. I wrenched my
head away, for suddenly we were once more on the Island and the
smell of his blood was burning in my brain. We lay gasping, too
spent to know anything but the rasp of stressed breath and the
beating of the heart's red drum. And then he lifted himself and
kissed me.

For a moment the taste of his blood and the taste of his lips
and the pounding pulse within me were all the same. Then all my
strength uncoiled in a single heave as I thrust him away.

"Do you think I am Gunarduilla," I hissed, "to be battled into
submission and raped like a prize of the sword?"

He lay where he had fallen. "What do you mean?"

I closed my eyes, remembering. I had never told him. When I
had returned to the Island after that dreadful wedding feast I had
tried to lock the memory away. I had said that I would never marry,
but not why.

I could feel him waiting. And so, sitting on the grass with the
sweat drying on my naked body, I told him how my two sisters
had been married.

"I will never force you . . ." Agantequos said at last. And then,
"At least your father is not likely to compel you into marriage with
me. . . ."

I looked at him with a sudden gurgle of laughter. There was a crescent of purple marks upon his arm, and bright blood beading up again where my teeth had broken the skin. I bent over him and began to lick the blood away.

He went abruptly still. I could feel the tension in him building as I touched him. His fingers clenched in the grass.

"Cridilla—" The words were forced from him. "Let me love you."

I licked my lips, tasting him. Though I had caught my breath, the blood was still beating in my temples. I could hear bees humming over the harebells, a whisper in the grass as a mouse slipped past. But on all that bare hilltop nothing else moved. I saw that his flesh was indeed ready to serve me, and heat flared beneath my skin.

"You have not conquered me—" I whispered.

"How could I ever say it, when it is I who will bear the scars?"

Once more, his eyes were dancing. I sank down upon his breast, and as I had done on the Island, I let my lips touch his.

The hands of Agantequos were tender as the shepherd's hands upon a newborn lamb; they were firm as the hands of the rider who leads his mount through the marsh in a storm. Everywhere that his eyes had worshipped his hands confirmed their praise, and where his hands went, his lips soon made their own prayer. I had thought myself cold as yesterday's hearth, but my flesh was tinder, waiting only for his touch to burst into flame.

I learned the sweet tantalizing brush of lip on lip, and found myself still thirsty when his kisses burned their way from the hollow of my throat to my breasts. As his bright hair brushed across my skin the flame flared outward. His tongue teased first one nipple, then the other, until they stood rigid. When he sucked at them I felt a fierce stab of sensation between my thighs. I whimpered, trying to push him away without letting go, and he laughed.

Once more I was panting. My limbs twitched with the need to move, but only the throbbing softness between my legs had volition, opening to the firm pressure of his questing fingers like a flower in the sun. Instinctively I thrust against them, and heard his breath come harsh as my own.

Has he conquered me? I thought disjointedly. *Or is it my own body? And is this betrayal or a victory?*

Consciousness focused to that single core of sweetness. Agantequos was fire, but within me, the sacred waters were beginning to flow. I gasped at the rising of the tide, and Agantequos slid back up against me.

"Let me into your heart, my queen . . ." he breathed. "Welcome me in. . . ."

Blindly, my lips sought his. I felt his weight upon me, his strong hands lifting my hips as my legs closed around him. Then I shuddered at the slow, sure sweetness of his entering in.

And then I was the falcon, wings beating the sky; I was the doe, bucking beneath the weight of the stag; I was the salmon, scales brushing scales in the stream. The force of his thrusting pressed me deep into the earth. The pleasure where our flesh joined was almost pain.

Once more I felt the gathering of a mighty tide. I let awareness flow outward, and gasped as the ecstasy exploded in a rush that swept up my spine. In that instant I *was* the earth, and the power I had sensed in the sacred springs was uncoiling within. I heard someone moaning, but the shout that built in my own belly and tore through my throat reverberated from hill to hill.

An eternity later, I became aware of the sound of water. Agantequos and I were still lying entwined on the hillside, but somewhere very close to us, water was flowing. I turned my head and saw a gleam of moisture in the grass. Perhaps it had been there all the time and we had not noticed. I reached out my hand to cup the water, and slaked my thirst from the clear spring that was bubbling up from the cleft in the hill.

Chapter

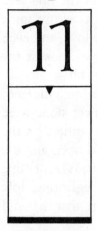

11

For it is the Prince's falsehood that brings perverse weather upon wicked people and dries up the fruit of the earth.

—Ancient Laws of Ireland III:25

That was the strangest of spring tides. I understood at last what my father had been looking for with all those women he had taken to his bed. With Agantequos I had found it, and when we came back down the mountain to the sacred springs I was sure that the glory that radiated from within me must cast a light on the leaves. But the eyes of the flesh could see nothing, though when my beloved was near me I felt his presence like a hidden flame. Perhaps Lady Asaret could have perceived my joy, but I took care to keep out of her way. And I returned to the dun alone.

My world had been remade, but outwardly, things remained the same. If it was known I had given myself to the outlander, my father would lose some of his bargaining power. Agantequos knew why I would not marry him. He said that it did not matter, but that was not true. He struggled to keep from reaching out to me when I passed; I strove to keep my eyes from following him. For both of us, our union had changed everything.

Now, when I drank water, I remembered the sweetness of that hilltop spring, and felt once more the tingling where love had touched me until my own juices began to flow. When I looked at the brightness of flame, what I saw was Agantequos's hair, and its warmth set my flesh afire. I found Earth herself in the hills and valleys of my own body, and with every breath of air my spirit winged free. All things were blessed because of my love, and even when the rainless days continued and folk began to look at my father and mutter once more, I could not be sorrowful.

Agantequos followed Leir's court as we moved through the land, burning from within. The times when we could meet alone were rare, though we did manage to slip away from the others on the Eve of Belotennia, when the gates of the dun stood open and the woods were all a-tremble with love's sweet grapplings. When I came in the next morning crowned with cowslips and eglantine, folk might guess what I had been doing, but I took care that they did not know with whom.

That was my first secret. The second I kept even from Agantequos; and that was the suspicion that I was going to bear his child. In those first days everything seemed possible. My pregnancy, gave me no difficulty—indeed, I had never felt stronger. My father was getting his strength back and all would go on as it had been. Even if my lover returned to his own land, I could raise my child to inherit Briga alone.

And so matters continued as the dry days lengthened toward Midsummer. I took advantage of the heat to adopt the old style wrap of cloth held by shoulder brooches, whose folds obscured my thickening waist and left my bare arms free. All the talk was of the approaching Council, and the road up the hill to Ligrodunon had been ground to white dust by the feet of messengers. To the casual eye, Leir seemed to have recovered. He had slowed, but his stride was steady and his speech was clear. And if his temper was still short, well, he had never been known as a patient man.

And then, suddenly, it was the Eve of Midsummer and the Council was tomorrow. All day the king's hall had reverberated with argument. Now the people were gathering around the bonfire that had been prepared in the field behind the dun, but as I returned for a cloak my father wanted, I realized I was not alone in the hall

"And I say that to make such a sacrifice is an admission of

responsibility—" Artocoxos's ringing tones startled me. "Let the sacrifice be a bull. We have had droughts before, and never a finger pointed at the king. Folk will say my lord admits this one to be his fault if we offer a man!"

"Fingers are being pointed at him now," came Talorgenos's deeper reply. "The people are saying that he has lost sovereignty and blood must feed the land. Give thanks that a substitute will satisfy them. If the crops fail entirely, the gods may demand the life of the king."

I stood with my hand spread in an instinctive gesture of protection over my belly, listening, but the fear and the fury that warred within me held me still.

"The gods, or men who have grown fat in the peace that Leir won for them and now are greedy for his power?" asked Artocoxos bitterly.

I let out my breath in a long sigh. Men—it must be men who were behind this talk of sacrifice—but they would see how Leir's daughters could call down the wrath of the Goddess if they should try.

"Do you think I interpret the omens to serve the will of any man, even the king?" Talorgenos's voice had sharpened. "Leir has broken his own *geas*, and there must be a payment. He himself has agreed to it, and tonight we will make the offering."

"To still your tongue I would agree to anything . . ." muttered Artocoxos, but softly, and then, "You have a man?"

"Chosen by lot from among the captives taken in last summer's warring. They will be feasting him now, and when the sun goes down they will bring him to the fire."

Their voices grew fainter, and then someone opened the door to the hall and I heard a distant murmur like the far-off roaring of the sea. I shivered, though the air was still warm, and stopped to get my own cloak before I went out to them.

The rolling ground to the east of the fortress had sprouted an unseasonable harvest of skin tents and bothies woven from green branches. Only the meadow was free of them, and in the fading light of the long summer dusk it bore its own crop of heads, brown and red and fair, as the people moved into position around the wicker cage upon the piled logs.

A muted murmur of sound flowed and eddied as I made my way toward the platform they had made for the king. The voice of the people had carried because they were so many, and perhaps because of the suppressed excitement that lent an edge to each word. The Quiritani had never been used to give so much attention to Midsummer, but it was a great day among the Painted People, and now that the oak priests had learned from the wisemen of the older race how to calculate it exactly, they had begun to add their own rituals to the ancient festival.

Many of the valley folk had come up for the ritual. *"The Lady . . . the Lady of Briga . . ."* came the whisper behind me as I passed. Once more I thought of the sleeping power of the little waves as they hiss against the shore.

I was halfway to my father when I heard someone call my name. Gunarduilla and Rigana were standing together with their escort behind them. I had avoided them since they arrived, but now I answered the summons, for in the half-light I thought I could support even my sisters' scrutiny. After tomorrow it would not matter if they knew about the baby. After the Council, I would tell everyone.

"Cridilla, where have you been all day?" asked Rigana. "Are you well?"

"She must be," answered Gunarduillia, "with the bloom on her like a new-curried horse, though she's grown fat, lying about our father's hall!"

"I'm well enough—" I said shortly, "but run off my feet settling all the chieftains and their wives. Forgive me. I meant to come to you, but I knew that both of you and your households were well provided for."

"What need for forgiveness among sisters?" asked Rigana sweetly.

Her eyes were brilliant in the gathering gloom. The years had only confirmed her beauty, while Gunarduilla, who had been a handsome girl, had coarsened as time went on. I thought of the things that Agantequos had said to me and wondered how he would see me in a few years. Would his eyes still follow me in uncomprehending adoration, as Senouindos looked at Rigana when he was not too drunk to see? Or would he forget his wife to flatter whatever girl he fancied, as Maglaros had courted me?

"It is no matter," added Gunarduilla. "We will all be more than well provided for soon." I looked at her sharply, and she laughed. "Do you still play the innocent? Do not you know that tomorrow the chieftains will force Leir to divide his lands among his kin?"

I had not known. Focused on Agantequos and my child, I had not been going among the people and listening as I used to do. And Crow, who always heard everything, had not told me. Perhaps he had thought I knew already, or that I did not want to talk to him.

"But why?" I managed finally.

Rigana's eyes opened in astonishment. "He has already shown himself unfit to rule! And surely the time of the queens has been long in coming. Cridilla, this is the moment that I promised you! Do you remember, when you were made a woman—I told you then that one day we three would rule the land!"

"But surely there is time—"

"Not for me! I have served an old man's whim too long already!"

"And I have bled for my land. It is my right to rule!" echoed Gunarduilla. "Do you mean to wear out your maidenhood with nothing in your lap but a dotard's two feet?"

"They are the feet of a king!" I retorted, thinking of the new life that lay in my belly. "We would be warring like wolves if he had not made us all one!"

"We are wolves, kept from tearing each other's throats by the pack leader's growl," said Gunarduilla grimly. "Only the authority of the Mother can make us one. And there are three of us, as the Mother has three faces. It is our destiny."

I sighed, remembering how my spirit had encompassed the land when I lay in Agantequos's arms.

"We are the life of the land, it is true, but not alone. No good can come of dispossessing the king. . . ."

Gunarduilla made a sound of disgust and turned away, but Rigana gripped my arm.

"Fool, do you think he will give you everything? Do you think that you can share his high seat because he dotes on you? Or is it his bed you want to lie in, bitch? What vengeance do you think the Goddess would wreak upon this land for that sin?"

"The Goddess be my witness that no man has lain in my lap save as Her law allows, nor have I desired it, and may I be crushed by earth and sea and heaven if I lie!" I managed, but I could not keep the tremor from my words.

"Sister, you go too far!" Gunarduilla sounded as shocked as I.

"Then you make her see reason! Goddess knows she has no cause to be so ungrateful after all that we have done!" Rigana pulled her shawl around her.

"It will all come right, Cridilla," Gunarduilla said quickly. "If you flatter the old man he will let you choose your own husband. Nextonos might be best for you. He's old enough to be vulnerable if you pretend to love him, and too well established to be greedy. And the other chieftains know him well. . . ."

"I need no permission from my father to choose my man!" I found my voice suddenly, shuddering at the thought of Nextonos touching me. At last my rage burst free. "And certainly no help from you! Beat your own husband back to your bed, Gunarduilla, for be sure that I will slice his balls off if he comes fumbling after me again!"

Rigana was laughing, and I turned on her. "Nor you either, who have made a high road of your marriage bed! The Goddess gives Herself in Her own time and season, but all seasons are alike to you!"

Even in my rage I had kept any voice low. But the quality of the silence as I finished was like the stillness in the depths of my vigil cave, echoing with soundless screams. There was truth in my words, but not in the way I had said them. I stretched out my hands in appeal, but the faces of my two sisters had become stone.

From the gate of the dun the carynxes blared. The bleached robes of the oak priests glimmered in the gloom as they marched forward with their prisoner. With a sob, I pushed through the circle of guards and fled toward the sanctuary where my father awaited me.

On the royal platform, the chieftains were drinking. The king's face was in shadow, but I knew his silhouette and the silver glint of his hair. For a moment, looking up, he seemed immense against the fading sky, then I was standing beside him, and he was my father again. He turned and I thrust the cloak into his arms.

"I am sorry," I began.

"Hush, child, it's no matter. I am not cold yet . . . but you are trembling!" He reached out, and I moved into the curve of his arm and nestled there gratefully. In the darkness, nothing had changed. This was the powerful father who had sheltered me throughout the years of my growing. I sensed Agantequos somewhere nearby, but dared not look for him.

"I don't like this," I muttered as the ghostly procession neared. They had put one of Leir's cloaks on the prisoner, and the straw halter around his neck looked like a royal torque in the fading light. Two of the priests held the man to steady him, for the fellow was looking around him as if he did not know where he was, and once he laughed.

"When the black drink gives wings, the spirit sings . . ."said a shadow at our feet.

Of course, the victim would have been given some drug to help him along. I looked down. Crow was huddled on Leir's other side, almost invisible in the gloom.

"Want a drink, then, *amantanos*?" said one of the chieftains.

Crow looked up at him for a long moment, then shivered. His eyes were losing focus, but he spoke before I could stop him—

"Warrior, drink deep . . . when next the feast dost keep . . . wilt drink in Dana's mound, beneath the ground!"

"Curse you for a bird of ill-omen!" the man exclaimed, his fingers flickering in the warding sign.

He moved away, and I heard his voice, low and angry, as he reached his friends. My fingers closed on Crow's shoulder and he shuddered.

"Could you not have pretended to drink with him?" I exclaimed. "The talk will begin again, and we cannot afford it now."

"Drink bears the spirit 'way, where demons stay— If this one drank, would speak nothing but prophecies!" I saw the feral gleam of his eyes. "Dost remember when this one swung from the tree?"

I nodded, for I had never forgotten how I had found him.

"Once this one wandered in the spirit world; they crunched his bones. But not all, not all the way. Spirits gather now, and this one is afraid!" His fingers closed on the hem of my gown.

There was a little hiss of indrawn breath from the crowd, and I looked up again. Crow's babble had distracted me—perhaps he had meant to. Now the prisoner was at the pyre. As they lifted him toward the wicker cage, some understanding seemed to return to him, for he began to whimper weakly. But the oak priests were stripping him with grim efficiency until he was as naked as my father when he performed the sacrifices.

Still silent, the priests tied their victim, and after a moment's futile struggle, he slumped in his bonds. In the stillness of held breath, his harsh gasps were the only sound.

Then the sudden flare of a torch drew all eyes. Talorgenos came forward, lifting the flame so that between the twisted withies we could see the gleam of sweated skin.

"Thunderer, we send you this sacrifice, that the rumbling of thy chariot wheels may wing us welcome rain!" Talorgenos cried. Then he plunged the torch into the pyre.

The oak priests surrounded the bonfire as smoke began to billow from between the branches. This furnace would leave nothing but cinders, so they must take their omens from the way the man died.

The wicker cage quivered as the flames leaped higher, as if the poor man were jerking at his bonds. Was it the noose or the drug that kept him from screaming?

"He fights it, good!" muttered the king. "It is what I would do."

The victim stood for the king. But it was not good—even I knew that the sacrifice should go willingly.

Presently the movement ceased. The smoke, or perhaps the drug, had driven the man from his senses. In moments the pyre had become a cone of fire within which the poles of the cage were like bars of iron. And then the poles caught, and the sacrifice was prisoned in fire. The ropes that held him must have burned through then, but all we could see was a rippling sheet of flame. It was only when the scent of burnt meat came chokingly on the heated air that we knew that the offering was accepted.

We had to watch until the pyre fell in upon itself in a heap of glowing coals. The king had to see it all, and while he stood, I could not turn away. Crow clutched my ankles in a grip that would have been painful if I had allowed myself to feel. I wondered why he had not gone to the arms of one of the warriors, his usual refuge when he was afraid. But perhaps they no longer wanted him now that there was silver in his hair. After a time I reached down and touched his head, stroking the coarse strands as if he were a hound.

When the fire had consumed enough so that men could approach it, the people began to come forward with unlit torches in their hands. One by one they brought them away blazing. Then they ran to bear the holy fire to their fields.

Now the whole great crowd was moving. I gave a convulsive shudder and turned my face against my father's shoulder.

"It is all right," he murmured, patting my hair. "It is over, and no one has hurt me. Do not be afraid."

After a time I straightened. Sparks crawled like glow worms through the fields below the dun as farmers carried fire through their crops to sain them against all ill. But had the offering been accepted? Would the Thunderer send rain?

I looked upward, and saw the fiery stars like scattered embers in the cloudless Midsummer sky.

That night I dreamed that Bear Mother came to me, armed for war. Her lips moved, but I could not hear her. Then for a moment the scene changed, and I saw in the distance the white shapes of flying swans. I tried to go after them, but I was earthbound.

I woke early, with tears still wet on my cheeks from my dream, and in the dim hour before the Midsummer dawning, went down to get water from the spring. There were serving girls to do that, of course, but the first water drawn on the day of a high festival had special power. Other women had come out with the same idea, but they were not so foolish as to deny me precedence.

We waited in silence, listening to the awakening birds. Then from the dun above us came the blare of the oak priests' horns, and I saw the light of the newborn sun kindling among the leaves. I let the cold water fill my small bronze cauldron, a lovely thing with elegant curves and spirals in the new fashion on the fittings and around the brim. The others were waiting behind me, for sacred or not, everyone needed water to start the day.

I smiled. "I will pour a little from my cauldron for each of you, and the virtue of the water will empower the rest. See, there is enough for all, and I will still be able to take the dawn drink to the king. . . ."

Suddenly there was laughter and a chattering that drowned out the birds. They were still talking when I started up the path.

"She is a gracious lady," said someone. "Does she know that the chieftains of the north are sworn to cast her father down?"

"It will make no difference to her," came the answer. "She is still Briga's queen."

I hastened on. It was more important to make sure that my father knew what was being said than to make fools understand the meaning of loyalty.

Halfway up the hill I paused beside the old oak to catch my breath, and found myself pulled into the shadows behind it. Water slopped over the rim of the cauldron but I did not cry out, for my flesh had recognized that strong hand.

"Agantequos . . ." I lifted my face to his kisses.

One of his hands clenched in the falling masses of my hair, the other slipped along the smooth skin of my neck and sought my breast beneath the loose folds at the neck of my gown. It had been two weeks since we had been alone, and his touch burned like fire. He tried to draw me to him, but I was still clutching the cauldron.

"Cridilla—we cannot live like this!" he said hoarsely. "Come away with me, whatever happens this afternoon."

"I love you, but have I asked you to give up your own land to stay with me?"

Agantequos sighed. "It was easier on the Island . . ." He moved so that I could lean against him. "I will not abandon the men who fought for me. . . ."

"And I will not desert my father. Why is that so hard to understand?" Longing had carved out new hollows in his face, and I saw the purple bruises of sleeplessness beneath his eyes.

"My mind understands," he whispered, "but my heart is in agony, and my body is crying out with need." His hands slid over my breasts, and the familiar tingling spread through my flesh. I told myself that I ought to run back to the dun, but I could not move.

It was Agantequos who stopped, the current of desire abruptly cut off as he cupped my breasts in his hands.

"Cridilla!" His voice vibrated like a gong. "Are you with child?"

"I am carrying . . ." Worrying about my belly I had forgotten how full and hard my breasts had grown.

"My child," he repeated. "Now you must come to the Great Land with me."

"Why? Do you think I cannot protect it?" I jerked from his arms and more water poured out onto the ground. "The babe is mine! I swore only that if I took a husband it would be you. But I am still free!"

"I will stand up before the Council and claim paternity!"

"I will deny it if you do!"

"And what will your father say? Oh, Cridilla, will you always give him the love that belongs to me?"

"You are a part of me!" I cried. "The love of my heart is yours! But I am a part of him as well, and if I desert him how can I be true to you?"

"Cridilla, I want you! I want my child!" Agantequos reached for me and the remaining water splashed from the cauldron as I whirled away.

I want to love my mate and my child and my father as well! I was weeping now. *Is that so impossible a dream?*

"If it is a daughter, she must be born here in her own land," I gasped. "But if it is a son I will give him up to you!" Still clutching the empty cauldron, I ran back to the dun.

Surely that Midsummer Council was the greatest convocation of the Quiritani that the Island of the Mighty had ever seen. The chieftains sat with their retinues around them, radiating outward from the black scar where the bonfire had been to chequer the meadow with color. The king sat in the center. He *was* the center —it was his strength, and his stubbornness, and sometimes his scheming, that had multiplied a few shiploads of crazy young warriors into this throng. Could they not see it? Could they not find in their hearts, if not mercy, then at least some gratitude?

I leaned my cheek against one of the poles that supported the sunshade. Other hangings, not so high, sheltered my sisters and their husbands. Retainers held stretched mantles over the heads of the chieftains, and some had pulled their plaids up to shield themselves from a sun that radiated heat like a molten shield. A few had even been desperate enough to put on the flat straw hats the farmers wear. This noon might mark the moment from which the sun's strength must decline, but so far there was no sign of it. Even the heavens seemed faded, as if earth's drought were extending to the skies. Heat shimmered in the air. *It will not improve their tempers,* I thought, wiping perspiration from my brow. *Or mine. . . .*

"Who slices the hero's portion when this roasting's done?" said Crow as he surveyed the sun-reddened faces of the crowd. I laughed in spite of myself. Then the drums annihilated all sound but their own thunder. When they ceased, the Assembly was still.

Father, the heart of your grandchild beats beneath your feet, I thought as I settled them in my lap. *Cannot you feel?* But at the moment he had other concerns. The chieftains sat up like hopeful dogs. It had begun.

"Who speaks first?" murmured the king to Artocoxos.

"Nextonos—"

The man to whom Leir had given lands and gold stood up in the blackened circle left by the fire and took the speaker's staff. But by the time he had said five words, the king had stopped smiling.

"—and so I speak for the chieftains. Leir can be king no more. You say that we will make up our losses with the plunder of the south and feed earth with the blood of the Ai-Zir. But how shall a king govern another land who cannot rule his own? Shall Leir's curse be extended to the country of the Ai-Zir? It is with sorrow that I say this, for I have eaten at his table; I have shed blood at his side. But no one who cares for his folk can deny the evidence.

Justice and victory he has given us, but the fruits of the earth are failing. This king's time is done."

There was a mutter of agreement, muted, as if they feared the heavens would strike them even though they spoke in lawful Assembly. But the treacherous skies remained clear.

Leir laughed harshly and held out his hand for the staff.

"I will not do it. You elected me, but the gods sanctified the bond. You have no power to sever the link between me and this land!"

"The gods have broken it!" came the cries. "The omens say so. Your queens are dead, your totem fled; your reign is sacred no more."

"The omens are good!" said Artocoxos furiously. "Talorgenos, tell them—" The oak priest looked troubled, and in my belly the cold serpent of fear began to uncoil.

"Speaker of the Sacred Words, tell us," challenged Nextonos. "Was the heart of the sacrifice consumed?"

"It was not. . . ."

"And the skull?"

"Cracked, but not consumed—"

"Are those omens good or evil, priest? It is the people who require this answer," came the implacable demand, "and you must reply."

"The omens are not good," the priest answered at last.

"Are you children?" Artocoxos burst out furiously, "to be frightened by a bit of burnt meat or the flight of a bird? Is there no man here with the courage to abide by his sworn word?"

"I will!" came a strong voice from behind us.

"I stand by the king!"

"And I!" "And I!"

At least Leir's Companions and his retinue were faithful, and many from the north of Briga, and the other lands that Leir had won, but only scattered echoes came from the rest of the Assembly.

"Old man—" Nextonos's gesture embraced them. "You may still have teeth, but can you fight us all?"

Slowly Leir rose. He was trembling, and I feared for him.

"I can fight you!" Rage rasped agonizingly through every word, but his voice was clear. "I have faced worse odds and claimed the victory! But even if I fell I would be no easy prey—" his lips drew back in a humorless grin. "Ye would be a long time licking the wounds this old wolf could give, and it would be you who must bear the guilt of a kingslaying, while I laughed as my blood soaked into the thirsty ground!"

A shudder passed through the Assembly. I bent, cradling the life in my womb, but I saw only red through my closed eyelids, blood staining the heavens, blood all around. . . . I had fought, but never such a war as could come from my father's words. The air was clamorous with the edged clash of voices as others foresaw the same doom.

"Will you bring this ruin upon your people—you who for so long have served this land?" I opened my eyes, and saw Lady Asaret standing like a shadow in sunlight in her dark robes.

"As you say, I have served them, so how can I abandon them now?" the king asked with suspicious sweetness. His glance rested for a moment upon me before he went on. "But even a great king must bow to the will of the gods. Fortunately the old line continues in the three kingdoms. Let them continue to support me as befits a king, and I will step down."

There was a stark silence. Men looked dazed as by an offer of faerie gold, wondering if it would become dry leaves if they touched it, or something worse that would turn on them and slay.

"Not a wolf, a fox," said Crow very softly. "But even old fox gets caught sometimes. Will these hunters go astray?"

"And what of your other lands?" said someone finally. "What of the clans whose kingdoms were broken? And the Ai-Zir lands, if we can take them—to whom will they belong?"

Surprise played deliberately across Leir's features and he stroked his beard. "I suppose I must divide them among my daughters now. . . . Will you agree to these conditions? Will you swear to them by earth and sky and sea?"

He was playing them! I grimaced to keep from laughing. My father had not gone mad—I had seen him do this many times before. He had not been king so long without learning to bend a little to serve his purposes. No doubt he meant to add his own conquests to Briga, and rule through me. It was a fair wager that when the others began to kick at each other like an untrained chariot team they would be glad to have his strong hand back upon the reins.

With gathering enthusiasm the confirmation came. If some of the young men were disappointed there would be no fighting, clan leaders who saw war's red shadow receding from their homelands were not tempted to question.

"It is a great gift I am offering—" Leir smiled craftily, and I saw Maglaros's face change as he began to understand. He bent to whisper in Gunarduilla's ear as the king went on. "And how shall I decide? I have loved and defended my daughters since they were born. Now let each one say how she shall repay me!" He eased confidently back into his chair and I took his feet into my lap again.

Ask me to take up arms and be your champion, I stared up at him in silent appeal, *or to prove my love by some impossible quest across the sea. But do not require me to stand before all the Island and say how I feel!*

Grim-faced and sweating, Gunarduilla was already coming forward, the sun striking dull sparks from her tarnished hair. *At least she's no better with words than I!* I thought with satisfaction as she took the speaker's wand.

"Always it has been my pride to be the daughter of a great king . . ." she said slowly. "I trained to be a warrior so that I could be like him. I prayed to become a man so that I could be his son, but the gods denied it and gave me to a husband."

I stiffened in astonishment, remembering our talk on the road through the Dales. *"In my heart,"* she had told me, *"I am my mother's child."*

"Now I have a son," she went on, "and I look for signs that he will be like his grandfather every day." That might even be true, though not because she was hoping to find a resemblance. All eyes went to the boy, who stood twitching beneath the strong hand of his father, but Morigenos made no sound, and I could not.

But Gunarduilla was not done. "But what are the claims of husband or child beside those of such a father? Leir is the sun and the stars. He is a god who walks among men." She turned to Leir, and her face was a mask. "Shall you not therefore always receive the Champion's Portion at my table, father, and sit upon the High Seat in my hall?"

Father! I looked up at Leir and saw that he was smiling. *Can't you hear how she lies?* I glared at Talorgenos's bowed head. *Truth-sayer! Make her admit the falseness of her words!* And Maglaros—Gunarduilla had never made any secret of her feelings—he must know this was hypocrisy. But of course it must be he who had told her what to say.

Crow made an odd choked sound, but he was hidden by the folds of Leir's robe and I could not see whether it was anguish or laughter.

Abruptly Gunarduilla seemed to come to the end of her learning. She looked uncertainly around her, and Maglaros frowned. She knelt then and abased herself, grinding her forehead into the ashes of the sacrificial fire. I remembered suddenly how splendid she had looked as she stalked out to fight Maglaros for her sovereignty, and in that moment, I felt only sorrow at the desperation that could undermine so magnificent a pride.

Because of course Leir, who read men so well, must know how she really felt about him. I relaxed a little, certain that only policy prompted his complacent smile.

"My oldest daughter loves me as I love her," said the king. "And she shall be confirmed in Alba with the husband I have given her. The rest I will decide when I have heard what her sisters have to say."

As Gunarduilla stumbled back to her husband, Rigana took her place in the circle, brilliant in crimson, with gold blazing balefully against the pale skin of neck and wrists and in the shadows of her hair. The men had nodded sagely as they listened to Gunarduilla, but Rigana they watched with hungry eyes.

"My sister speaks well, but coldly. I come from a gentler country—" Rigana's voice rolled caressingly over the crowd. She, at least, had not learned her words from her husband. Senouindos seemed to be asleep beneath his shade.

"And I have never wanted to *be* a man. . . ." A little stirring echoed her low laughter, then her gaze fixed on the king. "And so, my lord, I have always been grateful that your strong arm was stretched out to shelter me. Growing beneath such protection, how could I not love my father? Surely you know how I have adored you—"

Surely you know that she too is lying! I thought then. *Father, look at me now with laughter in your eyes,* I begged him silently, *so that I will know you see!*

"My lord, there has never been a man to equal you. There is no measure to the feelings you stir in my heart. No greater glory could I know than for you to make your home with me!"

"Do ye hear how my children love me?" Leir cried.

"A wolf-bitch will come to any carrion," muttered Crow, but the king did not seem to hear. *What is he hearing?* Panic fluttered in my belly. *Is this all a play to impress his chieftains, or does he really believe these flatteries?*

"Let my second daughter rule in Belerion with my old comrade, since she has proved her devotion!" Leir drew breath, then set his hand upon my shoulder.

"And, Cridilla, dear heart, now it is your turn. Speak well, child, and let my spirit rejoice in you." Such love was trembling in his voice that my eyes stung with tears. I reached up to grasp his hand.

"And what truth do you think to get from her, lord king—" came a man's voice, resonant with scorn, "who has not even told you that the belly upon which you rest your feet is bulging with a child?"

Chapter

Sit we here over the strand;
Stormy the cold;
Chattering in my teeth. A great tragedy
Is the tragedy that has reached me.

—*The Book of Invasions of Ireland*

The hush was like the stillness before a storm.

"Is it true?" Leir's voice tore the silence. "Do you go with child?"

I looked from Maglaros, who was smirking in vicious triumph, back to my father. Surely, I thought numbly, he ought to be pleased.

"What if I do?" I began, but the king was already swinging his feet from my lap as if it had become unclean. He whirled to face me, his white rod of kingship clutched in his hand.

I struggled to my feet, lest anyone think I was kneeling for mercy. How had Maglaros known about the child? Had my sisters guessed last night and told him, or had he set one of my women to spy on me?

"Who is the man?"

It was the voice of a king when he gives judgment. Where was Agantequos? Despite the friends he had made among the Companions, I was his only ally here. *Be still!* I thought. *For your life, my love, say no word!*

"Talorgenos!" cried Leir. "Touch her womb with your staff so that the creature within will cry out its father's name!"

[211]

My hands moved to protect my belly.

"I am a free woman and the child's father is a free man. That is the only question you have the right to ask. There is not a warrior in your hall can claim this child!"

"It is true—it is the law. She has done nothing wrong . . ." came the murmur from the assembly, and Talorgenos nodded confirmation.

"Lord king," said one of the chieftains, "you have not finished the questioning. . . ." An anticipatory silence spread through the crowd.

"Tell me then how you love me . . ." Leir said heavily, "you, whom I loved above all things. . . ."

I opened my mouth to answer him, but no sound came. I gazed at the sun-reddened faces around me, seeing rampant curiosity, in some few faces a malicious satisfaction, and in the eyes of the Briga men a fierce loyalty that heartened me.

"You are my father, and all my life you have cared for me. How could I do other but love you," I said finally.

"Because of what I could give you?" said Leir bitterly. "Your sisters were eloquent. Can you say no more?"

I glared at him. What more was there? If all the hours that we had spent together these past years had not proved my devotion, what could mere words do?

"Your sisters love me more than husband or child, more than life even," he added, mocking. "What is the measure of *your* love?"

And they are lying! I thought furiously. *I was willing to give up everything to stay with you—cannot you tell the difference between false gold and true?*

"I will hazard my life to defend you—"

"That duty any warrior owes his lord," Leir interrupted.

Bear Mother had beaten into us the conviction that a chieftain must have truth from those sworn to him. By the truth of the prince the kingdom prospered. Because Leir was my father and my king, even now I could not betray him with flattery.

"And I owe you also a daughter's love. But the love that I would give a husband has nothing to do with you—"

"What kind of love did you give to *him*—to that serpent who slid between your thighs?"

I blinked, not quite believing what I had heard.

"What kind of love did you offer my mother, if you cannot understand? I gave my lover what I owed the father of my child, as I will give this babe in my belly a mother's love. What use would that be to you?"

The king swayed, and Artocoxos leaped up to steady him. Was he even hearing me?

"She swore . . ." he muttered, "swore that th' child was mine . . . But never sure. . . ."

"Father! *Listen* to me!"

"Do not call me father!" He focused suddenly. "*There* are my daughters!" The sweep of his arm as he pointed to Gunarduilla and Rigana overbalanced him, and he was kept upright only by the old warrior's strong arm.

"They love you for what you are worth to them—cannot you see?"

But Leir was still muttering. "Not my daughter . . . not mine. A faithless bitch . . . laughs at me, like all of 'em . . . when she thinks I cannot . . . hear." Like receding thunder, his complaining faded away. Wind fluttered the edges of the sunshade, a hot wind that dried the mouth and brought no relief.

"The unclaimed lands," said Nextonos finally. "How will you divide the kingdoms, my lord?"

"North and south let Gunarduilla and Rigana divide them," he answered querulously. "What's it . . . matter now?"

"I would take your daughter and rule Briga for her, even with the child . . ." the chieftain said softly. The men of my own country had begun to mutter, but they stilled as they waited to see what the king would say.

"What daughter?" Leir began to laugh wildly. "Not mine! Can't give her away! By earth and oak and fire . . . I swear it," his breath was failing. "Sea rise up . . . swallow me if I deny my words!"

"Gunarduilla, Rigana! Don't let him do this to me!" I cried, but their faces seemed carved from the oak he had sworn by. Talorgenos grasped Leir's arm, whispering furiously, but the king thrust him away.

"I know what I do! You, Speaker, proclaim her banishment! Think me . . . crazed? She is disowned and disinherited. Cursed . . . I curse her . . . like her dam!"

I flinched from him, shivering. He must not curse me. . . . There was a reason he must not, but even if I could have remembered, there was nothing I could do. I had always been the one who tried to calm Leir's furies, but now I was the heart of the storm.

"And Briga?" asked Nextonos desperately.

"Will you take the girl without it? Or will you?" He turned on Loutrinos, and laughed as the other man backed away. "The both of ye were hot enough for the bitch before!" His gaze slid across me unseeing, as if I had disappeared.

"I will take her—" Suddenly Agantequos was at my side. "With or without an inheritance." The westering sun blazed like a beacon fire in his hair.

"The outlander?" the king peered at him. "You're a fool, then. She'll abandon you too!"

Agantequos's expression did not change. He held out his right hand formally, as if I had never touched him before.

"Take her! Beyond the ninth wave do you bear her away! Let Briga be orphaned too!" Leir giggled suddenly. "Gunarduilla and Rigana can slice it up between 'em—" He slashed at the air with his wand. "*They* are true daughters. They'll take care of me! Ye wanted the power?" He grinned round at the Assembly, lips lifting so that his teeth showed long and yellow as the teeth in a skull. "Take it, then—" Leir snapped the white rod of sovereignty in two and hurled the pieces away.

"*Two sister cuckoos in the nest . . . now rest . . .*" a thin voice sang plaintively into the silence.

> "*The swan's egg broken on the ground*
> *is found—*
> *When none this jest can understand,*
> *woe to the land!*"

The wind rose with the coming of darkness. Lightning stalked the distant hilltops as if the gods were at war. In the close darkness I waited with Agantequos for Zaueret to finish packing my belongings and bring them out to me. The dun was hushed as if someone lay dead, and perhaps that was more than fancy. *Cridilla daughter of Leir is slain,* I mourned, *and who is this who weeps for her?* Sweat trickled between my shoulder blades, but I was shivering.

"Hush, love, you are safe with me, and soon we'll be away from here. . . ." Agantequos smoothed the damp hair back from my brow. Behind us I could hear his men murmuring uneasily. Keir and Gruncanos were the tall ones, Cuno the more solid shape behind. Nabelcos leaned against a wall nearby.

I had not known that I was whimpering. I turned my face against his shoulder, and he drew his mantle around me. Even though the chill came from within me, it was comforting, so long as I could keep myself from remembering the many times it had been my father whose arms had kept me safe and warm.

The hides across the door to the hall were moving. I tensed as someone pushed through them, but it was only Zaueret, her outline misshapen by the bundles she bore. Someone else was coming after her, similarly laden. I recognized Crow's ungainly grace as he slipped past the barrier.

"The horses are waiting?" breathed Zaueret as she reached us.

"Outside the gates," answered Agantequos.

We redistributed the bundles and made our way through the shadows, as invisible to folk who feared to look upon the king's cursed daughter as spirits on Samonia Eve. Outside the dun it seemed lighter. Five ponies tugged at their tethers beyond the gatehouse, nervously sniffing the charged air. We began to load the gear.

Then metal scraped harshly behind us, and the horse I was holding tossed its head in alarm. Agantequos whirled, reaching for his sword, and Cuno and Gruncanos leaped in front of him. The bard Nabelcos took a quick step forward to speak for his master.

"There's no need for that, now—" came a northern voice from

the shadows. "Ye'll be safe enough an' ye just come peacefully with me!" The darkness quivered into motion; we were surrounded by armed men.

Agantequos froze with his blade half drawn.

"Where?"

"Why, to the queens your sisters, lady, that is all."

I peered at the dark silhouette and thought I recognized one of Gunarduilla's tribesmen.

"Don't trouble about your goods—" he went on. "We'll leave a lad on guard lest any should question your men waiting here. Now do come along. They've waited a time for ye already, and ye're none so patient a family!"

My hands had curved into claws at the thought of my sisters, but there seemed no help for it. I nodded, and heard Agantequos' sword slide into its sheath once more.

"Sister, be thou welcome!" said Rigana smoothly.

I blinked at the blaze of light and color. They had joined many hangings to make a feasting hall in the open, and a circle of men with torches formed the walls. I saw the tall figures of Quiritani warriors and others who were broader, Ai-Utu and Siwanet warriors of the old blood, in arms for the first time since Leir had won the land.

But all the brilliance seemed to radiate from the figures of the two queens. Rigana still wore crimson, and Gunarduilla a tawny robe like fallen leaves, but both of them were laden with gold. I was glad for the richness of Agantequos's blue and green chequered mantle over my gown.

"'Tis a fine hospitality that presents its invitations at the point of a sword!" I spat back at her, and Maglaros grinned at me like one of his black hounds. Senouindos was at the far end of the enclosure with his attendants, blinking as if he wondered how I had come there.

"Wast hurt?" asked Gunarduilla. "Well then, consider it a swift way to bring thee here. Indeed, we mean thee no dishonor!"

"Indeed," I mocked her, "how can one dishonor the disinherited?" I was beginning to feel my anger now.

[216]

"Disinherited?" asked Rigana coolly. "But who gave this up-start Quiritani lord the authority to cast down Briga's rightful queen?"

I stared at her as Gunarduilla filled a drinking horn and leaned forward to hold it out to me.

"Come, child, sit with us, and let us talk. . . ."

I cast a quick glance at Agantequos and saw one eyelid twitch in encouragement. Then he sat down among the warriors and I went forward to a cushion at my sisters' side.

"Your sisterly concern was not so visible this afternoon!" The mead was cool and sweet, and I drank eagerly.

"Cridilla, we *could not* help thee!" said Rigana. "We were fighting for our own rights then. But now we have won!"

"And you don't want Briga?" I asked. There was the faintest of hesitations, and then Gunarduilla laughed.

"It is Briga that would not want us, my dear. It is thy country, and now the time has come for thee to take thy rightful place as its ruling queen!"

"I do not understand—" I looked from her to Rigana and took another drink of mead. "Briga was mine already. All that lacked was for *him*"—I found I could not speak my father's name—"to confirm it. In a moment he would have done so, if thy husband, Gunarduilla, had not turned him against me!"

"Maglaros?" Gunarduilla laughed. "It was Leir's own outworn unwisdom that destroyed his love! Blame us, if thou must, for having forced him to reveal his madness and cause thee pain, but do not blame us for thy father's crime!"

"The queen of Briga must not owe her royalty to any man, nor let him rule for her!" said Rigana. "Thou wert only a tool for him, a means to power. But wouldst thou have believed it without being shown?"

"You lied to *him*! Why should I believe what you say to me?" I sat back, glaring at her. A gust of wind set the torches to flaring wildly. My sisters' faces were a confusion of light and shadow.

"Because thou hast known us since thy birth, and what we desire, and do intend," she answered me. "Remember thy passage into womanhood, Cridilla. Did we not tell thee then?"

The meadfire that burned in my belly lit a vision of three queens reigning in glory. But in those days I had never asked where, in this golden dream, was a place for the king?

"Now will we reclaim our rightful places," said Gunarduilla, and her voice rang like bronze. "Now will we bring back the old ways. The Great Goddess will rule once more, Her priestesses regain their precedence and Her priests come out of hiding."

"To Her the praise and the offerings, and the God Her consort shall be the first to honor Her," Rigana picked up the refrain, and I realized that they shared the dream.

Just so I had sometimes heard children in play. And then perhaps they would fall to squabbling about who would win the greatest glory, or the play would change to searching for bilberries, or casting stones at a mark on a tree. But these were grown women talking —these were queens.

Yet as I listened to Rigana, I found myself desiring her vision, and realized that I too had been bred up on this dream.

"Then will the Age of Gold return," said Rigana triumphantly. "Then will the sun shine and the rains fall in season, the winters be mild so that we can reclaim the open land on the downs. When the Goddess gives of Her abundance, then shall all men prosper. There shall be fat cattle in every meadow; every grain pit shall be filled with corn. And no man will call another master, for there shall be good land for all, and fields shining with peace beneath the sun. . . ."

"That is how it was, in the time of the queens," said Gunarduilla softly. "That is how it will be in Briga when thou dost rule. . . ."

I opened my eyes, shocked out of the dream by memory.

"What rule have I anywhere? My life is forfeit if I am still here when the sun sets nine nights from now!"

"Forfeit to whom? These are Leir's lands no longer!" Rigana laughed triumphantly. "He himself renounced his sovereignty. He left Briga's fate in our hands, and we will shelter thee."

"Do ye believe it is done so simply?" I stared at them. "There are many who will still call him king! Queens ye are by birth, but by his gift only have you sovereignty. And for my whole lifetime,

Briga has called *him* king! Hard will it be for any other to rule there now, and it cannot be done against his will."

"We know it. Indeed, did he not to mean to rule through thee? We could see it—it was another reason we must seem to betray thee—or nothing would change!"

"So then—what is this talk of making me queen?"

Rigana leaned forward and took my hand. "Belerion and Alba will follow us as the herd files after the bell-cow. But Briga must be won. The new lords that Leir has put in would resist you. But the old ways are stronger than you might think. For a generation the Painted People have licked their wounds and their anger has grown. The Ai-Akhsi would fight for thee, Cridilla. Thy mother was greatly loved."

I rested my head in my hands. It was hard to see through the torches' red haze. If I brought war to Briga there would be blood and fire.

"The Quiritani lords hold the fortresses," I said slowly. "Stone Fort commands the northeast and Rigodunon watches the dales. And here in the south there is Ligrodunon itself and the High Dun that Nextonos holds—" Slowly I ticked off the names.

Did my sisters know how strong these places were? They had not listened to the interminable disputations about their building, whereas I could number every stone in their walls! But in those heedless days when I listened to the chieftains it had never occurred to me to question why the king needed such great fortresses. My sisters must be right thus far—that in Briga the Painted People had never entirely accepted Quiritani rule. The duns were meant to keep them down.

And it seemed to me that in any clash of forces they would probably succeed.

"It cannot be done without destroying the people I wished to serve." I cast a quick glance at Maglaros. Where did he stand in all this? He was Quiritani too.

"Then they must be divided," said Gunarduilla practically. "Take Nextonos or another as thy consort and add his strength to thy own!"

"And what about my child," I said gently.

"Nextonos has already sworn he would accept it. And it is well to establish from the beginning that to bear to whom she chooses and in her own time and season is the privilege of a queen."

"And so I must marry for policy? Where then is the *freedom* of a queen?"

Rigana shrugged. "We did so, and with less choice than thee. Thou must not expect to come into thy power without some sacrifice!"

"I have lost my father's love already!" I burst out suddenly. "Must I now reject the father of my child? I have a husband! He is the only one by whom I have never been betrayed!"

"Keep him then!" snapped Gunarduilla. "He does not matter! Wilt claim Briga and join us, sister? That is the only decision required of thee now!"

Once more wind swept through the encampment. I heard a distant shout as someone's tent caught fire. If I chose war it would be like that everywhere. . . . And for what? It would not win me back my father's love.

I turned to Agantequos.

"You have the right now to advise me," I said stiffly. "What do you desire me to do?"

He swallowed, but his face did not change. "I say . . . that you must choose. . . ."

Suddenly I was laughing. "He understands me! He knows that to be faithful I must be free! Why didn't my father know that? Why?" Someone pressed the meadhorn into my hand and I gulped more of its sweet fire.

"Choose—" hissed Rigana.

"Sister," echoed Gunarduilla, "thou must choose!"

I struggled upright. "Doom take ye all! War as ye will—I'll not set my own fields aflame! You've tried to twist me to your own purposes, all of you, and my father the worst because he pretended it was out of love! I'll go with the one man who has never lied to me. At least he's honest about what he wants me for!" As I staggered Agantequos caught me in his arms.

"Go then!" cried Gunarduilla. "But don't think you can come

begging for the kingdom you're throwing away! You are our sister no more!"

"Get her away! Get her gone!" Rigana was shrieking, but it was my father's voice that I heard. Lightning flared; I saw my sisters' faces stark as skulls, and behind them the spectral shape of Bear Mother, weeping.

"Our protection will cover you to the coast, outlander," said Gunarduilla, "but it would be well now if you were away."

Sorrow wracked me, and I sobbed aloud.

"It is you who will weep! It is you who will burn!" I had never found words easy, but they tore through me now. "I see smoking fields and blood upon the ground. Woe to those who are forsworn."

"She is mad," said Gunarduilla to Agantequos. "Go while you can." The rest of her words were lost as the thunder came.

The battle of the gods continued as we hurried back to the horses. Lightning had struck one of the roundhouses and the thatch was afire. People darted in and out of the buildings, shouting to each other to get blankets to beat out the flames. And close behind each bolt of brightness came the clap and clatter of thunder, absolute, deafening. Agantequos's strong hand on my arm was my lifeline as we ran, one pair among the many shapes scurrying in and out of the dun.

Crow and Agantequos's men were still waiting with the horses. But Maglaros's guard had been replaced by someone bulkier. For a moment I hoped. Then light from the burning roundhouse flared and I recognized Artocoxos.

"Lady," he said hoarsely in a gap between claps of thunder, "when you leave us the light will go from this land. But tonight there is no reasoning with him. And truly, I did try."

"Oh, we are all mad tonight—" I heard the shrillness in my own laugh. "Stay with him. He will need your counsel more than ever now. Send word to me of what passes if you can find a trustworthy messenger."

Artocoxos brought my hand to his forehead as if now, in this moment of my most complete dispossession, I had become his queen. I flinched as a wisp of burning straw brushed my arm. Thunder rumbled again, but more distantly.

"And thou—" Changing languages, I turned to Crow. "Thou must stay to make him laugh. . . ."

Crow gulped and hiccoughed and shook himself like a dog.

"When in daylight no one sees—
While burning, men freeze,
and the daughter is mother,
then one fool knows another!"

He slid to his knees and threw his arms around me. "This one is laughing, lady, canst hear him?" Crow said, but his tears were wet on my arm. Then the shifting wind brought the smoke smell to the horses and my mare reared.

"Mount quickly," Agantequos shouted. I clutched at the pony's mane and let him push me up onto her back.

Then we were all moving down the hill. Behind me I saw the dark shapes of my friends backlit by the embers' red glare. But Bear Mother's transparent figure floated on before.

A cold voice within was asking why I looked back at all. Let the old fool live alone, since he had rejected me. The disaster I foresaw was of his own making, and a new life waited for me across the sea. Why was I weeping for Leir now?

But I could not stop the tears as we rode away from Ligrodunon. The lightning flared fitfully from the far hills now, and thunder muttered a sullen commentary, but there was no moisture in it; never a drop of rain.

After that first night I stopped weeping, but it was the husk of a woman that Agantequos brought to the chalk cliffs in the Banalisioi lands. The trading bark that would take us to the Great Land was waiting, round-bellied and sturdy as the ponies we were leaving behind.

"And this is the bride?" The trader was a little, sallow-skinned man of no tribe that I knew. "That's a wager I've lost, then, for never did I think ye would bring her home. But she looks sickly. Breeding already, is she?" He eyed Agantequos with respect.

I sat on the shore and sifted the coarse grains through my fingers as if I had never seen sand before. A low mist clung to the heaving waters. Fog had settled in behind us too, cutting us off from the fishing village and the cliffs and the dry rustlings of the oak woods and the downs where the grass was already ripening to an unseasonable gold. Only this circle where land met sea was real.

"Cridilla, it is time to go—"

There was a reason why I did not want to get into the boat, but I could not remember it. I let Agantequos help me to my feet and drape his heavy cloak around me. Then he lifted me in his arms and splashed around the side of the bark so that he could load me, wrapped securely as some treasure he was stealing, on board.

I huddled where he had set me, watching the pallid sand and the grey shore dissolve into the mist as we pulled away. Then the leathern sail flapped, the boat slid sickeningly down the swell, and my guts cramped in warning. A second lurch, and I was scrambling for the rail and spewing my breakfast over the side.

I had thought myself past this sort of thing, after several years of puttering in a skittish leather curragh around the shores of the Misty Isle. But that had been six years ago, when both my body and mind were strong.

"My poor love—" Agantequos's arm went around my shoulders. "I had forgotten it takes you this way. Never mind, you'll grow accustomed."

He was wrong—I could tell already that this was going to be as bad as it had ever been, and if I starved to death before the passage was completed, I would not care.

To either side the mist closed in around us. So close to shore, the water was still aswirl with sand scoured up by the waves. Below the haphazard ripplings of the sea forest, but beyond that the water was cloudy, pulsing with movement that had nothing to do with the tide. My senses were in turmoil; I perceived the world with preternatural clarity, but as if through a veil.

I leaned farther and farther, trying to see.

"Cridilla—you'll fall in, beloved. What were you staring at down there?" Agantequos gathered me into his arms again.

"There's a serpent . . . in the deeps. Lady Asaret told me. Once it tried to eat my father . . . now it wants to eat me. . . ."

"Not while I am here—" Agantequos murmured, cradling me against him. "Not while I can keep you from harm!" There were things against which neither his strength nor mine were any protection, but it helped a little to hear the words.

"Is she mad?" came the whisper above the lapping of the waves. It was Cuno, I thought—his voice was deeper than the others'. "Did not her father think himself a swan and try to fly?"

"It was her grandfather, fool—" Dimly I wondered where the bard had got that story; I knew so little of the family my father had left behind. But I was too miserable to care.

"Her family, anyway—all mad. What an alliance! Won't the Council just be pleased!"

"Hush! She is our lady now. . . ."

Had Agantequos heard? Well, that did not matter either. The new land to which I was going could hardly be more cruel than the one I was leaving. I groaned and clung to Agantequos's strong arm as the ship leaped beneath us. A damp wind skimmed spray from the waves.

"It will be better in the Great Land . . ." he crooned. "Moridunon has stout walls braced with wood and filled with earth and stone. Each night a hundred brave warriors eat and drink inside my hall. There are fat cattle and sheep heavy with wool, and there is no fruit so sweet as the apples that grow on our trees. . . ."

I managed a smile. "On the Misty Isle, you spoke of mist veiling the sun as it rose above the marshes, and the scent of the apple blossom in the spring."

For a moment the boat wavered sickeningly at the top of the wave, then it wallowed down the other side. I whimpered and dove for the rail. The sail flapped loudly, and the captain yelled at his men. Then the sailors got the unwieldy thing around and suddenly the boat surged forward before the freshening wind.

"Even the ship wants to be on her way," said Agantequos. He moistened a cloth and gently wiped my face clean. "And look—the wind is blowing the fog away!"

I lifted my head. The grey pall that had weighted my spirits was moving. The swooping seabirds appeared and vanished through the currents that swirled in the air, but something glimmered beyond them.

And then for a moment the breeze blew strongly, and I saw behind us white cliffs like the walls of a fortress mightier than any of my father's duns. A fortress, indeed, for those chalk cliffs defended the Island of the Mighty, and against me its gates were closed.

I rested my forehead upon the boat's side, and the salt sea received my salt tears.

Chapter

13

An Assembly without reproach, without deceit,
Without injury, without shame,
Without dispute or seizure,
Without theft or reparation . . .
Wheat and milk on every height,
Peace and fair weather, because of her
Have been given to the tribes of the Greeks
To maintain justice.

—*The Metrical Dindshenchas*, IV

For three days and three nights we sailed out of sight of land, guided by the watery sun and a glimpse of the stars. Or perhaps it was an age of the world. By the time we sighted a low grey streak upon the horizon I was hollow with hunger and light-headed as a spirit approaching the shores of the Otherworld.

But it was a very earthly landscape that appeared as we drew in to the shore. Beyond the dunes rose a thickly forested, rolling countryside, with an occasional wisp of smoke to show that people lived here. There was a flutter of movement on the headland, then the faint clear call of a horn. We had been seen.

We rounded a point and of a sudden saw rearing out of the quicksands a great upthrust of stone. This rock was far greater than the sacred seamount in Belerion, its summit crowned with standing stones.

"The Hill of the Horned One!" exclaimed Cuno. "Now we are near home!"

We eased in toward a cluster of thatched stone houses that clung to the inward curve of the headland. On the stony shore folk were gathering. I looked at Agantequos uncertainly.

"They will have been awaiting us," he said confidently. "They will rejoice when they see that I have brought them a queen!"

I had been born Lady of Briga, but by what right could he give me a country I did not know? It was not only the treacherous waters beneath the keel that made me anxious.

"They will think you have brought them a hag—" I patted clumsily at my hair, tangled and lank after two weeks of traveling.

"Not when they see your belly!" He laid his hand upon my womb, which in the last week had begun to curve, as if the creature that swam within was unaffected by its mother's aversion to the sea. I set my own hand over his, and for a moment it was all right again.

Then stones scraped our keel and a last thrust of the poles ran us up upon the shore. The boat canted sideways and stuck there, quivering to the lapping of the waves, and people surged toward us. Agantequos lifted me onto the land and I set foot upon the earth of my exile. As we moved up the slope to the village it grew steadier and I took a deep breath, feeling the first real stir of interest since I had left Ligrodunon. This land might be alien, but at least it was solid ground.

Agantequos's stronghold was located on a rise surrounded by thickly forested rolling hills. It was not so imposing as Ligrodunon, and the marks of charring on the timbers of the great gate were still visible beneath the new building that Agantequos had done. But Moridunon was stoutly built and well manned. And for me, the center of safety was our boxbed in the hall. When I lay warm in his arms I knew that here was the heart of the world.

In the fields the grain was paling to gold as the season turned toward harvest. The village folk were cutting grass in the meadows, but many of the young men and women of the clan were still in the hill pastures with their cows. In the dun there were fresh flax and newly shorn fleeces to be dealt with, just as at home. I was glad to fall into the routine of labor with the other women, and for once I had no desire to exchange the spindle for the spear. My condition made a bond between us, and if I had brought no treasure in bride-gifts, I was giving the people the greater gift of an heir of the princely line.

It was easy enough to tell which of the women had shared Agantequos's bed before I came. They were mostly village girls, brought in to serve in the dun, brown-haired like my mother's folk—like me. These folk had nearly lost their memories of a time before the Quiritani came. When the girls saw that I did not hate them they attached themselves to my service. Brenna and Eloret in particular became my constant companions. This did not recommend me to the bright-haired women who had hoped to be his queen, but it was good to have someone who was loyal to me.

And so the Horse Moon waned, and the Moon of Claiming began to swell in the sky. Each day the farmers tested the seed heads for ripeness, folk gathered the goods they would take to the great market fair, and the oak priests began to prepare for the festival there.

"Of course we are going to the fair!" exclaimed Agantequos as we lay entwined beneath the bedfurs. "I must take the role of the Young God in the ritual. And we'll go to the cattle market as well. I owe you a bride-price, and there you can begin your own herd."

I kissed him, being enough of a Quiritani to count wealth in cows. He had known how I must feel, with no resources of my own.

"And when you have the cattle, it will be easy enough to find men to run them for you, young warriors, eager for prestige. You can have your own Companions, and, after the child is born, lead them as well."

"Then you don't desire me to dwindle into a spinster who sits by the fire?"

His fingers traced the tattoo upon my belly, bulging now with the growth of the child, and I shivered and reached for him.

"Now would I have wooed a warrior woman out of the north if that's what I was wanting?" His hand strayed lower and I giggled, knowing what he wanted now.

Then the babe within me kicked and we stilled, watching in wonder as the Bear on my belly flexed and stirred.

"He will be a great warrior that grows beneath the sign of the Bear. . . ."

"She," I corrected him.

"Like her mother!" He grinned and kissed me, and then our limbs were sliding together in the sweet convolutions of love and neither of us said anything for a long while.

It was the Feast of Lugus and the harvest was under way. As we rode past the ripe barley a wind sprang up, bending the seed heads so that the light lay along the beards. Suddenly the field was a-shimmer with silver and my heart lifted. In another clearing they were reaping, and the stubble glistened in the sunlight, all a-flutter with gleaning birds.

Behind us came the folk of Agantequos's retinue and my own. We made a fine sight in the sunshine, cloaked in our brightest mantles and glowing with amber and gold. My husband chattered with a kind of feverish excitement. I understood. Leir had always gone silent and snappish before the ceremonies. And then we were riding into the marsh meadow before the great Rock of the Horned One, dry enough at this season to serve as a fairground. Looming over the festivities was a pole to which had been fixed a straw image of the god, with bull's horns, a serpent belt around his waist, in one hand a purse, and in the other a staff upon which ram-headed serpents twined.

The oak priests came forward to ready Agantequos for the ceremonies, and his Companions scattered to look at cattle or join in the games. I was left with my women to enjoy the fair. Everyone in Morilandis who had anything to sell was here, and merchants from all over the world seemed to have come as well. Men of the Carnutes had come north with cattle for the market, and Hellenes with amphorae of heady southern wine. And there were Etruscans as well, selling bronzework and pottery, and Ligurians and Turdetani from Iberia with silver jewelry and fine patterned cloth, complaining about how the struggle between Tartessos and Gades had hampered trade. And it was not only around the Middle Sea that the world was upset by war.

"Fighting to the east o' here, so they say—" came a man's voice nearby. I continued sorting through embroidery threads, but I found myself straining to hear.

"Always is fighting. Cows or women, 'tis all the same!" His companion laughed.

"Not this way. This be a new people, moving west with their womenfolk and little ones in great carts and driving their herds along behind. 'Tis not cattle they're wanting, but land, and will fight to the death to take it, having nothing to lose."

"Let 'em. The kings will settle it come Samonios meet. Now I'm thirsty, and old Brochagnos, he makes good ale. You come along!"

"Think you it's no matter?" the first man asked as their voices grew fainter. "Where will the tribes they drive out go? An' they turn up at your gates, old man, you'll fight them or lose your land!"

I traded some of my precious salt for the crimson thread and moved onward, mulling over what I had heard. I used to discuss this sort of thing with my father in the evenings when we sat before the fire. I tried not to wonder who he talked to now. It was odd, though, to think that the sort of thing that had happened in my homeland was going on everywhere. And who was pushing these newcomers? They were like the froth of the flood that rushes down from the dales, fed by rains that have fallen on invisible heights far away.

I was seeking the herb sellers, hoping that they would have yarrow here, and near the edge of the fair I found them. The first one I saw was a plump woman of middle age, ginger-haired as any Quiritani, but wearing a gown of a blue so deep it was almost black, like the priestesses at home.

"About four moons along, are you not, and past the first queasiness?" The woman's bright eyes went from my belly to my face again. "And it is your first, I think, for your muscles are still firm. But your hips are broad enough; you will do well—"

She had not needed an answer. Flushing, I asked for the herbs.

"'Tis not yarrow ye'll be wanting, my child. Too much could bring on an early labor. Try the chamomile for a soothing tea and raspberry leaf for a toner now."

"You seem to know a lot about it—" I said as she hunted through her baskets.

"I am a midwife—"

"Are you a wisewoman, a priestess?" Did the Quiritani even have such things? Something serene and self-possessed in this woman's face reminded me of Lady Asaret.

"Of course—ah, you are the half-blood foreign queen. But why are you surprised?"

"Only the women of my mother's people are priestesses in my land."

"All peoples must have priestesses as well as priests, child, and honor the Lady, or how could they survive? Our own tradition here has simply added to the knowledge of those who came before."

"Where do you live? When my labor begins, will you come to me?" Until now I had not realized how much I feared to bear a child with no woman of the old wisdom by.

"Oh, we all know Mother Nesta," said Brenna, behind me. "She travels from dun to dun, treating the cases that our own women do not understand."

The priestess looked at me. "You are the daughter of the swan, and a warrior-maid. I have heard much of you . . ." she murmured. "And I see that in the Island of the Mighty they still train the queens in the old ways. But you will have no need to send for me, child. When your time comes I will know."

"What do you mean," I asked, "about the swan?"

Before she could answer, the shrilling of horns split the air. A sudden deep drumbeat throbbed through the encampment. The sun had already sunk nearly to the horizon; the ruddy light of its westering kindled the sea with sparks of gold.

"The ceremony begins," Mother Nesta began to pack the bunches of herbs back into her basket, and Eloret helped her to roll up the hide she had been sitting on. "I will tell you one day, but now we must see the sacrifice."

They had laid hurdles on the marshland below the Rock to make a platform. The white-clad priests were already in position for the ritual; the flames of their torches flickered pale against a still-bright sky. People were gathering in a rough crescent on the firmer ground, a shifting, multihued throng whose colors were fading with the light.

With my girls and the priestess, I took my place in the bower. The pulsing of the drum was like the heartbeat that the child hears in the womb. A chill pebbled the flesh along my arms, although I was not cold, as one of the priests came to the center of the platform and lifted his staff.

> *"The grain feeds on the earth,*
> *The folk feed on the grain,*
> *Earth feeds on the folk;*
> *So it is, so it was, so it will be—*
> *Eater and eaten, feeder and fed,*
> *All that dwell on earth must become."*
> *Hail to the hero who shall harvest them!"*

This was like the rite that Talorgenos and his fellows performed when we brought the cattle down from the pastures in the hills. Behind the priests, the western sky flared as if it already consumed the sacrifice, but the face of the Rock was becoming an open door to darkness.

Upon the platform appeared a figure that glistened with the harvest gold of the straw from which cape and mask and skirt had been made. Even his shield and spear were of cleverly plaited straw. The drums woke to sudden life and pipes twittered madly. The figure began to dance about the platform, brandishing his spear.

My own body twitched in sympathy as my muscles remembered the training dances that both Horse and I had learned. I knew the dancer and the dance, but I had never seen the energy that blazed around him. I could not look away.

He is tranced, I thought. *He cannot fall!*

The drums were beating in my blood. I only realized that I had taken a step toward him when Mother Nesta gripped my arm.

"Not yet, child. You cannot go to him now—"

A shiver ran through the crowd as another figure joined the Bright God there. This also was male, but the straw that clothed him was blackened. I saw plaited horns, and around the waist a serpent of straw. Like the image above the marketplace, he carried a staff around which twined snakes with the heads and horns of rams.

A hissing of rattles had joined the throb of the drums. The Black God moved ponderously toward his rival, but each slow step was full of power. They circled each other like the champions who meet before the war-bands clash.

"Why does he wear serpents?" I whispered. They had not done it this way at home.

"He comes from the Rock," said the priestess, "and the power of the Serpent grows within. From the deeps He comes, in the name of the Serpent Mother who dwells there. It is Her power that the Rock contains. He comes to deny Her fruits to men."

I stared at her, trying to remember—in my vision in the cavern I had not seen the serpent, I had *been* the serpent, spiraling into the sky. But my power had flowed freely into the world.

"Why?" I whispered. "Why must it be this way?"

"Do you take the gifts of the Goddess for granted? When your time comes you will understand the cost of bringing life into the world. But She is not without mercy. The Young God is Her child and Her champion."

The two gods stamped and twirled, feinted and parried in a deadly dance. The other man was good, and though he did not have Agantequos's grace, he moved with disturbing power. The Bright God must win, but when the rite was properly performed, one always wondered if perhaps this time he would fail, and the people be doomed to starve.

The oak priests began to circle the fighters. The figures flickered dark and bright in the spaces between their white robes. They closed in with a shout, and for a moment there was silence. Then came a bellowing that seemed to arise from the belly of the earth, and something struck the platform with a rhythm that was not that of the drums.

The priests moved apart again. The Dark God had been transformed into a monster that roared in the torchlight. I blinked, and saw that it was a black bull like the wild cattle of the hills, with wicked twisting horns. In the last of the dusk, the Rock reared up like the Bull's black shadow, a gaping doorway to that land from which no one returns. I shivered, for I could feel the power in it now, and it was angry.

The Bright God had exchanged his spear for a long-handled axe with a butterfly blade of bright bronze. The bull stamped and lowered his head, snuffling angrily. Now the oak priests drew back to form a barrier of white behind him. But before him the beast would be seeing freedom, with only a single straw figure to block the way. And he would smell an enemy.

If the platform had been covered with fallen leaves, not a one would have stirred as Agantequos eased forward. But the wind was blowing from behind him. The bull snorted angrily; great muscles rippled in his massive neck as he began to move. This was no fleet stag such as Horse and I had hunted on the Island, but a creature of malevolent might. Once more it was Nesta's hand that kept me from going to him.

"He must do it—" whispered the priestess. "He must slay the Old God. You cannot interfere. . . ."

I would have been too late if I had tried, for the bull was charging. Agantequos pivoted; the bronze blade flashed down, and the whole world echoed to the bull's roar of rage. Then the sound was lost in the great exultant clamor of the crowd. The bull staggered, and the bronze blade bit once more. A great wind rushed past us, and the oak priests dragged the thrashing body to the edge of the platform to catch the life that was bleeding away in the vessels below.

"Now," said Nesta with satisfaction, "the Mother sets the harvest free. They will pour the blood upon the Rock, and She will take the spirit of the dead into Her womb to be reborn, but we will eat the flesh, and live."

"Is there no other way but this?" I asked. "That the old must be brought down in destruction to bring new life to the world?"

"Of course there is another way." She patted my stomach. "As you will learn. Though even that is not without dangers. But the cycle of the seasons must move on. The Goddess must be free."

I sighed, remembering things my sisters had said to me. "If we were in my country I would bring you to Lady Asaret. It would be interesting to hear what you and she would say."

"I would like to meet a woman of the old wisdom," Mother Nesta replied thoughtfully. "I would like to know what we have learned, and what we have lost."

The posts of our bower shuddered as people swirled around the platform. The head of the bull had already replaced the image of the Horned God on the pole, and the body was being swiftly butchered for the cauldron. The Bright God stood on the platform, brandishing the bloody axe triumphantly.

"The God must lie down with the Goddess!" someone shouted. "Give the hero his bride!"

I cannot do it . . . I thought as the swirling crowd swept back toward me. *The old king's blood is still on his hands.* But it was like being caught in a flood. The flimsy barrier of branches went down and it was all that Mother Nesta and my women could do to keep me upright as I was borne toward the king.

The poles were slippery with the blood of the bull. Straw scratched my skin as they thrust me into the Bright God's arms. I swayed; was he my support or my captor? I knew only that I could not move away.

"Behold your lady!" Agantequos cried. "Behold your queen!" And the crowd roared in answer as the bull had roared; I felt the power of their belief filling me like strong mead.

"The God! You are the Young God, the Champion!" the people cried.

"And she is the Goddess, the fertile Mother of mankind!" Agantequos drew the cloth of my gown tight across my belly. His strength flowed into me from behind, and the need of the people before me beat against my awareness like the heat of a fire.

"You must respond to them—" came his whisper in my ear.

I faced the folk to whom my marriage had bound me, and began to lift my arms in the ancient blessing. One of the priests pressed the ram-headed serpents that had twined around the staff of the Black God into my hands. Vision wavered, so that at one moment

I saw serpents of plaited straw and in the next real snakes writhing in my fists.

But I was not afraid. I *was* the Serpent. I held the snakes higher, smiling. Surely I had done this before. . . . In some other time and place I had blessed a rejoicing crowd. But my breasts should have been bare. Power surged through the great pile of stone behind me, and in that moment I understood what I must do.

Slowly I brought the serpents forward, opening myself to the energy. If there had been no outlet, it would have destroyed me, but the patterns in which the serpents had been plaited allowed them to channel the power. It rushed through me and out through the spirals woven into the straw, over the waiting people, over the land. For an eternal moment I stood, arms extended in an ecstasy of blessing. Then the rush dwindled, and I sagged back into Agantequos's arms.

"Indeed, they teach their queens the old ways, over there . . ." Mother Nesta had spoken those words, but I did not hear them with my ears. I was aware of many voices. The land that I had thought so alien was calling my name.

"Thou art Goddess!" came the cry, and in that moment it was true.

That night Agantequos and I feasted on the flesh of the slain bull. Then they conducted us to the summit of the Rock. Along the shore below us, couples that had pledged each other at the fair were celebrating their union. Torches sparkled among the fields like scattered stars. But for the king, a bed had been prepared beside the standing stones.

"You did not tell me about this part of the ceremony—" I said when our attendants had gone.

"I did not know," Agantequos replied. "I have performed the role of the Young God, but I have never married the Goddess before." He unlatched his belt and tossed his kilt away, then he reached out to me. For a moment I resisted the response that in these last weeks had become instinctive.

"You have never married anyone before . . ." I said slowly.

"Bringing me across the sea may count as marriage by capture, but there was no wedding. What we did that first time was mating, not marriage. I told you so—"

"I remember." His gaze held mine, a little unfocused with passion, or the mead he had drunk at the feasting, or perhaps with memory. "Cridilla, I remember everything that you have said to me. But I have known ever since we were children on the Misty Isle that you were the only woman I could wed."

"And now you have me. Are you satisfied?" I listened to my own words in wonder. My flesh tingled with need for him already, but my spirit had somehow become detached from it.

"Do I?" He stared at me. "Does the ship possess the sea? Do you know how often in the night I have watched you, afraid to close my eyes lest you disappear? Marriage by capture! Is that what you think of me? I am trying to be a king, Cridilla, and you are my queen! After this evening you cannot deny that. I felt the power flow through you to the land."

"My body understands," I whispered. "As it understands how to respond to you and how to cradle your child. It is my mind that still mourns what I have lost." A night bird called from the slopes below, but here it was still. Against the stars I saw the thrusting silhouettes of the standing stones.

"The stones are watching us," I said then. "What do they want from me?"

"They wait for you to do the office of the queen," he said hoarsely.

"But I do not belong to this land. . . ."

"You are a woman. There must be another way, or how are the rites continued when a queen's line fails? Tonight you served the people as a priestess. Does the Goddess care where those who do Her will were born?"

I remembered that sense of having shown the serpents to the people in some other place and body, many times before. That power owed nothing to my bloodlink with my land.

"If you can give yourself to the land, then you will belong. If you give yourself to me, I will be king," Agantequos said desperately. The sense of something listening around us grew stronger.

"Did the oak priests teach you that?"

"Spirit Bear taught me, on Caiactis, after you went away."

His voice had faded to a whisper, but I laughed, for suddenly I understood a number of things, including where he had learned the love skills that had kindled my desire.

Agantequos knelt and set his palms against the moist earth.

"Lady of this high place, hear me. Speak to this pigheaded woman who does not understand that she is Your image to me. I love her, but it is You I must serve. I beseech You, make her understand!"

I held my breath, for pressure was building around us, and I saw a haze of light flicker above the stones.

"Touch the ground, Cridilla—" Now there was iron in Agantequos's tone, and I sensed behind him the power of the Young God.

But it was the energy of the Earth Herself that drew me to the cool grass. Agantequos and I were both on our knees, but his features were in shadow. He was a man, and ready to serve me, and suddenly that was all that signified. I reached out, and our hands met, palm to palm. Light was beginning to shimmer around us. I saw his face pure and resolute as the face of the god whose image he was to me. His eyes widened as he looked into mine.

"Son of Vorequos, will you lie with Me?" The voice was not my own.

"I will—" he answered steadily, though I could feel the fine tremors that ran through him. I was trembling too, but I had no will to stop what was happening.

Someone was taking form behind me.

It was Her voice that spoke through me, Her hands that unfastened the brooches that held my gown; She who lifted breasts grown heavy as ripe fruit. The king licked his lips as he saw the brown nipples hardening.

"Will you give your life and your strength to serve Me?"

"I have sworn it already, when they gave me the white rod of sovereignty—"

"Then come to Me. . . ."

That Other overshadowed me entirely now. I eased back on my

haunches, unfastened the woven sash of my gown and pulled the folds of fabric away. Soft hands stroked sensuously across the smooth curve of my belly, and the king's eyes went unfocused with desire. Then I slid my fingers between my legs and parted the sweet petals of flesh there, and he moaned.

A fine tremor traveled through Agantequos's flesh and I laughed softly. He bent to kiss first one breast, then the other, and my own breath quickened. Then he bowed down before me and saluted the doorway that I had opened, and I began to ache with need. The moist breath of the night was heavy with the scent of my desire. Agantequos drew a deep breath, his nostrils flaring.

I fell back upon the grass, thighs opening, and the king came to me, lowering his body over mine with agonizing control. As his phallus brushed me, the slow heat that had been building within my body burst into sudden flame. Then my fingers closed around the hard strength of his manhood, and I guided him through the door.

As my legs locked his hips the king clutched my shoulders. His power was filling me, but it was not enough. I whimpered and wrapped my arms around him, nails digging into sweat-slick skin. This was something more than the familiar sweet friction of flesh against flesh that my body had learned to welcome. With each thrust, the light around us grew brighter, but however desperately he drove at me, She who possessed my body demanded a deeper fulfillment.

"Please . . ." he whispered. "Please. . . ."

"*What will you give Me?*" I did not speak aloud, but Agantequos stilled, quivering like a bent bow, and I knew that he had heard.

"Blood and seed, blood and seed . . . my very life if there be need!"

"So be it. . . ." Appalled, I heard my own lips accepting his offering.

But already my body was constricting. Agantequos cried out in an agony of release and I felt the rush of his spirit pouring through me, and the emptiness at the heart of the world was filled.

And then for a time, there was neither Agantequos nor Cridilla, but a single completed Being that encompassed the two human forms entwined upon the summit and those that lay clasped in each other's arms along the shore, and the cattle, and the trees, and the growing grain, with the same uncompromising love.

Human awareness could not long support such knowledge. Presently we fell back into our separate bodies again, and Agantequos had just the strength to draw his cloak around us before sleep's dark wing brought us blessed oblivion, warded by the watchful stones.

But though my husband embraced my body, in the still hours of the night my spirit wandered. I found myself back in Ligrodunon, but it was warriors of Belerion who slept beside the fire in the feasting hall, and my sister Rigana and Senouindos who lay in the royal bed. I drifted toward one of the smaller buildings. My father's Companions lay rolled in their cloaks in a kind of shed against the wall of the dun, snoring. From inside came the faint thread of a song.

> *"A wolf to ward the sheep, a cow the bulls to keep—
> what wonders there be . . ."*

I must be a spirit, I thought then, for with a thought, I passed through the hide across the door. An oil lamp was flickering beside the cold hearth, and my father lay stretched on a pallet of straw. It was Crow, crouched on the floor beside him, who sang.

> *"The man becomes a child . . .*

He broke off, staring, and I realized that he could see me.
"Hast come to mock us," he whispered, "shining like the sun?"
"What is my father doing in this place?" I asked.
Crow shook his head as if he could not hear. "Thou didst well to depart. Leave the witless ones to their sleep, night wanderer! There is nothing for thee here!"
His hand moved in a sign of dismissal, and I found myself whirling back through the dark.

I woke in the dawning, clasped securely in my husband's arms. My body still remembered the sweet satisfaction that follows love, but my eyes were sore, and when Agantequos asked if I had been weeping, I had no reply. He pulled me close, and this time we shared the comfort of our bodies as mortal man and woman, and all was well again, for a little while.

Chapter

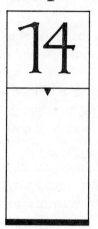

O Nessa, thou art in peril;
Let every one rise at thy birth-giving . . .
Be not sorrowful, O wife,
A head of hundreds and of hosts
Of the world will he be, thy son.

—*The Birth of Conchobar, Irish Text*

A fter the festival, there was a period of peace when I felt that the Moriritones had accepted me and that I had been linked with their land. In that time I wanted no more than to be Agantequos's fertile queen. And so we moved through the golden days of harvest, and the darker days as winter drew near.

At the Feast of Samonios Agantequos left to attend the Assembly at the sanctuary of the Carnutes. I was already too big with child for traveling to be comfortable, and I stayed with my women in the dun. It was there that the messengers from home found me.

For days the world had been murmurous with the sound of falling rain. Rain beat dully against the thick thatch of the hall and splattered into the spreading puddles. Even when no rain was falling, water dripped and trickled everywhere. Those who had to tend the beasts came back mired to the knees. Inside, the hearthfires did valiant battle with the damp air, and the smoke that curled into the high peak of the roof added its own harsh pungence to the reek of wet wool.

"Still raining . . ." One of the serving men shook out his cape of oiled skin and hung it on a hook by the door. The puff of damp air that had followed him dissipated as the heavy hides that covered the opening were hooked securely once more.

"Goddess pity those who must ride in it," said a man who was mending harness farther down the hearth. "Especially now, as night falls."

"Think you that our lord will be returning soon?" asked Eloret, who was stirring the gruel. "We'll need to be grinding more grain, and the wheat from the storage pit by the south wall is almost gone."

"If we open a new shaft in this weather, water may get in." Brenna cast a quick glance at me and I nodded. "We would have to bring all the grain inside. Perhaps by the time the warriors get home we'll have had a freeze. A good hard frost will make all tight once more."

I plucked another handful of wool from the basket beside me, feeding it into the strand that spiraled between my fingers and down to the shaft as the spindle whirled.

"But I am thinking that it would be well to bring in another ham," Brenna went on.

"That is true—" I agreed, wondering once more that the woman who had managed this household for years before I came should seek my approval so cheerfully. "And I would that I could help you, but these days I am a walking stomach-sausage myself."

"Never fear, lady." Brenna laughed. "The wealth in your storehouse is worth more to our folk than food."

The babe within me kicked sharply, and I patted my stomach. "Peace, little warrior, they are praising you. . . . Wealth indeed—I feel like a cow in calf."

"It will not be forever," said one of the older women, "and you will think it soon enough, lady, when you lie heaving in the straw."

I set my spindle turning again. Wherever there were women together, there was always someone who was bearing, and old women to frighten her with tales of their own deliveries. After my womanhood rites I had been allowed to assist in the birthchamber, and I had seen the wonder of a child's head emerging from between its mother's spread thighs.

I knew all about birthing—or I had thought so—but as my body swelled I began to wonder. I had at least a moon before my delivery. Unless things went very wrong, it would be a week at least before the king returned. I could not wish him back again and I must wait for the baby to be born. But there was no harm in wishing for an end to these storms.

"Sing to us, Sobuiaca." I smiled at the youngest of my girls. "I am wearied of the patter of rain and the crackling of the fire!" She began a riddling song, and soon the chorus was echoing around the hall.

From outside came the sound of male voices and a horse's neigh. We stilled, staring at the door as if our singing had brought the men back early after all.

But the first figure who pushed past the hides was one of our herdboys, followed by two strange warriors in plaids too sodden to recognize. Then the taller of them stripped off his cloak and handed it to one of the women, and I stood up, the spindle slipping unheeded from my hands.

"Vorcuns!" I exclaimed. "Is it really you, man? In Briga's name, what are you doing here?"

"It is," came the answer, "or a poor drowned ghost of him! Lady, I will tell you everything, only let me lie a moment by your fire!"

The second man shook badger-grey locks and I realized that he must be Nodontios, though both of them were half masked by splattered mire.

"Find dry clothes for them! Sobuiaca, bring some of that hot broth." I clapped my hands and women went scurrying.

"A queen in her own hall! Ah, 'tis worth being worn to the bone to see you," said Vorcuns.

I smiled, but I was too busy pulling the wet clothes off of him to reply. By the time we had the two men settled by the fire he had sobered again.

"How fares your lord?" I asked then.

"As the herd stallion who has lost his last fight but is still too strong to be driven away," said Nodontios slowly.

I stared at him, trying not to let pity replace the anger that had sustained me. Had Leir sent them to beg me to return to him?

"Or too stubborn," added Vorcuns. "He is still my king, mind you, and I will likely die serving him, but a more stubborn old man it was never my misfortune to meet!"

"Do you think that he should have let the queens disband the war-host without a word?" asked his companion, frowning.

"Reassigned, Gunarduilla put it—the meanest men taken into her guard and the prettiest into Rigana's," said Vorcuns, spitting into the fire. "And a poor chieftain he would have been not to protest. They say that one of Zayyar's nephews has begun to gather men of his own. But it was not reasonable in Leir to insist on keeping them all with him as he moved about the country."

I looked from one to the other. "When was he ever a reasonable man? But what word did he give you for me?"

They exchanged a quick glance and looked away.

"Is it an ill word? Do not doubt my courage to hear it!"

Again there was silence. I stared at them until finally Vorcuns met my gaze.

"It was Artocoxos, lady, who sent us here. . . ."

Once more I must keep my feelings from my face. Would I have pitied my own father if he had begged me to return, or stayed loyal to the father of my child? I could not say; I knew only the pain of not having been asked to choose.

"And what word does Artocoxos send?" I asked at last.

"He bids us say that when you left us you took the luck of the land," Nodontios replied. "You are flourishing, but this summer your sister Gunarduilla miscarried of a child. Coming here we passed well-stocked steadings and well-fed folk. It is not so at home. The rains came too late to help the crops, but in good time to ruin the harvest. This year there was a great autumn slaughtering of cattle and sheep, for there was not enough fodder stored to keep them through the cold, but the beasts we did kill were such poor things that the people will be hard put to make the meat last until spring."

"Do you know what the people are calling a Quiritani ox?"

Vorcuns grimaced in a poor imitation of a laugh. "It is a man's wife, for with the beasts dead, come spring planting she will have to pull the plough."

"Do you lay that at my door?" I exclaimed. "The drought began before I left the Island!"

"Shall we lay it then upon the head of the king?" Nodontios asked. I was abruptly silent. For the sake of the king they had killed a man already. There was only one greater sacrifice.

"The king?" I asked. "But my father is high king no longer. Surely it is for my sisters and their husbands to placate the gods!"

"He still goes attended like a king with his Companions," Vorcuns said. "Truly, no one knows where the sovereignty is seated anymore. But there is no doubt that the Goddess is angry with us, and angrier since you have been gone."

"Do you desire me to save you?" I was becoming angry. "To leave the land to which I have been bound by the Great Marriage, and desert the father of my child? Where were you when I was driven out of Ligrodunon?"

The child in my womb kicked sharply and I crossed my arms over my belly to calm it.

"Lady!" Vorcuns held up his hands in surrender. "We are your father's men, and when you left us he was already out of his mind with rage. We wept in our hearts that night, but we did not dare to anger him."

I turned away. That night, I had wept real tears.

"He is confused, and he is a stubborn old man," Nodontios said carefully. "He has got it into his head now that you abandoned him."

"Well, I am a stubborn woman, and you yourselves have digged the pit in which you lie. Perhaps I will listen if Leir himself sent to plead with me!"

My father's men were still guesting with us two weeks later when Agantequos came home.

"They say that they will wait until the child is born and carry the word home," I explained as I helped him into clean clothes. There were shadows of sleeplessness around his eyes, and a grim set to his mouth, but no one was wounded. That relieved one anxiety, for there was always a chance of it when proud men met with swords to hand.

"Home . . ." Agantequos frowned. "Your home is here. I don't want them stirring up old memories!"

"These old warriors taught me how to draw a bow and put me on my first pony! My father's men have guest-right here; you will not turn them away!"

"Nor will I," he surrendered, "unless they have eaten up all of the stew. If you want your babe to have a father, you had better feed this starving man!"

That night we lay curled together in our boxbed, and all was well once more. The beard Agantequos had grown for the cold weather tickled my neck as he nuzzled it.

"Were there no girls to warm your bed at the Council?" I whispered, turning my head so that he could kiss me.

"None so round and firm. . . ." His hand moved across my belly, then stilled as the child within began to shift position, jabbing with a tiny elbow.

"Is it a badger in a bag you have here, lady?" he said when the baby was once more still.

I laughed. "I think sometimes that she will dig her way free. But not yet. Now, tell me about the Council!" I could feel the laughter leaving him. "The truth, love, not the heroic phrases you will give your men."

He sighed. "There are new peoples on the move. The Veneti and the Venelli, they call themselves, and there are others behind them—fierce warriors, and hungry for land. If the tribes in their path fail to hold them, soon the survivors will be weeping at our gates, and presently the invaders themselves will be trying to knock them down."

"And then?" I asked softly.

"We will do like the others," he said bitterly. "We will fight and die, or we will run away!"

"Where, Agantequos?" I whispered. "If it came to flight, would you bring your people to the Island of the Mighty?"

"For this land has my blood been shed, to this land I am sworn!"

he groaned. "*You* above all others know by what oaths I am bound! As well ask me to love another wife as another land!"

"That is what you asked me to do. . . ."

He grew rigid and I held my breath. Would he say it was not the same?

"Cridilla—" his answer came at last. "Are you regretting your promises to me?"

"Oh, my love, it was I who needed a refuge! I hold by my oaths, but I have reason to know that one cannot always keep them! *If* it should come to that, at least consider the possibility!"

"I will—" he said dismissively. "But I pray there will never be the need. If it does come, it will not be this winter," he added, holding me closer, "or even this year."

Winter deepened and the weather grew worse. They called these the black months here, and it seemed to me that even in the north, when deepest winter left only a few hours of light each day, I had never known such cold. As the solstice approached, the women brought in fragrant boughs of pine to hang above the doorways, and trails of wood ivy and stiff sprigs of holly to tie around the posts that supported the hall.

"Soon the sun will be reborn from the Lady's darkness," said Brenna, "like the babe from your womb. Do they not feast this day in your home?"

"They will celebrate the sun's returning," I answered, swallowing to release tight throat muscles, "in every village in the land."

I was remembering the bull-feast at which we had found Crow, and another district where the men danced bearing the horns of great deer. One year I had kept vigil with the priestesses through the longest night and gone out to watch the sun rise above the standing stones. Each place in its own way would reenact the great story of the renewal of the light, midwifing that mighty birth with whatever magic they could command. And this Midwinter there would be desperation in the ceremonies. In a year in which so much else had gone wrong, folk might well fear that spring would never come. And men did evil things sometimes when they were afraid.

The longest night drew in and we butchered a boar in honor

of the earth gods. Outside it was getting up to storm once more, but in the long hearth the oak log that had lain seasoning since Midsummer blazed merrily, encouraged by the libations the men poured over it to release the fire within. All of Agantequos's Companions were gathered at Moridunon for the feasting, and many of the chief men of the country who were pledged to him as well. We had made sure there would be mead enough for a night's drinking, and the strong brown ale of the countryside was in good supply.

"Sit down, love. I have saved the tenderest pieces for you—" Agantequos called out to me. The man beside him whispered in his ear and he laughed long and loud.

"As soon as I have seen to the bread—"

I wiped my hands on the cloth I had tied over my gown and arched my back, trying to ease the backache that had been plaguing me all day. Then I hurried awkwardly toward the back of the hall to see if they had brought in the new loaves from the ovens in the yard.

"Lady, you should be sitting down!" Brenna hurried toward me, the warm bread bundled into her shawl. "We have everything well in hand."

"What about the boiled beef and barley? Is the goose on the far spit done roasting? If that rain gets worse we shall have to bring the rest of the food inside."

"They are cooking just as they should, lady, and by the time the storm hits all will be done! Sobuiaca, child, come and help the queen to sit down. . . ."

"I don't want to sit down!" I said crossly. "I ought to be carrying round the mead, but if I bend over I will likely fall into the fire! Still, I can bear a loaf of bread without danger. Give me those—"

The two women exchanged a look of affectionate exasperation as I snatched the bread from Brenna's shawl.

"Here's bread for you, and the blessing of the season as well!" I tore off pieces to hand to Vorcuns and Nodontios.

"Let's . . . toast th' lady!" Vorcuns swung up his horn expansively. "To th' Lady o' Briga . . . health an' long life!"

"Do not be calling her by that name! She is Lady of Morilandis now!" the voice of Agantequos cut across his. I turned, gaping, as the conversations around me faltered.

"Jus'. . . a blessing!" Vorcuns gestured expansively and I realized that he had already consumed more than his share of the mead.

"She does not need your blessings, old man! I can protect her!" Agantequos's tone sharpened.

"Little king"—the warrior peered across the fire,—"you be tryin' t' *insult* me?"

I recovered from my astonishment and stepped between them as Agantequos's men started reaching for the weapons that hung from the hooks on the wall.

"Nobody is insulting *anyone!*" I exclaimed. "My husband, they are your guests! Vorcuns, are these the manners you learned in my father's hall?" The older man ducked his head in apology, but Agantequos was still glowering.

"Cridilla, come here! Your place is at my side!"

I moved carefully toward my husband, but I did not sit down.

"Listen, thou!" I said in the old speech we had used on the Misty Isle. "The she-bear lairs where she will! Were I not heavy with thy cub, I would teach thee to bespeak me so!"

He was on his feet in a single smooth motion, reaching for me. I struck out at him and swayed, overbalancing. He caught me by the shoulders and I glared at him, hating my helplessness.

"Art my woman, Cridilla, hast forgotten? These men are nothing to thee!"

"I am my own!" I spat back at him. "Drink the night away, but wilt drink alone!" I wrenched away from him then, and stumbled across the floor to the hide curtains that hid our bedbox, followed by a gust of male merriment.

There were wolf pelts on the bed, well tanned and warm. Awkwardly I lowered myself down. Silent sobs rippled through me as I burrowed into the furs, seeking escape from my misery. When I became aware once more, the noise from around the fire had diminished and rain was gusting around the hall. I still ached. Brenna had been right, I thought dully. I should have sat down.

"Cridilla?" Firelight glowed for a moment across the furs as the curtain was drawn aside. "Are you all right?" The bed gave to Agantequos's weight as he sat down.

"I hurt," I mumbled into the furs, "and you are a beast!"

"No . . . only a man with a tongue too well oiled by mead. A man who still cannot believe that the queen of all women lies every night in his arms. . . ." His embrace enfolded me.

Rain thundered against the thatch above us. I sighed and straightened, turning so that Agantequos could kiss me, and at that moment felt a rush of warm wetness between my thighs.

"Curse it, I've pissed myself!" I exclaimed. "Call Brenna!" More liquid flowed as I struggled upright. I was already half out of my gown, shivering, when the other woman arrived.

"Oh, I'll change the bed—" She looked closely at my ruined gown and then began to laugh. "But not for you. 'Tis the waters of your womb that you feel flowing, lady, and the birthing bed in the Women's House where you must lie now!"

Another shudder rippled through me and I clutched at the post until it passed. "But 'tis too soon!"

Brenna shrugged and began to help me into a clean gown. "It is the babe who chooses the time!"

Agantequos heard the end of that and stopped short. "The child?"

"Indeed, my lord, you will have something to drink to presently, but you must leave your lady to the women now!"

"I will carry her," he said hoarsely. I started to protest, but that odd ache swept through me again, and I was glad enough to put my arms around his neck and let him bear me through the windy darkness. "I love you," he whispered as he lowered me onto the straw bed that had been prepared for my lying in.

I wanted to answer him, but another pain was gripping me, and I could only squeeze his hand.

Throughout the hours of darkness the power of the storm rose and fell, and with it the pains that were reshaping my body. *When dawn comes it will be over,* I thought as I caught my breath between pangs. But when at last a thin grey light filtered through the skins that covered the windows, my body was still laboring.

I heard Agantequos's voice at the door, and the women cheerfully shooing him away. But I heard also what they said when they thought I was dozing. I wondered vaguely why it should be wrong for the pains to slow. Perhaps then this relentless wrenching would go away. But here was another one beginning—I stiffened and bit my lip. I was a warrior woman, and I would not scream with the pain.

"Lady, you must not resist it!" Brenna's voice was soft in my ear. "Loosen your muscles, flow with it, let go!"

"I'm tired—" I mumbled. "Let me rest...."

"Does a warrior sleep in the middle of a battle?" the other woman asked.

"A warrior *fights* in a battle!" I sighed as the fist that was squeezing my belly began to release its grip. "But now I am the battlefield! Let me rest—I'll try again another day!"

"My dear, once the waters have broken you must go through with it, or you and the child could die." She wiped the sweat from my skin with a damp cloth. "Come now, drink a little more tea—"

I swallowed the bittersweet mixture of yarrow and raspberry leaf and lay back again, listening to the steady patter of the rain. Falling water was flowing into a hundred tiny rivers that snaked toward the stream. Could I follow those swollen streams into the grey river that sought the sea?

I tried to let my muscles liquefy, but at the thought of the sea a new wave rose within me and I began to struggle once more.

All I could manage was to endure. Sometimes they made me walk, and one or another of the women would uphold me during the pains. When I lay in the straw they took turns kneading my back muscles, or laid warm cloths across my contorting belly. But a time came when I no longer had the energy to rise. I could hear the anxiety in the women's voices, but I did not care. This year the Goddess had decided to keep the light prisoned in Her womb, and we were all going down into the dark.

Only when the door opened and I felt a gust of damp wind did I rouse.

"Is it Agantequos?" I whispered. Men were kept from the birth-chamber, but suddenly I wanted him.

DIANA L. PAXSON

" 'Tis someone you'll be glad to see!" Brenna spoke with the resolute cheer she had maintained throughout my labor, but now I heard beneath that brightness a note of profound relief that made me open my eyes.

Mother Nesta was dripping into the straw beside me, her gaze sweeping over my swollen body like a warrior at first sight of his foe.

"Reinforcements . . ." I whispered. She laughed and began to strip off her soaked garments.

"I told you that I would be here!" She laid out bags and bundles on a cloth.

"I . . . have waited for you."

"I see that you have," she said briskly. "Well, perhaps matters will go more swiftly now."

Brenna was giving her a whispered summary of my labor, but I did not listen, for another pain was on its way. When it passed, the priestess had finished arranging her gear. I felt a light pressure as she moved her hands above my body though her palms were several inches away.

"Here, Sobuiaca, you have the Sight—" She touched the girl on the forehead. "Look at her and tell me what you see."

"I see . . . the lifeglow around her," came the hesitant answer. "It's brightest over her belly, and when the pains come it flares out an arm's length away."

"Now look deeper. Can you see a point of brightness there?"

"The child's light? Is it that small steady glow?"

"It is." Mother Nesta nodded with satisfaction. "I can feel the lifeforce, but 'tis useful to have someone who can *see*. Keep watching, child, for I will be busy, and tell me if there is any change."

I understood now how a frightened chariot team must relax when the horses feel an experienced hand on the reins. Even when the priestess oiled her fingers and poked and prodded inside me I was less afraid. She was like one of the wisewomen in my own land.

"Mother," said Sobuiaca, "the baby's light is flickering a little now."

"It is time we were ending this." Mother Nesta pulled up a low stool beside the bed and took my hand. "Will you trust me?"

I nodded. Men came to this place in battle sometimes, when they did not care whether they lived or died so long as it was done.

She gave me a drink then, whose honey sweetness did not quite cover the bitterness of bay leaves and the odd, acrid taste of the black stuff she scraped from the blades of rye grass, and as I lay back she began to trace symbols over my womb. I could feel the movement of air against my skin as her hand moved above it, and something shifted deep within me. My eyes closed at the firm pressure of her hand on my brow.

"Sa . . . sa . . . there, my lovely, you must let it go. Go with it, flow with it, like the river to the sea. . . . The waves will roll through you, but you feel only their power. . . ." I drifted away on the murmur of her words.

Then the first great wave struck my womb and I screamed. Again and again my muscles constricted.

"Stop it! Make it stop!" The great waves were dragging me down. I kicked out, then the firm pressure of Mother Nesta's hands brought me back to focus again. Another wave built, but this one was different. Suddenly I began to understand. This time I shouted, and as the convulsion eased I felt the women lifting me. Now Brenna was supporting my back and two other women braced my knees. I wriggled, desperate to ease the strain.

"Not yet—" The priestess crouched between my thighs and made a warding sign above my womb. "Wait until your body moves and push with it or you will tear. Hold your breath, child, it will not be long."

I could not answer, for the bear on my belly was flexing and stretching again and already I felt the power growing within. I let out my breath in a thin thread of sound that built and built as the hands of the priestess swept downward in strong decisive strokes that focused and intensified the energy.

"You are a seed within the soil," she was chanting,

"You are a fruit upon the tree,
You are an egg inside the swan,
Now comes the time to set you free!"

[255]

Again and again I pushed. I was being split apart, but nothing mattered except ridding myself of that pressure within.

"Almost there!" cried Sobuiaca. "Oh, see—there's the top of the head, and it has fair hair!" I struggled for breath, wondering where I would find the strength to push once more.

"Sing! Shout!" Mother Nesta cried. "This is your battle! Call out your battle cry!"

I remembered Bear Mother, shouting as they struck her down. Could I do less to bring a new life into the world?

"Ai . . . ai . . . ai . . . an Adder am I!" I cried.

New energy flared through me, and as I bore down I felt something slippery between my thighs. I glimpsed a purple face contorted in protest and one tiny arm.

"Now hold, while I get the other shoulder—"

But I could not hold back now. Snarling, I pushed again, and felt a rush of warmth and sudden blissful release as the babe burst free.

The chamber was pulsing with light. There was a thin, angry wail, and then they were holding up a small, squirming creature with a nub of a penis and a swollen purple scrotum. Brenna wiped his mouth and nostrils and laid him on my flaccid belly. At the touch my womb clenched again, and there was another warm rush as the afterbirth slid through.

My son, I thought, but as the infant frowned it was my father's face I saw.

I sagged back into Brenna's arms. Mother Nesta murmured the birthblessing as she cut the cord. From outside came men's shouting and the sudden thunder of swordblades drumming on hide shields. Someone was pressing cloths between my legs, muttering anxiously, but I didn't care. It was over, and I was floating on a calm sea.

Agantequos's face swam into view and I smiled. "A son . . ." My lips moved, but no sound came.

"She is still bleeding," said someone. But women always bled a bit after childbirth. Why were they concerned?

"Her lifelight is flickering," came Sobuiaca's voice, and I saw Agantequos's face change.

"Cridilla, don't leave me!"

He was gripping my shoulders, but his voice seemed very far away. For a moment I seemed to be looking down at my own body. Agantequos cried out and Mother Nesta handed the child to Brenna and turned to see. But the room was awash with light. With a sigh I let it carry me away.

I floated in a sea of light, wondering why the ocean had ever made me afraid. But presently the waves began to heave. I started to struggle, but I was sinking, no, I was being sucked down a slippery dark gullet that swallowed every sensation but fear. Through endless serpentine coils I descended, and gradually I realized that there was someone ahead of me, a sturdy, fur-clad shape that moved steadily on.

"Bear Mother!" I exclaimed. "Wait! Where am I?"

Abruptly I could see the space around us, lit by a curious moony glow. Thrones hewn from living stone were set in a circle around a pool.

"Art in the Womb of the Goddess, child," Bear Mother spoke to me. "Ever and again She is thrust into the deeps, but it is still from Her womb that all must be reborn. And when the God dies His blood begets Her into the world again."

"Am I dead? I don't understand."

The light grew brighter around us, and I saw that there were figures seated upon those thrones.

"Death and life are alike to the warrior, did not I tell thee so?"

Upon the nearest throne was a woman with the royal insignia of Briga upon her brow. I moved past Bear Mother and the grey eyes focused on me.

"Art thou my mother?"

"If thou art my daughter, why didst thou leave thy land?" came the question.

"Why didst thou leave me alone?" I shot back at her.

"I gave my life to leave the land a queen."

Now I could see that women sat on all of the thrones. The circle grew larger the longer I gazed.

"I have given mine to leave my lord a son!" I replied.

"Not yet!" came a new voice, faint but clear. A hazy figure was taking shape between me and the pool. "Your body yet has life if you will return to it!" I gazed in astonishment. Mother Nesta was a greater priestess than I had thought if she had the power to follow me here.

"Why should I return to pain?"

"Your husband is weeping. Your son needs his mother's love."

"What do they matter?" came a whisper from around the circle. "They are only men!"

"I was a girl-child, and thou didst abandon me!" I cried to my mother. In this place, in this time, I could recognize how desperately I had needed her. Then I realized that her cheeks were wet with tears.

"Will you condemn your child to the same loss?" Mother Nesta asked.

"I dared thy birth for the sake of our people, and that the land might live," my mother answered me. "I offered my life willingly and in love, that it might be a valid sacrifice."

"Who was there to show me what that means?" I exclaimed.

"How shall the sons learn to love the Mother unless a woman nourishes them?" Mother Nesta cried.

"How shall the warriors learn not to fear death unless a woman guides them?" Bear Mother echoed her.

"How shall the fathers learn to serve the land unless a woman teaches them?" my mother asked.

All my mothers from the world's beginning were waiting for my reply. The figures blurred as if I saw them through rain.

"Mother, only hold me, and then I will go back again!" I stumbled toward her.

As she opened her arms she became brighter. And now she was grown huge, or I was becoming a child once more, cradled close to a soft breast, lulled by the steady rhythm of her heart. Radiance pulsed through me. Here was the perfect protection I had always desired.

"Mother, don't let me go . . ." I whispered, and the answer, when it came, was all around me.

"Now that thou has known Me, know that there is nothing that can separate thee from My love. . . ."

Around us the glory was fading. I floated toward the world's dim light. . . .

And then I opened the eyes of my body and saw the anguish in Agantequos's face give way to astonished joy, and reached out for my child.

THIRD
SPIRAL:
THE
SERPENT
OF THE
DEEP

*Winter: First Year of the
Rule of the Queens*

Chapter

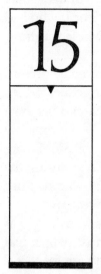

15

Before I was bent-backed, I was handsome,
my spear was in the van, it drew first blood—
I am crooked, I am sad, I am wretched . . .
Boisterous is the wind, white is the hue of the edge of
*   the wood;*
the stag is emboldened, the hill is bleak
feeble is the old one, slowly he moves . . .
I am bent in three and old, I am peevish and
*   giddy,*
I am silly, I am cantankerous;
those who loved me love me not.

—*Canu Llywarch Hen*

My singing was a whisper of sound in the darkness, no louder than the breathing of the man who slept at my side. I had learned to love these moments of peace when the only reality was the babe in my arms and the flow of milk that nourished him. My breath caught as the child bit down on my nipple and the milk descended with a rush that was almost pain.

Belinos had nursed vigorously from the beginning, but even nine months after his birth my body's response to his suckling still took me by surprise. He had been in a hurry to enter the world, and in haste ever since to grow. Sometimes I fancied that he had been waiting for the first chance at conception, as if all I had been through had taken place just so this child could come into the world.

I ought to be grateful. My son was as fair and fat a babe as any mother could hope for, like the lambs our ewes dropped that spring, and the calves, and the foals. There was now no doubt among the people that I was Agantequos's rightful queen. Why, then, could I not be as content as any other fertile animal with her child?

I shifted Beli's solid weight against my belly by touch, for the embers of the hearthfire had faded hours ago, and at harvest-tide it would be an hour or so yet before the sun rose. An occasional snore came from the warriors who slept in the hall. But I, who had once been able to sleep through the revelry of the whole war-host, now roused at the first mewling of a child.

The women of the dun had feared I would never be able to nurse the child. Keir's wife had given birth just before me and for a few days, her milk had been needed for both Beli and her own girl. But Mother Nesta's herbs had great power. By the time my child was ready for his Naming, I was on my feet again. Since then, both I and the baby had been flourishing. I still fed him during the day, but there was not a nursing mother in the dun who had not fed him as well. It was only at night that he was all my own.

"Peace, small warrior—" I broke the suction with my finger as Beli began to fuss and shifted him to the other breast, which had been flowing like a spring in sympathy. "There is enough for thee." He fell to sucking eagerly and I closed my eyes, for my words had reminded me of the tale told by the last messenger from home.

Corn in the meadows and milk and honey on the heights there might be in the Great Land, but in the Island of the Mighty it was otherwise. There, the Goddess had decreed a terrible year for men. Babes that were carried to term came into a world in which the powerful walked warily and the poor sold themselves for bread. Beneath the standards of the queens the warriors were hosting, and what food there was went to feast them. Woe, in such times, to those who wished to till their fields in peace.

Sensing my tension, Beli released my nipple and started to fret again. I lifted him to my shoulder and began patting him.

"Be still, little one, and I shall tap out a sleep song upon thy crown . . ." By the time I had finished, Beli had become a limp weight in my arms. Carefully I untangled his fingers from my hair and laid him in his nest beside the bed. Even when I changed his clout he did not waken; I could hear the whisper of his breathing as I covered him up again.

"Does he sleep?" came a murmur as I eased down into the cave of warmth my husband's body had made beneath the furs. My breath caught as Agantequos drew me against him and began to lick the last of the milk from my nipples. For a long time after the birth he had not dared to touch me, but my healing was complete now, and my thighs opened to receive him as the flower opens to the sun.

Each time we joined in love it seemed to get better. Even when we had hunted and fought and lived together on the Misty Isle we had never known each other so perfectly, for now there was no place held secret, no response or sensation in either of us that the other had not explored. I breathed his breath; his sweat flowed with my own. And when the moment of release could no longer be delayed, we sang a single song and slid into sleep entwined in each other's arms.

But in the still hours before the dawning, I dreamed; and in my dreaming I was alone.

I was floating in a world of mist. Dizzied, I sought for substance, and found myself standing in the darkness on a moor. I forced the vision to solidify, and realized that I was on the path that crossed the moors from the dwelling of the priestesses to the Down Fort. Mist swirled around the hilltops; I could see the path ahead of me, and the dark bulk of the barrow to one side. Sounds came muffled through the damp air. From somewhere ahead I heard cries, and the clangor of swords.

Three ravens flapped toward the battle music. I ran past the humped forms of sleeping cattle up the slope toward the dun. Mist lay heavy here as well, but the air above the dun glowed with the light of hidden fires. As I approached, the shouting grew louder, and two blurred figures shot through the gateway, followed by a noisy crowd still clutching their drinking horns.

I stopped, amused by the uproar. From the sound, one would have thought somebody was attacking the dun. Such commotions had been part of my upbringing. They were inevitable when young warriors or hunting dogs were kept in packs together, a way for the combatants to vent tensions and a sometimes welcome source of excitement for everyone else in the dun.

The blades clanged and scraped as the two fighters swayed together. The older man shoved his opponent away, and the young warrior rolled down the hill and came to his feet again. The tall man leaned on his blade, panting, and I recognized Vorcuns. That did surprise me, for he had never been a quarrelsome man.

Then the younger fighter was charging uphill, losing momentum as the slope grew steeper. Vorcuns greeted the attack with his snarling battle cry. Both men struck at the same time, but it was the younger man who staggered backward, blood spurting from the join of neck and shoulder, and crumpled to the ground.

There was a moment of shocked silence. Things were not supposed to go so far. In the stillness, two new voices could be heard.

"And I tell you, I will not suffer such lack of discipline!" The last time I had heard that voice it had been counseling me to rebel against the king. "A queen's court is no place for untrained hounds. Even when you were young, 'tis little enough pretense you made of controlling them. What trust can I place now in your assurances?"

"As much or as little as I can place in yours!"

This was a man's voice, strained with fury, that I did and did not know. The speakers came through the gate, and I saw my sister Rigana and an old man who had once been a king.

Shock blurred my focus. I forced myself to concentrate.

"You said you loved me—" Leir's tone was petulant. "They all heard you—" A wave of his hand summoned his Companions, who had trooped out of the dun behind him. "But you and your sister have disbanded my war-host, and the warriors and servants who remain to me are insulted by your people at every turn. Did you lie to me?"

"I agreed to house *you*, father. Nothing was said about your men!"

Rigana eyed the Companions balefully. In the torchlight her exotic beauty was amplified. She had pulled the sash of her gown tight, and men's eyes followed her even as she railed at them. She saw them looking, and her own glance became brighter, her walk more languorous.

Only Artocoxos, glowering at his lord's shoulder, seemed immune to the spell.

"Father, we can defend and serve you. What need have you for a royal retinue?"

Leir was shaking his head as if he did not understand.

"He is a king, woman," growled Artocoxos. "He may not go unattended. It is the law. . . ."

Rigana laughed suddenly. "Law? But he himself cast his kingship away. Listen therefore to my judgment—" Abruptly she looked taller, cloaked in the authority she had claimed. Leir, who had always towered over any company he was part of, now seemed small.

"One of my people lies dead before me. This is the compensation I require—neither gold nor the life of the manslayer, father, but the dismissal of your Companions. Five men only out of the thirty shall you retain to serve you. The others may return to their own clans or seek service where they will. In the names of earth and heaven have I vowed this. Thus will it be." She knelt, and her fingers closed on the soil.

Crow had crept to his master's side. As Rigana finished Leir's hand went to that silver-streaked dark head and began to pat it, mindlessly, as one might stroke a horse or a hound to still its fear.

"It is a queen who has spoken, and the third of your *geasa* broken, lord," came the voice of Talorgenos from the shadows of the gateway, with a groan in it like the sound a blasted oak tree makes as it goes down. "You have lost your following, you have cursed a woman, and you have slain the swan. Leir Blatoniknos, now is your sovereignty passed away. . . ."

"Father!" I cried, but as the priest spoke, a wave of shadow rolled between me and the torches, and the vision disappeared.

"Cridilla! Cridilla, my heart—what is wrong?"

I blinked stupidly as the hangings around the bedbox were thrown open to admit the light. I struggled upright, and Agante-quos's grip on my shoulders relaxed.

"You were shouting—"

I let out my breath in a long sob. "What did I say?"

"You cried out three times, *'The luck is lost from the land!'* What did you mean?"

Frowning, I sought truth through the mists of dream.

"I was dreaming about my father . . . and Rigana. Something is badly wrong at home."

"This is your home!" He let go of me. "Is not the child enough for you to worry about that you must be dredging up sorrows from the past?"

"This did not feel like the past. It was as if I were there, Horse! Last night my spirit walked in Belerion! It has happened before that I dreamed true. Once I even saw you and Spirit Bear. But I have not dreamed in that way since I crossed the sea."

He had reddened a little at Spirit Bear's name, as if I could be other than grateful to the woman who had taught him to be so tender and skillful a lover.

"And a good thing too, if it is going to upset you . . ." he said more softly. "Come now, love—I can smell the morning gruel cooking over the fire." He laid his hand on my arm.

I jerked away. "Rigana has driven off my father's men. He will be alone. I should never have come away!"

"Cridilla!" Agantequos shook his head. "I recall very well that it was your father who exiled you! Your sister will hardly allow him to starve."

"Will she not?" I muttered. "She lied before! Why could my father not see that she would break those fine promises as soon as it suited her?"

"He knows it now, I suppose. But, Cridilla, there is nothing you can do. Come eat, or you will have no milk for our son."

"Our son!" I exclaimed. "And how do you mean to raise him, my lord? What kind of a son will Belinos be to us in our old age if he is brought up on tales of how we abandoned his grandsire when *he* grew old? It was Leir's wrath that railed against me, not his love. I knew that—his moods have ever been stormy as the sea. He would have soon forgiven me—if I had stayed. . . ."

"In the name of the Mothers, Cridilla, you babble about your father as if he were the only one who ever loved you! What about your duty to your baby? What about me?"

Agantequos was really angry. But his words could not seem to touch the sorrow within me. I was like a warrior who suddenly discovers pain in a long-healed wound. How could my father's griefs still have the power to upset me?

Upset by our raised voices, Belinos began to cry. I lifted the child, patting his back and murmuring wordlessly. But my voice sounded thin and unconvincing, even to me.

> *"Grandmother, tell me, what is that sighing?"*
> *"'Tis only the wind, child, the wind all alone—"*
> *"Grandmother, it whispers that something is dying!"*
> *"'Tis the old year, child, the year that is gone."*

Nabelcos's voice rose and fell like the wind around the dun, clear and piping for the child's questions, cracked for the replies.

> *"Grandmother, tell me, who is that calling?"*
> *"'Tis only the raven, who summons her kin—"*
> *"Grandmother, what is it that I hear falling?"*
> *"The snow, for a white shroud to wrap the world in."*

Winter was fast approaching, and there was a bitter nip in the wind. Agantequos and his men had gone out after venison, but everyone else was staying close to the hearth.

I sat mending a bridle while Belinos pulled himself up on uncertain legs to progress from one to another of the women who sat around the hearth, or plopped down, entranced as a kitten with a wisp of cloudy wool. It was hard to believe that almost a year had passed since I gave birth to him, and even longer since any real news had come from home.

> *"Grandmother, tell me the source of this stillness—"*
> *"By cold and by ice all earth's children are bound."*
> *"Where are the green things and what is their illness?"*
> *"The bear guards the seeds sleeping safe underground."*

Bear Mother and the Island seemed a lifetime away, and next year's springtide almost as distant. I stood at the crossroads of past and future, and neither one seemed real.

> *"Grandmother, say why the night's end comes never—"*
> *"It will end when the sun-child from winter is born."*

"And when will that happen? I've waited forever—"
"Sleep, child, and you'll understand come the morn . . ."

My own sun-child reached for the harpstrings. The bard plucked a chord with one hand and with the other set him toddling toward Brenna once more. The firelight faltered, leaving his hair backlit and her face in shadow. I saw Youth and Age sitting there.

"Grandmother, tell me, why is your shape shifting?"
"I am the same, 'tis the shadows that flee—"
"Grandmother, say why the darkness is lifting!"
"Look into my cauldron, child, then you will see . . ."

It was only an old rhyme, but suddenly I was afraid. I set down my tools, scooped Belinos from Brenna's lap, and hugged him until he squirmed. The awl clattered to the floor, and Belinos began to cry.

Brenna reached for him and stopped, staring past me. I gave her the babe, hardly noticing this time how soon she had him smiling again. My attention was on the stranger who stood in the doorway. He had the slack skin of a man who has lost flesh, but the stained tunic beneath his cloak had once been snowy white, and though his flowing hair and beard were wilder than I remembered them, he still had enough presence to focus the interest of everyone in the hall.

What disaster could have compelled them to send *him* after me?

"Lady—" He moved toward me, and suddenly our meeting became a ritual. He saluted me as I had seen him salute my father long ago.

"Talorgenos . . ." I faltered. "Have they exiled you too?"

His eyes narrowed. "What do you mean?"

"In a dream I saw you. I saw Vorcuns fight, and I heard your words."

"Artocoxos was right to bid me seek you. . . ." For a moment Talorgenos's eyes closed.

"I am exiled indeed. The oak priests have been banished by the queens," he said heavily. "And some of us have been slain to atone for the priests of the old gods who were killed when we came into the land. The king's household is broken, his Companions driven forth, but it was not done easily. Nodontios and Zanis and several more were killed; others forced into exile. Some took service with the queen to save their lands. The king has gone north to seek redress from Gunarduilla and Maglaros, swearing that one daughter, at least, must keep faith with him."

I blinked back tears. "How does he? I only saw him for a moment in my dream. . . ."

"I read the omens. I do not make them. It is with him as with the husk of a blasted oak tree that the next storm may bring down. Now, only anger drives him. His strength is gone."

"Then he will fall, for Gunarduilla will do as her sister has done," I said bitterly. Sobuiaca brought a silver-bound cup of ale and I offered it to the old man. "But could you not have watched over him, if only from afar?"

"Rigana would have had my life, had I stayed," Talorgenos answered me. "But I have not come here to nurse my grief beside your fire. I have come to bring you home."

"Be glad that we have given you the guest cup already," exclaimed Brenna, "or my lord would have your head for trying to steal his wife away!"

"Peace, woman . . ." I said wearily. "One would think he were trying to elope with me. What does Artocoxos say?"

"He will stay by Leir as long as he can, but he also begs you to return, if not for your father's sake, then for the health of your land."

I turned to him. "What do you mean?"

"Things are not well in Alba or Belerion," Talorgenos answered, "but it is for Briga that we truly fear. Hardly a dale has not seen bloodshed as men incline to one queen or the other, or seek to uphold the right of the king, or to carve out chiefdoms of their own. The Goddess is angry, and the fields do not bear. Men will not sow where they cannot harvest, and what the fighting does not destroy, starvation will."

"What in the Lady's name could I do?" I exclaimed.

"In the Lady's name? You *are* the Lady of Briga. Do you think this a thing that only your priestesses can understand? The people would rally to you, and with your blessing the crops would grow once more."

"I am Lady of Morilandis," I answered him. "I have a husband and a child." I felt the blast of cold air as the doors were once more opened, and male voices raised in laughter.

Talorgenos's shoulders slumped. "It is true—but, lady, this land is at peace, and your own land has such need of you!"

"At peace?" came a new voice. "With the Veneti crawling down our throats?" Agantequos strode forward with the carcass of a young deer slung across his shoulders, his skin still glowing from the brisk air. He looked Talorgenos up and down warily. "What are you doing here?" Red drops spattered the rushes as the deer's head swung.

A moment before the old priest had looked defeated, but the challenge reminded him that once a kingdom had feared his frown.

"Agantequos!" I stepped between them, and I could see their bristles flattening once more. "Never shall it be said that any man of Leir's household lacked a place in his daughter's hall."

"I would rather have had one of his Companions—" said my husband more equably. "We can always use another good fighting man." He heaved the deer off of his shoulders, and one of his men dragged it away.

"Son of the Great Horse, I bear the words of Artocoxos who is the chief of those Companions! It is an alliance we are asking!" Talorgenos said then. "The king has been dispossessed against both law and nature. But his enemies are weak with fighting each other. Artocoxos believes that even a small force of disciplined fighters could set Leir in his high seat once more."

Agantequos looked at him. "I cannot do it. They will not have had a chance to tell you how the tribes to the east are pushing into our lands. Already the first wanderers are raiding our outlying steadings. One needs no skill in reading omens to see that their full strength must be upon us by spring. Then, I will need every warrior I can find. Perhaps afterward, when this threat is past. . . ."

"It may be too late for the king's forces by then, and too late for Leir."

"Bring him here to us, then—" said my husband, moving to the raised bench covered with wolf skins that was his seat in the hall. "We can shelter him."

"Do you think we have not begged him to do that?" said Talorgenos bitterly. "Even when *I* asked it—and he was used to accept my counsel. He will not speak his daughter's name. I think . . . he is ashamed."

Agantequos snorted disbelievingly. "Did he say so?"

"He will never say it. Old he is, but not yet broken. And I think he has fought too long for the Island of the Mighty to leave it now."

My husband nodded, easing back against the furs that covered his chair. "There came a time when my life seemed a small price to pay for my land. It would take more than fear for myself to drive me from it now." There was a deepening in the lines that anxiety had graven between his brows.

"Then you will understand that my mission is not for the sake of Leir only," Talorgenos went on. "Your lady is of the blood of the queens. The wise ones of the old race and the Quiritani agree that without her there will be no healing for Briga." He turned to me and once again the authority of the priest was in his tone. "Is that not so, princess? Did they not lay oaths upon you when you became a woman, to bind you to the land?"

I stared at him, remembering. I had thought all obligations canceled by my father's curse, but this link with the land was the root of all other loyalties. And I had abandoned it.

"Cridilla made her choice. Let Briga choose another Lady. My wife is queen here now!"

"Let the Lady answer me. Is she a slave, with no will of her own?" Talorgenos turned to me.

"The Island of the Mighty rejected her!" Agantequos exclaimed. "I gave her back her royalty!"

"Did you wish me exiled so that you could claim me? You will make me sorry I came away with you!" I found my voice at last. Our household had drawn away in a circle around us, apprehensive or entertained. Belinos was whimpering in Brenna's arms.

[273]

"Cridilla, they will never let you rule. Do you think that the flowers will spring up in your footsteps if you return to Briga? There is nothing that you can do!"

Agantequos was repeating the arguments I had offered myself not so long ago. Why could I not accept them now?

"I will not let you sacrifice what we have built here for an old man who was too blind to value you!" he went on. "He never loved you, Cridilla! He never understood you at all!"

I flinched at each word. Talorgenos's gaze went from me to my husband and back again, and I remembered that he had spent his lifetime counseling kings.

"Can I allow that to matter?" I forced myself to straighten again.

"Can you deny it? The rite we did on the Island of the Horned One binds you to this land. You cannot leave me! You cannot abandon our child!"

My temper snapped suddenly.

"*Cannot!* Whatever the right of it, no man may say that to me!"

A torrent of hurtful words was bubbling up within me, and I knew that if I let them flow, they could not be unsaid. Perhaps I was afraid to free them, or perhaps I sensed that Agantequos was not really the cause of my rage.

I strode to the doorway and grabbed my cloak from its hook, feeling the oak priest's gaze burning my back as I pushed through the door. I heard Agantequos's oath, and Brenna's voice calming him. She had seen me do this before, when Belinos's crying or the incessant chattering of women drove me from the hall.

A little mizzling rain was still veiling the hills. I passed through the gates of the dun and made my way down the slope. The cattle in the home pastures lifted incurious heads and then returned to their grazing as I went by. Beyond the stream at the foot of the hill the ground rose sharply to a cragged height where we set a warrior on watch when there was need.

My goal was not the summit, but the outcropping of rock just below it, where a trickle of water welled out from a cleft in the stone. I climbed quickly, and by the time I reached the top I was sweating. I waited until the pounding of my pulse began to slow, then knelt to bless myself with water from the hollow in the rock where it collected before spilling downward again.

"Lady of life, from the depths of earth upwelling," I exclaimed. "Help me, my Mother! What am I to do?"

The water was icy. I stood up again, listening to the music of water flowing over stone. Gradually the stillness began to suffuse my soul. Through the mists came the distant lowing of a cow and even more faintly the sound of the sea. In the past year I had learned to know these sounds, but suddenly they seemed strange.

Why had my father refused to seek refuge with me? Should I believe the oak priest or my husband? I was bound both to the land of my exile and the one where I was born. I swayed and pulled myself up on the brink of the precipice, staring at the swirling spray below and the sharp-fanged rocks that waited there. I had only to let myself fall. . . .

But if death solved anything I would have died when my child was born. Shivering, I turned back to the pool.

"How can I keep faith with both the old life and the new?" A mist rose from the still water as I whispered the question into the pool. "How can I care for husband and child when my soul is still weeping because I have lost my father's love? Even with the sea between us, I am not free!"

The grey gleam before me held no answer. I bent to drink, gasping as the icy liquid went down, and sat back, shivering. Then light flared from the water. Sunlight was pouring through a gap in the mists, and radiance surrounded me. The fields and forests were still hidden, but in the distance I could see the triumphant glitter of the sea.

And in that moment I understood what I must do.

As I made my way back down the hillside, a figure rose out of the mists. For a moment I thought it a spirit, but the veil of cloud was only a grey shawl framing Mother Nesta's blunt features, and the moving leaves were herbs that she had been gathering beneath the trees. I stopped short. Perhaps she could help me with the one part of my plan that was not yet clear.

"In the name of the Mothers," I asked her, "will you do a thing for me?"

She tilted her head to one side. "I sensed that you had need of me. I will do what is in my power."

"I am going to the Isle of the Mighty with the oak priest. Agantequos would stop me," I said quickly, "so I must go in secret. There are plenty of women in the dun who will be glad to nurse Belinos. You must tell my lord that I go only to rescue my father, and that I will try to bring back some of his men to swell our war-host. Before winter's turning we will be home again."

"I can tell him"— she closed her eyes, swaying—"but I sense things stirring that may upset all plans."

"What do you mean?" I asked sharply. "Do you see doom ahead for me?"

"I see . . . change. Nothing will fall as we foretell it. I see peoples moving, and fire and water. I see nine priestesses dancing about the sacred stones. . . ."

I shook her, and the grey eyes opened again.

"I do only what I am compelled to—" I cried. "Until I fulfill my old oaths I will never be able to keep the new. Will you help me?"

"I will. But on the day when you see me again you must do what I ask."

I promised. She had left me no choice, and in my heart I trusted her. And then I went back to the dun.

That night Agantequos and I made love fiercely, but we said no word. If he had tried to talk to me perhaps I would have told him everything, but our quarrel was like a naked sword between our spirits, and our bodies' frantic passion could not get past its guard.

And the next day, when he had ridden out to see what raiders had left of one of the steadings on our borders, I kissed my child and summoned Talorgenos and we rode to the coastal village where his boat waited to take us home.

Chapter

16

But from that moment she turned woman-
*   warrior, and*
with her company set out to seek the author of the
*   deed.*
In every district of Erin she destroyed and
*   plundered,*
so that her name was changed to Nessa after that,
*   because of*
the greatness of her prowess and of her valor.

—The Birth of Conchobar

Human skulls grinned whitely from the rough stones of the Giant's Dance. As the short day died, they framed the western sky like doorways to the Other-world. I shivered. I had asked Vorcuns to guide us here on our way northward when he met us on the coast, for I had never seen the great circle of stones, but I was sorry now.

"Someone has been sacrificing . . ." observed Vorcuns at my shoulder. "And not so long ago. Those bones have been boiled clean, but they are not old. Was it the Ai-Zir, do you suppose?"

Talorgenos shook his head. "The Painted People did not take heads before we Quiritani came into the land, and the priestesses would not shed blood on the holy stones. This is the work of folk too desperate to understand why the Circle was made. The stones do not like it. Cannot you feel their anger?"

I was surprised by the intensity with which I did feel it. The moment my feet touched the shore of the Island I had felt something reach out to greet me, and my sense of homecoming grew stronger with every step northward. But it was a welcome wracked by pain.

"The Circle gathers the sunpower at Midsummer's dawn and releases it into the land," Talorgenos went on. "There is no need for blood to feed the stones. The Ai-Zir know that. They have lived with the Dance too long to risk unbalancing its energies."

"Whoever they were, they had chariots—" Vorcuns resumed his wanderings around the perimeter of the Circle, moving sunwise and not crossing the path that led from the center to the weather-worn sighting stone that looked out across the plain. "War-chariots, and warriors who watched the ritual," he went on, "for here's the mark where someone stood leaning on his spear."

I took a quick look behind me, less concerned now with who they had been than with where they had gone. The great midland plain rolled away into the dusk. We had seen no one during this last day's journey northward, but scouts could have hidden among the trees that edged the watercourses, or in the long swales of tall grass. Vorcuns had thought the middle route would be safer than Rigana's west or the east where the Banalisioi were settling old scores. But the country where once the Great Bull had ruled was in no better state than the rest of the land.

Already there was hunger in the villages, for heavy rains had spoiled much of the harvest. Children stared hollow-eyed from doorways as we passed, and my belly clenched, as I saw in their faces the features of my own son. Morilandis could be equally devastated, if the tribes that were migrating across the Great Land proved too strong.

But the folk did not run from us. Perhaps they did not think three lone travelers a danger. Or perhaps they had nothing left to steal.

"Let us go—" I called. "I do not want to be near the stones when darkness falls." Samonios was nearing, and the barriers be-tween the worlds grew thin. The spirits that lingered here would not be good to meet—not if they had died, as I suspected, un-willingly, and in pain.

The light was fading rapidly. As we headed our ponies across the tangled grasses toward a line of low trees, my back ached with the fatigue of the day's riding. I would be glad to rest, but not here. Then the darkness beneath the trees stirred. My pony tossed her head and nickered warning. I reached for my sword, a pulse of alarm shocking all other awareness away. An arrow hissed past my cheek and I froze with my fingers on the pommel's cold knob.

"Make no move—" came the command in the old tongue.

The shadows solidified into the bulky shapes of bullhide capes, and behind the Ai-Zir warriors, taller riders wrapped in plaids gone colorless with the dying of day. Vorcuns swore and I strained to see. Then I understood, for the foremost of the Quiritani warriors had the running hare that was the device of my sister Rigana painted upon their shields.

Rigana had encamped a night's ride northward at the shrine of Ava. By the time we jogged past the winding avenue of standing stones that led to this second, and greater, circle, I was almost too tired to care what would become of me there. My sister's men gathered to watch us ride in, sturdy, brown-bearded fighters in crested helmets and armor of hardened leather or young ones with the warrior tattoos newly pricked into their skin. We halted before the largest roundhouse. I rubbed my eyes, trying to bring into focus the meanders painted on the whitewashed wall. To either side of the covered porch curved the crescent horns of the bull. Rigana must have done more than conquer these people. She had got them to accept her as their Great Queen.

The elegant half-blood boy who had escorted Rigana at the Spring Council and a tall Quiritani lad with a stiff roach of red-blond hair who stood guard before the doorway eyed us suspiciously, but from within I could already hear women's voices.

The hide curtain was thrust aside and a girl in a blue cloak came out and whispered to the guards. I swung my leg over the pony's side and slid stiffly to the ground.

"These men are in my household and are not to be harmed—" I said loudly as the Quiritani reached for Talorgenos's rein.

"Of course not!" came Rigana's voice from within. "Let Vorcuns lie with my warriors and the oak priest be committed to Lady Asaret's care. Those to whom you extend your protection I shall honor, even when they lie under my ban. Did you think you were a prisoner?"

I might have found out if I had tried to ride away, but as I entered the house I bit back the first few replies that had come to mind. Now that Rigana knew I was here, I might as well see what I could learn from her.

At the hearth she turned to inspect me, and though she had to look up into my face, suddenly I felt like a gawky girl. But apparently I did not show it, for when she let me go there was a hint of admiration in her smile.

"Marriage suits you," she pronounced suddenly. "You are growing into your bones."

I was glad that the hide curtain had fallen closed behind us, for surely my face must have shown my confusion. Agantequos had praised me, but he was no dispassionate observer. Women, and sisters especially, were more critical.

We sat down beside the hearth and one of the women ladled steaming tea into two cups of silver-banded horn. I fought to keep my hands steady, aware only now, with the heat of the cup radiating through the palms of my hands, how chilled I was from the long ride. *Don't reveal any weakness,* said the same interior observer that had kept me upright on the pony. *You are two queens together. You must not show fear.*

I gazed at my sister in the firelight, glad that courtesy forbade me to assess her in turn. Proud and powerful she might be, with gold gleaming from her neck and wrists and rich embroidery banding her gown, but she did not look well.

"And now you have a child—" Rigana went on.

"A son," I said. "Belinos . . ." My breasts ached at the thought of him, though my milk had almost gone. But that was a price I had known I must pay. I had not expected to ache with desire for his warm weight in my arms.

"Who would have thought that after all our vows, all three of us should have only sons . . . but you would not have heard. My little girls died of the plague a moon ago."

Her features twisted as the smooth surface of a river is momentarily distorted by a snag. I swallowed. What if something happened to Beli while I was gone? I had been prepared to hate her. I did not know how to manage sympathy.

"It is no more than others have suffered . . ." Rigana regained her composure, ". . . my sacrifice. Perhaps the Goddess will give me another daughter when we have peace again."

Who would her father be? I wondered, for there was no sign of Senouindos here.

"But I think the Goddess is already smiling," Rigana went on, "for if She had not brought you here, I must have sought you myself—"

"The last time we met you cursed me!"

"Oh, we are all cursed now!" There was no amusement in Rigana's laughter. "No doubt Vorcuns has told you about our disasters. You belong here, sister, and I am glad that you know it, for I think the Goddess will not bless us again until you are back in your own land."

I stared at her. "Are you blaming all this on *me*? I came here to rescue the king!" I bit my lip. She would never let me go if I told her that I meant to take Leir back across the narrow sea.

"Is that why you are angry?" she asked, sipping her tea. "At the time it seemed the only way. Our father is old, Cridilla, and whatever force he used to rule his retinue has failed. Bad enough to have a house with two masters, but worse still to have half the household under authority and the other under none! And Gunarduilla had even less patience than I. She has reduced his attendance to old Artocoxos and that wretched creature you dragged home when you were a child."

"His name is Crow." I swallowed. "Where are they now?"

"My informants say that Leir ran from Gunarduilla as he ran from me. They are pursuing him, for mad as he is, he can still cause trouble in Briga, and Gunarduilla, or perhaps I should say Maglaros, has a great ambition to make one kingdom of Briga and the north."

"Your informants?" I was still trying to assimilate what I had heard.

"They tell me that she has grown more stubborn than ever, and addicted to killing. But it has been six moons since Gunarduilla communicated with me," snapped Rigana. "I am not your rival, Cridilla. The south is mine and I want no more. I will break with the Albans and help you to recover Briga if you will be my ally."

Slowly I drank the rest of my tea. It was cold, but I needed time to decide what to say.

"Install the old fool in your dun and call him king if you will," she went on. "It will not matter now. But you must be here to perform the rituals. It is well that you have come in time for Samonias. If the sacrifices are sufficient, perhaps the gods will be kinder in the coming year."

I was still seeking an answer when the curtain flapped behind us and Lady Asaret appeared. It was clear that Rigana had assumed my agreement and I did not disabuse her. If I had not sworn to return to Agantequos, the temptation to accept her proposal would have been extreme.

And yet—there were things afoot here that I did not understand. Until I had found my father I must make no decision that would bind me more straitly than I was now.

That evening I was finally able to speak with the priestess. I had slept most of the day, and by the night meal I felt strong enough to begin asking questions. No one had ever lived near the Giants' Dance, but at the Shrine of Ava the houses nestled among the stones. I felt as if they were welcoming me.

Wherever I went in the camp I was guarded, but everyone talked freely. Despite plague and war my sister had a force of many hundred, and more who would come at her call. The old Bull's nephews had killed each other, and the last princess of the Ai-Zir had died. Some ancient link with Rigana's bloodline gave her a claim to the sovereignty. In her encampment, the men of the Bull Clan outnumbered Quiritani, but Lady Asaret was the only priestess I had seen. Senouindos was in the Down Fort, and according to rumor, he was dying. Rigana moved through her camp with an escort of splendid young men, but at least in public she gave no hint who would share her high seat when the old man was gone.

While the queen was in Council, Lady Asaret came to me.

"So, you will take your place in the dales at last?" She seated herself beside me and poked another piece of kindling into the fire. She still had the quality of serenity that I remembered, like a deep, slow-moving stream on a still summer's day.

"Do you wish me to?" I said softly. "Rigana says that it is necessary for the queen-born to perform the ceremonies."

"It depends," she answered very slowly, "on which ceremonies you are planning to do. . . ."

I let out my breath. "I was at the Giants' Dance. I saw what had been done there."

"Abomination!" the priestess hissed suddenly. "The blood pollutes the stones. Lady Urtaya has withdrawn to Sulis, and I have stayed only in hopes of preventing a worse thing here. But Rigana will no longer listen to me!"

"I have always been taught that when the gods are angry men must sacrifice."

"Do you think that the only acceptable offerings are made in blood?" she exclaimed. "Sometimes blood is required, but that is not the purpose of the stone circles. And what blood is shed must be given freely! The queens and their consorts rule only because they are willing to give themselves to the land, to live for it, or to die at need. The old lord has been cast down, but no one else has taken up his burden."

"My sisters told me that when the queens ruled, the Golden Age would return. . . ."

Lady Asaret sighed. "I myself had hoped it. But the Quiritani have been here too long. You can never go completely back again."

"Is that why you have spent so long in talk with Talorgenos?"

She gave me a faint smile. "It seemed time. For a generation the people have been changing. Even the gods are different. They answer to Quiritani names; to our seeresses they sometimes appear with Quiritani faces now. The old ways are gone, and the land is laboring to bring something new to birth. But I fear it will be stillborn."

"I understand," I answered her. "I nearly died bearing my child."

She turned her grey gaze on me and I could not look away. "Why did you live?"

"There was a Quiritani wisewoman there, Mother Nesta, who followed me into the Otherworld. She made me choose"—the memory was drawn painfully from the darkness—"to serve the Lady and the land. . . ."

[283]

"So—" said Lady Asaret quietly. "You have done what neither of your sisters would do. I should like to meet this Quiritani priestess someday."

"I should like to hear what the two of you would say!" My smile faded as I heard voices beyond the door.

"Tonight the guards will be very sleepy," the priestess said abruptly. "When the owl calls thrice outside, take up your bundle and come out to me."

That night and all the day following we pushed northward as fast as the ponies would bear us. When the sun rose, clouds were already moving in from the west, trailing grey fringes of rain across a land leached of color by the dying of the year. Our ponies splashed through the puddles and labored through the soggy mats of last summer's grass. But Lady Asaret had come with us, and perhaps the spells that she and Talorgenos cast befuddled the pursuit as well as delaying it, for there was never a flicker of motion behind us as we pressed on.

The evening of the second day Vorcuns led us to a steading on the edge of the downs where one of the Companions, lamed in Leir's service, farmed now. Water dripped from the eaves of the snug roundhouse and stood in pools on the ground, but there was a shimmer of smoke above the peak of the thatched roof and a smell of cooking food.

"Is it safe?" Lady Asaret's voice cracked with fatigue. I looked at her in swift concern. I was tired myself, and I had only been riding, not maintaining a warding.

Vorcuns shrugged. "We need food and fire. Ilix and I have been each other's shield on the battlefield. He will not betray us if once he lets us in."

When we rode out the next morning, Ilix came with us, his son by his side. And he was not the only one. As we continued north the word ran before us. Men were flowing out of the hills like the rivulets that fed the swollen streams, trotting up on sturdy ponies with their weapons clasped under their cloaks to keep them dry. The Quiritani came to me because I was my father's daughter. Even

Nextonos rode down from his new fortress as we went by, and though he would not meet my eyes, I believed his promise of loyalty.

But there were others who came on foot with no weapon but a crudely hammered spear—sturdy men with the curling brown hair of my mother's people and the tattooing of warriors showing blue beneath the sleeves of their tunics, and half-bred boys with every mix of features—who came because I was the daughter of my mother as well.

At first I accepted their escort for protection. But between one day and the next, it seemed, the escort became a young army. My decision was being made for me. As we moved north toward Udrolissa, their numbers swelled until I had a war-host at my heels. It was too late, by then, to send them home. I told myself they might be needed to get me and Leir to the coast. And perhaps some of them would follow me back across the sea.

Two days before the Eve of Samonia I glimpsed the Arrows, stark against a dull winter sky. But I had no time for memories, for Artocoxos, ragged as an old bear at the end of winter, was riding down from the dun. He was alone.

I sat in the high seat of the house where I had been born, shivering. Fire leaped in the great central hearth, but it had been over a year since the queens had disbanded its garrison, and the folk of the household had gone back to their kin. The damp that permeated the thatch would be slow to yield. Artocoxos had gathered many of the Companions, and others had come with me. It lacked a day yet to Samonia, but as I looked at Drost and Catuueros, at Red Leg and Tomen and Zanis, Dogbelly and Ilix, I felt as if we were all ghosts come back to feast in our old home.

Across from me, Artocoxos gnawed on a piece of venison, but I had no stomach for food. The firelight cast an illusory gilding across his grizzled hair, but it could not put the flesh back on his bones or hide the half-healed scar that twisted down his arm.

"Did Gunarduilla order the attack on you?" I asked again.

"The offal shouted her name as if they thought so," he mumbled. "Leir believed 'em. It was a foul night anyhow, with a wind that would fair slam you into the stones. The king called on the skies to crush him, and the thunder came hammering down, but he couldn't command his own body, and Crow dragged him away. The place was rocky, and I got between two boulders and held the northerners until they were away. . . ."

I held out the jug of ale. Artocoxos took a long swallow and sat back, wiping his long moustaches with the back of his hand.

"How many of them did ye take out?" Vorcuns's eyes were blazing.

"Six, maybe—drove 'em off—but I'm not what I was. Tried to follow the king and fell, and if a herder out after a lost ewe hadn't tripped over me, my bones would be bleaching on the moors." His hand beat down upon his thigh. "Lady, forgive me! I've lost my lord!"

I gripped his wrist. "Listen, Bear-leg, the blood you lost would have stretched a younger man upon the stones. The wonder is that you live!"

"Cridilla," said Vorcuns. "Your sisters are devouring their people like maddened sows! The Goddess has given you an army. You must claim your kingdom now!"

I clutched my cloak to my aching breasts. "I only came to see my father safe! Have you forgotten that I have a husband and a child?"

"And what about all those other fathers and husbands and children?" Vorcuns returned. "Will you let them—"

"Peace!" Artocoxos growled. "What does any of this matter without the king?"

"You've set every shepherd in the dales to searching—" exclaimed Drostagnos. "He is dead or the Old Ones have taken him! Lady, you are our leader now!"

"Not until I know what has become of my father—"

"You'll be a long time waiting, then," rumbled Dogbelly.

"If you have the courage," came a voice from behind me, "there may be a way to learn where he has gone . . ." The men drew back respectfully as Lady Asaret threw back her dark blue cloak and knelt, holding out her hands to the fire. "I can send you out on the spirit road."

From the corner of my eye I glimpsed one of the men making a warding sign, but I leaned forward. "When?"

"If you like, tomorrow."

"But that is Samonia!" Talorgenos exclaimed. His gaze locked with hers.

"A good time to contact spirits, by your people's reckoning." The priestess smiled.

There was poor fare for the Samonia feasting—a few deer that the men had brought down, flat barley bannocks and hard cheese, and some dried fruit that one of the village women had stewed. The pigs and cattle that in a better season would have been kept until the winter slaughtering had been eaten long ago. I was ashamed to have to ask even this much from the village, but they offered it willingly, seeing in our presence a return to days that were golden in memory.

After I had blessed the feast I left Talorgenos to preside over the drinking of the memory ale. Tonight the duty of welcoming departed comrades belonged to the warriors. Lady Asaret and I had a task of our own.

As we came out into the darkness a cold wind swirled down from the dales to pluck the last of the dead leaves from the trees and moan forlornly through the tattered thatch of the hall. Or perhaps what I heard was the whispering of the spirits who had come back to keep the festival. Seeing the dun so cheerless, did they think they had missed their way? I remembered how I had seen the spirits the night my woman's blood first flowed . . . it was not that time in my cycle, but perhaps childbirth had sensitized me, for with every breath I tingled to the unmistakable pulse of power.

"They say that this night was no different than any other, before the Quiritani came—" said Lady Asaret as we made our way down the hill.

"But the spirits do return! Cannot you feel them in the air?" I exclaimed.

"I can feel them," she said shortly, "and for one trained as I was, that is an uncanny thing. For a generation they have been summoned on this night. They have grown accustomed to returning now."

"Do you mean they would stay away if we ceased to welcome them?"

Her face was a white blur in the darkness as she turned to me.

"Do you think the Otherworld is somewhere distant—beneath the earth, perhaps, or over the sea? It lies upon the world we know like the folds of a cloak, some parts touching closely, some far indeed from the knowledge of men. For some folk, the doors open easily and unawares, while others can find them only with senses heightened by time or place or ritual."

"A place like the Arrows?" I asked. Ahead of us the four columns of stone bulked featureless against the stars.

"And a time like Samonia," she agreed. "The great tides of the seasons ebb and flow in man as in the earth, regardless of his will. But the forms that folk give spirit have their own reality. They may fade, but like the marks we make on the land, something always remains. Even if your father's people should be cast down as mine have been, still something of their spirit would survive, and one who called the old names with will and knowledge would be answered. I have seen stone circles overgrown by forest where there is still power."

"The Arrows have power—" I remembered how I had sensed it when I was a child.

"They lie at a crossroads on the spirit paths. They exist in both worlds. If you are determined to dare this journeying, they will be a beacon to light you back again."

I have done this sort of thing before, so why am I afraid? I wondered then. Fear coiled in the pit of my stomach, but I quickened my pace down the hill.

Wood for bonfires had been stacked to north and south and east and west of the Arrows. I set down my cloakful of kindling and Lady Asaret added the sticks to the piles. As she coaxed each one alight I stood behind her, cloak spread to shield the embers she was carrying, and the wind spun out the flames in skeins of sparks that whipped against the stars.

"Lie down in the center, along the line of the stones," said the priestess, "and wrap up warmly."

The bells on her branched staff jangled as she paced the circumference of the circle. As she completed the first circuit, I felt the wind fade. Beyond that perimeter the bare twigs of the hawthorn hedge still rattled, but suddenly the leaping flames of the balefires were burning steadily. As Asaret began the second round, a droning undertone joined the sound of the bells. The pressure within the circle dropped abruptly.

Not until she began the third circuit did I realize that it was her voice I was hearing. The rhythm of its vibrations resonated in my bones. But by then I was already ceasing to feel the half-frozen earth on which I lay. My limbs had turned to lead but my mind floated, translating her words into images.

I saw the fires linked by a shining path of light as Lady Asaret wove the barrier. All was vague outside it, but the clarity within fountained upward, swirling sunwise with an energy whose sparkling motes I now could see. My spirit jerked like a tethered boat, but still the flesh held it. The priestess finished the seventh circle and spiraled inward to stand at my feet. Spirit sight perceived light flaring outward from her lifting arms like mighty wings.

"Serpent of Briga, go forth! Now the gateway is open. Fare freely, my daughter, the shining path awaits thee." The words rushed through my awareness and whirled me away.

I was aware first of sound, a directionless resonance like the shimmer of harpstrings. When my vision steadied, I saw the land below me veined with light. One bright branch flowed from the great stones where I lay. The sacred grove on the river below Udrolissa was the center of a sunburst of rays. Another shining path ran from farther down the river north and south as far as I could see.

For a time I was lost in wonder.

I thought at first that the tracks were like rivers of light; then I realized that what I was seeing was the movement of many man-shaped motes of light that thronged the spirit paths like folk on their way to a festival. I recognized Uxelos, who had been one of the Companions, and realized that they must be drinking the memory ale in the hall. The old warrior was clad in all his war-gear, but his age seemed to have fallen away. His hair appeared freshly bleached and stiffened, his shield new-painted with the image of a black boar. What would he think of the tattered men who had called him home?

Indeed, all the warriors who passed were a-gleam with finery; the men and women, even the children, were brightly clad. But there were so many! They thronged toward their villages, crying out to the women to conceive and make new bodies so that they could live again. But I saw dead spots in the web of life in places where there was no one left to welcome them. The wailing of spirits who no longer had an earthly home troubled the air with discordant harmonies.

Onward they hurried, the new dead and the old. I thought I glimpsed Waterdog and Willow, who had been my hearth-kin on the Misty Isle. I saw Loutrinos, who had died of the plague, and Senouindos, dead of old age in Belerion. Companions killed defending my father passed me, and then one whom I recognized with shock as Cuno, who was one of Agantequos's men. Had there been fighting in Morilandis?

I strained to see more, but my spirit was tethered. Below me was a brighter sphere of light that I recognized as Lady Asaret. She was standing guard over a long, cloak-wrapped bundle, and I realized with a start that this was the body I had left behind. I was out then, and I had to discipline myself to the task at hand, but on this night when the spirit roads were so crowded, how was I to locate one living man?

I too would have to do some summoning.

"Bear Mother! Artona!" I cried. "Your daughter is calling! Warrior woman, by the blood you shed I summon you!" I waited, but nothing stirred. Before, she had always come without my having to call. Where was she now? "Mother, remember how you taught me to track the red stag on the rocks and the otter in the stream. Mother, I need your trailcraft! Hear me, help me, come to me now!"

The web of light rippled around me. When I could focus, I saw Bear Mother before me, wrapped in her fur cloak as I remembered her.

"Tonight in Alba they feast. Thy sister roasted a young ox an' poured out the blood for me. Her warriors drink to me in golden mead."

I stared. Should I have made an offering? It had seemed to me that the living needed what food we had more than those who were gone.

"I can give thee no more than the bones of the buck that fed my men," I said bitterly. "And it is sour ale in which they drink to the brothers they have lost. But without thy help, there may be neither men nor ale next year."

I met her flat stare defiantly. I had never understood her when she wore flesh; why should she be more comprehensible now? Then she smiled.

"Bones are the seed. Will be content with bones."

"Canst find my father?" I asked.

"To see where he is, must know where he has been. Remember thy woodcraft! The spirit leaves its traces here!" Her form began to dislimn, arms extending, and suddenly she was an osprey, lifting away from me on outspread wings. "Come!" came the screech from above.

For a moment I panicked, then I remembered my testing, and with a surge of joy stretched out my arms to embrace the sky with the wide white wings of a swan. The osprey wheeled northwestward, and I followed her.

The night was wild with energies for which I had no names. I willed them to take familiar forms, winds that my spirit-shape could ride, shaped by recognizable contours in the land below. The web of light extended in all directions, and I sensed that some led to places very far from the world I knew. They called me, but I resisted their music and flew on.

Artocoxos had lost the king where the road that led south from the shrine of the Young God wound up through the fells. It was a wild country of thickly forested valleys and stone-crowned hills, hard for a foot traveler, even one with Crow's woodcraft, to pass. But the spirit road rolled straight and true.

Suddenly the osprey dropped downward.

My wingbeat faltered. There was something there, like the ghost

of a scent, or a half-heard, half-remembered song. I let myself glide
in a long spiral toward the storm-lashed land, and saw at last two
glimmers that were neither beast nor tree, huddled in the lee of an
outcrop of stone.

"Father!" my spirit cried.

Both men stirred; I saw the wind of the world whip at Leir's
hair. He lurched to his feet, shaking his fist against the sky.

"Strike, curse you—lightning sear my soul! Upon my head let
fire and thunder fall, if only they will crush my enemies! The
wretched earth is wounded to her death, what do ye wait for? Strike,
and make an end! All that I willed to do has been destroyed. Why
do I struggle on? O dreadful gods, when ye have had your sport
with me, in mercy, slay!"

Lightning flared and I saw him double-visioned, seamed features
carved in sharp relief and spirit-shape like a trapped wolf howling
out its pain. I angled my descent toward the darker shape that clung
to his knees.

"Crow, can you hear me? I am here!"

The lifeshimmer around the second man shifted as he looked
up.

"Don't hurt! This one does no harm!"

"Crow!" I called again. "It is Cridilla! Gods be thanked we've
found you!" The osprey's talons found a perch in a wind-twisted
birch tree and I settled awkwardly to the ground. "How did you
get here? Do you have food? Why can't my father see me?" As I
moved closer the words tumbled out.

"Everyone looks for him, but this one knows the hidden paths,"
said Crow. "Can do nothing, Adder. Be safe asleep. Go home!"

"I am in Udrolissa," I replied, "with Artocoxos and the war-
band. Stay here and we will come for you." Lightning flared again
and I saw Leir's face, all its strength disintegrating into despair.

"Father!" I cried. "Can't you hear me? I've come to take you
home. . . ." Leir's lifelight wavered like a torch when the wind
shakes the roof of the hall.

"The armies of the dead are coming home . . ." he whimpered
as more thunder battered the sky. "Their chariot wheels come clat-
tering through the clouds! Listen, can't you hear them? The cruel

wind flings accusations at my head like rain!" He dropped to his knees. "Mercy! I did try to save you, lads! The bitches have betrayed me! Oh, their eyes, there are so many, far too many dead! Damned and doomed, oh, leave me! Let me be!" He covered his eyes with his veined hands.

"Father, I am alive! Crow, you can see me—tell him I am here!"

For a moment Crow shook his head, shivering. Then he levered himself stiffly to his own knees and shook my father's bony shoulder.

"What? What is it should I see?" Leir muttered. "Already I have seen too much that's ill!" But he turned, staring, as I stretched out my pinions to embrace him and for a moment felt myself neither swan nor woman, but something in between.

"*Cridilla*—" Leir came upright suddenly, pointing at me, and his voice was terrible. "A spirit! Demon! Deceiver! Why have you come to me? It is Samonia, when the dead come! She's dead too! Two daughters have turned demon and the third I drove away to die! If I do speak with spirits, then am I a spirit too?" Suddenly, appallingly, he began to laugh. "You are dead and she is dead, and I! I killed the one I loved the best of all!"

"Not dead!" Crow said desperately. "Her spirit walks the dream roads in shape of swan!" Once more he turned his master toward me. I beat the air with my wings, and Leir's thin locks lifted in the breeze. His eyes widened.

"Do not mock me. I murdered you! It was I who shot the swan!"

Chapter

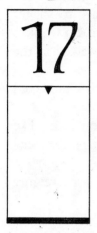

17

After wine-feast and mead-feast they hastened out,
men famous in battle-stress, reckless of their lives;
... For the retinue of Mynyddawg I am bitterly
sad, I have lost too many of my true kinsmen; of
three hundred champions who set out for Catraeth,
alas, but for one man none came back.

—Aneurin, *Goddodin*

O
vernight, a mass of cloud had moved in from the
north, and the pale sky was flaking into snow that
left icy kisses on cheek or brow but melted when
it touched the ground. In the midst of the bustle
of a camp awakening, the man who had been high king of the Island
of the Mighty sat alone. The snowflakes caught in Leir's eyelashes,
so still was he, and starred the heavy cloak Crow had draped around
him. Once, he reached out to cup a falling flake and smiled as it
melted in his hand.

A man carrying a roll of blankets slowed as he neared the king,
then moved carefully around him. While I had been waiting for
the cauldron to boil it had happened thus a dozen times. It was as
if my father inhabited a separate reality.

My spirit flight had been exhausting, but by the following afternoon I had picked two hands of men from the war-band to go
after the king and we were on the road. It was a force large enough
for defense against any chance-met foes, but small enough to move
swiftly, and it included all that were left of Leir's sworn Companions. The rest of my army I left in Udrolissa with Talorgenos,
promising to send for them if there should be need.

Even so, it had taken us nearly three weeks to reach my father and Crow, following the main road through the dales, for after the Feast of Samonia the weather closed in again, and the horses made slow going on muddy trails. Crow had found a cave to shelter himself and the king while they waited, but they were too weak to travel quickly. And since Samonia, Leir no longer walked in the waking world.

"He grows no better—" I said to Crow, who was hunkered down beside me, gnawing on a rind of cheese.

"He wanders in dreamfields. He plucks snowflakes like flowers—" Crow's voice wavered painfully. "Perhaps he is the lucky one. . . ."

Perhaps, I thought, but to see so complete a loss of sovereignty shook my faith in what was real.

"Crow, how is it with *you*?" I touched his shoulder.

He looked up at me, eyes wide and dark as a startled deer's. The eyes I remembered, but his face was worn to the bone. When had that happened? I had been so concerned with my father I had scarcely looked at the man who had saved him.

Crow licked his lips.

> *"At end of year, ill signs appear—*
> *Spirits cry in empty sky,*
> *Ravens call, warning all—"*

He shrugged painfully, the clever hands for once stilled. "This one is afraid—ran from hills long ago, but Old Ones are not forgetting. Too fearful to live, always. But not yet like *him*—" He motioned again toward Leir. "Still earthbound. . . ."

"Crow—" I began, but what could I say to him? If we got safe to Udrolissa perhaps I could put some meat on those sharp bones. At least I understood what to do for Crow. I had no notion what might be required to heal the king.

I filled a cup with chamomile tea from the cauldron that hung steaming above the coals and handed it to him. Then I carried another to the silent figure on the other side of the fire.

"Father, here is tea. It will warm you." I knelt and held it out to him.

"The drink of the Otherworld is fragrant." He lifted the cup and breathed deeply of the steam. "Maiden, I thank you. My daughter used to bring me tea in the mornings. I wish that I might see her, but it is forbidden." He nodded wisely. "She has been transformed into a swan. . . ."

"Father, I *am* Cridilla, alive in the flesh, and so are you!" I laid a hand on his arm, wincing at the feel of old bones so near the surface of the skin. "Father, *look* at me!"

He bent forward, and I forced myself to meet his unfocused gaze.

"You have the look of her, indeed, but my daughter was just coming to her womanhood, while you are grown. . . ."

I sat back on my heels, brushing snowflakes from my eyes, or perhaps it was tears. He did not see me. Had he *ever* really seen me, I wondered then.

"Lady, the men are ready to ride." Artocoxos looked from Leir to me. "My lord's mount is waiting, if you will help him." His mouth twisted painfully, then he mastered his emotion and brought up his arm in salute to me. "The men are waiting for your orders now."

I got to my feet. I had hoped that finding my father would relieve me of the weight of the war-band's loyalty. Perhaps it would be different when we reached Udrolissa, but the loyalty of the men here seemed set on me more than ever, and I could not deny them. It was seeing me that had snapped Leir's last link to reality.

The snow had ceased falling, and below the ceiling of cloud the air was clear. Ahead of us, smoke rose from the rock walls of the fortress of Rigodunon, a flat-topped hump crowning tier upon tier of living stone. It had been raining when we came north, and we had gotten by the fortress unobserved, but by now Bituitos must have heard of our passage and be waiting for our return.

"By noon we'll be under the lee of the dun," said Artocoxos, following my gaze.

"What do you think they'll do?"

"Bituitos owes much to the king, but from Rigodunon he could rule the dales. 'Tis not for nothing they name him Landmaster. He was ever a careful man, and he has sat tight in that fortress since the troubles began. He will not anger the queens by aiding us, but perhaps he'll let us go by."

The pitiless grey light showed me every line that a lifetime in Leir's service had left in the old war-leader's face, and I reached out to him in sudden gratitude.

"Artocoxos—let me say what my father cannot—thanks for his life, little though he may value it. It would have been so easy to simply go away. . . ." I flushed a little as I met his bleak gaze. That was what I had done, after all.

"At first I blamed you for seeking another home across the sea—" Even as he echoed my thoughts, Artocoxos began to smile. "But you have grown. I am hearing you have chosen a strong man to match you. I look forward to seeing your son."

I nodded, unable to answer, and took up my reins. Did Agantequos still love me? Would Beli remember me?

The night before I had dreamed that I was crossing the narrow sea. But this time there was a great company of ships around me; the reflections from the lanterns in their prows danced on the waves. In the boats, folk slept huddled together. From somewhere I heard a baby cry. But in the stern of the first boat one man sat waking with his hand on the rudder and his eyes on the moon. It was Agantequos, but his face was all white planes and dark shadows above the stubble of new beard. I cried out to him, and saw his eyes follow the flight of a seabird that wheeled across the moon. I had awakened still hearing the cry of the gull, or perhaps it was my own.

Had that been a true seeing, or only a fantasy of my own fear? I told myself that I could not allow it to matter. I could only go on, trusting that Bituitos would honor old loyalties. It was a long way to Udrolissa and the weather was not going to improve as Midwinter neared.

Rigodunon was a brooding presence at my left shoulder as we turned eastward. But no one challenged us as we crossed the Doe and began to skirt the mountain. To the south, the hillsides were hidden by a dim haze of leafless trees. Above, the rocky bones of the mountain broke through the mat of dead grass in weather-bleached scars, as if the entire peak were a buried fortress, and the human walls that crowned it only a model, like the earthworks that children build in the sand of the shore. With senses focused by my journey on the spirit road, I knew that its apparent solidity hid chambers and passages and streams that never saw the sun. Crow eyed the heights uneasily as we passed, but I did not ask him what omens he read there.

A little past noon we saw smoke rising through the chill, damp air. Ahead and to our right fields had been cleared in the woodland, and presently I made out a cluster of huts that seemed to have been grown from the native stone. Sheep bleated on the grassy slopes above us. A small figure detached itself from among the sheep and dashed for the village. At least they still had livestock. I wondered if we could buy one of the beasts for our dinner. There had been no time for hunting here.

We moved on more slowly as the hill curved away into a broad ravine where a good trail edged the beck that came rushing down from the fells. Another path ran across the slope to the village ahead of us. I was turning to ask Artocoxos if he would send a man down there when my pony whinnied urgently.

I stiffened, reaching for my sword.

Another horse bugled in answer; there was a moment of stillness, and I heard clearly the sound of many hoofbeats on the stony road. My belly clenched. Traveling had toughened me, but it had been two years since I had gripped anything more deadly than a spindle shaft, and the day when I had fought my way into the Bear Clan was almost seven years past.

Swearing, Artocoxos shrugged his oblong shield from his back to his arm and reined his horse past me. Then I saw the first of the riders coming around the outcrop ahead of us, a dark-haired man with the skin of a mountain cat slung round his shoulders and blue tattoos spiraling up his arms. Those were Ai-Zoma tattoos; the Albans must have made alliance with the wild northern tribes. Others clattered after him, skin cloaks and tattered plaids whipping back over leather tunics as they kicked their ponies into a gallop. Horns brayed wildly.

Then came one with a standard, streamers of dyed horsehair trailing beneath the bobbing figure of a stuffed hawk with outspread wings. Behind it two horses bolted toward us as if pursued by the chariot that lurched after them, the charioteer urging them on. Clinging to the rail beside him was a big man glittering with golden ornaments. It was Maglaros of the Banalisioi. Maglaros of Alba. At last I recognized my real enemy.

"Siwanet! Ai-Siwanet! The hawk strikes true!" they cried, spreading out as the road widened. A lance flashed past me and rattled across the stones. Another hurtled through the air; I heard a cry and saw Catuueros down with a spear in his gut. There were so many! Gunarduilla might be leading the other half of the Alban war-host, but the men Maglaros had here were more than enough to roll over my little band. Now indeed I wished for the men I had left at home.

"Crow, take the king's rein and get him behind us—" I cried, tightening the chinstrap of my helm. More spears darted toward us. A horse screamed.

Artocoxos hauled his pony round on its hindquarters, yelling, "Everyone get back or they'll surround us! Retreat to the ravine!"

That made sense. Where the walls narrowed, a small band might hope to hold off a larger one. My mare fought the bit as I booted her back the way we had come. One of the northern warriors careered toward me. I struck out clumsily, cursing as he swerved. In the Great Land there were tribes who fought a-horseback, but the Quiritani clung to their chariots, and my mother's people were foot fighters one and all. I could feel my saddle pad slipping already and gripped harder with my knees; it would be under the mare's belly and I on the ground if I tried that blow again.

The slope curved away before me and I urged my mount to greater speed. The others were scattering like blown leaves before me. I caught the glitter of rushing water and yanked the mare's head around to keep from going into the stream. One horse was already thrashing in the water. Iron clanged as its rider traded blows with the enemy who had dismounted to attack him as he struggled out of the stream.

A horse stumbled ahead of me. I pulled back and glimpsed a shadow beside me; a spear jabbed and I grabbed for the shaft, dropping my reins. The shock nearly wrenched my arm from its socket as the other pony leaped out from beneath its rider and my enemy's weight came full on the butt end of the spear. I let go and saw him flung against the rocks, screaming, but the jerk had snapped my girth and all I could do was to grab a handful of mane and swing myself off the mare before I was thrown.

I landed hard on my back and heard my shield crack; its strap parted and it fell away as I rolled, but my sheathed sword was still at my side. A shadow lifted above me, then pebbles peppered my face as the horse that had leaped over me plunged on. I struggled to my feet, fighting for breath, and grabbed a fallen spear.

Men and horses were strung out along the ravine. A few paces away, Dogbelly lay groaning on the ground. The chariot had come to a halt below me and dismounted men were gathering around it. I heard Artocoxos shout from somewhere above at the same moment as one of the Albans caught sight of me and they started up the path, baying like hounds.

My arm swung back and I cast, knowing even as the spear left my hand that I had thrown true. The battle-serpent sped through the air and a man screamed as it pierced his eye and bore him down. But the others were still coming, and even for one trained by Bear Mother those were poor odds. I wrenched my sword from its sheath and forced my limbs into an awkward run.

"Cridilla, *behind you!*" Artocoxos screamed.

I twisted, glimpsed a blur in the air, and felt iron rip through the top of my shoulder as I flung myself down. The spear slithered across the stones ahead of me and dug itself into the side of the hill. My shoulder was on fire. The ground shook as my foes ran toward me. No time to wonder how badly it had bit me; I struggled upright, almost dropping my sword at the first wave of real pain.

I saw pounding legs and the flash of blades and ducked, thrusting up beneath the first man's guard. As my sword went into his belly he doubled over on top of me with a grunt and we both went down. I felt the impact as a blow meant for me went into my enemy's back, and warm blood spurted over my arm.

My own pain had been shocked away. A tangle of thrashing arms and legs flickered above me. I shoved the dead man off and jerked my sword free as another blade swung down. Still rolling, I jabbed ineffectually, then slashed the back of someone's knee and came up onto my own knees as he fell.

Spear shafts whipped above me like branches in a storm. Something snapped at my head and instinct brought my sword up to bat it aside. There was a roar of rage and suddenly a bulky shape was between me and the spears. I blinked and recognized Artocoxos, gulped air and staggered to my feet, sword swinging up to guard his back as more Albans charged in.

The fire in my shoulder burned away my fatigue. I felt as if someone I could not see were fighting beside me. When Horse and I battled, we used to become one being in two bodies, but what I sensed from this presence was a single-minded delight in fighting that set my spirit ablaze. Then all the skill Bear Mother had beat into me awoke to furious life, and my sword scraped the length of an enemy blade and slid through leather padding into the heart of the man who wielded it. Another foe took his place. Above the brutal clang of iron I could hear my own laughter as we traded blows.

At least this man had some skill. His sword scythed toward me from above and my own flicked up to meet it. Iron hissed as the blades met, for a moment I held him, then I gave way suddenly and as the release of pressure drove his weapon down I stepped aside, bringing my sword in a wide circle back and around to slash across his chest.

Two riderless horses came galloping past us and splashed through the stream. Others were milling at the edge of the trees. There was a flurry of motion behind me and a head flew toward the stream like a hurley ball. Artocoxos stepped back with a grunt of satisfaction. Then two more men came after me.

"Take the woman alive!" came a shout from below. "I want the woman living, and the king!" The attack faltered, and beyond the

Alban warriors I glimpsed Vorcuns and three of the others pounding back down the slope toward us, shields bobbing on their arms.

"Run for it, Cridilla—" gasped Artocoxos. "I'll hold 'em . . . here."

"We'll hold them together!" A spear's cast up the slope the rest of our men were gathering. The trees were thicker there, and from their cover some of our men were snapping arrows at their foes. "A step back, and then another, now while they're wondering! Move!"

I reached behind me, grabbed the skirt of his tunic, and pulled. He gave a bark of laughter and then, between blows, we started up the hill.

In another moment our rescuers were crashing into the enemy. Artocoxos gave me a shove and the others closed in around me. After a few curses I realized that I might as well save my breath for fighting. We were moving anyway, all together toward the shelter of the trees.

"There's a way through the dale up onto the fells," said Drostagnos, who had been born in these hills. "If we can cover a retreat up the ravine."

Artocoxos grunted, and the mass of us moved back a few feet more, bristling like a hedgehog with swords and spears. Then we were into the trees. I sped forward and heard branches crash as the others followed. Ahead I saw daylight, and Leir, still hunched on his pony with Crow hanging on to the reins.

"Keep going!" I yelled, and smacked the pony's flank with the flat of my blade.

The beast snorted indignantly and went bucketing up the trail with Crow scrambling after it, and the battle knotted and unwound behind them as our rearguard stopped to fight or broke free to run once more.

The walls of the dale grew steeper, and suddenly we saw where the stream burst forth from the naked stone. Beyond it the valley was floored with turf beneath pale limestone scars all pitted with the entrances to caves—good footing for fleeing or fighting, and I saw plenty of both ahead.

The clouds settled slowly onto the hills above us as we fought our way up the dale, Artocoxos covering our retreat and Maglaros ever in the forefront of his men. A rising wind moaned through the rocks and my face tingled to the first sting of snow. The gash in my shoulder had stopped bleeding, but blood loss had weakened me; the world narrowed to the next lifting blade, the next foot of ground. Then the path forked, the right-hand track leading up to a broad dry bowl of pasture broken by a few outcroppings of stone, and the other curving into a rocky gorge.

"To the right," cried Drostagnos, grasping the rein of Leir's horse and dragging it along.

Maglaros yelled and came after, but despite his superior numbers we had given him a good battering. We started up the path, then stopped short as every rock in the bowl sprouted an armed man.

There was a moment of appalled stillness as both sides strained to identify the warriors. Then an arrow from above took Drostagnos in the throat. As he fell I leaped to catch Leir's rein, and, looking up, saw a still figure wrapped in a crimson cloak watching from the crag.

"Bituitos!" Artocoxos's roar echoed from wall to wall. "Are ye grown like all the others then, sniffing under the skirts of the queens? Will ye lift blade against your sworn lord?"

"I am Landmaster. I serve neither king nor queen. Go back. You shall not pass this way."

"You belly-crawling shit-licker—" Artocoxos began. He took a step up the slope and another arrow struck quivering at his feet.

"I will not attack, but for you Rigodunon is no refuge."

I longed for an arrow to shatter that serene complacence, but we had spent all our arrows against Maglaros, who was listening with a grin that grew broader with every moment that passed. Artocoxos took a deep breath and looked around him, and I felt sick once more. Just so I had seen a trapped bear give one last glare around the circle of hunters before he charged upon the spears.

"What is it?" Leir roused, blinking. "Do the heroes practice their swordplay even here?" A gust of wind swirled snow between us and he leaned forward, trying to see.

"Even here, my lord," said Artocoxos gently. "We show our

skill for your pleasure. It makes no matter. In death as in life I am your servant, and I never thought to make old bones by the fire. . . . Maglaros!" He turned back to our enemy. "Artocoxos son of Esuscutios challenges you! Let us show the king how Quiritani warriors die!"

A combat of champions? I stared at him, wondering if we could trust the Albans to keep their bond to let us go if Maglaros was killed. Artocoxos was grinning through his beard, but he had spoken as if he saw his doom before him. Could he win? There was no telling how much of the blood that covered him might be his own. The chill of half-frozen earth seeped through the soles of my shoes and I shivered convulsively.

The old warrior gave me a sharp glance, and I realized that he had said nothing about terms. Leir's pony tossed its head restively and I pulled it toward the other path where the cliff might give some shelter. If we edged along a step at a time, perhaps they would not see.

Those Companions who remained had drawn in around us—Vorcuns and Sigo and Ilix. Vorcuns's blade had bent in the fighting, and he was surreptitiously straightening it against one of the stones. His face had a grey pallor to it that would have worried me if there had been time. Maglaros's men were arguing around him. He shook his head suddenly and grasped his lance, and Artocoxos laughed.

"Oho, Gunarduilla is not here to protect you! Come on, and I will eat you, queen's man!" he cried.

Maglaros swore and wrenched free of his warriors. "Let me be—do you think I cannot handle an old fool?"

"I may have twice your years, but I've twice your battle-craft. I have slain more men than march in your war-host. I have conquered three kings!" Artocoxos shouted back.

He dropped his battered shield, fumbled with the pin that held the tatters of his cloak, and used the rags to wipe some of the blood from the leather that protected his chest. Somewhere in the fighting he had lost his helmet. He turned to me, and I dragged shaking fingers through his coarse hair and twisted it into the warrior's knot at his crown.

Silently Vorcuns handed him his long-headed spear.

"Your shield is chopped to kindling," said Ilix gruffly. "Take mine."

The bronze of the boar-shape that backed the boss of the shield gleamed dully as Artocoxos slid it onto his arm. The failing light struck a last glint of gold from the arm ring he had been awarded long ago by his king.

"Maglaros son of Magloscutios accepts your challenge," came the call from below. "From the islands of the north to Uotadinion the bards proclaim my deeds. You were great once, but your day is long past. You and your lord are ghosts, *old* ghosts, and it is time to send you back underground!"

Artocoxos straightened. "You will see whether age has sapped the strength from my arm! You have betrayed your king, and the gods will give you into my hand."

Maglaros stalked toward us, and I remembered how he and my sister had circled on the grass.

"Kill him—I want to see his blood on the ground," I said to Artocoxos, and the old warrior snarled and strode out to face his foe.

Maglaros was waiting for him, his own lance gripped fast. As Artocoxos approached, his enemy began to run, and in the supple dip and backswing as Maglaros poised his weapon and threw I saw a blurred echo of Bear Mother's training, and knew that Gunarduilla had broken her oaths and taught her husband the Bear kindred's warrior-craft.

Artocoxos took the cast full on his shield. The lance pierced the bronze boar on the boss and the layers of leather beneath, but stuck fast in the lindenwood that backed it, and the weight of the shaft bent the spearhead so that the wood hung quivering. But already Artocoxos's heavy frame was swaying to his own swing, and only a quick twist saved Maglaros from being spitted as he came on. There was no time for either man to regret his failure. The old warrior jerked the spear from his shield and flung it away, then drew his sword.

Both men had good weapons, made of star iron that did not blunt or bend. Maglaros drew, his blade scraped across the bronze boar on Artocoxos's shield. The old warrior's return blow boomed on that of his enemy and Artocoxos pressed forward, but his foe slid sideways and away. Leir leaned forward to watch them, his eyes brightening with interest.

Maglaros darted in again, his blade flashed up on his enemy's sword side, met Artocoxos's weapon with a bone-jarring screech and slid away. He whirled, but the older man's arm snapped forward and down, shearing the corner of Maglaros's shield away. Swiftly he followed up on his advantage; the heavy blade rose and fell and the shield split where the planks behind the leather covering joined.

Maglaros danced backward, lips curling in a feral snarl as he flung the remains of the shield away. "Glad . . . to be rid of the weight!" he gasped, gripped his sword two-handed, and whipped it round in a low arc that brought the tip across Artocoxos's thigh just above the knee. I saw bright blood welling through the tear in the wool breeches as the Alban leader spun away.

Perhaps it had been a mistake to destroy the shield, for Bear Mother's style had always been strongest in swordwork. And though Maglaros was no youth, he was still twenty years younger than his opponent, and now his speed was beginning to tell. Artocoxos stood like a bear at bay as the younger man danced round him, slashing. Soon the edges of his own shield were disintegrating, and blood was dripping from gashes on his legs and arms.

I stamped numb feet and never felt the cold. Leir swayed with every blow. We strained to see as the wind flung veils of sleet between us and tore them away again.

Finish him! I prayed silently. *Lady of Ravens, make it stop now!*

As if he had heard me, Artocoxos cast away the fragments of his shield, and though he left a trail of blood upon the ground, he drove forward with a series of two-handed scything strokes that beat Maglaros to his knees. For a moment they were still. Maglaros was panting, sword lifted in a wavering guard. Then the old warrior heaved up his blade for the final blow.

Maglaros glared like a cornered ferret. As the blade fell, he jabbed his own sword upward. There was a sound like breaking ice, and half Artocoxos's shattered sword arced outward while the lower part smashed into the shoulder of his enemy.

Maglaros's unbroken blade was thrusting at his foe's gut, but it was the force of the old warrior's downward motion that drove it in. Maglaros curled sideways to clutch his ruined shoulder as the body communicated its pain. Artocoxos reeled backward with the sword still stuck to the hilt in his belly, jerking it from his enemy's grasp. For a moment longer he remained on his feet, as the lightning-riven oak trembles in the blast. And then, so slowly that I forgot to breathe, he fell.

For a long moment there was no sound but the whimpering of the wind.

"Why doesn't he get up?" Leir's voice broke the silence. Beyond the bodies, the Albans were beginning to stir.

"In the Otherworld you will see him fight again," I answered, and wondered why I was weeping, for surely we were all going to be reunited soon.

"Run for the other passage," Vorcuns whispered hoarsely. "Don't waste his sacrifice."

I grasped the reins and pulled, and as Leir's pony broke into an awkward trot my sister's warriors roused from their own stupor and came after us.

"Where are you taking me?" asked my father. "Why are we leaving Artocoxos behind?"

To our right, the rising bank was all grass, but the left side was sheer stone, and the slope between them was steepening rapidly. The horse stumbled and went to its knees. I dragged it up again, but now it was limping, and in another moment it came to a trembling halt and would move no more. From behind me came the crashing of sword on shield, the kettle-mending clangor of clashing blades.

"Father, get down!" I clutched at his sleeve. "We must go on foot now or we'll be killed!"

"But I *am* dead—" he began, then Crow shoved from the other side and he came down in a tangle at my feet.

I glimpsed the blur of a blade above us, then another body pushed between. It was Sigo, with his throat slashed. The man who had killed him raised his sword for another blow, but Leir's hand had closed instinctively on Sigo's dropped blade. He struggled upright, swinging, and the enemy yelled and fell away.

Mad the king might be, but his reactions were still those of a warrior. As we scrambled up the scree between the narrowing cliffs he accounted for more than one of the enemy. But now there were only five of us, and Crow without a weapon, and though the Albans fought less furiously without Maglaros to drive them, more than a dozen remained.

"Crow, you could at least throw rocks at them—" I gasped as a thrust from Ilix's spear sent the leader sliding back into his fellows. "Do you *want* to die?"

Crow's face worked, but he did not move. His glance was flickering over the rough walls beneath the ribbon of sky. The passage was so narrow now that we blocked it if we stood together. It protected us from the worst of the wind, but we had to dodge an occasional falling stone. Suddenly Crow tipped back his head and gave voice to an eerie, high-pitched squeal.

I gritted my teeth as the sound faded into the rising howl of the wind. Then there was another noise, and the ground shook as loose stone cascaded onto the path below. Snow whirled down behind it, cutting off vision, but screams told me that at least a few of our foes would trouble us no more.

"It's our chance," cried Ilix. "Come on!"

We staggered forward, and suddenly I felt the loose rock give way to turf. Snow slammed into us as we left the shelter of the gorge and I grabbed for the king.

"Hold on to each other!" I shouted into the storm.

I glimpsed smooth slopes curving away to either side, and the increasing fury of the wind told me we were coming out onto the open moor. In this weather we would be hard to find if we could locate some cave mouth or tumble of rock to shelter in.

Cautiously we moved forward, grasping cloaks or clutching belts to keep together. The wind was a dangerous ally, numbing hands and driving sleet down every gap in our clothing even as it hid us from our enemies. And the light was going fast.

My feet told me when we left the crag and blundered out onto the broad limestone bench at the foot of the mountain. We staggered from hard stone to squelching peat bog, then to turf again, and went on.

A few moments later Leir stumbled and went down. The rest of us collapsed in a huddle around him, breathing hard. I was not the only one who was almost at the edge of endurance. How long would it be before we began to regret the swifter deaths waiting for us on the points of our enemies' swords?

"Here . . ." gasped Ilix. "There's a hole. I think we can get in!"

I felt my way after him. The last of the light showed a narrow rift angling into the earth before us. A tossed stone rattled and bounced through what sounded like considerable space before it came to rest, but we did not need to go very far—just deep enough to get out of the wind.

One after another, we wriggled into the cleft.

We had to crawl for what seemed a considerable way before we found a place where all of us could cling in anything like comfort. Ilix continued on toward the larger cave he was sure must lie farther in. We heard the scrape of stone and an occasional oath as he worked his way down.

"There is space here! I can feel it," came his shout finally. I was already sliding toward the farther passage when I heard stone crack and then a cry of surprise that turned to terror as it faded. Then it was gone.

"Gods below!" exclaimed Vorcuns, crawling down beside me. For a moment we listened, but there was nothing more.

"I should go after him—" I began, but Vorcuns's big hand closed hard on my arm. His harsh breathing was all I could hear.

"He is gone, Cridilla. There is nothing you can do."

"Hungry gods . . ." Crow giggled behind us. "Safe now. They have sacrifice."

Vorcuns cursed him, but I was shaking too hard to speak, and I recognized the edge in his laughter.

"Leave him alone. We're all on the edge of madness," I whispered finally. "We must rest now. Find what comfort you can on the stones."

I dragged myself back to the ledge and pulled my cloak around me. I could hear the others settling themselves: Crow's breathing light as a beast's, and Leir's occasional cough, Vorcuns's labored breaths growing slower as he stilled. The stone was cold beneath me, and my shoulder was throbbing again. I would not sleep, I thought and in the same moment plummeted unresisting into a darkness as deep as the chasm into which Ilix had disappeared.

When I woke, a shaft of pale light was filtering down from above. My wounded shoulder had stiffened. Indeed, every muscle in my body was shrieking its pain. And I was cold. The others lay un-moving, Leir and Crow huddled together and Vorcuns by himself with his sword clutched to his breast and his head lolling at an awkward angle on the stone. I crawled over to him, whispering his name.

But even when I shook his shoulder, he did not answer me. I touched his face, and felt it chill as clay. Had it been the cold, or had his heart at last given way? I looked from the dead to the sleepers and wanted to bawl like a baby. I had never felt so alone.

"Vorcuns, did you bring me to this pass, or did I bring you?" Tears pricked behind my eyelids and I could no longer contain them. I bent over the cold body, weeping for Vorcuns and for Ilix and Artocoxos and the others, and for myself most of all.

"Let him lie. . . ." Leir's voice brought me upright, staring. "This is a worthy barrow for such a warrior. It is we who must go on."

Crow caught his master's hand and kissed it, and Leir patted him absently. Carefully he extended one leg, then the other, and levered himself up the passageway. Speechless, I followed him.

We came out into a new world. Above us the plateau sloped gently toward the summit of Rigodunon. Before us the land fell away in frosted folds. But here on the heights, all was whiteness. A pale sun sparkled on last night's snowfall, and though the crisp air nipped at cheek and brow, all was still.

"Father?" I ventured finally. The king turned, and I flinched at the grief I saw in his eyes.

"I would rather still be mad—" he spoke slowly. "If the gods are kind, I will be mad once more. But today I remember my shame. You should have left me to die in the hills."

"I love you . . ." I said helplessly. It was all the answer I had ever known. I stumbled toward him and after a moment he opened his arms to hold me. I could feel his trembling.

"The gods are playing with us, Cridilla. But at this moment they are busied elsewhere. Long ago I used to hunt these hills. If we go eastward, we can get down to the river. There are folk in the dale who might share a little food and fire."

Leaning on Crow's shoulder, and with me on his other side to steady him, the high king led us across the moor.

Chapter

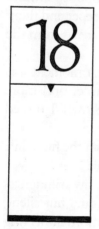

Dismal is this life, to be without a soft bed;
a cold frosty dwelling, harshness of snowy wind.
Cold icy wind, faint shadow of a feeble sun,
the shelter of a single tree on the top of the level
  moor.
Enduring the shower, stepping along deer-paths,
traversing greenswards on a morning of raw frost.

—Suibhne the Wild Man, *Buile Shuibhne*

S now puffed glittering from the branch I was grabbing to
slow my way down the trail. Rough bark scraped my palm
as my wounded shoulder betrayed me, then I was sliding
down the bank in a spray of snow. I came to rest with my
nose in a clump of broom, and in the stillness that followed heard
the high peal of Crow's laughter.

Squinting against the sun, I glared up at him. The night before
we had found shelter with a family who scratched out a meager
living at the edge of the fells. I thought that food and warmth had
restored me, but clearly it was going to be some time before I could
depend on my left hand.

"Otter is new totem!" Crow said cheerfully. "But better go down
this way—" He tugged one of his tattered furs across his belly,
dove forward, and slid headfirst down the bank after me, avoiding
the stones with a neat wriggle that brought him up by my side,
grinning from ear to ear. There had been no sign of searchers, and
ever since we had left the huts that morning he had been in appallingly good spirits. Abruptly I could endure them no more.

With my right hand I grabbed a handful of snow and flung it
at him. Crow rolled away and returned the favor, and I forgot both

our journey and its reason in my determination to smother that grin. The bank erupted into a blur of white, as if the snow that covered it were trying to return to the sky. Crow bobbed around me, agile as an otter. I stayed where the snow was deeper and flung snowballs in all directions as once I had frightened crows from the cornfields with a sling and a scrip full of stones.

Then I heard an oath in Quiritani, and in the next moment was hit on the back of the neck by a ball thrown harder and more accurately than anything Crow had hit me with. Slowly I turned around.

My father, who had managed to get himself down the hill while Crow and I were busy, was brushing snow from his beard.

"I got you—" he said uncertainly. Did he doubt my willingness to play or his own? Since yesterday he had been sane but silent, conducting himself with a careful courtesy almost more unnerving than his madness.

"I can still throw straight, it seems. . . ." Leir coughed, but I could not keep from grinning and suddenly his eyes began to dance in answer, brilliant blue as the winter sky. For a moment his hair seemed not white but golden, and I was a child again at Udrolissa. The laughing young man who used to play in the snow with me looked out from my father's face now, and suddenly I was filled with joy.

I clambered to my feet, flinging wide my arms as if to embrace all this terrible and lovely land. We had been making our way down the dale along a sheep trail that skirted the edge of the scars, never showing ourselves against the skyline, and avoiding the more traveled road that followed the stream. The cliff behind me hid the summit of Rigodunon, but across the river the Hill of the Winds crouched like a great white cat watching over the dales.

Water gleamed bright through the trees below us, where the river meandered south and eastward to swell the Verbeia, which led in turn to the Udra and in the end to the sea. We had only to follow it to be free. My breath caught; I felt those waters as if they flowed through my own veins. I felt every underground rivulet, every secret pool that never saw the light of day. Suddenly the vision of my initiation was as vivid as it had been when they carried me out of the cave six years ago.

In that moment I stood at the center of safety. What could those puny creatures that hunted us do? I was the land.

More snow flashed through the air as Leir and Crow targeted each other simultaneously. My father laughed, and the sound sparked through me. I saw the laughing god dancing across the fells, and he was the spirit that made the land live.

Then another snowball splattered against my arm, and I returned to the fray.

After a time we ran out of breath for play. The sun was overhead, so we settled on a bare rock to eat some of the cheese and barley-cakes for which we had traded Leir's cloak of crimson wool the night before. The other part of the trade he was wearing, a loose garment made from a sheep's pelt that looked from a distance like dirty snow. My cloak was a mottled reddish-brown like last year's bracken, and Crow, who always responded to winter by simply layering on more hides and furs, moved through the landscape like some odd animal.

When we started out again the sun was beginning to arch west-ward, and I was feeling the strain of the day's march despite last night's sanctuary. Or perhaps it was the horseplay that had tired me. On our way north we had stopped at a settlement just past the road from Rigodunon. It was only two stone huts with their backs against the scar and a croft with a bit of fenced pastureland, but the folk had been friendly. As we came around the edge of the scar I searched the sky for the smudges of their hearthfires, thinking of food and rest. But the sky stayed clear. I stopped, holding out an arm to slow the others.

"What is it?" Leir's hand was firm on my shoulder.

"Nothing—that is why I have stopped. There were two families and a fold full of sheep here when I passed this way before. They should be making some sound."

He nodded. "Crow, lad, creep around the rocks and tell us what you see." He suppressed another cough.

The furs blurred Crow's outline as he dropped to all fours, or perhaps it was the way he moved, for suddenly I was watching a thick-pelted dog trot forward to survey the fells. Too soon, he returned.

"Dead. . . ." He looked as if he wanted to howl. "All dead, all gone!"

Leir and I edged forward. There were no cookfires, but the stones that had formed the walls of the huts were blackened, and charred roofbeams had fallen in. The snow around them was trodden to mire.

"Go back," whimpered Crow, "ghosts will hate us! Go away!"

Perhaps, I thought dismally, since the place had most likely been burned for having sheltered me. But the storage shed built into the wall of the croft looked as if it might still keep out the wind.

"We need shelter. Ghosts there may be, but I would rather appease them than Maglaros's men. Have they left anyone on guard?"

Even Crow could see no one, but we waited until dusk to cross the trail and make our way up to the ruins. We dragged the twisted bodies of the slain into the largest of the huts and piled rocks and the remains of the turf roof on top of them. It was a poor enough burial, but it would keep their bones from the beasts and their spirits from wandering.

The attackers had been more vicious than thorough. In one of the storage pits there was grain that we parched over the fire, and the carcass of a sheep kept fresh by the cold gave us meat. We ate well enough, but even though we had buried the bodies and made offerings, Crow would not sleep there. I suppose he found some hole among the crags to nest in. When he reappeared the next morning he was stiff and tousled and he pressed my father's hand as if he were not quite sure of its solidity.

The next morning we crossed the river and began to look for a way across the fells. There was no question now of taking the easier road along the river. Our best chance was to hold to the wilder country to the north. Crow looked unhappy, but it was he who found us the deer trail, and I could not spare the energy to wonder what was bothering him. Leir walked more slowly today, and the sky was clouding over again.

[316]

It was well past noon when Leir stopped, coughing, and I realized that we were going to have to rest yet again. We were well up onto the fells by now, with the Hill of the Winds looking over our shoulders. The going had been easy enough, for the rising wind had swept most of the snow away, but even the rocks here hugged the ground. The fells seemed to go on forever. I steered my father to a patch of dry rock and he collapsed onto the stone. I tried not to hear the harshness of his breathing as I shared out a few strips of hard-roasted meat left from the night before. His cough was far worse than it had been yesterday, but the rest would restore him. It must.

A shadow slid across my outstretched hands. I looked up and saw a falcon wheel away across the slope of the hill and then circle back again.

"What do you see, sister," I whispered. "Is there any sign of our enemies?"

"It is the hare she is stalking," said Crow. "Many hares here."

With each circuit the falcon slipped a little lower, focusing on some invisible prey. Now I could see the pale ruffled feathers of her breast. The twitch of a pinion brought her upright in the air; for a moment she hovered, fighting for position, and wind rippled along the edges of her wings.

Then suddenly she was falling. The foliage beneath her thrashed as something grey exploded from hiding and bolted across the open ground. The falcon came in at an angle; wingtips skimming the dry grass. There was a single sharp cry as she struck and lifted heavily into the air with her talons hooked firmly into the flesh of the struggling hare. As they passed overhead a single drop of blood fell onto the stone.

"The gods are like that . . ." said Leir conversationally.

I looked at him sharply.

"All my life I have fought my fate. I forced the sea to bear me to these shores. I conquered queens. But even as I lay with them, they laughed at me. Yesterday the land smiled on me; today I am a stranger. I ruled my people, I made the sacrifices. What more could I have done? No matter how we labor, the gods wait to strike us down. It is no use trying to run away."

[317]

He was gazing westward, and as my glance followed his, I saw rolling up along the horizon great bastions of snow-heavy cloud.

"What was it all for, then?" he cried. "All the fighting, and the dreams?" He shook his fist at the clouds. "Why am I still alive?" His voice wavered alarmingly, and I could feel the madness in him waiting like a wolf to seize its weakening prey.

"Because I love you." It was the only answer I had. "Shall we go back then and offer our throats to Maglaros's sword?" Fear edged my words—of what he had said, and of him. There was a feverish glitter in his eyes. Exposed as we were, I feared we might come to think even an Alban sword kinder than the elements if the storm should catch us on the open fell.

"This one ran—" said Crow quietly. "And now the circle brings him back again. It is *Her* way, always—" He gestured upward and I was not sure whether he meant the falcon or something more. "Wouldst hear a tale?"

Leir stared at him. For a moment I thought he would strike, then the wildness began to fade from his eyes.

"Long ago, in the beginning of things, *She*—the White Lady —was cooking up a brew in Her cauldron. She sets a boy to stirring it while She gets more herbs; for a year of moons he's stirring it, and one day more. She said not to drink, but three drops splashed him and he licked his hand. Then he knows all Her secrets, and he's afraid. . . ."

"I know that fear," said my father slowly. "I learned it looking into women's eyes."

"What did he do?" I asked sharply.

"What can he do? He runs—but now he knows Her magic. He runs in the shape . . . of a hare." We all looked at the red spot on the stone. "She chased him as a black hound, and so he had to change again, became a fish swift-swimming in the stream. She changes into an otter to catch him, but he slips through Her paws, flies up like a grouse, and now She's become a falcon to snatch him from the air. So he thinks he'll outsmart Her—turn to something so small She'll never see." He paused, smiling faintly, and brushed his fingers across the gravelly soil. "He became a single grain upon the ground. But She knows every stone. She became a grey goose and swallowed him down."

"That death I know also," said Leir.

"But it was life She gave him," said Crow. "Nine moons in Her belly he grew, and when he's born She casts him into water and the stream carries him away to be a great singer of spells in the lands of men. They called him Radiant Brow."

"If he had not run from Her he would never have changed—" I said slowly. "He would never have learned to use the knowledge the cauldron gave. . . ."

For a long moment Leir looked at me; then his gaze went back to the clouds. Crow's eyes were closed; his clever fingers clasped in his lap like resting birds. As I watched him, another idea came to me.

"Crow, you know this country . . . you've been looking at the stones like old friends—or perhaps old enemies. Were you born in this part of the dales?"

He gave a little sigh that I took for agreement.

"Then you know where we can find shelter. We need a settlement off the main track, or a good cave. . . ." He began to shake his head and I licked my lips and went on. "Or an encampment of your own people. Do the Senamoi live on the high fells? Tell me! It may mean life for us—for *him*." I nodded toward the king.

"He has the ghost sickness," said Crow softly. "Already he burns. But the Painted People killed the Old Ones first, and the Quiritani kill them after. Why help you now?"

"For your sake, then—a son of their hearths?"

"For this one they have long ago blackened the face and cut the hair . . . No hearthright for a spirit, Daughter of the Swan."

I felt his pain, but I dared not be merciful. "Still we must chance it," I said instead. "Lead us there, Crow, or all three of us will join the ghosts, unblessed and unburied, that wail across the moors."

Darkness fell early, hastened by gathering clouds and just enough snow to make both footing and vision deceptive. Progress was slow, for it took me and Crow together to keep the king upright. My own face was stinging with cold, but Leir's brow radiated heat like a hearthstone. He muttered to himself as we stumbled onward, and though I knew it was the fever speaking, it was enough like his madness to have chilled me even without the storm.

"Tired!" he spoke suddenly. "Want to lie down!" He jerked to a halt and I almost fell.

"Not yet, love—only a little farther and you can rest." Just so I had soothed my child.

"Why?" He turned to peer into my face, swaying so that I almost fell.

"Don't you want something hot to drink, and a warm bed by the fire?"

"Hot already . . ." He turned his face upward to the sifting snow and laughed. "Swan feathers! Soft and cool!"

"Whatever you want, only come along!"

"Stop soon," said Crow. "Walk now—" It was the first thing he had said for quite a while. I wondered if it was true.

We stumbled a few more steps and Leir's mutterings grew louder. Suddenly he jerked from our grasp and staggered away. Crow shouted and flung himself forward. I heard the scrape of feet on stone, and then the grunt as they fell. I stumbled after, tripped over someone's leg, and came down on top of them.

"The swans . . ." muttered Leir beneath us. "Can't you see the swans?" He heaved an arm free and waved at the sky. "White ladies, carry me away! Now I see her! She is calling me!"

The wind was fierce here. I looked up and saw the sky all alive with flurrying whiteness and frowned, for in the darkness of the night I should not have been able to see anything at all. I pushed myself to my knees. Light was coming from somewhere nearby. The faintest of changes in the gloom told me where the stone ended. Beyond it was the abyss, but when I crept closer, I could see that below there was a fire.

Somehow we got the king back from the brink of the cliff and down the path. When we reached the bottom the wind was cut off abruptly. I smelled woodsmoke and heard the bark of a dog. Even Leir seemed to understand finally, for he stumbled forward. I glimpsed the low, humped shapes of brush shelters, and Crow called out in his own tongue.

Suddenly there was a stirring all around us. A deep voice challenged and I stopped short as the skin of my throat shrank from the icy edge of a well-honed bronze spear. Crow was answering, but the other voice was still hostile. Someone pushed us toward the fire. Leir fell then and they let him lie, but the glint of metal kept me where I was. I looked at the faces around me and saw curiosity and anger, and fear. An old woman gabbled something and Crow turned to me.

"They say no food here for outlanders. The black pack hunts the fells and we bring dangers. They say to go—"

I looked at my father's crumpled form. "Let him kill me himself, then!" I screamed, wrenching at the neck of my tunic. "Better a swift stroke now than Maglaros, or the storm!" The worn material gave way suddenly, baring my breast and belly to the cold air.

But the spear was swinging away. Staring, the old woman pushed through the crowd. She asked Crow a question, and suddenly he laughed. She glowered at him and turned to me once more.

"Where . . . dost get Bear?" she asked in the tongue of my mother's people.

"On the Misty Isle—Caiactis . . ." The answer was surprised out of me. "Bear Mother pricked it on."

For another moment she stared at me, then she spat a series of orders at her men. Crow was still laughing.

"What is it?" I asked him as they hurried us toward one of the shelters. "What are they going to do?"

"This, the Bear Clan—" He grinned. "Is you that wins hearth-right here!"

I stared at him, but my vision was blurring already. As I bent to follow the old woman into the shelter the ground came up to meet me and I knew no more.

I floated up into consciousness from wells of sleep deeper than the bottomless lakes of the caves. Through closed eyelids I sensed golden light; the warmth of sleeping furs enfolded me and in that moment I was content. Then I tried to move.

I must have made some sound, for almost immediately someone was helping me to sit upright. I forced open sleep-gummed eyes and saw a face as worn as the stone of the fells. Then I realized that it was not time only that had carved the old woman's features— like Crow, her cheeks and brow were ridged with scars.

"My father?"

"In other shelter. Hot . . . not good for old man to walk in storm."

"Is it the lung sickness?" That was how the old usually died. And for some, it was a mercy, but for Leir to die of a fever now devalued the lives that had been sacrificed to save him and the sufferings that we had survived.

"We give herbs, but spirit wanders in Otherworld. . . ."

I looked at her sharply, noticing now the necklace of bear's claws alternating with an adder's vertebrae, and above it the necklet of jet and amber beads.

"Lady—" I saluted her as if she had been Mother Nesta or Lady Asaret. "Canst help him?"

Her face did not change, but her eyes glowed.

"Dost believe, Painted Woman?"

"My name is Adder. I have traveled the spirit roads and worn shapes not my own. Wise One, I *see* thee."

"And I, thee— Art the child of two bloods that the spirits told me would come."

I stripped off the golden arm ring I wore. "Wilt help him then, and take this for thy fee?"

"Between Adder of the Bear hearth and Speaker-to-Spirits of the Bear Clan there is no fee." She did not even look at the gold.

The curing ceremony was set for the next day. That morning I went ranging out with the hunters to bring down a deer for the offering.

When we returned, the last light of afternoon was gilding the eastern face of the cliff over which Leir had nearly fallen. From its base, a small stream flowed. The hide tents of the clan had been pitched on green turf sheltered by a great cove carved out of the living stone. Woodsmoke scented the air.

As darkness fell, some of the brush was pulled away from the sides of the wisewoman's shelter so that people could see inside. Already the clan was gathering. Four hands of folk as dark-haired as Crow were hunkering down in a silent circle around the perimeter. They were thin, and even the women with babes at the breast seemed old. But the few children were bright-eyed and healthy, and it was clear that they were loved. I clasped my arms across my breasts, wishing desperately that my own babe nestled there.

But it was my father I had to care for now. Leir, well wrapped in furs, lay next to the firepit with Crow on one side and one of the clan mothers on the other.

"Sit thou at his head," Speaker-to-Spirits told me, "and *thou* at his feet!" Her gesture halted Crow as he started to creep away.

He stared at her, eyes white-rimmed with fear, and I remembered abruptly how he had fled his pursuers the first time I ever saw him, and how fearful he had always been whenever the priests worked with power.

"When the drum speaks, this one is lost— *Thou* knowest!" he stammered, but the wisewoman laughed at him.

"Just so, and shalt track thy master through the spirit world. Didst think I would not know thee, son of the Winged Ones? Thy master told me all the tale before he died. Do not fear, little bird. This time *I* watch over thee. . . ."

He gave her a frightened look, but said no more. I touched his shoulder encouragingly as I went past. Despite the weathering of lines around his eyes and the sprinkling of silver in his hair, he was still the long lad I had rescued so long ago. It was I who was growing old.

Then I saw how sallow my father's skin had become, tight-drawn over the bone of the skull as the fever burned the flesh away, and I had no thought but fear. I settled myself and took Leir's head into my lap, carefully so as not to jar him, but he never stirred. Each breath rasped his lungs. I looked around the circle of faces and all—even Crow's—were alien. Why was I making my father's death a show for strangers?

Then an odd sound set every nerve to twitching. A little sigh stirred the crowd. Speaker-to-Spirits was standing on the other side of the hearth, her angular old bones swathed in a cape of painted hide. From her throat came the low discordant humming, and presently the others began to join in. The sound deepened until I could feel the vibration in my bones. Speaker-to-Spirits faced the north, and her voice rose above the chanting in a shrill call. For a moment she waited, and a sound like the groan of an awakening bear answered her. To the east she turned and this time the answer was the thin cry of a hare. From the south came the belling of a stag, and from the west, the call of a seal.

She moved around the circle with an odd, halting step, and the bone and metal ornaments on her cape clacked and jingled rhythmically. She paused beside me, peering into Leir's face, and the other woman handed her a painted drum. In a single movement the old woman squatted, holding the drum between her knees.

"Drum tell her direction of demons now," whispered the clan mother who sat beside me.

Speaker-to-Spirits bent over the drum, whispering. Its surface was covered with designs half-effaced with age. From a snakeskin pouch the old woman took several bits of carven bone and placed them in the center. The chanting grew louder, then she lifted her knobbed wand and gave three sharp taps to the drum.

The bones leaped from the struck surface and fell back in a new pattern. The wisewoman peered at the drumhead, then gathered up the bones once more. Three times she repeated the procedure, muttering, then she swept the pieces back into their pouch and got to her feet, beating furiously on the drum. Crow shook visibly as she approached him and gabbled out a shrill command.

"She tell him demons are in south," said the woman beside me. "He go look for them—"

Crow was shaking his head in denial, but when the drumbeat took him his motion became part of its rhythm. The figures around me pulsed in and out of vision. I felt as if I were falling, though I had not moved.

Then the old woman touched Crow between the brows and his eyes rolled up in his head and he fell over, twitching. The wisewoman gestured for silence, then began a new chant, a repetitive, demanding line that the others echoed as she bent forward, staring into Crow's face as she had peered at the drum and whispering. After a few moments a shudder passed through him, and he began to answer her. I was aware of their voices, but I could not feel my body anymore. I had a sense of vast gulfs and rushing waters, of winds that whispered at the edge of sound.

"He go very deep now, says what he sees. Spirits try to stop him, but Speaker's power stronger," came the whisper at my ear.

With doubled vision I saw the old woman dancing and beating on her drum while Crow twitched at her feet, and a grizzled she-bear who followed the erratic flight of a black bird across a shadowless land. Dim shapes rose up to oppose them, but they fared onward until they came to an island in the midst of a fiery lake, and found there a weeping child.

The face I glimpsed was that of my own son, and emotion shook me out of the vision. When I came to myself, the wisewoman was crouched, panting, before me, but Crow lay still. I felt my father stir and look down. His eyes were still closed, but I could see awareness flicker through his features and with it, pain.

"Mother . . ." he muttered. "Where are you going? Why have you left me alone? You are in the fire; you are going into the ground!"

"We got him back, but fever spirits still attacking—" said Speaker-to-Spirits. "Lift him. Now we cure. . . ."

I braced myself, sitting on my haunches with my thighs apart. Leir moaned as we pulled him into a sitting position leaning against me with his hands clasped over his belly. I curved my body around him, holding him with bent arms and thighs. Once more the singing shifted. Speaker-to-Spirits squatted before us, moving the drum up and down his body as she beat out the rhythm.

My posture was oddly familiar and as the singing increased in intensity I realized that this was the position in which I had given birth to my child. I gripped my father's wasted body harder, but I felt as if it were Beli whom I held in my arms. If I died here, would he think I had abandoned him?

Speaker-to-Spirits tapped the drum above Leir's head and then moved down his torso, listening intently. At last the drum came back to his chest and I could hear the liquid in his lungs as he strove to breathe. Carefully the wisewoman laid the drum aside and moved closer, cupping her hands above Leir's body as if she were trying to capture a wild bird.

My father gasped, and his head moved restlessly against my breast. Suddenly a flare of energy rushed up my spine, and in the same moment Speaker-to-Spirits pounced upon Leir's chest, then jerked away again. She exclaimed triumphantly and opened her palm—a flint arrowhead lay in her hand.

Leir had gone limp in my arms; he was taking in breath in deep, shuddering gasps. But the dreadful bubbling sound was gone. I dropped forward onto my knees. As I lifted my father's head I felt the sweat rolling off of him, but his skin was cool.

That night I dreamed that I floated above a great company of folk who were slowly making their way across a plain. Carts heavy-laden with bundles lurched across the uneven ground. Children rode on top of them, or clung behind women on slow-plodding ponies, or around the necks of walking warriors. Their shields and lances were in the carts, and sheathed swords banged against their thighs. They looked thin and sleepless, but determined.

I dropped lower and realized that some of them were familiar. Surely that gaunt man was Nabelcos the harper. I recognized Mother Nesta's blue robe. Eagerly I spiraled over the column, and was rewarded at last by a glimpse of red hair.

It was Agantequos; even in the dusk of dream I knew him. His face was grim, but as he listened to the thin crying of the children behind him his eyes glittered with tears.

"Agantequos, I love you. I am with you. Can't you see me?" I cried, but he did not hear.

"Old man travel soon," Speaker-to-Spirits told Crow, "but thou, stay here. . . ."

My gaze jerked from Leir, who was sitting on one of the boulders above the stream, soaking up the thin Midwinter sunshine, back to the fire. Beyond the cove the country fell away in long swells like the smooth limbs of a sleeping woman. Leir had spent most of the past two days still as the stones, looking out over the land, but Crow was all tension, caught like a frightened bird by the old woman's implacable gaze.

"This one will go with the king," he said harshly.

"Why? Dost desire to be his hound always? Stay with me and I teach thee to hunt spirit world. It does not matter about thy clan. I make thee my son, eh? Dost journey better than any I've trained. Who will go out for the people when I am gone?"

"Too late . . ." whispered Crow. "The water that has flowed to the sea is gone. The heart once given does not return. This one has seen where the circle ends. . . ."

The old woman grunted. "Thou, afraid? What is to fear when dost walk worlds?"

Crow lifted his head. "Death. This one fears to be lost."

"Huh! Art still a child. All things die. When the old man is dead, come back to me."

The spear fell from my hands.

"What is this talk of death? My father is cured!"

Speaker-to-Spirits looked at me and I understood why Crow had been afraid.

"He is old as I am old. And the land spirits are angry. He and thou both—" She shook her head at Crow. "Thou canst not always run away!"

But Crow and my father did understand, I thought, seeing the bleak look in his dark eyes. They both had said as much, when we were on the moor. It was only I who would not accept futility.

From the slopes below the cove came the call of a hunting falcon. By the third repetition, Speaker-to-Spirits was on her feet. And then, closer, we heard the low grunt of a swan and the whinny of a mare. If I had not seen the wisewoman's reaction I might have been deceived, even knowing how rarely the swan's voice is heard, and how rare a visitor it is to the winter fells.

"Riders coming—" said the old woman. "Ye go to hiding place now!"

But Crow was already running toward my father, and I was leaping for the shelter to grab my weapons and gear.

The tribe had been told what to do if Quiritani warriors should come. As one of the hunters hustled us away toward the cave in the cliffs there was nothing in the encampment to betray our presence, only a new tension in the bodies of the tribesmen as the wind bore up to us the howling of the hounds.

Night had fallen before the falcon's whistle told us that it was safe to come out of the cave. But even now, when we could talk again, Leir was silent. Through the long hours of hiding I had watched him chew the ends of his moustaches and gaze unseeing at the stones. It was not like him to be so patient. What had he been thinking of?

I gazed around me in swift appraisal as we came in. The soft ground was trampled into mire and one of the shelters was in pieces, but I saw no blood. Only one of the women was weeping soundlessly.

"What did they do?" asked Leir. "Go we must before they return. We are a danger to you, not so?"

"Threats! Always threats!" Speaker-to-Spirits spat at the ground. "What they will do if we aid you—but they took a hostage. They took Vixen's son."

There was a murmur of sorrow from the people and Vixen wailed aloud. I bit my lip. I was not at all sure that Leir was fit to travel, but even my anxiety could not gainsay him if it meant the lives of those who had sheltered us.

"Tomorrow morning you go—" said the wisewoman. "Before true light. Will raise a mist to confuse those others, and give you a guide."

"How can I thank thee?" I asked her later, when the provisions they could spare us were packed and we were ready to go. "Hast saved my father once more."

"Have saved thee!" Speaker-to-Spirits placed her palms flat against my breast. "The blood of two peoples and the spirit of three is in thee. Live, Adder, bring peace to the land!"

The next night we sheltered with a woman of the Senamoi who was married to a sheepherder in the next dale. Their hut was dug into the earth with a domed roof of brush over branches resting on low rock walls, and the forest grew up to its eaves. We were off again early, though, for there were sizable settlements just to the south and to the north as well, and a band of Maglaros's men was still quartered in the village downstream. The southern road was closed to us, but the woman's half-blood son guided us up past the scar behind the village and out onto the fells.

Much of the snow had melted, though the weather was dank and chill. Leir moved slowly, but he kept going. He did not speak though—from lack of breath or because he was thinking? I did not dare to ask.

That night we camped in the lee of a small, flat-topped hill called Mu'her. It was a sacred hill, said the boy, and the purplish cliffs just visible beyond it were even holier—the walls of the great god Acora's house beneath the fells. They glimmered above us as we marched northward the next morning, glowing in the dawnlight as if lit from within. This was a country where men did not wander except when they were seeking visions. I listened to the wind howling among the crags and shivered with something deeper than cold.

At midmorning we climbed up from the path to drink at the well at the edge of the scar. The water was clear and sweet, but I looked into the pool and saw my face drawn with fatigue and my hair all silvered with rime, and knew that I was seeing the face of my own old age.

As our path turned eastward I began to realize that though this land held few folk, it was populous with stones. Crow stayed close to my side, but Leir strode out more strongly. As we started the descent to the Nith, our guide stopped us, pointing southward and then to the east, ahead.

"See—the stone people. Once it was they who ruled this land. They are quiet now, but sometimes in the moonlight they dance, and on the festivals. . . ."

I squinted ahead and was suddenly glad he had told me they were only rocks, or I would have been sure someone was standing there. I blinked, for they seemed to be in motion. Across the vale I could just glimpse what looked like two tall forms with floppy caps like those the farmers wear.

"That is the chief of them," the boy followed my gaze. "That is old Jan-et, the queen!"

I twitched, for I had thought that only the priestesses knew that name.

"Fieret—" said Leir suddenly. I reached out to him and he smiled reassuringly. "She would stand just so, gazing out over the hills. I find myself thinking about her often these last days. She loved this land."

I tightened my grip on his arm as if he might vanish away. His fever seemed to have burned away all of the craziness, but since then he had been strange, as if a part of his spirit still roamed the Otherworld.

"Your mother was the queen," Leir turned to me. "And now it is you who must tell us how to serve the land. . . ."

Speaker-to-Spirits had said much the same thing. But neither of them could tell me what I must do. I stared at that distant figure and felt the power that surged upward through the stones. There was one kind of magic in deep forests, and another in the sea, but this was the magic of earth Herself, and as the turning of the suntides neared, it was drawing ever closer to the surface.

"Not now—" I whispered. "Not where She can hear us. Let us go on."

Chapter

While we were seven thrice seven dared not attack us, nor made us retreat while we lived; alas there are none but three of the seven, men unflinching in fight.

—"Elegy on Howel ab Owein," *Llawysgif Hendregadredd*

"Father! Crow!"

I drew breath to call again and coughed as the mist swallowed my words. The fog had come up so quickly, collecting in the hollows and flowing along the folds in the fells. Walking with gaze fixed on the far vistas, one did not notice the white serpents that coiled about the skirts of the hills. When I went aside to relieve myself I had no thought of danger. It was only when I tried to rejoin the others that I met the mist rolling up the moor and was lost.

I called once more and then stilled, straining to hear a reply. For a moment I thought there was something, but the sound faded as soon as I moved. I stopped, listening to the harsh sound of my own breathing in the damp air.

Across the Nith our guide was out of his territory and would go no farther. But from there our route should have been clear. This was for the most part an empty land. We could see our way; we had only to follow the Nith southeastward until we came down from the dales. But the mist had drowned all directions now.

No use seeking a path in this white sea. But the fog had rolled up from the river bottom; perhaps it would be thinner above. I clambered diagonally across the steep slope, bruising my hands on the rocks and stopping every few feet to draw breath and call again.

Beneath my feet and fingers the land was becoming stone. Rock bulged through a thin skin of soil in knobs and pinnacles, split the surface with crevasses floored with mosses and yellow sand, sheered away in sculptured faces of gritty stone. The smell of damp rock was heavy near the ground, but the pressure of moving air upon my cheek was growing stronger as I climbed.

As I came out onto level turf a gust of wind swirled the mist away. A dark shape loomed up before me and I crouched, gasping.

It was only stone . . . or something that stood as still. The tall, twisted form was like a priestess with her shawl drawn over her head, standing with folded arms as she watched over the moor. Only when I reached out and touched the cold, gritty surface was I certain it was stone. I made my way past the pillar carefully, for the ground was treacherous too.

Mist brushed my face and I looked behind me, shuddering as the outlines of the rock blurred into something monstrous. The standing stones near Udrolissa were imposing, and the Giants' Dance had inspired an uneasy fear, but they had been shaped by the hands of men. These stones still stood where the gods had set them, intact in pride and power.

The shapes grew ever more terrible as the light dimmed, but I dared not stop, for I had the uneasy sense that every move was observed. When I turned, shapes that had seemed benign took on an ominous significance. And yet I risked a broken ankle or worse if I tried to cross this rough ground in the dark. My steps slowed, and when the last of the light showed me a clear area I halted. However illusory, the protection promised by the stones that circled it seemed the closest to safety that I was likely to find. I moved carefully forward and called again, but the only sound I heard was the crunch of sand and the whisper of wind among the stones.

The open space dipped toward the center; I felt like a pebble rolling around the rim of a bowl, being drawn inexorably down, but I resisted the attraction. Shivering, I settled myself halfway between the midpoint of the circle and its rim, and wrapping my cloak tightly around me, prepared to wait for dawn.

The chill, and the darkness, were oddly familiar. Abruptly I remembered the cavern in which I had kept my initiation vigil. That had been almost at the same time of year, and not so far from here. But the seven years since then made it seem a lifetime ago. For a time, sheer physical discomfort kept me from remembering, but when my body grew numb, there was nothing to distract me.

Lady Asaret had said that there were places where the Otherworld lay close upon the one that mortals know. Surely this was one of them. The powers that dwelt here took forms that had little to do with the world of men.

My expanding awareness sank deep within, and suddenly I could see time like a flowing stream. To the senses I was leaving behind, the stones stood stark and still; if I drew back to watch them, I could see them altering to the touch of wind and weather like icicles shapechanging in the sun. But if I dove into the stream I saw that each pile of rock itself was a pattern, and each element within those patterns a rhythmic structure that spun its own circles to draw me deeper in. Within infinite space points of brilliance whirled. The light defined the darkness, the darkness provided a context for the dance. And I was both the light and the darkness, the ebb and the flow.

Nothing is eternal. . . . Nothing is mortal. . . . Everything changes. . . . Everything endures. . . . It was as if a voice spoke from the silence, but what I sensed was not in human words.

"I do not understand—" cried my spirit. "Show me shapes my mind can comprehend!" I felt something waiting with patient attention while I tried to reconstruct my identity.

In the space before me a light began to grow. I stared, for only my eyes had volition, and saw gradually revealed the pebbled soil and then the shapes of the circling stones. But they no longer seemed sinister; their grotesque proportions were like the straw costumes the men wear at village festivals, that make the grown folk laugh and the children cry.

Or perhaps they were costumes—stiff and baggy garments for

beings whose shape and proportions bore only a rough resemblance to those of humankind. But they put the same energy as the village folk into their dancing, stamping and swinging round the circle with a rhythmic boom of stone. And then the circle became a spiral, peaked silhouettes swirling together as they did when they danced the Midwinter rites at Ambiolissa. But this serpent was shaped from living stone. Around and around the serpent wound its coils; once more there were words—

> *"Crack rock, crack—round and*
> *back!*
> *What has been, comes again!*
> *Stamp and stump!—clap and bump!*
> *Choice is chance, join the dance!"*

Now I was looking at an earth adder whose black and white patterning flickered dizzily as it spun. Fanged jaws gaped wide to engulf the world. And then, when light and darkness had become one rainbow radiance, it disappeared.

"It is true—" I responded. "But what is that to me?"

Perception shifted once more. At the center of the circle lay an egg that shone like the sun. Steadily the brightness expanded. I blinked, and suddenly I could see a shape within it—human, and as it grew clearer, male.

"Who are you?" I asked as the vision cleared. I saw a bright-haired youth who held a spear of light, and when he grinned I could not restrain an answering smile.

"You may call Me the Son of the Rocks—" came the answer. "If you would see a wonder, follow Me. . . ."

I do not know if my body moved or my spirit alone floated after him between the stones, but with his radiance to guide me I felt no fear of them. In moments, it seemed, we were before a mass of rock pierced by an opening like the holed flints the folk seek on the southern coast to ward evil away.

"Through this portal that which will die can be reborn . . ." said the youth. "Look and see—"

I drifted closer. At the other end of the passage I saw daylight.

In that world it was summer, and sunlight shimmered on wind-fluttered leaves. Beneath the trees folk were walking. A kind of radiance glimmered about them that made their features hard to see, but it seemed to me that Artocoxos was among them, healed of all his dreadful wounds. I strained closer, calling his name, and in that moment all the light in the scene began to swirl. For a moment my vision was filled by a great wheel of stars in a midnight sky, and then I saw nothing at all.

When I woke, the clear light of early morning was gilding the stones. I staggered to my feet, staring around me. The way that the Son of the Rocks had gone in my vision lay clear before me. Still blinking away sleep, I followed it to the holed stone. But this time when I peered through it what I saw was my father, curled in the lee of a rock formation like a sleeping cow. Crow lay a few feet away. Beyond them stretched the mist-shrouded slope of the moor.

I ran around the stones, shouting. They were alive! We came together in a huddle, laughing to find ourselves solid and living after all. Somehow Crow had ended in the middle of our embrace, and in that moment I felt the link with my father more fully than ever before, mediated by the ambiguous energy of the one who stood between. Then we were pulling apart again, laughing with delight in the day.

Dry stems from the heather made us a little fire, and we broke the ice in one of the rock pools and scooped up water to make porridge with some coarse-ground meal. The wind was clean and chill. In the daylight the rocks lost their terror, though their fascination remained. As we ate, we watched the changing play of light and vied to see who could suggest the most fantastic names.

"That rock is like the holed stone in Belerion—" Leir said suddenly, pointing to the tunneled stone I had looked through. "It was forbidden to men to approach it, but this place is not subject to the rules of priest or priestess. I would like to crawl through it now. . . ."

"Do not!" Suddenly uneasy, I tried to tell him of my vision of the night before. Crow was shaking his head and holding onto the skirts of the king's robe. But Leir only smiled.

"All the more reason to try it then. After all the mistakes I have made and the evils I have done, I have a great need to be reborn. . . . Do not fear, daughter. I too have dreamed in the night. All will be well."

I examined him carefully. There was a new serenity in his gaze and as he approached the rock his step had a firmness that I had not seen since before he killed the swan. For a moment he stood before the opening, then he lifted his hands.

"This is the sacred center," he cried. "This is the heart of the kingdom, the place before men. This is the womb. I come to this place to be renewed. Let what I have been be forgotten. Now I offer myself to the spirits of this land to be used as they will. . . ."

"He must not—" Crow started to rise. "He will be changed. Here there is too much power!"

But the king was already making the passage. Crow stood swaying. Immobilized by the sudden heaviness in the air, we could only watch, torn between worry and wonder as Leir forced his long body through the opening in the stone. I could tell when he passed the barrier, for the sense of pressure lifted. Released, Crow and I hurried around to ease him out the other side.

"I have taken no harm, child. Why are you fussing so?" Leir insisted as we readied ourselves to go on. I shut my lips and managed a smile. I knew that there had been a change, but I could not tell what it had been or what it might mean.

Upon the moor the mist was already moving as the wind came up with the brightening day. Leir, Crow, and I picked our way along a deer trail that curved through the heather, keeping the moist breath of the wind upon our right cheeks as we moved along. Half-frozen stems crackled beneath our feet, and when for a moment the swirling fog lifted, the spreading plain before us glittered with light. Then the mists would close in, and all we could see was the ice-rimed heather at our feet once more.

The next time the mist thinned Crow halted suddenly. I peered where he was pointing and glimpsed a grass-covered mound rising from the brown sweep of the moor. I looked at him inquiringly.

"Go carefully," he whispered. "Be very still. This place is the barrowplain. Spirits of dead warriors walk here, even by day."

I blinked. In the mist it was easy to imagine ghosts rising from those barrows. I tried to recover the awareness of eternity that had comforted me the night before, but I heard ancient battle cries in the wind. I told myself we had nothing to fear. These were only memories; I had seen myself how the spirits of dead warriors fared in the Otherworld.

We moved a little more quickly as we passed the first barrow. When we came to the second, I was sure I saw movement, and I heard the howling of the dogs of war. As we approached the third barrow the howling grew louder and four dark shapes burst from the mists and loped toward us, red tongues lolling, hot breath smoking in the chill air.

Crow made a warding sign but I reached for my sword, because as the dogs began to bay once more I suddenly understood that they were real.

"What is it?" said Leir, lifting the spear he had been using as a staff and straining to see.

"Warhounds. Their masters must be close behind them—" We moved back-to-back, facing outward. There was no cover in the midst of the plain, and even if we could have evaded the eyes of men, the dogs would have tracked us down.

The wind blew more strongly. The distorted black dog-shadows leaped across the frosty heather, almost upon us now. The howls shattered into a chorus of yips and hoarse barking, but beneath their challenge I could hear also the rapid drumbeat of clawed feet upon the hard ground. I readied my blade.

The air shivered to the long calling of a horn. The dogs veered off, whining, and in that moment the mist lifted finally. The top of the barrow was spiked with armed men.

Bobbing atop one man's lance were the spread wings of the hawk. The standard of Alba. . . . Leir stirred angrily beside me. We had come so far, and with such pain. How could Maglaros have trapped us now?

We waited in silence. After a few moments the line of warriors parted to let a dun pony through. The rider rode slumped, his cloak misshapen over the bandaging that swathed his shoulder, but his voice was strong.

"Take them!"

"I mean you no evil, Cridilla! You are my sister! Why will you not be reasonable?" Gunarduilla's voice cracked as if her throat had been scraped raw by shouting her own battle cry.

"Sisters do not take each other prisoner," I spat back at her. "Reasonable proposals are not delivered at the point of a spear!"

"You have not been hurt, have you? A ceremonial summons would not have brought you here." My sister waved at the cluster of round stone huts tucked into the lee of the moor, sheltered by a few birch trees from the worst of the winds. Behind us the largest of the birches stretched out wind-wracked limbs. The moors rippled away in white waves to the southeast and westward. To the north the forest lapped the lower slopes like a dark sea, pierced by an occasional gleam where the Verbeia's winding waters caught the sun.

The settlement consisted of two round houses with walls of filled stone. Gunarduilla and Maglaros had taken up residence in one of them. Leir and I were put into the other, while the warriors camped under stretched hides. I could see them moving about, and the plaintive warbling of a bone flute was drifting to us from somewhere down the hill. I did not yet know what they had done with Crow.

Once, before the world changed, the place had supported a thriving community, and the tumbled stones of older buildings were all around. Now it was mostly used when the herds were driven up to the summer pastures. But today it was war ponies, not cattle, that were nosing away last night's snow to get at the grass.

"Sit down, child. Let this tea warm you and try to understand what I say." She pressed the bronze-bound beechwood cup into my hand. "You must have seen how the land has suffered since you went away. Unless we stand together behind a strong war-leader, this Island will become a hundred warring kingdoms, prey for any other barbarian with a war-band who comes over the sea." Gunarduilla settled herself upon a folded hide and motioned to me to do the same. It was not only her voice that had weathered. Time had leached the gold from her hair and battered her face like an old shield.

"What do you mean?" I remained standing, blinking as sunlight sparked from the spear of the nearest warrior. A rising wind was hurrying the last of the clouds away and setting the world a-glitter where the snowfall had powdered over the winter browns of the moor. It puffed ash from the firepit and a dying coal glowed red.

"There is only one man with the strength to unite the Island," said my sister. "Leir had three queens. Maglaros already has the support of the Banalisioi and Alba. Why should he not do the same?"

"But I am married already!" Astonishment sapped the force from my words.

"To the outlander?" Gunarduilla shrugged. "That was no real marriage—Agantequos only carried you away. Anyway, you have given him the heir he needed. Let him be content with his land beyond the sea."

"You've gone mad!" I struggled to master my voice. "Are you telling me to leave my husband and my child to become a second wife to the man who took you by force before the whole Council? Has Rigana agreed to this insanity?"

"Why not? Senouindos is dead. Rigana will give us the south as you will give us the middle. Even Leir never brought the whole of the Island under his hand!"

"Leir is still alive, and it is he to whom my mother gave the right to defend this land. And the gods themselves have blessed my marriage to Agantequos!" I exclaimed. "There is no power that can force me to deliver Briga into Maglaros's hands!" I flung the cup away and the tea splashed Gunarduilla's boots and soaked steaming into the ground.

"Is there not?" said a new voice behind me.

I jerked around and saw Maglaros, surrounded by the shifting black shadows of his dogs. He was as grizzled as my sister now, wrapped in a cloak lined with wildcat fur against the cold. But there was no warmth in his smile.

[339]

"You were trained in the same school as your sister, and I defeated her. I felled the greatest fighter in your father's war-band. Do you think I cannot master you?" He stroked my cheek with his left hand.

My flesh shrank from his touch. Maglaros was good with a sword, or at least he had been. But he listed a little to one side, as if the pain of the shoulder that Artocoxos had smashed with his last strength was bearing him down.

Perhaps you can force me, monster, but until that shoulder heals you won't do it alone! I thought viciously.

For a moment he stared, trying to force down my gaze. Then he swore and turned to Gunarduilla.

"The bitch is stubborn and we have work to do! Put her back inside!"

"It is nigh onto Midwinter by my reckoning," said Leir.

I peered at the sliver of light that showed where the bullhide did not quite cover the doorway and saw the shadow of the warrior who was guarding us pass. Outside it was another bright chill day.

The valley of the Verbeia was two days' ride south of the barrowplain. Since the snowstorm that had blown in the night of our arrival, the weather had settled to a frozen stillness as if nothing would ever change again. But if I calculated back through all the days of flight and fighting since Samonia I supposed that six weeks might well have passed.

The night before I had dreamed that Agantequos was in Udrolissa—surely a fantasy of my desire. It was more likely that by now he was in bed with Brenna, consoling himself because he believed I had renounced my vows. I tried to remember what it had been like when we were together, but it was like a harper's tale. And my breasts were empty and no longer ached when I thought of my child.

"Daughter, why are you weeping?" my father asked then. I touched my cheek and found that it was true.

"Because I promised Agantequos that I would return by Winter's turning, and now I am forsworn."

"You love him?"

His tone held only wistful curiosity. In the days when we had plotted how my marriage might work to his advantage, love had never been a factor in the plans. I had thought it the detachment of a king until Leir's reaction to my pregnancy showed me otherwise.

I shifted uncomfortably, trying to find a position where the damp of the ground would not seep through the bracken that had been spread over it, and the cloak wrapped around me. Our prison was not unkind, but it would take more than a few dry ferns to make the hut habitable at this time of year.

"Did you love my mother?" Leir had often told me so, but I thought that I would be able to discern the truth of it now.

"I loved her . . ." he said harshly. "But I never knew if she loved me, or if she only did what was needful for the sake of the land. She showed me the sacred places of Briga and taught me the obligations of the king. This moor was one of the spots where the Old Ones made magic for the land. I wonder if that was Gunarduilla's reason for bringing us here. . . ." He sighed, and for a moment I thought that he was done.

"I came here with Fieret and Talorgenos, it seems a lifetime ago," he went on. "They made new signs on the stones to link me to the land. She kissed me afterward, and promised to keep faith with me. But I knew that she must have sworn the same to the husband she had before. . . ."

I heard the truth in his voice and reached out to take his hand.

"I thought I could be sure of your love, at least. And then I thought that you had betrayed me."

Close as we were, he felt me stiffen and drew his hand away. For a moment our harsh breathing was the only sound. As if in mockery, the song of the bone flute rose and fell outside.

"I love Agantequos," I said finally, "as you loved my mother— I love him as a wife, and as a sacred queen. Is that the kind of love you had for me? I thought," I forced words past stiff lips, "I thought that between us there was something less common, and more wonderful. Cannot you believe it even now? At the Assembly I said that

I would fight for you, and I have. I said that I gave you a daughter's love. Are there no words for that? Even here, even now, cannot you understand?"

I threw myself down in the bracken, sobbing.

"I understand . . . many things." After what seemed a very long time I felt the gentle touch of my father's hand upon my hair.

"I understand that somewhere a man sits lonely, wondering whether you still love him as I wondered if Fieret loved me. I understand that there is a child who does not know why his mother is gone. I understand that because I was a fool the cycle of abandonment is beginning again—" His voice shook. "It must not continue!

"I had such dreams when first I came to this land—" he went on. "I went through the old rites of marriage to serve a greater purpose, but the purpose was my own. I willed to make the land my own by conquest, as a man thinks he can make a woman his own by planting in her his seed. I thought to set my name upon the land so strongly that I would never die. And now I am a prisoner, and finally I begin to understand that the power lies not in what I can take, but in what I am prepared to give. . . ."

I was still weeping, but now there was healing in my tears. I rested on the cold ground, and felt warmth spread through me as my father stroked my hair.

"All this time, we have been too breathless with running to talk," said Leir. "Tell me about the man who won your love. Tell me about this grandson whom I have never seen. . . ."

Still sniffling, I sat up again.

"His name is Belinos, and his hair is like the sun—" I began.

"I can force you—" said Maglaros, holding my face so that I could not pull away. My nostrils flared at the foul stink of his wound. I closed my eyes, trying to ignore the pain in my bound hands. The sunlight of another day was glaring from the snow. The phase of reasonable discussion had not lasted long.

"Try it!" I spat through set teeth. "I will give that shoulder a crueler buffet than Artocoxos did!"

He let me go and I opened my eyes just in time to see his fist coming and roll with it. There was a convulsive movement nearby and a grunt as Leir's guard wrestled him back down.

"Father, stay calm!" I blinked back tears as my mouth began to sting. "He can do me no real harm!"

"What if I order my men to hold you?" growled Maglaros, flushing.

I looked at the warriors around me. They were sturdy, dark-haired tribesmen from the hills of Alba. The tattoos of the Painted People showed beneath their kilts and the rough cloaks they wore above—and they were already beginning to look sidelong at the Quiritani lord they called king.

"Do you think they will obey?" Through swollen lips I laughed. "They know who I am . . . they know that the Goddess will shrivel their man's parts like withered apples if they assist in any such blasphemy. The Lady gives herself in her own time and season. And I have given myself to Agantequos of Moridunon," I said proudly. "He defended me when all I loved turned against me. I have borne him a son. I need no other man."

"*Him!*" Maglaros gave a harsh snort of laughter. "Where is he, then, now when you need his protection?"

"That is no fault of his. What reason had I to fear my own kindred in my own land?"

"Do you think your man is such a hero?" snapped Gunarduilla. "You praise him for having defended you at the Assembly. Who do you think told us that you were with child?"

For a moment that silenced me. Behind us someone was chopping wood. I felt each blow in my flesh, as I felt Maglaros's words. Could Agantequos have told them, knowing that the news would turn my father against me and force me into his arms? I closed my eyes, summoning up the image of his freckled face and blue eyes. I had seen the pain in those eyes when I was exiled. Surely I would have sensed dishonesty.

"*If* he told you, he might have had a good reason. There was no honor in the way you chose to reveal it, or the time! But all this changes nothing. Even if you could take me by force you could not make me give you the power! Even *she* knows that much—" I nodded toward Gunarduilla. "You are not king in Alba because you defeated her in battle, but because she agreed that the victor in that fight should rule!"

"He and I rule together!" my sister cried. "It is you who are opposing the will of the Goddess now!"

"Is this how you bring back the old ways?" I shouted back at her. "You no longer even know what they are! You are not his partner, but his slave. The old way was not to force the sacred queen!"

"Leir forced my mother!" Gunarduilla screamed.

"I won her in fair battle, and she agreed to take me as her protector," growled Leir. "And the gods blessed the land. . . ."

"I do not say the Quiritani conquest was justice, but you cannot turn the river back again," I cut in. "The old ways were not destroyed, or why do you need me? The blood of the Painted People and the Quiritani has been too much mingled for us to live in any way but by a marriage of traditions now."

"A marriage is what we are offering—" said Maglaros, and I saw that he had not understood at all. "And if I cannot take the kingship from you, there are other kinds of force that may persuade you to offer it to me. . . ."

I cast a quick glance at my father, and Maglaros laughed. Leir stood as if the thongs around his wrists were bracelets, more kingly in his captivity than he had ever been in his power, but with the pitiless sunlight shining full upon him I realized that even after his illness he had never been so fragile. The light seemed to shine through him. And surely he could not endure much pain. If they threatened him, what could I do?

"Peace, daughter. They dare not harm me for the same reason they will not harm you. My head is sacred, and old and ill as I am now, any mistreatment would likely finish me. But my dying curse could blast them all. My death is in the hands of the gods. . . ."

"There is another way—" said Gunarduilla harshly. Leir turned to look at her, and smiled.

"Only if I am willing, and you know that well. That is the mystery of the king. . . ."

"What do you mean?" I said sharply, feeling my belly clench with an apprehension I did not understand.

[344]

"I am safe, child. Whatever they do I cannot be harmed."

I heard the words as truth, but they must be lies meant to ease me, or were his wits leaving him once more?

"Father—" I began, but my protest was lost in the bray of a horn.

Echoing back and forth across the valley, others replied. For a moment I hoped, but the Alban horns were blaring not in challenge but in greeting. Then we heard the clatter of hoofbeats; a considerable company was approaching us. The swaying bullhide standard of the Ai-Zir appeared over the edge of the hill, and then came the riders, gaudy in the dyes they imported from southern lands and glittering with gold.

Rigana rode beneath a crimson canopy. The two warriors who bore it were both young; one of them with fair hair twisted up in a knot and the other dark and slim as Rigana herself. I had seen them in the south, eyeing the queen like two dogs with a single bone. I wondered which one of them she had chosen.

Her gaze paused a moment as she saw me, then she moved on. Gunarduilla was striding forward to embrace her. Maglaros waited behind her, and grinned as Rigana's posture became visibly more seductive. Her kiss of greeting was far too long and too warm to be sisterly, and her escorts glowered. I had been sure that Gunarduilla was lying when she claimed Rigana as an ally. My heart sank as I realized I was wrong.

"My messenger found you, then?" asked Gunarduilla, slipping her arm through Rigana's and drawing her toward the fire.

"Indeed—and we made good speed to be here by Midwinter. You have them, then, as you promised. You have been busy to some purpose, sister, but your persuasions appear to have been less successful than your sword. . . ." Once more Rigana's enigmatic glance rested on me.

"Cridilla is being stubborn, as always," said Gunarduilla. "But perhaps there is a way to compel her. She and Leir are not our only hostages!"

Maglaros motioned and two of the warriors came toward us, carrying what I thought at first must be some animal, all blood and dirt and tattered fur.

But no hunter would willingly so mangle his prey. As they threw it down I saw that it was a man. Then he stirred, and I recognized the silver-streaked black hair. Crow whimpered as Maglaros prodded his ribs, and I swallowed bile. My father had closed his eyes for a moment, but now he was staring at Crow with a face like stone.

"The Senamoi!" Rigana leaned forward eagerly. "Does the old fool still cling to the young one, then?"

"Well—do you?" Maglaros asked Leir. The king did not reply.

"They care," said Gunarduilla disgustedly. "Don't you remember? They used to treat the creature like a favorite hound. Listen, slave"—she kicked the captive—"you beg your lady to help us, or we will hurt you some more!"

Crow curved into a fetal ball, tremors visibly shaking the strained limbs. They had broken no bones, yet, but his skin was all one bloody bruise.

"Traitor!" spat Rigana, leaning over him. "Traitor to your own race and to ours! You had the old magic, yet you sold yourself into slavery for a crust of bread! You should have died fourteen years ago!"

"Spirits fly with fiery wings . . . raven sings . . ." came Crow's singsong muttering. "Old ones come with hands of bone, teeth of stone . . . soon will feast." Painfully he raised himself on one elbow and tried to focus on me. "This flesh belongs to them," he said clearly. He blinked, and for a moment his dark gaze held mine. "For the land and the people the price must be paid." Then he collapsed again, weeping. "Don't hurt! Do not be hurting this one anymore!"

"This was only the beginning," said Gunarduilla. "But you saved him once already, Cridilla. To stop this, you have only to say the word!"

"You will have time to consider," said Maglaros. "We have treated you too gently. You say we cannot touch you, but we shall see what the elements can do—"

His gaze went past us. The warriors were dragging a large frame of lashed birch like a giant basket up the hill. They came to a halt with the construction upended, looking expectantly to Maglaros.

"What is that for?" Rigana lifted one eyebrow.

"We have made a pretty cage to keep two royal birdlings in—" Maglaros replied. "Perhaps the sun and the snow will strengthen our arguments!"

"A cage?" Rigana turned away from it in disdain. "You are not thinking, sister. Would you dishonor our blood by treating our kindred like slaves? This will do us no good with the people when they hear of it, Gunarduilla; it will diminish our own prestige. . . ."

My older sister frowned. "Perhaps, but talking to Cridilla is like arguing with a stone wall, and the old man never listened to anything but his own will."

"Ah, but with two of us to persuade her she is bound to see reason. At least let us try!" She turned to Maglaros and smiled brilliantly. "Come, my lord, I can be most persuasive. Would you not rather get the girl willingly?"

He licked his lips a little, then gestured at his men.

"Let it rest for now. It is ready if we should need it after all."

Rigana moved smoothly toward me, and her skirts brushed Crow's body as if he had been no more than a pile of worn-out furs. I stiffened as she enveloped me in a scented embrace.

"Bend, sister! Bend to me—" came her whisper as she pulled my face down to be kissed. "Maglaros is a madman. I will try . . . to free you, and Gunarduilla as well, and we three will rule together as we planned. But you must at least pretend to agree!"

Chapter

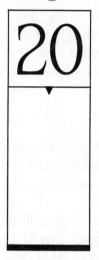

I shall not see a world that will be dear to me.
Summer without flowers,
Kine will be without milk,
Women without modesty,
Men without valor,
Captures without a king . . .
Wrong judgments of old men . . .
Every man a betrayer,
Every boy a reaver . . .
An evil time.

—*The Second Battle of Mag Tured*

I was a leaf aloft in the windy darkness . . . a branch adrift in night's stormy sea . . . I spread wings and rode the conflicting currents of the air as a swan. With powerful wingbeats I drove through the darkness, free . . . free . . . free!

For a time it was enough to be in motion, unbound even by memory. Then need for some certainty began to grow. Where in this chaos could I find a resting place?

I let the wind hurry me onward, and ever more clearly came the image I wanted, warmth, fire. Beside a rushing river I saw the dim glow of coals with huddled forms around them. Only one fire still flickered. A figure sat upright beside it, and his hair was as red as the flame.

"Horse!" I called. *"It is Cridilla, cannot you see?"*

He looked up as I swooped past and his hair fluttered to the wind of my wings. I swung away, shocked by his pallor and the marks like old bruises beneath his eyes.

"Where are you? Why are you so sorrowful?" I cried. He shivered as I circled him and pulled the folds of his cloak over his head.

"Horse, I need you! Come to me!"

Once more he looked up, but this time he made the warding sign as men do when they feel some spirit near. I saw his mouth twist with grief, then he bent to add more wood to the fire. I fluttered helplessly. Did he know who it was that rode the night? Or worse still, did he think it was my ghost that called to him?

"Horse—I love you!" My cry was the mute voice of the swan. . . . Then chaos swept me down into the dark.

"Canst doubt I love thee?"

For a moment I thought the words were part of my dream. But when I opened my eyes I was lying on a pile of bracken, and I was cold. It had been a woman's voice I had heard, and now a man was answering her, his voice urgent and low.

"Have I not chosen thee?" the woman replied. "They call me changeful, but that was before thou and I were one!" Her voice trembled with passion. For a moment there were only sounds without words. Then she must have pulled away, but she was breathless when she spoke once more. "Be patient, my hero, patient as I have had to be. The deception is only for a little longer, and then our time will come—"

The voices were fading. But the woman had spoken with the accent of Belerion. Was it Rigana or one of her women? And who was the man? Still wondering, I lay listening to the wind till dawn.

"Sister, be thou welcome. . . ."

I stopped short, remembering the last time I had heard Rigana say those words. Then she had worn crimson. Now she sat swathed in furs through which came the glint of gold. The push from my guards was firm, but not ungentle. I let them lead me to a sheepskin at her side. When my sisters had forced me to conference after the Assembly I had been defiant. But matters had gone beyond simple anger. Wordless, I sat down.

Last night's wind had scoured away the snow from before the huts, and they had spread cloths for the Midwinter feasting there. The last of the breeze brought me the rich scent of the beef that was boiling with parched grain in cauldrons made from the cows' own stretched hides, and sheep that had been roasting on spits over open fires since dawn, as well as the hunters' offerings of hares and deer. What food I had been given in these last days had seemed tasteless, and my stomach growled with anticipation despite my anxiety.

"If I have seemed cruel, forgive me," said Gunarduilla, "but courtesy is a luxury. Too long I've been fighting. I know only how to answer the time's demands, and have no skill in soft words. Sister, wilt thou not see reason at last?" Beyond the golden torque at her neck she had made no concession to the occasion. She sat stiffly in her stained leather tunic and woolen breeches, her chequered cloak wound around her in heavy folds.

"There has been no change in me," I said wearily.

"Wert headstrong from childhood, Cridilla," said Rigana. "After the Assembly we desired thy cooperation, but now 'tis necessity. All that we have cherished is failing. If we three cannot agree, the Goddess will turn Her face from us and we will be lost!"

I thought of the promises that had been made to me when I hovered between life and death after giving birth to my child. Had that been the voice of the Goddess speaking, or only my own need?

"Soon comes the shortest day," said Gunarduilla grimly. "This place holds some of the oldest magic in the land. This is our final chance to bring back the old ways, for if we fail, the new sun may die stillborn and winter reconquer the world. Already we have poured the blood of sacrificed bulls into the cup marks on the spirit stones down the hill. Later we will make other offerings. If the Goddess accepts them perhaps She will lift Her hand. By our lives or our deaths, Cridilla, She must be served!"

I looked at her and felt the first real shiver of fear. Which face of the Lady was the true one—the black sow who devours her offspring or the radiance that had comforted me? I looked up and saw two ravens flapping heavily northward across the wind-scoured sky. Talorgenos would have known how to interpret that omen. I wondered if the oak priest or Lady Asaret would have agreed with my sisters' interpretation of the will of the gods.

"And what about Maglaros?" I asked instead.

"I am my husband's only wife," said Gunarduilla, "but I will share him for the sake of the land—"

"Oh, Gunarduilla!" Suddenly Rigana was laughing. "Such generosity! All the world knows how long it has been since thou didst share his bed! If he takes other wives, wilt thou even care?"

"And all the world knows with how many thou hast shared thine!" Gunarduilla shot back at her. "I care not for bedplay but for power, and Maglaros lets me do as I will. I will share him as our mothers shared the old man, so long as I be sole queen in my own land! Unity without conquest we will have—and peace. . . ."

Unity, perhaps, but I wondered if there would be peace in any land that lay beneath Maglaros's heel. And neither of my sisters had said what would become of Leir.

"Let us agree to stand together, Cridilla," said Rigana. "Let us be as one!"

From behind us I heard the shouts of the warriors and the excited barking of dogs. Then there came a stifled cry of pain. My fists clenched. What kinship had I with these? But I remembered Rigana's whisper, and I preferred her plan to Gunarduilla's. I had to buy time.

"I do not know what to do," I whispered brokenly. "I cannot answer. Give me until Midwinter Day to decide."

Gunarduilla looked at me somberly. "Midwinter Day? Truly, at the sun's turning all will be decided, with or without thy will!"

Male laughter shook the air. Maglaros and his men were coming toward us, escorted by a celebration of dogs, and after them, separated by a few formal paces, the more brightly dressed men of Rigana's retinue. Many of them already had full drinking horns in their hands. Still laughing, they set their swords on the ground behind them and sat down in long rows facing each other across the spread cloths.

Maglaros eased down carefully beside Gunarduilla and his dogs flopped expectantly behind him. Leir was led to a place beside me while they braced up Rigana's canopy to shade us. I suspected that the red cloth before us was also hers and the wooden platters to hold our meat, for I had seen no such amenities among the Albans.

In the distance I could hear the rest of the dogs squabbling over the offal. Two of the men came marching up and set the hero's portion, still steaming from the cauldron, before Maglaros. For the queens they had reserved the most tender portions of the inner thigh. But to Leir they served the heart of the bull.

I saw how his face changed when they set the platter before him. His glance met Gunarduilla's and she looked away. His gaze came then to Maglaros, and it was the look of a warrior who goes onto the dueling ground to meet his foe.

"What is wrong?" asked the Lord of Alba. "Do you not appreciate my hospitality?" There was a silence while more and more heads turned, interested or uncomprehending, to see what Leir would say.

"I accept it," the king answered at last. "But if I take your gift, then you must also accept what you will get from me. . . ."

Maglaros frowned, but it seemed to me that he breathed easier when Leir had eaten. Suddenly I had no stomach for the juicy morsel in my hand.

"Father, I don't understand—" I whispered as he sat back again. "Has he insulted you?"

Leir looked down at his platter with a twisted smile. "It was no insult, child. He has given me the portion of a king."

"Let us drink to our new alliance!" Maglaros tossed the remains of his meat to his hound and motioned to his warriors to bring up the casks of ale.

"Wait, my lord—" Rigana's mellow voice interrupted him. "I have brought mead of my own brewing from the fields of the south, and a gift for you to drink it from!"

The dark young warrior from her escort handed her something wrapped in a linen cloth, while her Quiritani lad knelt with a bronze-banded cask cradled in his arms. Rigana flipped the fabric aside and held up a drinking horn covered with gold foil. As the queen presented the horn to Maglaros, a murmur of admiration swept through the crowd.

"A princely gift indeed!" Maglaros grinned, savoring his triumph. He took the horn, examining the figures of men and gods punched out in low relief on its sides. Then he held it out to Rigana to be filled. For a moment the cheerful glug of pouring mead was the only sound.

"A toast to you, my king—" Rigana handed it back to him and filled her own cup from the cask. "May you always be as happy as you are now!"

I stared at her in disgust. Where were all her promises? Rigana sipped her mead, watching the man she had promised to marry, while the others upended mugs or horns.

"Life to the king!" they cried. "Life and prosperity!"

"Death!" came a shout as Maglaros set the golden horn to his lips. "Stop! There is death in the horn!"

The chieftain looked up, uncomprehending, as Rigana's dark youth threw himself upon the speaker and brought him struggling to the ground. It was the Quiritani boy.

"Seize them!" cried Maglaros, still clutching the horn. In another moment both combatants were pinioned securely, still spitting at each other in a garbled mixture of Quiritani and the old tongue.

"What does this mean?" Maglaros got to his feet, still holding the horn. His voice was steady, but the color had ebbed from his skin.

"Lord, do not drink," gasped the Quiritani. "Poison. . . ."

"Nonsense," Rigana said into the silence. "I drank from the same cask just a moment ago. But pour it out and fill it with horse piss or sour ale, whichever you favor, if you are afraid!"

Deliberately she refilled her cup from the cask and drank it down. Her voice was as steady as his, but above the furs at her throat I could see a rapid pulsebeat. Maglaros matched her scornful glance and lifted the horn once more.

"Not the mead, but the horn—" said Gunarduilla suddenly. Her face had become a mask. "The poison could be in the horn itself. Give it to someone else to test—" Her stony gaze swept the rows of gaping warriors, then she pointed. "Give it to *him!*"

Rigana had risen, her cup rolling unheeded at her feet.

"What are you doing?" she cried as Maglaros passed the horn to one of the men who was holding the dark warrior. "That is one of my guards!"

"He is indeed," said Maglaros tightly. "Drink, lad, and let us see what manner of gift your lady intended for me!"

The young man straightened, took the horn from his captor, and lifted it in salute to his queen. Then he set it to his lips. We could see his throat muscles working strongly as he drank it down. He drained it and handed it back, his eyes fixed on Rigana. And all that time she watched him with the same fixity. Both of his captors now had let him go, and the others were edging away from him so that they faced each other in the center of a circle of men.

The boy stood, and I saw hope leap in Rigana's eyes. Then his face twisted. He stiffened, he was fighting it, but the convulsion that locked his muscles was greater than any will could overcome. As if in final salute one arm flailed wide, then he went down, twisting helplessly. But it was not for long. In another moment he arched like a bow, fell back, and did not move again.

Rigana brought her fist to her mouth. The young warrior's eyes were rolled up in sightless agony, but he had not made a sound.

"A brave death, but useless . . ." said Maglaros evenly, but I could see the fine tremors of shock beneath his skin.

"So perish all who live by treachery," Gunarduilla replied.

Leir reached out to me and I felt his grip tighten on my arm, but I could not look away.

Rigana knelt beside the body. "Ilf," she whispered. "Ilf, I waited for thee!" There was blood on the boy's lips where he had bitten back the pain. She bent and kissed it away. Then she felt beneath his tunic, as if, even now, she were seeking a heartbeat there.

But when she straightened I glimpsed a flicker of metal in her hand. She stood up unsteadily, hugging herself as if she were cold, but I could see the thin shape of the blade concealed in the folds of her furs. She faced her sister. In the dead-white of her face her eyes were like holes.

"*Thou!*" Her hiss carried clearly in the still air. She moved toward Gunarduilla like someone stepping across thin ice. "Fool! Dost claim power? Thou hast become the shadow of this monster who rules thee, and he has stolen all thy virtue away! It is thou who art the traitor to thy mother, Gunarduilla, and to the old ways, and to me!" Rigana took a step closer and spat.

Gunarduilla did not flinch. Not then, not until the little knife flickered into visibility in Rigana's hand. Then Gunarduilla blurred into action, scooping up the sword that had been laid behind her and drawing it in the single smooth motion that Bear Mother had taught us, arm flaring out and around in a spiral loop that flicked the tip of the blade through Rigana's white throat while she was still striking at the place where Gunarduilla had been.

Blood sprayed across the red cloth. The knife flew sparkling from Rigana's fingers. She fell as a tree falls, all of a piece, and the last of her blood moistened the hard earth in a red stream that wound toward her lover's outstretched hand.

"Rigana," whispered Leir. "My child!"

I looked down, saw blood dripping from the piece of beef I was still holding, and cast it from me. A raven that had been sitting in the birch tree launched itself downward, caught the morsel while it was still in the air, and, screaming triumphantly, bore it away.

The sound broke the spell. One of Rigana's warriors lunged for the Quiritani lad, who grabbed the knife she had dropped and struck out at him, shouting. Suddenly men were fighting all around us; Gunarduilla's Albans against the men of Belerion, Quiritani against the old race, the Ai-Zir warriors striking out at both sides until they could reach their ponies and gallop away.

By the time it was over, more blood than Rigana's reddened the ground, and the ravens were hosting hopefully in the pale birch trees. Maglaros stalked back to the remains of the feast and stared at his wife, who gazed stonily back at him with her red-tipped blade still clutched in her hand.

"I did well to wed a warrior maid," he said harshly. "I did a good day's work when I conquered you!" He prodded Ilf's contorted limbs with his toe. "Set this out with the rest and build a pyre to burn them. But we will give the woman to the earth and raise a barrow over her body, for she was a queen. . . .

"Like you—" He faced me suddenly. "But I am done with begging for alliances as I am done with mercy. I will take what I need, and your only choice is how much pain I will inflict upon those you care for before you give in to me!"

I got to my feet and reached down to assist my father, thinking that with my hand-to-hand fighting skills I could at least hurt a few of them before I went down. Leir leaned upon my shoulder, gripping it painfully.

"It begins," he said softly. "Thus it begins. Daughter, save your strength. We have a weary way to go. . . ."

"Bring the cage," said Maglaros, "and put the girl and the old man inside."

Gunarduilla had not moved. Not during the fighting, or while they were forcing us into our prison, or when they carried Rigana's body away. Throughout everything she stood as silent as the sister she had slain.

"Cridilla . . . sister, listen to me. . . ."

I shivered as I felt the first wet kiss of snow. But that was not what had awakened me. Someone was standing beside the cage. I turned over carefully, so as not to awaken my father, and saw a darker shadow in the gloom.

"I have nothing to say to you." I kept my voice low.

"Agree with Maglaros, or pretend to," she said as if I had not spoken. "He is not himself. I do not know what he will do—"

I believed her, remembering the shoulder wound. But though health might restore Maglaros's self-control, I doubted it would alter his ambitions.

"He will kill us, Gunarduilla," I answered coldly. "And then you will be alone."

"Cannot you bend a little for the sake of the land?"

"Cannot you help us out of this cage?"

"It would do no good," she whispered. "His dogs . . . would hunt you down."

"Then stand up to him. You are the queen!"

"Maglaros is the king. No one else is left who can rule. Did you think we had done all this for our own pleasure? I must support him, or it will all have been for nothing. Already Rigana's blood cries out to me from the ground. Cridilla, you must give in!"

Her voice trembled like an overstressed bowstring, and I realized that she was telling as much of the truth as she dared to see.

"If I do, will he let our father go free?"

[357]

There was silence. I lay down again, and after a time, the shadow that was my sister moved away.

Two nights in the open had taught me to sense every drop in temperature, every shift in the wind, and since the afternoon grey clouds had been advancing from the west, preparing to drop their burden of snow. Leir lay still beside me. I curved closer to his warmth both for his sake and my own. They had taken our cloaks when they caged us. How long, I wondered, did Maglaros expect us to survive?

But at least my father and I were free to share what warmth remained in our bodies. They had lashed Crow to the big birch tree, and he hung between earth and heaven alone.

I heard my father's breath catch, then he coughed. I held him tightly, feeling the pain rack his body as if it were my own. It was not the deep, tearing cough of his illness—not yet, but it was already painful. I reached out to stroke his hair and let my palm rest upon his brow.

"Am I fevered?" he whispered.

"Be easy, father—" In truth, his skin was too cool.

"If I begin to babble, you must tell me. All I have left to fear is the fever. I am afraid of its madness. I am afraid of dying uselessly."

"Is death ever useful?" I asked bitterly. "I saw no purpose in the way Rigana was cut down. . . ." I felt more snow and curved myself around him in a vain attempt at protection.

"Even she"—he coughed again—"was faithful to something. But she did not die as a queen. That is the mystery. For many years I forgot it, but I can run no more. That is the one weapon I still have, the thing Maglaros fears."

I held him more tightly. "I do not understand."

"There is power in the death of a king—to curse, or to cure. . . ."

I had gone down into darkness and not feared my own death. Why was I so frightened by the thought of his? Was it perhaps because in childbed I had run the risk natural to women, who lie down to give birth to their children as men march out to defend them? Or was it because then I had not been in my own country? I had thought that I was intended to teach Leir what he owed to the land he had ruled, but he was teaching me.

"You are bound to this place, is it not so? Is that what you meant when you told me how my mother brought you here? I belong to Briga by blood and birth, and you by the ritual. Is that why whatever happens to us here will have so much power?"

"Gunarduilla knew it," Leir replied, "and she has told Maglaros. He only half believes, as I did, but he dare not let me live and he desires the power my death can give him even as he fears me. Already the land is sick. The weather grows ever colder. Which will I choose?" He moved his head restlessly against my arm. "To make my death a curse to bring down the one who is destroying all I tried to build, or to make it a gift to restore the land?"

And what choices did I have, I wondered then. Whether my father lived or died, what decisions were left to me?

Snowflakes melted on my cheeks like tears. A rope creaked in the birch tree and I wondered whether Crow's dying would have a purpose too. Gradually Leir's head grew heavy on my arm, and when I knew he slept I fell into an uneasy doze.

I dreamed that I was back with Bear Mother on the Misty Isle. We had just brought down a deer. She slit its throat and held the head while the life drained away in a slow stream.

"Remember," she was saying, "always let th' blood feed th' land."

Then the scene faded, but Bear Mother was still before me, shimmering as she had when I went out on the spirit road.

"Mother," I cried, "like a beast they have caged me. What can I do?"

"Cage only holds body," she replied, "not you. . . ."

"I cannot do it!" I cried. Whether it was the cold or fear that if I left my body now I could not return, I had not been able to enter the Otherworld from the cage.

"Remember your song, Adder! Remember the song!"

As if it were part of my dream, I became aware that someone was singing. But it was neither Bear Mother nor me. The ache in my feet told me that I was awake. A few stars twinkled mockingly through the bars of our cage. The sky had begun to clear and the temperature was going down.

"One and twenty blackbirds you can see . . . hanging in the tree. . . . Three nights from the yew tree in the hills . . . and one night from the ash tree in the dales . . . and two nights from the birch tree that grows on the fell. . . ." The monotone of sound was coming from Crow. "Who can tell"—he giggled suddenly—"what the end will be?"

"Crow—can you hear me?" Raising myself on one arm I called softly.

"Two swans in a cage and one crow in a tree," he answered. "But this one is closer to the stars. . . ."

"Crow, forgive me. I should have sent you away!"

"This one ran from the yew and was caught by the ash tree. You and the bright one rescued him—" he chanted. "Fourteen turnings of the sun he evaded fate, but the birch tree is eldest, and she has trapped him at last."

I recognized one reference in these ramblings. It had been an ash tree from which I had cut him down.

"The spirits wait below, with snapping jaws, with gaping maws. They will consume this body, and when the wind sings through the bones the spirits give a new body, and this one climbs the worldtree to the stars!"

I blinked back tears. Crow had always lived in his own version of reality, but his odd wisdom had saved my father in his madness. Now Leir was sane in a way that frightened me, and it was Crow whose wits were gone.

"Do you not understand your danger—" I exclaimed. "You have been beaten to a pulp and now you are hanging in a tree!" In the camp below, one of the dogs howled and the others echoed him.

"Do not weep. Do not weep, Adder—"

How could he hear me, in his pain?

"This one was meant to be a singer for the people . . . like Speaker-to-Spirits." His voice cracked painfully. "This one hung on the tree of testing, and was frightened, and ran away. . . ." His breath caught as the rope creaked again.

Crow, Crow—go mad again! my spirit cried. *Let madness take away your pain!*

"The spirits wait," he went on. "It must be finished. But Crow is afraid. . . ."

I could hear them whispering just below my hearing; the air

was all ashiver with their wings. The sound grew. Was it the howling of the hounds or the spirits calling Crow and my father away from me?

Crow's moan strengthened as the howling grew louder; his throat opened in a high, clear cry, and his anguish was echoed by the baying of the hounds.

"Sing, Crow," I whispered, "sing your song of power! I too am afraid!"

"Are you warm enough? Are you well fed?" Maglaros's mockery came dimly through the weight of sleep that had come upon me with the dawn. Groggy, I raised myself on one elbow and squinted through the glare of sunlight on fresh snow.

"Are you ready to serve me?" Maglaros went on.

"When the tides run backward—" I mumbled. "When the stars begin to fall!"

"Dare you defy me? Woman, I hold your life in my hand!"

I shrugged and lay back again. It was not much of a life I had now. I could see Gunarduilla standing in the doorway of the house behind him, but she neither spoke nor followed him.

Maglaros shook the crosspieces of our cage. "I can *kill* you!" he shouted. "Don't you understand?"

Leir stirred beside me. "You dare not let our blood feed the ground," he said tiredly.

Maglaros swore. I could feel him staring at us, but I did not open my eyes to look at him.

"Not yours, perhaps," he said finally. "But there are others whose blood is not so sacred. This slave has amused you long enough. Now he shall make sport for me. . . ." He grunted and moved away.

I heard him giving orders, and sat up to see. His warriors were building a fire near the birch tree. Others stood leaning on their spears and fending off the dogs who tried to carry off the branches in play. They had already stripped off the rest of Crow's rags. He looked like a skinned hare, his meager flesh all mottled with scrapes and bruises, and he was shivering.

I shivered too, but not with cold.

"What is it?" asked Leir.

From the direction of the tree came laughter, and a gasp of pain. The king sat up, saw what the men were doing, and groaned. Already blood was running from a dozen spear pricks in Crow's breast and sides, and the dogs licked the bright drops from the ground.

"That is a sorry repayment for all his service to me—" said the king.

"Indeed, he ate at your table," said Maglaros, coming back to us. "He guarded your sleep. He guided you through the wilderness. Will you let his life be the price of your pride? Save him, you who were a king. Give over your lordship to me."

Leir was silent. Maglaros shrugged and pointed, and one of the warriors drew a long dagger with a blade of the ancient bronze that was more brittle but far sharper than any iron sword. He got a good grip on Crow's leg and began to carve off the flesh as one carves a piece from the haunch that hangs in the smokehouse to bring it into the hall.

My cry was lost in Crow's first yell of agony. I clutched at the crosspiece of the cage. Maglaros took the bloody strip of meat from his man and shook it, and I jerked back as the warm blood spattered my hand.

"Are you not hungry?" he snarled, and I gagged, suddenly glad they had not fed us for two days. "Well, 'tis often enough he shared the dogs' dinner. Now he shall feed them!"

His hounds leaped, eyes alight with innocent appetite, as he tossed Crow's flesh into the air. As it fell their whining disintegrated into a tumult of yelps and snarls. The man with the knife grasped Crow's other leg in his bloody hand.

"This is abomination—" said Leir. "This is not the work of a warrior, or of a king!"

Maglaros's face twisted. Suddenly I realized that he had held Crow's flesh in his *left* hand, the same one with which he had done everything since he took us prisoner.

"He is a warrior no longer!" I cried. "Artocoxos's blow crippled him. Men of Alba, listen, will you follow a maimed king?"

Some of the warriors turned, but most were too intent on their sport to hear. One man pressed a heated spearpoint to Crow's wounds to stop their bleeding, and the stink of burning flesh polluted the air. My empty stomach heaved and I retched bile.

"When you give me your power I will be healed," hissed Maglaros.

"When I was mad I harmed none," said Leir, "but you are a rabid dog! Do you *want* me to curse you? Do you want me to make the earth swallow your bones?"

"You can stop me. Is the slave's life important to you? Is there meaning in his pain?" He stared at his victim.

The crows were already gathering in the tops of the birches, stark black against the white of the tree trunks and the snow. Crow hung in his bonds unmoving. The dogs had eaten his flesh eagerly, and the birds, who were also his kin, would not refuse their share. I had a moment's hope that he was dead already, then I saw his rib cage rise and fall.

"Sing, bird!" One of the men set him swinging and he gasped. "You prophesied doom for so many—do you have a song for your own suffering?"

"Beg for your life, slave!" snarled Maglaros then. "Beg the old man to save you, plead with the girl!"

"The king is the light, and Crow is the shadow—" came Crow's harsh whisper. "The queen is the star, and Crow is the night."

"Don't you understand? We can make your suffering short or carve your flesh away bite by bite until you count your bones."

"The bones are the seed of the soul. . . . Bare the bones and set the spirit free!"

"I'll set you free!" Maglaros grabbed the knife and began to hack at the twitching body before him. "Don't you know I have the power to save or to slay?" Crow's next scream thinned to a single high note like the ending of a song.

"The bones are the earth; the blood is the sea—" he chanted. "The breath is the wind, the spirit is free. . . ."

"Do you defy me?" screamed his tormentor. "You made yourself a woman for so many—now we will make a woman of you! Will you sing so sweetly then?"

I hid my face against my father's shoulder and heard the dogs feeding once more. Leir's fingers dug into my arm.

[363]

"Stop them—" I whimpered. "Da, make them let him go. I will marry Maglaros and kill him when he lies with me. Say you will give in, father, tell them now!"

Leir held me closer, and the beat of his heart was like a broken drum beneath my ear. "Child, child, it is too late for that. He cannot live now."

"Free . . ." The scream tore the air.

> "When flies white skies the crow—
>   black on snow, swift shadow
> of night and day;
>   away the sundered spirit flies to be;
>   I am free. . . ."

Again his cry seared the air. I moaned and heard in my own tone its echo, swinging back and forth in denial of the sweet sung pain.

> "By the blade I was unmade;
>   reborn within a black dog's skin.
> I am the sound of the hound,
>   carried on the wind, fruit of the tree—
>   I am free. . . ."

Free . . . free . . . I found in the release of sound an answer to agony. Did his voice grow stronger, or was it my own?

> "I am the running deer, leaping clear;
>   I am the rooting boar; I am more,
> And the bear; everywhere
>   I find myself, and all life lives in me—
>   I am free. . . ."

I beat frantic wings and soared into the open sky.

> "I am the light and might of storms—
>   I am the silent song, I belong

to the starry skies.
The wind's wing I shall be—"

As I swept upward I saw a dark bird flying beside me—no, he was the shining one and I the shadow; black and bright, light that lifted while heavy wings beat slower, straining to follow that luminous presence that arrowed toward a light that was more radiant still—

"I am free. . . ."

Then he was gone, and I was alone in an empty sky.

I circled the settlement, seeing with sharp swan's sight the old man who wept over the girl in his arms, and the more profound stillness of the bloodstained body that hung on the tree.

My father's need dragged me down. Slowly I spiraled inward into unconsciousness once more.

Chapter

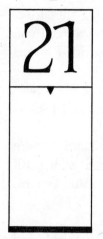

I invoke the seven daughters of the sea
Who fashion the threads of the sons of long life,
May three deaths be taken from me!
May seven waves of good fortune be dealt to me!
May no evil spirits harm me on my circuit!
In flashing corslet without hindrance
May my fame not perish!
May old age come to me,
May death not come to me till I am old!

—5th-century Irish

We rode out from the settlement in the bleak hour before the dawning; and the red light of the torches flowed like blood across the snow. They had put new crimson robes upon me and Leir, as if we were going to a festival, but our hands were bound, and Leir had a man behind him on the pony lest he should fall.

But I did not feel the pain of my bonds. Since I had seen Crow's spirit winging outward my body and spirit had been but loosely linked. The night was starless, the men who guarded us dim shapes in the gloom, but I could see their lifelights flickering and from time to time I would find myself floating in the windy darkness, looking down at the line of lights that bobbed across the moor. We were going to our deaths. I knew that, but it did not seem to matter anymore.

Presently we halted. I heard Leir's cough nearby. The torches were spreading into a ring around a humped shape almost man-high and nearly twice as long. My focus shifted and I saw a dimly luminous mass all marked with lines and rings and pocks through which radiance shone as if the brightness were somehow imprisoned beneath the surface of the stone. That was odd enough to attract my attention, and then I realized that I had seen some of those patterns before, scarred into the faces of Speaker-to-Spirits and Crow.

"Listen, spirits of the land," said Maglaros, facing the stone. "By the lord of club and wheel and cauldron I swear to feed you well if you will favor me—" He motioned to the warrior who led my pony. "Pull her down."

Leir's cry was stifled by the man who held him. I felt a swift flash of fear, then flesh and spirit divided once more and I knew that whatever they did to my body I would not feel.

"Father"—my voice seemed to come from a distance—"I am not afraid. It is Maglaros who should dread the wrath of Briga if my blood stains this stone, and Gunarduilla who should fear his impiety."

"Woman, do you think to threaten me?"

Slowly I turned to face my foe. His light pulsed sluggishly and I knew that death had laid its hand upon him already. He was like a cornered boar that would rather take its hunters down than break free.

"Maglaros, I am beyond both threats and pleading. I am free."

Clearly he thought I had gone crazy as Crow. "You are my prisoner!"

"Gunarduilla!" I looked past the butterfly axe in his hands to my sister. Mortal sight showed me her face haggard in the torchlight; the radiance of her spirit was leaping and sinking like a guttering flame. I looked for the sister who had once loved me, but I could sense only pain.

"If I must die, then do thou kill me. For thy husband's sake thou hast become a kinslayer already. Who will protect thy rights when thou thyself dost destroy them? Rigana is dead and all thy dreams lie broken. The Goddess hides Her face from thee because of thy crimes. Soon thou wilt be alone!"

"It was not my will—" grated my sister. "Why dost thou torture me? Already Rigana's blood burns my hand!"

"It is the truth that torments thee—" I began, but Maglaros swore and shoved me toward the stone.

"Woman, do not listen!" he told Gunarduilla. "I'll stop the bitch from babbling!" He poised the axe to swing, grimacing as the weight came down on his right arm. "Here is my offering!"

I let my spirit slip free and watched my body sag against the stone. Fire blazed from the bronze blade, and then Gunarduilla blurred into motion once more. But her sword caught in a fold of her cloak as she tried to draw it. Maglaros whirled, and the axe slammed against her skull.

She fell forward, knocking the weapon from his grasp, and clutched at the stone. Its light pulsed angrily and began to dim; it was not death but life that was written there. She heaved onto her back, leaning against the rock, and the light of the torches fell full on her shattered skull. Maglaros backed away one pace, then another, and stood shuddering.

"Cridilla . . . forgive me!" Her face twisted, and suddenly I was back in my body. But before I could reach out to her she tried once more to free her sword. "The Goddess will destroy—" For a moment the wavering blade pointed at Maglaros, then her strength failed her. I saw the life go out of her eyes and the blade fell harmless into the snow.

From the darkness above us came a crow's harsh call.

"The Senamoi has cursed us!" shouted one of the men. "Maglaros is doomed! He has killed the queen!" There was a commotion of men and horses, and then the fading hoofbeats of ponies galloping away across the moor.

Maglaros retained barely a score of men—the sworn Companions who had come with him from the land of the Banalisioi. One of them was the man who had carved the flesh from Crow's bones.

"My lord," came his deep voice, "what shall we do?"

"Sling the body over one of the ponies, and set the Lady of Briga on her horse again," Maglaros replied. "Since she has cheated death she shall serve me living, but I shall make her wish she had died instead of the other one."

"Why not kill me, Maglaros, as you are killing my girls? My deathword will destroy you." Leir coughed and then began to laugh. "I will not go consenting while the last of my children is in your hands."

Was it the fever, or only the king's anger that burned in the air?

Could not Maglaros feel how the land itself was trembling now? I tried to call out to my father, but the hard hand of the rider behind me cut off my words.

"Do you think that your will matters?" asked our enemy. "Between them, the bitches have closed all ways to me but one. We are going to the sun stone—we are going to the king stone, old man, and there we shall see who has the power!"

The torchlight rippled around us as we moved on. It seemed to me that I saw Bear Mother's spectral figure floating before us, and she was weeping, but behind us Gunarduilla's blood marked our trail across the snow.

When we stopped once more, the darkness had faded to a featureless grey. We were on the brink of a stream that rushed furiously downward from the moor above us, dashing itself against rock and rapid before plunging into the dark forest below. One man was left to hold the horses while others carried me and Leir across the stream. Then I was set on my feet again and prodded up the steep bank and out onto level ground.

A broad ledge ran between the long slope that led up to the spine of the moor and a rocky escarpment that looked over the dark mass of trees in the dale. Cloud concealed the crown of the ridge and brushed the treetops, closing us in. At the edge of the cliffs a patch of ground had been cleared of heather. In the middle of it was a flat mass of rock half-covered by snow.

From the stone I sensed a waiting stillness that I was too exhausted to probe. One of the warriors dropped me onto his spread cloak and tied my feet while another shoved my father down beside me. Leir burned, but I was cold in body and sick at heart. I had hated my sisters; I had loved them. Now they were gone.

"At Midsummer, the moor is white with heather, not snow," said Leir softly. I raised myself to look at him, but his gaze was clear. "I am not mad—yet—though at this moment I could wish it," he answered my unspoken question. "It was at Midsummer that your mother brought me here."

"Why here?" I asked. "There are so many carved stones—"

"The others are different. Your mother's people honored them, but even they could not say who had put those markings there. But the carving on the stone here is new. It is the sun sign of my people, linked with the cup and ring mark of the ancient ones. Talorgenos chiseled it into the rock at Fieret's direction to bind me and my blood to the land. And when it was done, she gave me the bride-cup of sweet water from the stream."

I peered at the rock from which Maglaros's men had swept the snow away, and though the light was still as directionless as the light of the Otherworld, now I could see clearly the four-armed outline that swirled around the cross-pattern of cup marks pecked into the stone.

"You said there was a promise—"

His mouth grew grim. "I swore . . . that if there was need, I would give my life for the land. . . ."

I turned over and saw Maglaros watching us. His face was sallow; the hair that had once been burnished auburn was dull and shot with grey. A sense of baffled fury pulsed around him, like a mist of blood in the dim air.

"I will not give it for *him!*" said Leir.

I rolled back and buried my face against my father's shoulder so that he should not see my tears. I could hear the irregular beating of his heart and the suck and rasp of air in his chest. The serenity of the night had left me. I was weeping with frustration because I was too weak to break these bonds and answer Maglaros's anger with my own. I felt the sprinkling of water and heard one of the warriors muttering the words of purification as he went by. From somewhere nearby came an irregular thunk and clatter as if someone were throwing stones. My nostrils twitched as the smoke of sweet herbs filled the air. It was beginning, and there was nothing I could do.

"Bring the old man to me."

I struggled upright as they dragged Leir to his feet and carried him toward the stone.

"Leir Blatoniknos, you are high king no longer. Now your sovereignty passes to me!"

The lifting mists revealed a tangle of bare-branched hazels that had rooted themselves in a cleft in the escarpment behind Maglaros. I blinked as something dark flapped heavily downward and settled among them, watching him.

"Do you think so?" The king was drawing strength from his anger. "It is my curse you will inherit, not my power! What will the lordship of Briga be worth to you if the year-wheel turns backward? What will you do when the serpent of darkness eats the sun?"

"Maglaros, you have lost!" I echoed him. "You will get nothing but dead meat from either my father or me!"

"Do you think I *need* your blessing?" snarled Maglaros. "You have left me no choice. With Gunarduilla and Rigana both gone, the old lines cannot be restored even if that were what I desired! Woman, I have brought your father here not to take his power but to destroy it. Your life will win me a foothold in Briga whether you cooperate or not"—his voice rang with a desperate pride— "long enough at least for everyone to understand that I have annihilated all other authority. I claim the kingdom by right of conquest, asking favor from no power but my own!"

Even his own Companions stirred uneasily at the sacrilege. The air grew heavy with fear, and from the hazel copse came the hoarse cry of a crow.

"I am Lady of Briga!" I cried, "and you will not rule this land while I live!"

"Silence her—" he screamed. The warrior nearest seized me. I saw his fist coming, but I could not avoid it. The blow rocked me; I felt myself falling and heard my father's cry.

"Have you killed her? Have you murdered my last child? She was the best of them—the most loyal in adversity and the most fierce in valor. How could you do it? Did you not know that her life was the justification for the world?"

I could see and hear him, but I could not speak or move.

"If the bitch is dead then I am glad of it—" came the reply.

"Maglaros, you have brought your doom upon you—" grated the king. "By the blood once shed, and by the oath once said, to me the powers of this place are bound. Therefore I call upon the eternal earth to witness, and the winds of heaven, and the great serpent that dwells in the deeps of the sea!" His voice grew in power and the air itself seemed to congeal.

"By the sign of the sun that empowered me I call upon the gods of the Painted People and the Quiritani. Black sow, consume the golden boar you farrowed—Great Mother, take back the infant sun into Your dark womb once more!" He drew breath to continue—

"Stop him!" screamed Maglaros.

"Arise, ye ancient powers—" The next words came garbled as the warrior's paralysis broke and he covered Leir's mouth with his palm.

"In the name of your oath you have called on the ancient powers!" Specks of foam dotted Maglaros's lips as he shouted the words. "But where was your oath when the floods came and the crops died and death stalked the land? I do not want your blood, old man. Oathbreaker I name you, and by the triple death of the traitor I shall strip your powers away!"

The thong in his fist snapped like a whip as his arm jerked. One of the warriors grabbed it; I saw the noose already tied and began to strain against my own bonds.

"By the Earth and Air and Water that you have invoked you shall die! Let your wrath stay locked within you! Here is the thong to cut off your breath; the water to fill your lungs runs down the hill; and all around us lie the stones that will weight your unblessed body while yet you live. . . ."

His words trailed off in a gasp of laughter as a swift twitch slipped the noose over my father's head and the warrior began to pull. Leir kicked out and twisted in his grasp, but he was an old man, and bound. In a moment the hand across his mouth was unnecessary. It was air itself for which he was fighting now.

The crow flew screaming from the hazels. I gasped, and the world around me grew dim. I sucked in breath, strangled by the malevolence of my enemy as surely as Leir was being strangled by his cord. The air was expelled from my lungs in a scream of denial that echoed across memory. I had screamed defiance in battle, and pain when I gave birth to my child, but never had such a sound as this wrenched through me. Dark wings beat heavily across my vision as the rage surged through me again.

"Ai . . . ai . . . ai . . ." Once I had sung it. Once, when I had power.

Leir slumped in his captor's arms, his face livid above the sharp crease of the strangler's cord. They began to drag him toward the stream.

"*Ai . . . ai . . . ai . . . the Adder am I! All of ye here, behold me and fear!*"

Words yammered in memory. Bear Mother had not lived to teach me their meaning, but now her figure hovered before me, and the knowledge was within my grasp. They were my words, my magic . . . The world dimmed around me, but I could feel a dark power uncoiling deep within.

"*Among bears a bear, face me if ye dare—*" I sang. "*Serpent hid in the grass, swiftly I pass . . .*"

I felt cold and wet and knew that they were holding Leir beneath the chill flow of the stream. The suffocating weight of that water bore me down into darkness. The image of the adder in the grass was dissolving. Shapes flickered in my awareness, but I released each one in turn, sinking deeper and deeper into the abyss where scaled coils huge beyond the range of human vision shifted and slid . . .

They lifted beneath me. They surged within me. It was I whose power was uncoiling in the vastness of that primordial sea. From a throat as deep as eternity came the echo of my song.

"*Serpent of Night . . . swallowing Light . . .*
Drowned in the Deep, no longer asleep . . .
All ye who hear, behold me and fear!"

The power that Leir had summoned was here.

Awareness arose into a dim world where puny mortals ran and cried. Bonds snapped like threads; *I* did not heed them. *I* was the Serpent, swinging back and forth above the ledge and the men who stood there, seeking my prey.

[374]

By the stream someone had dropped what looked like a bundle of sodden red rags. They did not concern me. It was the ones who were running whose fear I savored, their energies that whetted my appetite as they died. And it was the man in the cat-fur cloak for whose life I lusted. I dipped lower, opening fanged, fringed jaws.

"*Maglaros, Maglaros . . . come to Me!*" My calling echoed through all the worlds. "*I am the fear of the women you forced: I am the agony of those you killed; I am the rage of those whom you have manipulated and imprisoned and denied. . . .*"

The man edged backward, staring wildly about him. He stumbled and scrambled up again, hands clapped over his ears, and scuttled toward the sun stone. I swung after him, growing steadily more solid to the eye.

"*Come to Me, Maglaros, and I will consume you, for I am the Darkness within . . . I am She whose work is done by Woman. From My body all things were born, and I am She who unmakes all things. . . . I am the unwinding of all that binds and the ending of all that Time begins. I am Emptiness . . . I am the final Understanding. All other powers are food for Me. . . .*"

Inexorably I flowed forward. Driven by terror beyond ordinary perception, Maglaros could see Me. He took one step back and then another. The edge of the precipice was just behind him now.

For a moment Maglaros wavered between fear of the Abyss above him and the void below. Then I struck, and as he leaped into emptiness I engulfed him. His body fell through My shadow to shatter on the rocks below.

I reared upward, roaring my hunger, for despite Maglaros's malice, his little life had been barely a morsel compared to the emptiness within. Some of his men I had eaten, others were scuttling like lice across the moor. I lifted higher, seeking them, and saw a world of frozen life awaiting My jaws. My shadow darkened the mists that boiled around Me; thunder rumbled My rage through the air.

On the trail that led to the settlement more figures were moving, on foot or on horseback, pulling carts across the rocky ground. They had nearly reached the stream now. More living beings, a world of living things was coming to be consumed. I surveyed them with an impartial hunger. Nothing could halt Me now. For Me, all beings were food.

"*Adder—it is over . . . Go back to the depths now . . . be appeased —your enemy is gone. . . .*"

Before me stood a great she-bear, and each hair of her luxuriant pelt was tipped with light. On her shoulder perched a crow whose feathers glistened blindingly. My shadow swept toward them, but they did not flinch, and their radiance did not dim.

"*I am still hungry. . . .*" My jaws opened wide.

"*Serpent, we have been consumed already. We are not subject to You. Your task is accomplished. It is time to depart. . . .*"

The human horde had come to a confused halt on the far side of the stream. One of them bent over the body in the red rags, others were chanting; the air throbbed to the frantic beat of a drum. Did they think their silly spells would frighten Me? Only one of them was still approaching—a male with a small one in his arms.

"*Come back into your body now. Your people have need of you—*"

I swung back and forth in confusion. What did they mean?

The man dropped to his knees below Me. I heard the wail of the child. I contracted further, trying to see. What were they doing there? Could not they feel the shadow that loomed over them? The shimmering bear-figure stood between us and the man looked up suddenly. The child wound small arms around his neck and clung.

They were life, warm and breathing, sweeter than anything I had eaten before! Why should I hold back from consuming them? I drew closer until all the plateau was in darkness, but as My shadow engulfed them, the two human forms became points of light that continued to glow even though the figure of the Bear had drawn away.

"*Who are you?*" I demanded. "*Why are you not afraid of Me?*"

"*Without You we cast no shadow. Without You, we cannot grow. Return, and give us shape within the world . . .*"

His radiance grew until it balanced My darkness. I had seen that face before, on the Isle of the Horned One, and in the Kingdom of the Stones. My emptiness began to fill with His energy.

There was a moment when we were in balance. Day and Night together manifesting all Time in a single moment of unity. Then

Light and Darkness exploded together and interchanged. I fell inward forever, and then I was swimming upward through a stormy sea.

No, I was being shaken, and someone was crying, "Cridilla, my love, what have they done to you?" But why should he cry over me?

I reached out blindly and my fingers closed on rough wool. I blinked and saw a freckled face crowned by tangled red hair. There was a whimper, the man's hand closed over mine and moved it down to touch the baby's fair curls.

"Cridilla . . ." The man was weeping. "Please, hear me!"

And then my flesh remembered his, and recognized the sweet scent of my child. . . .

Light blazed from the ice that rimed the heather, and flashed from every stone. The mists were dispersing rapidly, and the world shone in the light of the new-made sun. I stumbled and Agantequos's grip tightened. Only with his support did I realize my own exhaustion. I touched his face again, unsure if it were the light or some dream that dazzled me. I remembered him hale and strong, but in my dreams I had seen those lines around his mouth and those shadows beneath his eyes.

"Have you been eating?" I asked stupidly. He gave a grunt of something that was not quite laughter.

"Have you?" He shifted the child on his hip and blinked as if he too were not quite sure what was real. But he was warm and alive.

Now I could see the encampment ahead of us. Those wagons had been in my dreams too. Someone there had begun restoring order. I thought I saw the dark blue of a priestess's gown.

"Was it the Veneti?" Dimly I could guess that his journey northward with the remnant of his people might have been in its own way as terrible a testing as my own.

"They came just before Samonios and took us unawares—Moridunon was already burning by the time I got to my sword."

"How many of the folk were you able to bring?"

"Two score families, some unmarried men. There were ten hands of children when we started, some of them orphaned, but on the journey many of them died."

I wondered how many of the people who had been so kind to me in Morilandis were gone.

Beli peeked out from the protection of his father's cloak and ducked his head back again. For a few moments he had clung to me, but how he was shy again. I would have to win him back. But at least he looked healthy—I could guess where some of the food his father had not been eating had gone.

"And your Companions?"

He swallowed. "Nabelcos. Keir. A few more. But Cuno and Gruncanos and the others died to cover our retreat. Our fighting strength is but a tithe of what it was."

"But down there I see many warriors—" And not only men— several priestesses were moving among the people, and I recognized the striped cloaks of oak priests as well.

"They are yours," Agantequos said gently. "We came first to Udrolissa, and found the men you left there, half-mad with worry. But it was Lady Asaret who led us here."

Someone saw us then and the first ragged shout became a wave of cheering. Belinos whimpered at the noise and Agantequos shifted him into my arms.

"Ma . . ." Small hands clenched in the wool of my gown. I nuzzled his soft hair and felt for the first time a flicker of certainty.

"I am here, my heart, and I love you," I whispered. "I will not go away again."

Then folk were crowding around me, grief fading from their faces as the clouds of a spent storm part before the sun. They touched my hair and my robe as if they feared I would vanish. I wondered myself, for I seemed to move through a mist of brightness in which only Agantequos's strong arm and the warmth of my child were real.

I knew I was at the end of my strength, but there was one last thing to do.

"Where have they put my father's body?"

"He is by the stream, lady," said Nabelcos, pointing. "And he is still alive. . . ."

I blinked as sunlight flashed from the rushing water, trying to make out the figures that knelt beside the body in the crimson robe. Surely the man beneath the tattered cloak was Talorgenos, and Lady Asaret and Mother Nesta were the two women beside him. Agantequos helped me toward them. They had got blankets around the body and a fleece for a pillow. Mother Nesta was holding a cup to his lips. I wondered why.

The king was dead. I had seen him strangled. I had felt him being drowned.

The others moved aside to let me kneel beside him.

Leir's skin was corpse-pale and clammy, but ever so slightly, his chest rose and fell.

"Father—" I laid my hand upon his breast, feeling the heartbeat flutter like a trapped bird. "The sun has been reborn and we are all alive again! Father, come back to us! We are free!"

Light glittered from the ice that sheathed the alders. My sight was blurred with weeping, but laughter was bubbling up within.

For a time I thought he had gone too far to hear me, then his eyelids fluttered a little and he sighed.

"Cridilla. . . ." I had to bend to hear him. "You were dead. But so was I, and I deserve death, for I wanted to destroy the world. . . ."

I tried to hush him, for his wrath had been but a shadow of my own, and now I was reaching for life as the first tendrils of green seek the sun.

"Father, it does not matter! Agantequos is here, and all will be well!"

Leir's eyes opened fully. In those eyes I had seen the laughter of the Young God and the lightning of the King. I had seen them filmed and foolish or clouded by wrath. I had never seen this utter clarity, as if he already gazed upon us from the Otherworld.

For a long moment his gaze rested upon my face, then it moved slowly to Agantequos and the child.

"You see me here a suppliant, lord," Agantequos said bitterly. "I am your man if you will give your protection to the remnant of my tribe, for my own land is laid waste, and the ravens nest among the charred rafters of my hall."

"I see . . . a warrior. I see a father. I see . . . a king." Leir tried to smile. "This body is broken," he said then. "It will not serve me long."

"Father," I protested, "when we get you to shelter—"

He closed his eyes against me, and looking up, I saw grief in Talorgenos's seamed face and a bleak certainty in Lady Asaret's dark eyes.

"Let him go," said Mother Nesta. "Would you keep him prisoned in pain?"

"You do not understand—" I began, but Belinos felt my turmoil and began to cry. I held him closer, as if the life that beat in him so strongly could repel the shadow that I felt approaching, and presently he stilled and began to chew on a strand of my hair. The music of the stream was louder than the sound of Leir's breathing. His eyes were as clear as the sky.

"There is a time for leaving and a time to hold on. You know that, child—you above all."

I sighed, remembering how I had almost died at Belinos's birthing and why I had returned. The choice had been offered me. Could I deny my father the same right, especially when a sight that had not entirely regained normality showed me his lifelight flickering so low? I looked up at the alder sapling whose branches overhung the stream and saw a crow sitting there, but light glimmered along the edges of its wings.

"I have been very foolish, but now I understand many things," whispered Leir. "I understand what I have been given, and what I must render back again. When I am dead, Cridilla, you must take my body back to Ambiolissa, to the heart of what I tried to build. Give me to the river, and I will watch over the land."

For a few moments all his energy was bent on the struggle to keep breathing. The rush of the bright stream sounded like a river in floodtide. I could feel the waters rising to carry the king away.

"Agantequos . . ." came his next words. "Lend me your dagger—"

My husband's face went pale beneath his freckles, but his eyes were steady as he drew the bronze knife, the blade of sacrifice, that was sheathed beside his sword. Leir's fingers closed around the hilt, of staghorn bound with gold wire.

"It is well. It is the blade of a king." He turned it and the bright bronze flamed in the light of the strengthening sun. "To you I give the kingship that Maglaros wished to wrest from me, if you will take the oath as I did, and when your time comes, make the offering."

Agantequos swallowed and gazed at the snow-veiled land around us. The people, Moriritones and Ai-Akhsi and Quiritani, had made a semicircle, silent witnesses to the mystery. I bit my lip, understanding at last what was happening here.

"To Briga?" my husband asked, "or to *her*?"

Leir smiled gently. "Are they not the same?" A spasm contorted his face, and he coughed. "Clasp hands above the river," he whispered then.

Mother Nesta reached up to take the child from me and Agantequos helped me to the side of the stream. It flowed deeply, but two flat rocks emerged from the streambed as though they had been intended for places to stand.

"Before the gods my people swear by, I declare this—" Leir coughed again. "Say the words!" he said, and Agantequos's strong voice repeated them. In my heart they were echoed as well.

> *"That my bones are the bones of the earth—*
> *That my flesh is the soil from which life grows—*
> *That my blood is the water of life and my breath is the wind.*
> *I am the earth and the stars of heaven;*
> *I am the offering. . . ."*

My mother had lived for the land, burying grief and teaching a new lord old ways until she gave her life for it, bearing me. In childbed I also had made the offering and been sent back again. To live for the land, or to die for it at need—to this both king and queen were bound.

In the silence that followed, I gazed into Agantequos's widening eyes.

From the stream I felt the upwelling of energy. My skin tingled; how could mortal flesh bear such power? And still it rushed up my spine; in another moment I would fly in glittering fragments—

then I felt something open in Agantequos and the power blasted through our clasped hands. He staggered, but I was a pillar of light, upholding him. Did the brilliance that dazzled me blaze from the water, or was it the eyes of the man before me that were so full of light?

Then a sound from Talorgenos drew us back to the world. Leir had drawn the razor tip of the dagger across the flesh of his arm. The dark blood was dripping slowly into the stream.

"I give my life to renew the land. . . ." His voice was suddenly full and clear. "I am the offering!"

The crow cawed once and launched itself into the sky.

In a moment Agantequos and I were on our knees beside my father, but the hilt was already slipping from his grasp. As I watched, he drew one harsh breath and then another, and then there were no more. As gently as water seeps from a broken vessel I felt the life in him flow away.

I sat back on my heels and light blazed against my closed eyelids. Awareness of my body faded. The crow was still circling in the heavens, but he was white now. Leir stood before me, looking around him with wondering eyes.

"It is finished," I told him. Here, I felt no need for tears. "You have the victory. And see—Crow is here to show you the way. . . ."

It was no bird but Crow in his own shape who stood before us, straight as a sapling, dark curls tumbled, laughter sparkling in his eyes. He held out his hand, and the illusion of age with which Leir's spirit had clothed itself vanished away.

"Go in peace, my father—I release you," I said then.

For a moment I glimpsed the golden god I remembered. Then brightness flared between us. They were rushing away from me, or perhaps it was I who was moving, for suddenly the whole world lay spread out below.

Leir's blood was a shimmer of light in the water. As the stream carried it away I saw its radiance suffusing the land. Every cup and ring mark on the stones of the moor was limned in light. From the heights a river of light danced downward; a bright flicker followed each tributary that sought the sea, sparked through the hidden channels beneath the soil, seeped through rock to bubble upward in well and spring. To north and south, to east and west it was flaring, and the land grew luminous where it passed.

As once I had yearned to devour, now I desired to give. In an outpouring of blessing I extended white wings, and living light bloomed throughout the land.

"*When falls the father of men—*" Talorgenos's voice echoed on all the planes. Gently awareness focused within my body once more.

> "*Spirit to the source returns again,*
> *The power once surrendered,*
> > *blood healing Earth—*
> *Brings back to birth,*
> *from Her dark womb life's ecstasy,*
> *Incarnate sovereignty. . . ."*

He finished, and the world grew still.

The people were waiting, but one task remained to me.

I bent to the stream, cupped water in my hands, and offered it to the king.

"There is blood in this water," Agantequos said.

"There is life in it," I replied.

EPILOGUE

The healing of the Island of the Mighty was not accomplished in one day, or even in many. The wounds were too deep, and the land had been weakened in ways not easily seen. But the king's sacrifice had been a beginning, and gradually that blessing took root and began to grow.

By the time the last storms of winter rolled in from the sea, my husband's folk were settling in the country around Udrolissa that had been emptied by war. In the labor of that replanting Agantequos found some solace for the loss of his land, and my own grief was numbed by the myriad details with which I had to deal. Guards of honor escorted the bodies of my sisters to lie in the earth of their own lands, and trusted warriors were sent to take their sons into safe fosterage. Then winter closed its white fist around us in a final spasm of cold, and we could only wait for proof of the healing I had sensed as Leir's blood flowed into the land.

I tried to be patient, remembering how slowly I had recovered from the birth of my child, and as the Feast of the Maiden drew near I hailed each small sign of emerging life as a promise of returning harmony. But I could not be sure until the morning I walked out along the banks of the Udra beneath a new-washed sky and heard the sweet calling as the greylag geese came home.

As I watched I felt a presence at my shoulder, and found Talorgenos there.

"It is beginning, do you see?" I pointed, as one after another the great grey shapes settled among the reeds.

"It is," said the priest, and his eyes brightened with memory of the hours we had spent discussing how to heal the wounded land. "Now will you summon the chieftains to Council?"

"At the Spring Turning—and do you send word to your folk. The seed is planted. Let us see if anything will grow."

By the end of that Council the shape of the new order we were creating could already dimly be seen. There was a wary hope in the eyes of the chieftains who came to my call. The beasts that had survived the winter were giving birth now, and all the young lived. Game that had hidden itself the year before came as if to the hunter's call, and the waters echoed with the cries of returning waterfowl.

One by one the chieftains told their tales, and I marked the wonder in men's eyes. It would not last. I knew how soon even good fortune could fuel ambition and rivalry. But for now, they accepted me and Agantequos as lord and lady, and they would do whatever I desired. We chose warriors to rule in Alba and Belerion until my sisters' sons were grown. I had heard that the boys blamed me for the deaths of their mothers, but they had the blood right in those lands. Perhaps if I built well enough, I could leave something that would survive the worst their hate could do.

My secret hope was in the oak priests and the Ti-Sahharin. Talorgenos had gathered all those of his order who survived, and while we argued in Council, they met with the Dark Sisterhood, which had been expanded by the addition of Spirit Bear and Mother Nesta. And so, as she had seen once in vision, there were nine priestesses now to dance around the sacred stones.

Before we dismissed the chieftains I had one more thing to ask.

"My lords, the body of the high king still lies unburied. It is because of a promise my father required of me as he lay dying on the moors. He wished no barrow to weigh down his bones, nor would he allow his spirit to be released by fire. It was the will of King Leir that his bones rest beneath the river that flows past Ambiolissa. From beneath the Soretia, he said, he will watch over the land."

There was a murmur form the men. "Is it even possible?" asked Nextonos aloud.

I turned to Giahad the builder. "What do you say? I will not give my father's body to the fishes. Can you build him a barrow that will withstand the river of time?"

But already I could see his blunt features hardening with interest.

"It can be done," he said finally. "I can dig a channel to divert the waters and dam the river with hurdles. It can be accomplished if you will give me the men."

I turned to the chieftains. "So—it falls to you. Will you send your people when the spring planting is completed and the cattle have been driven to the hills? We will need every man who can be spared from the pasture and the plough."

In their eyes, fear warred with wonder. But my father's name still had power. By the time the Council was over, the chieftains had promised to send their men.

The triumphant sun of Midsummer blazed overhead the day we put my father in his tomb. The stone chamber had been dug into the bed of the river with one end pointed upstream like the prow of an upturned keel. Its top was rounded to let the water flow over it, but set into the curve was a stone head with two faces, placed so that one gazed forever upriver and the other down. An opening had been left in the stonework, and through this we eased the cedar chest that held my father's bones.

Talorgenos had made of it a ritual, one more in the continuing cycle of ceremonies by which our lives were bound. "It will comfort the people," he told me. "A new rite, performed by priests and priestesses of the old race and the new. By such things they will be linked into one family."

The priests chanted Leir's praises to the music of the sweet-sounding harp as warriors placed the king's weapons in the tomb along with the vessels that held the offerings of meat and grain and mead. And then the time came to seal the chamber. Now the priestesses took the lead, throwing down offerings for the river goddess as the barrier was breached and the first muddy trickle of water snaked toward the tomb.

I stood silent at Agantequos's side, numb as if I had consumed the black drink they give to men before they are sacrificed. The whisper became a roar as the river raged forward, and the women wailed as the rushing waters devoured my father's body. I should have been weeping for my loss or exulting in Leir's final victory. But I could feel nothing at all.

Presently the grey waters covered the last stone, and the tomb lay hidden in the belly of the river like an egg of stone. For a time the ripples bobbed with bits of brush and straw, and then even they disappeared. The people were turning away now, the priests gathering up their gear and preparing to go. Agantequos touched my arm.

"The feast is ready," he said softly. "They will want us there—"

"You go," I snapped at him. "You are the king. I need to be alone."

At the top of the bank Nabelcos was waiting, and with him the men of Briga who were the king's men now.

"Speak to the people," I added more softly. "They need you to reassure them. But I must ask the river to flow gently over my father's bones."

"Does he yet bind you?" Agantequos's hands closed on my shoulders and his blue eyes held mine. "Am I not first with you, Cridilla, even now?"

I felt the strength in my husband's hands and remembered how he had held me in the winter nights when I woke shivering because I thought I was back in Maglaros's cage. And I remembered also how I had cradled him against me when he wept for his lost land.

"You are Lord of Briga and my beloved." I managed a smile. "Be easy. This is only to say farewell."

He left me then, but as the warriors fell in behind him it was not Agantequos my lover that I saw marching toward the feastfires, but the high king.

When he had gone I sat down with my back against a willow

tree. My father's tale was finished, and for the moment I found it hard to think why I should not simply let myself slide into the stream. Leir lay at peace in the womb of the waters. But though I was a warrior, the battle to bring peace to the Island of the Mighty would never end. Surely I had done enough for the land.

This is my exhaustion speaking, I told myself. *In a few moments I will get up and go.*

But the hypnotic ripple of water held me still.

"Live, Adder," words stirred the silence. "Art land's voice to th' people; and folk's speech to th' land."

I looked up and met the bright glance of a crow perched on a branch that swung out over the shifting surface of the stream. As I stared, new words formed from the waters' whispering.

"Look at the river, always changing yet always the same. This must thou know—all that has been is, and all that is, will be. The waters of the river are one with the sea." And I knew that this was the voice of my own mother, as I had heard it in the vision cave.

And then suddenly the air glimmered with radiance. I fell back, covering my eyes against the dazzle as a great white shape settled in the water before me, folding mighty wings. A new voice spoke then, and I knew it was Leir.

"Hear me, daughter—even death cannot separate us from what we have loved. You are the Serpent of Briga. In each age you cast another skin, but you will never die."

The last light of the longest day shimmers on the river and glows through every leaf on the willow tree. Each stone on the shore has its own radiance, and in earth and sky and water the lifesparks of living creatures glow. From the depths to my crown that light is welling. I am the heir of my father's hopes and the vessel of my sisters' dreams, yet I know now that my task is simply to let life flow through me into the land.

Beyond the willows my people are waiting for their queen. The shining coils of the river glitter with scales of light and the white swan wards the waters above the tomb of the king.

And Agantequos is calling me.

AFTERWORD

IN THE VALLEY of the river Soar below Leicester, the traveler who abandons the great highway for the roads that wander among the rich farmlands may pass a simple sign marked "Leire." The hamlet itself consists of a few farms and a stream, but the village has been there since the *Domesday Book* was compiled. The association of the Leicester area with King Lear goes back to Geoffrey of Monmouth's *History of the Kings of Britain*. From Geoffrey the story went to historians like Holinshed, from whom Shakespeare got the tale. It has had many versions, including several border ballads.

The kernel of the story is always the same—an old and powerful king decides to divide his kingdom among his three daughters as a reward for swearing a sort of loyalty-oath that will demonstrate their love. Two of the daughters swear an impossible fidelity and later betray him, while the third, tongue-tied by her truthfulness, is exiled and returns in a vain attempt to rescue him. But why? Why does Lear makes such a stupid decision in the first place? Why do the two elder daughters try to take over the kingdom? Where does the self-effacing Cordelia find the gumption to come to her father's rescue with an army?

The virtue of fiction is that it allows one to show not only the deeds of men and women but the motivations behind them. But where in the shadows of history or of the human heart can we find an explanation for the story of King Lear?

Literary Source

Our major written sources for the history of Celtic Britain are the *Mabinogion*, whose four branches tell the stories of the euhemerized Celtic gods, and Geoffrey of Monmouth's *Historia Regum Britanniae*, which determinedly traces the descent of the British kings from a great-grandson of Aeneas with no recognition of the Celts as a separate people at all. Geoffrey is, however, our earliest source for the story of King Leir and his daughters (though the name Llyr is also given to the sea-god in Welsh and Irish mythology, and to a legendary Irish king whose children were turned into swans). Another of Geoffrey's stories, his account of Brennius's attack on Rome, seems to enshrine a faint recollection of the sacking of Rome by the Celtic leader Brennus in 390 B.C.E. It is possible that some of his other stories had their roots in history as well, though probably not in the same sequence as Geoffrey gives them, and not necessarily in a single line of descent. According to Geoffrey's chronology, Leir lived at the time of the founding of Rome. I have moved him up about two centuries, to sometime in the fifth century B.C.E.

To the medieval and Renaissance storytellers, a woman who seized power was unnatural. But traces of a culture in which women were not second-class citizens survive in the old Irish heroic literature, so why not in Britain as well? It seemed to me that most of the motivational problems in the story of King Lear could be solved if he were a war-leader from a patrilineal culture who had come over the sea, and his daughters were his children by the queens of the matrilineal tribes that he conquered.

According to Geoffrey, Cordelia survived her father. This is how he continued the tale.

Leir's daughter Cordelia inherited the government of the kingdom of Britain. She buried her father in a certain underground chamber which she had ordered to be dug beneath the River Soar, some way downstream from Leicester. This underground chamber was dedicated to the two-faced Janus. . . . When Cordelia had ruled the kingdom peacefully for a period of five years, Marganus and Cunedagius began to cause her trouble. These were the sons of her two sisters who had been married to the Dukes Maglaurus and Henwinus. . . . They refused to stop their outrages; and in the end they laid waste to a number of provinces and met the Queen herself in a series of pitched battles. In the end she herself was captured and put in prison. There she grieved more and more over the loss of her kingdom and eventually she killed herself.

History of the Kings of Britain, Part II: 14–15

Medieval historians, culminating in the *Chronicles* of Holinshed, followed Geoffrey's lead in their account of the early history of Britain, ornamenting the old tale with a courtly embroidery without changing it. Even Spenser, in *The Faerie Queene*, only summarized the story in graceful stanzas. An earlier and extremely forgettable play on the subject familiarized the Elizabethan public with the tale.

It was Shakespeare who turned a story of dynastic warfare into an elemental conflict in which the fate of king and kingdom became one. He moved the story from the world of the court to the world of Nature, and though his vision was moral rather than ecological, the fascination of that connectedness endures. Man and Nature suffer from the same madness, and only the cryptic utterances of the Fool (another of his inventions) cast a flickering illumination across the scene. In Shakespeare's *Lear*, a great and terrible wind from the dawn of the world swept away the surface reality of Elizabethan England to reveal a landscape of archaic power in which human conflicts of love and loyalty acquire an eternal significance. It can do the same thing for audiences today. It is this world to which, in *The Serpent's Tooth*, I have tried to return.

Prehistory

The archaeologists are still arguing about the date of the first true Celtic migration into the British Isles, and whether the language spoken by the people they conquered was Indo-European. None-theless, during the fifth century B.C.E,. enough artifacts of the early La Tène style began turning up in Britain to argue for a Celtic presence in the island. At the same time, a climate shift was forcing farmers from the open uplands down into the heavily forested river bottoms that could only be cleared with iron tools. Could this be a historically defensible example of the conflict between an Indo-European culture and its predecessor, whose outcome was a rather more successful fusion than can be found on the Continent?

If there had indeed been such a fusion of cultures, its initial stages would be bound to be traumatic for all concerned. Again and again in European prehistory one finds tales of the conflict of peoples, of new tribes being forced from their homelands and dis-possessing or conquering others in turn. There are no truly native peoples; even those whose homelands are now at the edges of habitable lands lived first in more fertile countries. The paleolithic hunters who left the first traces of human occupation moved back and forth as the ice caps grew and withdrew, and challenged the great bears for rights to the caves. There are no stories of the coming of the first farmers into northern Europe, though in the Lapps and other peoples of the circumpolar culture, a remnant of the hunter-gatherers they displaced may survive. But there are indications that pockets of people different from their neighbors survived in remote areas into historical times, and awareness of their presence may have contributed to legends of faerie.

European mythology is rich in legends of nomadic or migrating tribes who overrun a culture of settled farmers as the Achaeans overran the heirs of Crete. These invasions are reflected in myth-ological syntheses such as the alliance of the Aesir and the Vanir and the intermingling of the Tuatha De Danaan and the Fomorians after their wars. These original fusions have been overlaid by later migrations and evolutions of culture. One historical survival of the original mix may have been the Picts, who according to K. H. Jackson (in *The Problem of the Picts*) consisted of a layer of proto-Brythonic Celtic aristocrats over a non-Indo-European people. The Irish *Book of Invasions*, Snorri Sturlusson's euhemerization of the Aesir/Vanir conflict, and what we can deduce about the Picts, all suggest that the original encounter between the Indo-Europeans and their predecessors resulted in a fusion rather than elimination of the latter.

Georges Dumézil's theory of Indo-European culture identifies three social functions: sovereign/priests, warriors, and farmers. However when a people migrates it loses its links with the land. In any case the Celts were originally a cattle-herding, not a grain-growing, culture, as the fact that their festivals are linked to significant events in the life-cycle of flocks and herds shows. But as soon as migrants settle down, especially if they consist of a band of raiding warriors without their own women along, they start looking for someone to till the soil. Who will do this, if not the former owners of the land?

If one takes Dumézil's analysis of the original Indo-European tribal culture and compares it to that which evolved in the British Isles, one finds a number of anomalies, characteristic of British but not of Continental Indo-European cultures even given successive waves of Celtic migration on top of the original synthesis. Celtic culture retained elements of this first fusion until its conquest by Rome in the form of the Church suppressed them, at least among the aristocracy. Even then, peasant culture preserved many practices and beliefs that can be traced back to the farming culture of Neolithic Europe.

The People

The Quiritani of the story are La Tène culture Celts—an iron-using people speaking an early form of the language that divided first into Brythonic and Gaelic, and later into the languages spoken in the Celtic lands. Thus, they have much in common with the Celts of the later heroic period chronicled in the Ulster cycle of Irish legend and in a medievalized form in the *Mabinogion*. I have tried to show some of these resonances through the chapter headings, which are drawn from material in Cross & Slover's *Ancient Irish Tales,* and Jackson's *Celtic Miscellany*. But in other ways they are more like the Homeric Greeks, the early Germanic tribes, or the people who founded Rome. Many of the distinguishing features of high Celtic culture, such as the Druids, do not appear until later. A rudimentary priesthood can be found among the ancient Germans, and in Rome and among the Vedic Brahmins at the other end of the Indo-European migration, the priesthood did indeed develop in ways that show a family resemblance to that of the Celts. But the Druids also developed (or retained) features found nowhere else in Europe, and the Druids of Britain were feared by the Romans as the custodians of an ancient and powerful magical tradition.

Very little can be known for certain about the inhabitants of Britain in the fifth century B.C.E. In writing this story, I have worked from the assumption that those characteristics that differentiate the historical Celts of the British Isles from those of the Continent might have been derived from the people who were there when they arrived. These would have been the descendants of the folk who built the megaliths, a people who farmed the open plains and the tops of the downs and moors, and whose agricultural and ritual system was based on observance of the solar year.

In all probability, there were many migrations into Britain before the Celts came. In order to achieve a distinctive characterization I have chosen to identify their immediate predecessors as relatives of the Iberians, part of a first millennium migration of people speaking a Hamitic language who spread westward through North Africa and then up the Atlantic coast. Their descendants include the Berbers, the indigenes of the Canary Islands, and the peoples who shared the Iberian peninsula with the Celts when the Romans arrived. Spanish sites show that they had developed a sophisticated culture, with artifacts of which the statue of the priestess at the Dama de Elche site is among the most remarkable. It may have been they who favored the round style of house building that becomes steadily less common as one moves eastward into the lands from which the Celts came.

Nonetheless, the Continental immigrants into Britain, whoever they may have been, were not the first inhabitants. Archaeology identifies the presence of hunter-gatherers who belonged to the circumpolar culture, heirs to the Paleolithic and Mesolithic cultures of northern Europe in Britain. Such cultures share a shamanic tradition found from Siberia to North America, and among the Lapps of Scandinavia. Pockets of such folk could well have survived well past the Celtic period, withdrawing ever deeper into the wild lands. It is these people whom the Celts in the story call the Senamoi, the first to inhabit and to be dispossessed from the land.

Places in the Story

A great many leaves have fallen since the fifth century B.C.E., and successive waves of settlement, not to mention the ravages of modern building, have obliterated much of the evidence that would have given us more certain knowledge of early Iron Age habitation. Wherever possible, I have set scenes from this story at known sites, filling in gaps in knowledge with extrapolation from other sites where more evidence has survived.

Leir's fortress of Ligrodunon is Burrough Hill near Somerby, Leicestershire. Although not the largest Iron Age site in the area, Burrough Hill is one of the best preserved. Excavation of the site has been minimal, and some of the information on construction has been carried over from other sites such as Danebury in Wiltshire. What evidence exists indicates that Burrough Hill had been inhabited since the Bronze Age, and that it was a significant site, since fairs and assemblies continued to be held there through the end of the nineteenth century. Rather than having a single royal center, Leicestershire seems to have had a number of hillforts. Presumably the king moved from one to another.

The Yorkshire dales are a limestone country rich in caves and natural formations that beg to be used as settings for dramatic events. The sacred spring in Chapter Seven is now known as St. Aldkelda's Well. The local church has a charming story of a Saxon martyr to explain the name, but its origin is more likely the Norse, "hal keld"—"holy well." It is located about a half mile from Giggleswick, next to a busy highway (the A65 road). The lead figure of the Lady was in fact found in the well at Giggleswick. Since it is of lead, it is impossible to date it, but the designs on the skirt and bodice are similar in style to those on an early La Tène-style shield found in a hoard at Merioneth. Both the shape of the figure and the symbols are also remarkably like those of some of the

Neolithic goddess figures found in Eastern Europe, a style that is continued in the stiff skirts and bare-breasted bodies of the priestesses of Minoan Crete.

The Womb Cavern is Victoria Cave, reached from the Stockdale road out of Settle or from Langcliffe. Recent excavation has opened it completely, yielding remains dating from the Stone Age through the Romano-British period, when it was a repository for votive offerings. Those who are interested in following the track of Cridilla and Leir's wanderings in the dales may do so with the aid of the Landranger series maps (#91, 98, 99, 104) and a good imagination or a pair of stout walking shoes. The Pennines are crisscrossed with paths and trails that have no relation to the motorways, for feet and hooves can go where wheels require engineering. Some of these are old drovers' roads for the moving (legal or otherwise) of cattle between England and Scotland, and of these, many are Celtic or earlier. My assumption is that Cridilla located Leir and Crow somewhere near the stones called Long Meg and her Daughters, on the river Eden above Langwathby. If one follows the Eden southward to its head, one can eventually cross over into Dentdale by an ancient track called Galloway Gate, and then west and south through Deepdale to Kingdale down another pre-Roman track, turning eastward around the southern flank of Ingleborough (Rigodunon) along the old road above the modern A65 that goes from Ingleton to Clapham. From Clapham, one follows the trail beside Clapham beck, past Ingleborough Cave (which was only opened to view by the use of explosives in the nineteenth century) to Clapham Bottoms, where the fight takes place. They retreat up onto the fells, where the pots and holes take their toll of both sides, and eastward through the crags to Ribblesdale.

The rocks of the southern Yorkshire dales, especially Rombald's moor, are famous among archaeologists for their wealth of pictographs. By far the majority of these are simple cup marks pecked into the stone, although some of them are surrounded by whole or partial ring marks or penetrated by straight lines suggesting the lingam/yoni symbols of India. Occasionally, however, one finds a pictograph that is different. One of these is the "Swastika Stone" on the hillside above Ilkley. According to Professor Anarti of Fiumi University, the only other example of a four-armed figure of this type is in northern Italy. One school of thought suggests therefore that this carving might have been added by the Celts when they arrived. The other stone mentioned in Chapter Twenty-one is the "Badger Stone," a rock within easy walk of the settlement remains that the Ilkley Archaeological Group was excavating when I visited there.

A Note on the Celtic Calendar

Our best evidence for the Celtic naming of months is a bronze tablet discovered in 1897 at Coligny. The Celtic year began at Samonios with the festival called the Samonia (later, Samhain). Herm, in *The Celts*, describes some of its other complexities. The months were lunar, and each day began at moonrise. The somewhat loose translations of the month-names, based on those of Caitlin Matthews, are my own.

OCT/NOV—SAMONIOS	NUTFALL MOON
NOV/DEC—DUMMANIOS	DARKTIME MOON
DEC/JAN—RIUROS	MOON OF COLD
JAN/FEB—ANAGANTIOS	HOUSEBOUND MOON
FEB/MAR—OGRONIOS	ICE MOON
MAR/APR—CUTIOS	WIND MOON
APR/MAY—GIAMONIOS	BUD MOON
MAY/JUN—SIMIVISONIOS	BRIGHTNESS MOON
JUN/JUL—EQUOS	HORSE MOON
JUL/AUG—ELEMBIUOS	MOON OF CLAIMING
AUG/SEP—EDRINIOS	ARBITRATION MOON
SEP/OCT—CANTLOS	SONG MOON

SOURCES

Arribas, Antonio. *The Iberians*. London: Thames & Hudson.

A Celtic Miscellany, translations from Celtic Literature by Kenneth Hurl-
stone Jackson. New York: Penguin Books, 1971.

Cross, Tom Peete, and Clark Harris Slover, eds. *Ancient Irish Tales*. New
York: Henry Holt & Co., 1936.

Cunliffe, Barry. *The City of Bath*. New Haven: Yale University Press, 1986.

Daniélou, Alain. *The Gods of India*. New York: Inner Traditions Inter-
national, Ltd., 1985.

Eliade, Mircea. *Shamanism*. Bollingen Series LXXVI. New York: Pantheon
Books, 1964.

Harding, D. W. *The Iron Age in Lowland Britain*. London and Boston:
Routledge & Kegan Paul, Ltd., 1974.

Hartley, Dorothy. *Lost Country Life*. New York: Pantheon Books, 1979.

Herm, Gerhard. *The Celts*. New York: St. Martin's Press, 1975.

Matthews, Caitlin. *The Celtic Tradition*. Longmead, Dorset: Elements
Books, 1989.

Monmouth, Geoffrey of. *The History of the Kings of Britain*, translated by
Lewis Thorpe. New York: Penguin Books, 1966.

Naddair, Kaledon. *Keltic Animal Lore and Shamanism, Vols. 1 and 2*. Edinburgh: Keltia Publications, no date.

Phillips, Guy Ragland. *Brigantia*. London and Boston: Routledge & Kegan Paul, Ltd., 1976.

Rees, Alwyn and Brinley. *Celtic Heritage*. London: Thames & Hudson, 1961.

Ross, Anne. *Pagan Celtic Britain*. London and Boston: Routledge & Kegan Paul, Ltd., 1967.

Shakespeare, William. *The Tragedy of King Lear*.

Waltham, Tony. *Yorkshire Dales: Limestone Country*. London: Constable & Co., 1987.